ALL
WE
HIDE

ALSO BY ROBYN GIGL

By Way of Sorrow
Survivor's Guilt
Remain Silent
Nothing But the Truth

ALL WE HIDE

ROBYN GIGL

Published by
Soho Press, Inc.
227 W 17th Street
New York, NY 10011
ww.sohopress.com

Library of Congress Cataloging-in-Publication Data

TK
ISBN 978-1-64129-806-3
eISBN 978-1-64129-807-0

Interior design by Janine Agro, Soho Press, Inc.

Printed in the United States of America

10 9 8 7 6 5 4 3 2 1

This book is dedicated with love to all members of the transgender and gender diverse communities.
Stay brave, stay strong, do not despair. We will not be erased.

ALL
WE
HIDE

AUTHOR'S NOTE

THESE ARE DIFFICULT TIMES for transgender and nonbinary people. On his first day in office, the president of the United States issued a series of executive orders declaring his belief that trans people don't have the right to exist. That's not hyperbole—just his words and actions taken at face value. And he's not alone in this view. Governors and state legislatures in approximately twenty-seven states have passed laws banning or prohibiting trans people from certain fundamental rights—like receiving appropriate healthcare, using a bathroom, changing their identity documents, or participating in sports. Policies that everyone from the Supreme Court of the United States to major media outlets have found no fault with.

I will confess that, as a transgender woman, it's hard for me to fathom why rich and powerful people fear me and other trans people. We make up a tiny fraction of the population, and like every other human being inhabiting this planet, all we're trying to do is live our best lives possible without hurting or interfering with anyone else's right to do the same. Yet, for some reason, powerful people view folks like me as an existential threat.

I certainly don't have the power or prestige that those attacking my community have, but, as a novelist, I do have a voice. As Walter Mosley once said, "Every novel that's worth its salt is about something other than the story." In my case, the something else is an effort to educate people who aren't trans as to what it's like to be a transgender woman and, hopefully, to show them that we're just like everyone else—no better, no worse—just trying to find happiness in this mixed up, jumbled up world.

Admittedly, there are times when I feel like my words are powerless against the forces arrayed against my community. But then I remind myself that I'm not alone—there are all of you. No matter what lens you view life through—cis, trans, nonbinary, or none of the above—we all should remember that we don't need to understand those who are different from us; we just need to be understanding of them. Together, let's reclaim the virtues of understanding, kindness, and empathy toward our fellow humans and once again embrace those virtues as strengths, not weaknesses. If we do, love can conquer fear.

With love,

Robyn Gigl
December 31, 2025

PROLOGUE

I WAS FIVE YEARS old the day my mother left. Just old enough to have fuzzy memories. I had gone to kindergarten in the morning. After I got home and had lunch, I remember sitting on the couch watching afternoon cartoons. When my younger brother Brian woke from his nap, Mom said we were going to visit Nanny—that's what we called my dad's mom. It must have been cold because we had to wear our winter coats, hats, and gloves. When we got to Nanny's, Mom told me she had to run to the store and she'd be back in a couple of hours. She promised me that we'd stop at McDonald's on our way home and I could get a Happy Meal. I remember the Happy Meal part because we had never eaten at McDonald's, but I had seen commercials and begged. She kissed me, and she left. That was it. There was nothing else special or different. Nothing except she never came back.

What followed is a blur. In the days and weeks after, Brian and I stayed with Nanny, or our Aunt Maeve, our dad's older sister, and her husband, Steve. I cried a lot. I missed my mom and I didn't get the Happy Meal she had promised. No one talked too much about her leaving. For a while, Dad said that she just needed some time to herself, but she'd be back soon. How do you explain to a five-year-old that their mom had decided to start a new life without them? I still have trouble making sense of it as an adult—as a kid, it was impossible. I blamed myself, sure that she had left because of me—because of what she had discovered about me. I recall lying in bed every night praying that if she'd just come back, I'd be the good little boy she wanted me to be.

Every year until I turned fourteen and my brother was twelve, she sent us birthday cards, usually with a ten-dollar bill inside and a note that she loved us. I still have the cards, tucked away in a file folder. Some were postmarked from California, a few from Arizona, and the last one from Las Vegas. I don't know how old I was when Dad stopped pretending and told us that Mom was happier where she was. I knew what he meant: She was happier without us—or at least, without me.

Brian always seemed less emotionally scarred by Mom leaving than I was—he was only three. His scars came from our father.

I can't deny that I probably wouldn't remember what Mom looked like except that, when I was eight, my Aunt Maeve gave me a picture of her. In it, Mom is bending over next to me as I blow out the candles on my fifth birthday cake, a cross dangling from her neck. I don't remember the party, or what I got, but I remember the wish I made. That photo has forever frozen my mom in my memory as a beautiful twenty-five-year-old woman with long wavy red hair, bright blue eyes, and a smile that seemed to radiate as bright as the candles.

When the birthday cards stopped coming, I tried—once—
to talk to my dad about her. He was a detective in the Donn
County District Attorney's Office. Surely, he must've used all
his connections to try and track her down and make her come
back. But even back then, when he still had all his faculties,
my dad was an unforgiving guy. He looked at me, his steel
gray eyes narrowed, and said, "Sometimes people just want to
stay gone." I guess even he must have realized his answer was
cold because he added, "If it's any consolation, she didn't leave
because of you. It was my fault."

It was no consolation. All it meant was that whatever had
happened between them was stronger than her love for me.
And that haunted me, leaving me wounded in a way that my
father's beatings never even came close to replicating—the
bruises he inflicted faded, the one my mother left never did.

CHAPTER 1

October 3, 2022

WHEN I WALKED INTO his room at Rolling Knolls Care Center, my father was sitting in the corner facing the television, his face devoid of expression. The channel was set to some daytime game show, boasting a brand-new car on full display, but there was no sound, just the light from the picture flickering in and out. He sported several days' worth of gray stubble on his hollowed-out face, and it looked like it had been just as long since a comb had been run through his disheveled, thinning gray hair. He was only sixty-eight, but years of hard drinking and early-onset Alzheimer's had added ten years to his appearance. I grabbed a spare chair from beside the bed, pulled it close to his, and sat down. His eyes finally shifted away from the television and found mine.

"Do I know you?" he asked.

"Not sure if you remember me," I replied. "I'm a sergeant in the Donn County District Attorney's Office."

He eyed me suspiciously. "I used to work there."

"Yes sir, I remember. And that's why I'm here."

"I have a son who works there." He hesitated, a look of profound confusion spreading across his face. "I think," he added. "Do you know him?"

"Yes sir, I do," I replied, knowing I should have said "I did."

"He never comes to see me anymore," he offered, rubbing his stubble.

"Yes sir," I said. "I was wondering if I could ask you about a case you worked on when you were at the district attorney's office?"

"Who are you?"

"Sergeant Lauren Kelly, Donn County District Attorney's Office."

"Kelly?" he repeated, momentarily lost in thought. "My name is Kelly," he finally responded, leaving me encouraged that today might not be a total waste of time after all.

If I had wanted to, we could've played this scene out for hours and never gotten beyond the fact that we shared the same last name, but I really did want to try and get some information. "It's a common name," I offered and plowed ahead. "Sir, I'm working on a cold case. Do you remember a case you worked on when you were in Homicide involving the murder of a sex worker by the name of Sherry Darling?"

"Sherry Darling?" he repeated to himself, then his expression darkened. "Not his name. He was a man."

"Actually, she was a transgender woman," I corrected.

His stare became more intense. "No, a man," he repeated, shaking his head, his voice distant, as if coming from some faraway place he once inhabited. "My last case. Someone else was lead. I don't remember. I retired after . . ." His voice slowly faded out like the ending of a song.

"Detective Richard Snyder was the lead. Does that help?" Snyder, who starting tomorrow would be the captain I reported to, had made no secret of his antipathy toward me, so I wasn't expecting any support from him.

His eyes wandered back to the television—a woman standing next to the car was jumping up and down with joy. I lost him. After a few beats, he looked back at me, his surprise evident. "Who are you?"

I tried a different tack. "I'm Lauren. We're working together on the Sherry Darling homicide."

His head bobbed. "Snyder has the lead on that. He can help you."

"Thanks, but I need to ask you something, and I need it to remain between us." The absurdity of my request for confidentiality was not lost on me.

"What's that?"

"Snyder is convinced the boyfriend did it, but I don't agree."

I knew from reading the appellate decision reversing the boyfriend's conviction that there was DNA from skin cells found under Sherry's fingernails that didn't match his. If my hunch was right—that she had clawed at whoever stabbed her—it wasn't the boyfriend.

His eyes clouded over, but then suddenly they seemed to shine. "Not the boyfriend," he mumbled, but it was hard to tell if it was a statement, a question, or simply a repetition of my question.

"If you don't think it was the boyfriend, who do you think did it?"

His face went blank again. "Do I know you?"

"Yes, Dad. I'm your daughter."

"I don't have a daughter," he said tersely. "I have a son."

"Brian," I offered, hoping he'd remember my brother who now lived in California. Beverly Hills to be exact, an address befitting his status as a well-known actor.

"Who the hell is Brian?" my father fired back. "That's not my son's name."

I watched him racking his brain, the synapses no longer connecting. It was the same routine every time I visited. I already knew how it would end.

"Yes, Dad. Your son Brian is an actor. He lives in California. You've seen him on television. He plays a detective on *The Gold Shield*."

It would be easy to blame my dad's refusal to acknowledge Brian on his dementia. But the real reason had little to do with his memory. Twenty years ago, when he was still compos mentis, Dad wrote Brian out of his life after Brian told him he was gay.

"Liam," he finally spit out, with a hint of triumph. "My son's name is Liam. Where's Liam?"

I wondered how I should respond today. It was like one of those *Choose Your Own Adventure* books I used to read in middle school. Was Liam dead? Was he away, working on a big case? Or should I go with the truth?

"Liam's away, Dad. He has a big case. You remember what it was like when you were a cop—duty calls."

"Yeah, I remember." He peered up at me, the mask of confusion returning. "Who are you again?"

"Liam's wife," I said, knowing that was my next line in the adventure I'd chosen.

"Oh. Thanks for coming," he said, a wisp of a smile

creasing his craggy face. "I forgot your name. What did you say it was?"

"Lauren," I replied.

He continued to stare at me. "That's interesting—Liam and Lauren."

I smiled. "Yeah. Funny how that happened."

"What do you do?" he asked.

"I'm a sergeant in the Donn County DA's Office."

"Oh, do you know my son? He works there. He's a detective."

I smiled politely. "Sure. I know him."

"He never comes to see me."

"He told me to let you know he's coming by tomorrow." I lied with no remorse, knowing the message had no chance of being remembered. "Do you recall the murder of Sherry Darling?" I asked, figuring I'd give it one last try.

"No scratches," he muttered.

"No scratches," I repeated. "What do you mean, Frank?" I asked, using his first name in the hope it would resuscitate whatever memory was lurking there. Instead, his gaze remained empty.

God, I hated this disease. What was truly ironic was, had I known that my father was going to be diagnosed with Alzheimer's, I could have saved us both a lot of agita by holding out until he didn't know me anymore. But that ship sailed four years ago. Life was strange. For the first two of those years, he wouldn't speak to me, because he was so angry with me. After that, the only reason I'd been able to see him was because he had no idea who I was.

"Who are you?" he asked.

I stood, equal parts anger, frustration, and loss stewing inside. My mixed emotions certainly weren't over missing someone I loved. Truth was, I despised him. He represented everything I hated in a man. "Thanks for your time, sir. I appreciate it. Have a good day," I said over my shoulder as I left.

Michelle sat at the reception desk, directly in front of the locked doors meant to keep the poor souls in the Alzheimer's wing from wandering off on their own. "How's he doing today?"

"The usual," I said with a sad smile.

She gave me a knowing nod and buzzed the door to let me out. "Oh," she said suddenly. "I saw in *The Harrison Gazette* that you're getting promoted today. Congratulations, *Lieutenant*!" Her lips spread into a genuine smile. "I'm sure your dad would be very proud of you."

"Thanks" was all I could say as I walked through the doors. Doors that were the portal to the world inhabited by folks like me who can't forget—even if they want to.

I THREW MY PURSE into the car, annoyed by my inability to communicate with my father. Surprising, given that the inability to communicate had been the hallmark of our relationship. All his dementia had done was add an extra layer.

I sat, contemplating the little my father had given me. "No scratches." *What the hell did that mean?* Patience, I reminded myself. Sherry's case was over twenty years old. The chances of solving it were slim. Talking to my father had been a shot in the dark.

My personal cell phone buzzed, and when I fished it out of my purse, I saw a text from Brian.

Flight gets in at 3:30pm. Hope to be on time. See you soon.

I looked at my watch. Shit. I needed to get home and change for the ceremony.

CHAPTER 2

I'VE SPENT MY WHOLE life living in or around Harrison, the second largest city in the state and the seat of Donn County. There was a time when I thought I'd escape its gravitational pull, but other than some trips to see my brother in California, my aunt in Florida, and a honeymoon eighteen years ago in Ireland, I never left. Built on the banks of the Dagda River, Harrison was originally settled by mostly Irish and German immigrants, whose Catholicism and evangelical Protestantism still shape the lives of many of the close to two hundred thousand people who live here. But it has also diversified over time, especially as a result of the first and second waves of the Great Migration of African Americans from the rural South. Unfortunately, the segregation they were fleeing still exists in Donn County, just more subtly, accomplished through redlining and job discrimination, as opposed to Jim Crow and lynchings.

The promotion ceremony was taking place in the ceremonial courtroom of the historic Donn County Courthouse, a relic of a different era—the Great Depression. Built in the 1930s by the Works Progress Administration, and then refurbished in 2000, it was the epitome of the majesty that the law could at times project. The judge's bench, counsel table, and all the railings were made of solid mahogany. The vaulted ceiling was adorned with frescoes depicting the Revolutionary War, and the walls were solid marble. Given the grandeur, one could envision Solomon himself sitting on the bench, holding forth, dispensing justice. Of course, the building where most of the real work of the Donn County justice system occurred sat across the street—the Courts and Administration Building, the home of the criminal courts and the DA's office. The ten-story building, built in the 1960s, was outdated before it was even finished, and unlike the splendor of the ceremonial courtroom, both the green glass exterior and the drab courtrooms fit in perfectly with this area of downtown Harrison—dated and dilapidated.

Ten minutes early, I took a seat in the back row. The courtroom was already crowded with folks milling about. Most were family and friends of people in the DA's office who, like me, were being promoted.

Despite the crowd, no one bothered with me. I'd become persona non grata in the DA's office four years earlier when I came out as a transgender woman. This is a red state, and Donn County is scarlet, so being an out trans person in this area isn't easy for anyone. Of course, as the only out trans woman in law enforcement in the county, I had the added bonus of trying to deal with cops steeped in machismo and transphobia.

It's been hard at times, but I recognize that I'm a privileged trans woman. To start, I'm white. I still had a full head of chestnut brown hair when I transitioned, so I don't need a wig, and I was able to afford facial surgery to give my face more feminine contours. As a result, I pretty much blend into the landscape. At five foot ten, I'm tall, but I lost a lot of weight before I transitioned, so at 140 pounds, I'm on the slim side. Having started estrogen at forty, I don't have a classic hourglass shape, but I'm not complaining. To paraphrase Springsteen, I'm not a beauty, but I'm all right. Unless you knew me before I transitioned—like just about everyone in the law enforcement community in Donn County—you probably wouldn't know I was trans. You'd just accept me as a tall, middle-aged woman. Of course, on the job, I don't have the luxury of anonymity or acceptance. I'll always be the tranny detective—the Hester Prynne of our time, just that I was branded with a scarlet *T*, not an *A*.

As I waited for my brother, I was bemused as many in the crowd were drawn, like moths to a flame, toward the front of the room where Ron Furst was holding court. Anyone who had political ambitions in the state needed to pay homage to Furst, who was not only the county executive, but also chairman of the state Republican Party. Meaning that any Republican running for office, from dog catcher to governor, needed his blessing. Without it, you might just as well have been a Democrat.

Furst and my father had known each other, so I'd met him a few times when I was growing up. How they were connected, I never actually knew. But from listening to some of my father's drunken tirades, it was pretty clear that there was no love lost between them. I'd bumped into him on the job from time to time, usually at retirement dinners for people in the DA's office. Fortunately, since I steered clear of politics, I'd managed to avoid having to deal with him—that is, until I'd threatened to sue the county. Which is how I wound up on his shit list, and also the reason why I was being promoted.

As I watched the political tableau unfold, my brother Brian appeared in the doorway to the courtroom. Between shooting new episodes of his show, various personal appearances, and everything that goes with being a celebrity, I would've understood if he couldn't make it, but there he was. That's one of the things I so admired about my brother: No matter how famous he was, our bond remained unbreakable. A bond that had been forged in the cauldron of our childhood when all we had to cling to was each other.

I always got a charge out of what happened when Brian walked into a room and the crowd recognized who he was. Sometimes it was like the Red Sea parting to let him pass. Other times he had to fight his way through. I wasn't shallow enough to think his success was based solely on his looks, but I wasn't foolish enough to think that a face and body that had him on the cover of every popular magazine didn't matter. A chiseled jaw, jet-black hair, bright blue eyes, and a beard that provided the perfect amount of stubble for an early morning photo shoot without ever making him look grungy had no doubt helped propel his career. On top of that, he was outgoing, funny as hell, and somehow, despite his fame, had maintained an aw-shucks humility, earning him the reputation of being one of the most eligible bachelors in Hollywood—an image nourished by him staying in the closet. For two people with the same parents, raised in the same household and only twenty-three months apart, we couldn't have been more different. Even before I transitioned, we didn't look that much alike, and my personality tended toward sullen introvert. Some of my personality came from hiding who I was, but even after I transitioned, I was not one to light up a room the way Brian did.

When Brian saw me and headed in my direction, it was the Red Sea effect. There were the mumbled whispers and finger pointing, but everyone stepped aside when he walked in, watching as he made his way over to me. The bear hug he gave me when I stood to greet him was as potent a statement of support as I'd ever gotten. Given my scarlet T, I'm not sure anyone would have even acknowledged my existence at the ceremony if Brian hadn't shown up. But within a few minutes, a number of people in the room, including some from my office who openly despised me, approached Brian and were even willing to smile with me in order to snap a selfie with Detective Sergeant Dan Hill. We made a good pair—he was a fake cop and famous; I was a real cop and infamous.

"Mr. Kelly, I'm County Executive Ron Furst, nice to see you again," Furst said in a rich baritone, his hand extended as he approached. "I think the last time I saw you was your junior or senior year in high school."

Brian shook his hand. "Please, call me Brian. Mr. Kelly is my father," he offered with a warm smile. "And it was senior year. The baseball team was county champs."

"Of course. I remember," Furst said, patting Brian on the shoulder. "And please call me Ron. How's your dad? Helluva detective. Is he here?"

Brian gave me a pleading look.

"No, he's not here, sir," I said, taking my cue. "Unfortunately, he's suffering from Alzheimer's." *Not that he'd be here anyway*, I left unsaid.

Furst looked at me, as if noticing me for the first time. "I'm sorry to hear that."

His tone was practiced—the kind that good politicians use to convey sincerity, even if they don't give a shit. He studied me for several seconds, his brow furrowing, his eyes narrowing, his disdain apparent. "Congratulations on your promotion, Lieutenant Kelly. I'm sure your father is very proud of you," he said, this time not even hinting at sincerity.

"Thank you, sir," I replied, trying my best to remain cordial.

He stepped closer to Brian and took out his cell phone. "Can I get a selfie with Donn County's biggest star?"

"Of course." Then before Furst could snap the picture, Brian reached out and pulled me in, his eyes full of mischief. "Sis, squeeze in here."

AFTER THE CEREMONY, BRIAN'S limo picked us up and we went to Franco's, the most expensive restaurant in Donn County, to celebrate.

"Nice dress," he said with a nod of his head when we were seated. "I couldn't help but notice you turned some heads with those legs."

I still had on the black dress, the white, collarless jacket, and the three-inch pumps that I had chosen in keeping with the DCDAO's policy that female law enforcement officers receiving a promotion were permitted to wear a dress or a skirt to the ceremony. I could have worn my usual pantsuit, but I do have nice legs, and sometimes I like to screw with the heads of the folks in the front office, just like they liked to screw with mine.

I laughed. "Trust me. Those heads didn't turn because of my legs. They were just pissed I was getting promoted."

"How'd you pull that off? The promotion part, not the legs." His lips tightened, suppressing a grin.

"I hired a good lawyer," I replied.

"Yeah, but it's not like you live in California. Isn't being trans a fireable offense in this state?"

He was right. Which was why I had hired an attorney before I came out, figuring they'd come up with some pretext to fire me. They tried, but when that failed, they decided to go with the tried and true strategy of making my life so miserable I'd quit. I was transferred from Major Crimes to the Grand Jury Unit where I basically served subpoenas—a glorified process server. I received notes and email messages addressed to "it" or "he/she." I was called a "tranny" and a "wannabe woman" and a few things I'd never even heard before. Despite the fact that sexual orientation and gender identity are two separate and distinct things, I heard "faggot" whispered so often I began to think it was my middle name—Lauren "Faggot" Kelly. Yeah, I probably could've sued for discrimination and harassment, but, with the results of a lawsuit far from certain, I made the decision to annoy them by waiting them out until I reached the holy grail—retirement. All I needed was to reach the magic twenty-five years on the job, and I'd collect a pension of almost eighty thousand every year for the rest of my life, plus lifetime medical benefits. For eighty grand a year plus medical, I was willing to take a lot of shit.

"I was lucky, and like I said, I hired a good lawyer. The luck part was the law changed, making it illegal under federal law to fire or refuse to promote someone because they're trans. So, six months ago, when the next round of promotions was announced, my lawyer, Wanda Pitts, threatened to sue the county. She's pretty well known around here because she's sued the county four times over the last six years and won each case."

"Sounds like she knows what she's doing," Brian said.

"She does," I replied. "One threatening letter from her, and here I am," I said, gesturing with my hands as if to say "Voilà."

"So, what's the new position entail, Lieutenant?" Before I could answer, he let out a laugh. "Hey, you now outrank me," he said. "Seriously, where are they putting you?"

"As of this morning, I'm in charge of the newly created Homicide Cold Case Unit."

"Cold case unit—that sounds interesting."

"It beats serving grand jury subpoenas." There was no point in me trying to explain that my purview didn't involve what everyone typically thought of as a cold case—an investigation where no one was ever arrested or charged with the crime. My role was limited to investigating homicide cases in the county where there had been an acquittal to see if there was another suspect to investigate.

"How many folks in the unit?"

"Just me," I said.

"Jesus," he said. "That sounds impossible."

"I think that's the point," I said with a chuckle. "Make it so frustrating that I'll just go sit in a corner and hide until I hit twenty-five years, retire, and disappear."

He gave me a knowing look. "You have a case in mind, don't you?"

I loved the way my brother could read me. Up until four years ago, I'd always played by the rules and done what was expected of me. But since then, I wasn't real good at doing what people wanted me to do. And since they hadn't assigned me any specific cold case, I was free to choose. "There was a trans woman, Sherry Darling, who was murdered twenty-one years ago. Dad worked the investigation."

"One of Dad's cases? Wow, your therapist will have a field day with that. Any leads?" he asked, sounding more like a real cop than a TV one.

"I haven't looked at the file yet, so don't know what's there. They did find some DNA, but as far as I know, it didn't turn up any matches. Sherry was pretty open about who she was, including being on a daytime talk show just days before she was murdered."

"Sounds like you knew her?"

"Yeah. We went to high school together," I said, trying to mask the regrets I still carried with me.

"Were you friends?"

I shook my head. "No. Back then, I was just a scared high school kid, paranoid that if I befriended her, everyone would figure out I was trans too. So, I avoided her and just tried to blend in with the rest of the guys."

"You did a good job—of blending in."

"Thanks, I think," I replied, knowing he was right; I had blended in for most of my life, but now felt a little conflicted over whether that was something I was proud of or not.

The waiter suddenly appeared, fawning over Brian, holding

out a bottle of the 2010 Dom Perignon he had ordered. Brian tasted it and nodded to the waiter, who filled my glass and then Brian's. After the waiter disappeared, Brian held his glass out in front of him. "To my older"—he hesitated—"sister," he said emphatically. "Who makes me proud as hell to be her brother. Congratulations!"

"Thank you," I said, taking a sip after we tapped glasses. "This is amazing," I offered, admiring the wonderful citric taste of the champagne, which was certainly not in my budget.

"Can I ask you a personal question?" he asked.

"Sure."

"Please don't take this the wrong way, but over the last four years we haven't gotten to spend that much time together, and when we did, you were either dressed casually or in cop mode. But this," he said, gesturing to me, "you're all woman." There was a tinge of surprise in his voice. "I mean you were a tough son of a bitch before. Now, I don't see that person at all. How'd you do that?"

I looked down at the table before looking up and allowing my gaze to settle on him. "You're an actor," I began. "So was I, in a way. I took on the role of a tough guy because I was afraid people might figure out who I really was. Being that guy—that was an act, and part of it was fueled by my anger at not being who I knew I was." I smiled weakly. "This is who I've always been inside."

His eyes told me he understood. "How's Dad?" he asked softly.

"Boy, you're moving right from the frying pan into the fire, aren't you?"

He shrugged.

"He doesn't know me anymore," I finally said. "But it's actually better that way, because whenever there's a flicker of recognition . . ." I paused to try and find the right words. "It's the worst version of Dad."

He nodded. Brian certainly had experienced the worst version of our father, culminating in the night Brian came out to him.

"Does he need money to cover his expenses?"

I studied my brother, finding it remarkable that despite all our father had done, he still had it within him to ask that question. "Thanks, but financially he's okay. The house is paid off and between his pension, social security, Medicare, and his savings, all his expenses are covered with a little left over." I was well acquainted with the details of our father's finances because eighteen months ago, when it became clear he could no longer handle his affairs, the court had appointed me his guardian. "At some point, I'm going to have to sell the house."

"You have a one-bedroom apartment, why don't you move into the house?"

I cocked my head, raised my eyebrows, and let my eyes say *Are you for real?*

"Sorry," he replied. "I don't know what I was thinking. I guess we'd both rather live in a box on the sidewalk in downtown Harrison before we lived there."

I sighed. "Actually, I am going to need to spend some time there. First, to clean it out, but unfortunately, Dad's insurance agent told me if someone doesn't live there, the homeowner's insurance will get canceled. So, I have to stay there at least a few days every month, until we sell it."

After we put my father in the nursing home, I went to his

house at least once a week to make sure the heat was on and that there were no problems. But living there, even if only for a few days, truly unsettled me. It had been more than twenty years since I'd lived in that house, but there was something that hit me whenever I went back that left me drained. It was as if my father's drunken tirades had seeped into the walls and, whenever I went inside, the remnants of his cursing and screaming would ooze out, dragging me back to the hellscape Brian and I had barely survived. The only solace I could take from staying there was it would give me time to look through my father's papers and whatever was in the safe I had discovered in his bedroom closet, to see if they held any clues as to why my mother had left—and where she had gone.

"Not that I care, but who gets everything when he's gone?"

"Nora," I replied with a smile. "He was a shitty father, but he's been a decent grandfather—well, until he forgot who Nora was."

"Glad to hear it's going to Nora. By the way, I thought Becca and Nora were going to join us. Is everything okay?" he asked, referring to Rebecca, my ex and Nora's mom.

"Yeah," I said, glancing at my watch. "They should be here any minute. No way Nora is going to miss seeing her Uncle Brian."

"That's another thing I admire about you. Through your divorce and transition, you maintained a relationship with your daughter—and Becca," he added quickly.

I chewed my lip, hoping the pain would keep me from tearing up. "Truthfully, Bri, there were times that Nora was the only reason I stayed alive. She means the world to me. And I know what it feels like to have a parent leave. I couldn't do that to her. I just couldn't. I know it's not always easy for her to have me as a parent, but I'll always be there for her."

I heard a familiar voice call out "Uncle Brian," and when I looked up Becca and Nora were heading our way.

CHAPTER 3

AFTER BRIAN'S CHAUFFEUR DROPPED me off at my apartment, I changed into my pajamas, plopped down on my couch and grabbed my laptop. Shortly before she was murdered, Sherry had appeared on a widely syndicated daytime talk show called *The Michael Dobbs Show*, which had been based in Harrison. I opened YouTube and typed "Sherry Darling on Michael Dobbs" into the search bar. Within seconds my screen filled with video links to the show. Sherry's episode was right at the top.

The show opened, as it always did, with Dobbs standing among his studio audience, holding cards and a mic, before the camera switched from him to three women sitting on the stage.

"*We have three young women here today, and all of them have a secret. Karen Mosley is twenty-one years old from Wichita. Susan Tinsdale is a thirty-year-old from St. Louis. Sherry Darling is twenty-three and lives right here in Harrison. Welcome to you all.*"

I hit pause and opened the YouTube window to full screen. There was Sherry. Her long, blond hair hung past her shoulders, framing her high cheekbones, button nose, and full lips. I tried to study her eyes—my recollection was that they were brown—but the video was a little grainy and the camera shot of the three of them was from a distance, so it was hard to tell. Her smile was winsome, and sitting there in a black sheath, with black heels, gold hoop earrings and a gold heart charm on a gold necklace, she appeared just as petite as I remembered her. The difference being that the skinny kid I recalled from high school had blossomed into a beautiful woman.

After Dobbs prattled on a bit, he said, "*Now each of you has a secret that you're going to share with our audience. Sherry, let's start with you. I understand that you do secretarial work for a temp agency during the day, but on weekends you have a different job.*"

"*That's correct, Mr. Dobbs,*" she cooed.

Her voice, and the way she used it, brought a smile to my face. Hazy memories of high school drifted back. Sherry was about five foot four and probably weighed a hundred and ten pounds soaking wet. Halfway through our freshman year, she dyed her shoulder-length hair blond and pierced her ears. West Harrison High had a strict gender-based dress code that Sherry relished flaunting. One day, Mr. Cox, our biology teacher, had confronted her because the shirt she was wearing was clearly a woman's blouse, with the buttons on the left side. She defended her selection, saying it was easier for her to button because she was left-handed. Mr. Cox had screamed, "How can you claim to be left-handed when I know you write with your right hand?" Sherry had stared down at her desk and replied, "Oh, Mr. Cox, don't you understand? Left-handed people are made fun of, and I just want to fit in with everyone else." She lifted her head, tilted it coquettishly, and batted her lashes, causing the whole class to erupt in laughter.

"*So, why don't you share with the audience, Sherry, what's unique about what you do on weekends?*"

"*I'm a performer in a drag show.*"

This being *The Michael Dobbs Show*, the audience hooted and hollered, but the smile in Sherry's eyes never faded.

"*A drag show? Are you telling us you're a man, Sherry?*"

"*Oh no, Mr. Dobbs. I'm definitely not a man. I'm a transgender woman and as soon as I have enough money saved to have my surgery, I'll be just like every other woman.*"

"*And is that why you do drag—to save up the money for your surgery?*"

"*It is. You have to understand. This kind of surgery is very expensive. But I'm almost there and I'm hoping that by Christmas I'll have enough money saved to go ahead. And then my boyfriend and I can get married.*"

"*Your boyfriend? You have a boyfriend? Does he know that you were born a man?*"

"*I told you, Mr. Dobbs. I'm not a man. I was never a man. But to answer your question, yes, he knows about me. And he loves me.*"

"*So, I assume your boyfriend is gay?*"

"*No! He's straight. I told you, I'm a woman.*"

"*So, you're having the surgery because he wants you to have it?*"

"*No, Mr. Dobbs. The surgery is for me, not him.*"

"*Are you saying he loves you the way you are now?*"

"*Yes, he does. Why do you sound so surprised that a man could love me, Mr. Dobbs? Trust me, I've made lots of men happy."* And just as she had done to Mr. Cox, she tilted her head coyly, with an expression that let you know there was nothing modest in what she was suggesting.

Fifty minutes later I turned off the video. She had been so alive, so filled with hope— and within a week, she was dead.

CHAPTER 4

THE NEXT MORNING, I headed straight to the industrial area on the outskirts of Harrison, where a storage facility housed the DCDAO's old paper files. It reminded me of the warehouse at the end of *Raiders of the Lost Ark*—not as huge, but still pretty intimidating. After I checked in, one of the security guards, Stan Kaminski, a portly gentleman with thinning gray hair, led me toward the area where the files were stored.

As we walked down the rows of metal shelves piled high with dusty file boxes, Kaminski looked at me. It's a look I get sometimes, along with the question that followed. "You're the detective that's transgender, right?"

"Yeah," I replied, in a tone that I hoped conveyed the message that he should drop the subject.

"You Frank Kelly's kid?"

I nodded. "You know him?"

"Yeah, I was with the sheriff's department for twenty-eight years before I retired and took this gig. He and I bumped into each other a few times. Shared a few beers in Stosh's. How's he doing?"

"Alzheimer's," I said.

"Oh man. Sorry to hear that. He was a tough son of a bitch."

I studied Kaminski. When I first became a cop in Harrison, my father was a sergeant in the DCDAO, and I quickly learned that there were two camps in the law enforcement community—those who hated my father's guts and those who revered him. I knew where I stood, but had learned to keep my opinions to myself.

I had to give Kaminski credit; he was a good poker player.

"Yeah, he was," I replied, noncommittal, even though I wanted to say, *Leave out the "tough." He was just a son of a bitch, period.*

We turned down a different aisle and stopped in front of four levels of shelves labeled 2001. "There you go," Kaminski said, pointing to a box at eye level. A paper taped to the side read *State v. Riccoli, Joseph—victim, Barr, Owen—DCDAO File No. 01-0542-H.* "There's a table at the end of the row if you want to take a look before you sign it out."

Kaminski started to reach up to grab the box, then stopped, as if suddenly realizing I wasn't worthy of his chivalry.

I reached up, pulled the box from the shelf, and placed it on the floor. "I think I'll take a look to see what's here before I go." I paused. "Let me ask you a question. You know anything about the facts of these cases?" I gestured to the boxes all around us.

"Don't have a clue, Lieutenant. I just babysit the files—take them out when someone needs them, and put them back when they're done. No idea what's in them."

"But aren't all the files on these shelves considered solved?" I asked.

"Yeah, I guess," he said, pointing to the label—*State v. Riccoli.* "Some kind of case was brought otherwise there wouldn't be a state versus on the file."

Great. I didn't know if storing the Barr file with the solved cases was intentional or not, or even if it was limited to just this case, but it was definitely going to make my search for potentially related open cases much harder.

Start with the easy ones, I thought—*the ones even the office considered unsolved.*

I nodded. "Okay. But they're obviously stored in some kind of order. Let's say I wanted to look at open unsolved homicide files where the murder occurred between 1980 and 2007," I said, stopping at the year the DA's office had started digitizing its files. "Is there a specific location you could direct me to, where those files are stored?"

His squint betrayed his incredulity. "I guess," he said, looking at me like I had two heads. "There are two places you can look. One if you know the victim's name, the other if it's a Jane or John Doe."

"Can you show me?"

He led me first to a section that had files for the unknown victims. There were twelve accordion files on that shelf. Then, he turned around and pointed to another set of shelves with about forty boxes. "Those are the cold case homicide files where we know who the victim is." He hesitated. "And, if they're sitting on one of these shelves, it means no one's looking to solve them either."

"Understood. Thanks for your help. I assume I'll be taking

this box with me," I continued, nodding to the box with Sherry's file inside. I allowed my eyes to settle on the cold case files. "And I'll probably take a quick look at these before I go."

"Whatever. Just see me before you leave so you can sign out whatever you're taking."

After taking a look through the Barr files, I went back to the shelves and did a quick inventory of the other cold case files, searching for cases with other trans victims and the possibility of a serial killer targeting trans women.

I found two files where the victims were trans. One involved a trans woman who was an informant in a drug case. Her dealer had been the prime suspect, but they couldn't get enough evidence to charge him, so the case went cold. The second involved a trans man who had been beaten to death behind the back of a bar and no suspect was ever identified. Neither held anything helpful for Sherry's case.

I made a mental note to search the FBI's National Data Exchange, N-DEx, for any crimes similar to Sherry's murder. But N-DEx hadn't launched until 2012, which meant anything prior to that was going to take a lot of digging. I always knew looking for connections to other cases was going to be tough. I just hadn't realized how hard it was going to be—especially without help.

I grabbed the box, signed the Barr files out with Kaminski, and headed back to the office.

MY NEW OFFICE WAS a drab, windowless box, not much bigger than the office I had occupied as a sergeant. At least it was large enough to accommodate two chairs for visitors on the opposite side of my desk, as opposed to the

standing-room-only size of my previous digs—not that I
expected visitors. The wall facing the hallway was glass, so it
didn't afford much privacy, but it was at the end of a corridor,
so there was no foot traffic. As I looked around and took in
the nameplate on my desk, it suddenly dawned on me that my
father had never been promoted beyond sergeant. Now here
I was, a lieutenant. I wasn't sure what it was—maybe some
"Fuck you, Dad, I outrank you" schadenfreude—but it did
provide me with a perverse bit of satisfaction.

I booted up my computer and, before logging into the network, opened up the online edition of *The Harrison Gazette*.
There at the top of the page was an article about the famous
TV and movie star Brian Kelly visiting his hometown.
Although the article didn't mention why Brian was in town, it
had a picture of him with County Executive Ron Furst—the
selfie that Furst had taken at the promotion ceremony, with
me carefully cropped out. Further down the page there was a
smaller article, "Transgender Detective Among Those Earning
Promotions," with a pre-transition photo of me from when I
was promoted to sergeant and a picture of me from yesterday's
ceremony. The proverbial before and after photo—just what
every trans person needs.

After finishing the article, I went to work, spreading the
Barr file out on my desk. I began reviewing the initial crime
scene report. Sherry's body was discovered in a dumpster
outside the Collister, a fleabag motel in South Central, a run-
down part of Harrison. Her body had been stashed in black
plastic trash bags, which were found mixed in with the bags
of food wrappers, plastic bottles, used condoms, cigarette
butts, and empty beer cans. She might have gone unnoticed,

except it appeared that vermin had chewed through a portion of the doubled-up trash bags, exposing a human foot. When the sanitation workers saw the exposed foot, a couple of them climbed into the dumpster and removed the body.

Because it was clear that foul play was involved, Harrison PD called in the DCDAO Homicide Unit. The first person on the scene from the DA's office was none other than Detective Sergeant Francis Kelly—my father. I remembered that my father had testified at the first trial, his retirement coming right after Riccoli's conviction was reversed on appeal, based on the failure to turn over exculpatory evidence. The report showed that he was later joined at the crime scene by Lieutenant Howard Clarke and Detectives Richard Snyder, Tom Hammond, and Barry Reed. Detective Snyder—who was currently my captain—was designated by the lieutenant as the lead investigator, meaning that Snyder had the responsibility of preparing the main investigative report—the one I was reading now—while others on the team prepared supplemental reports.

I pulled the crime scene photos from the envelope and laid them on my desk. Crime scene photos in a homicide case can be unnerving. Sometimes the victim stares up at you from the photos, eyes open, a hint of disbelief clouding their face. It's as if they're calling out to you. *Is this really the end?* It takes a certain mindset to insulate yourself from the emotional toll this job can inflict. Not sure what it says about me, but over the years, I've gotten used to dealing with death. Still, as I scanned the photos of Sherry, I grimaced. Maybe it was because I had watched the video last night, or because I knew her, or maybe it was what had been done to her. Whatever it was, these photos were going to haunt me for a while.

There were several photos of her body still in the trash bags, laying on the asphalt next to the dumpster, her one foot exposed. In the next group, a sterile, impervious sheet had been laid on the ground with the trash bags placed on top. Then things got real. There were twenty photos from different vantage points taken after the crime scene techs had cut open the trash bags. Her blond hair was a disheveled mess, matted with blood. Her eyes, which I remembered always flickering with a bit of mischief, were open but vacant, as if staring at something or someone off in the distance. She was naked and rigor mortis had set in. There was dried blood on her shoulder and chest beneath an approximate four-inch wound on her neck. Several photos showed slash wounds on her left hand and arm. And the last set showed that her testicles and penis had been amputated. Despite the devastating nature of those wounds, there was almost no blood around her pelvis.

I pulled out the autopsy report. The coroner opined that the cause of death was a sharp force injury, a single slashing wound to the neck that severed the victim's left carotid artery. The weapon was likely a knife with a blade approximately five to six inches long that had entered the left side of the neck just below the left ear and was then pulled across the neck toward the Adam's apple. The wound was approximately two inches deep. The seven superficial slash wounds to the left hand and arm were consistent with defensive wounds. The coroner had concluded that the victim hadn't taken more than twenty seconds to bleed out. The report also noted that the victim's male genitalia, which had been completely severed from the body, were not found at the crime scene. Based on an examination of the tissue in the pelvic area, it was determined that this occurred post mortem. No murder weapon was found.

I placed the autopsy report back in the file and closed my eyes. The image of Sherry sitting onstage sparring with Dobbs, determined to be joyful in being herself, was all I could see. Why had she been so brutally murdered, and what sick piece of shit had mutilated her after they slit her throat? After all those years as a cop, I should've known better than to underestimate the depravity of humans. But maybe it was good I could still feel outrage and compassion. If the day came when I didn't, I'd know I had become my father.

I couldn't remember if I knew at the time that the mutilation happened after she died. There wasn't a whole lot of press coverage—at least initially. The few stories that appeared after her body was discovered misgendered her and included reports from "unnamed sources close to the investigation" that the victim was a male whose genitals had been severed.

From Snyder's initial report and the supplemental reports from the other detectives, it was clear that at the time, no one really gave a shit about one dead trans person and the investigation was destined to go nowhere. But that all changed when folks at *The Michael Dobbs Show* learned that a recent guest had been murdered and put the story on the air. In the law enforcement world, press equals pressure, and suddenly there was a big push to solve her murder.

Sherry's boyfriend, Joseph Riccoli, had been arrested several weeks after her death and charged with first degree capital murder. Based on my review of the reports, the investigation leading up to him being charged had been cursory at best.

The evidence against Riccoli consisted largely of his

statement to the police: He and Sherry had argued the day she
was murdered about her engaging in sex work. A semen stain
was found in her underwear that contained Riccoli's DNA.
Riccoli had tried to explain that he and Sherry had engaged
in consensual anal sex shortly before their argument, but no
one bought it.

I emptied the musty cardboard evidence box, looking for
the lab analysis of the DNA from the skin scrapings found
under Sherry's fingernails. I knew from the appellate court's
decision reversing his conviction that they hadn't come from
Riccoli, but I couldn't find any lab reports that analyzed that
DNA. All I found was a handwritten note paperclipped to an
empty manilla file folder labeled LAB RESULTS that said,
No matches in CODIS. Det. B. Reed 6-26-01. CODIS was
the Combined DNA Index System maintained by the FBI.
CODIS didn't store the actual evidence. That should still have
been in the DCDAO's evidence vault. But, as I stared at the
empty folder where the lab analysis should've been, I couldn't
help but wonder if someone had purposefully lost the results.

I emailed the lab, asking for them to send me a copy of
the original analysis and to do an updated DNA search in
CODIS. Maybe I'd get lucky, and whoever had killed Sherry
would have committed some other crime in the interim and,
as a result, their DNA would now be in CODIS, providing
a potential suspect. But even if there was no match, DNA
analysis had advanced so much in the last twenty years that
other avenues, such as familial DNA analysis, might yet provide valuable leads.

I turned my attention back to my computer and did a
quick check of the DCDAO's database concerning everyone

from the office who had been involved in the investigation and prosecution of Riccoli. Lieutenant Clarke, who was now deceased, had retired after twenty-six years on the job, within months of my father. Hammond had died as the result of a self-inflicted gunshot wound before the second trial. Detective Reed had also left the office right after Riccoli's conviction was overturned, the reason for his leaving listed as "voluntary separation."

Strange, I thought. According to the information in the database, Reed was only twenty-six when he left. This case seemed to end a lot of careers. I needed to find out why.

The two assistant DAs that tried both cases were Vincent Chrystal, who had retired right after the second Riccoli trial and died from Covid over a year ago, and James Barry, who had left the office several years ago for private practice. I knew one thing for sure: I'd get no help from either Snyder or my father with my investigation, so my only hope was to track down James Barry and former Detective Reed.

As I was getting my things together to leave for my weekly Wednesday dinner with Becca and Nora, Captain Snyder stuck his head in my door.

"I heard a rumor you're looking at the Barr file," Snyder said.

Since the woman who provided me with secretarial support was also Snyder's secretary, I couldn't help but wonder whether it was her, Kaminski, or both of them who had tipped Snyder off.

"That would be affirmative, sir."

"What's up with that?" he asked.

"I was assigned to look at unsolved murder cases, and I thought I'd start with one of the oldest."

"It's not unsolved," he fired back, his face turning crimson. "Riccoli did it. He got off on a technicality."

I shrugged. "Just doing my job, sir."

"Figured you look at the fucking tranny case," he said with a sneer, then disappeared from my doorway.

Once he was out of sight, I flipped him the bird. Then, before heading out, I collected the folders from Sherry's case that were strewn all over my desk, placed them in my file cabinet, and locked it. I didn't think anyone would tamper with them, but there was no point in tempting fate.

CHAPTER 5

BECCA AND I SAT across from each other, her with a pinot grigio and me with a chardonnay. She had beautiful silver-gray hair, its texture like fine silk, with a gentle natural wave that caressed her shoulders. Her green eyes could go from as warm and soothing as a calm ocean to as fiery and piercing as a laser in seconds—and I had experienced both. She kept herself in great shape with a daily yoga routine. Her body seemed just as curvaceous and taut today as it was when we were married.

While Nora was learning how to become the next Taylor Swift at her weekly guitar lesson, Becca and I would meet for a drink at McBride's Pub next door. Then, the three of us would head out to dinner together at Giger's.

McBride's was located in the north end of Harrison, near the river. When Harrison originally developed, the south end of the city, where the courthouse and my office were located, was the center of activity. But in the early 2000s, the former industrial area of the downtown along the river gentrified with the old warehouses now renovated into riverfront condos, a new art center/theater, a Marriott hotel, three gleaming twelve-story office towers, and an arena for the Harrison Hawkes, a minor league ice hockey team. The aptly named Riverview section was now teeming with nightlife—a far cry from the dark, decaying underbelly of the city that we were warned to stay out of as kids.

When I was growing up, McBride's, then called Stosh's, was your basic corner ginmill. Most of the clientele were cops and firemen, there being no firewomen back then. Besides, no woman in her right mind would have set foot in Stosh's. Not surprisingly, my father had been a regular. But with gentrification, Stosh's was reborn as McBride's, with high-top tables and a wine list longer than Trump's enemies list.

Six years after our divorce, I was still trying to make amends for failing as a husband and being a mediocre father. But I was grateful that Becca had given me the space to try. Well, not the good husband part—that was no longer in the cards. But at least to be a decent human being to the woman I still genuinely loved, and a good parent to a daughter I adored.

We sipped our wine, the conversation touching on how good it had been to see Brian again and then, as it always did, focusing on Nora. As we chatted about the play Nora was trying out for, I watched Becca in the dim light of McBride's and realized that as much as I had changed, my love for her hadn't. I tried desperately not to let my mind go there, but it did.

As if she read my mind, she suddenly shifted gears on me. "You know I've been seeing someone."

"You told me. Roger Martin," I replied. Martin was the evening anchor for our local CBS affiliate, and considered the handsomest newsman on television. At six foot two, with brown hair, he looked like a younger version of Brian Williams.

"I just wanted to let you know it's getting serious," she said.

"So, you're telling me there's no hope of you coming over to the dark side," I offered with a droll smile.

"That was never happening and you always knew that," she said emphatically.

I couldn't argue. She had always been upfront in letting me know that if I transitioned our marriage was over. "All I ever wanted was for you to be happy," I managed.

"Thanks."

"He's certainly very handsome," I added, raising my glass. When she did the same, I tapped mine against hers and said, "To your happiness."

"Thank you." Her eyes held a mixture of joy and regret. "Are you seeing anyone?"

"No. I can't see myself ever being with a man. And I'm still learning how to navigate driving on the opposite side of the street," I said, knowing that I faced a steep learning curve in assimilating myself into the local lesbian community. The truth was I hadn't even tried. It wasn't that I had anything against the community, but up until four years ago I hadn't been eligible for membership, and even now I knew there were some who didn't think I belonged. Plus, cops had a reputation for being homophobic, transphobic, and a lot of other phobics, making us less than desirable dating material in some circles. But if I was being honest, those were just excuses. The real reason I hadn't tried to date anyone was the woman sitting across from me and my hopeless unrequited love.

"You're an attractive woman. You'll meet someone," she said.

I gave her a bemused smile, grateful for her effort to soften the blow. One thing I couldn't argue with was that Roger Martin was a marked improvement over the former me. Truth be told, I'm not sure what Becca saw in me when she married me. I was a decent enough looking guy, and back then I did a better job of hiding the anger and guilt I carried around with me, but Becca was stunning—still is—and so smart. We met the summer between our junior and senior years of college when we both landed internships at the DCDAO. Me, because my father worked there, and her, because when they saw she was number five in her class at Amherst, they just assumed she wanted to go to law school. It also probably didn't hurt that her father was one of the top lawyers in the state. But, much to her father's dismay, Becca only wanted to work inside a district attorney's office to use it as a stepping stone to becoming a journalist.

Becca's parents despised me. According to them, I wasn't good enough for their daughter. My mother had run off. My dad was a cop. And I was a criminal justice major at State. Her family lived in Royal Oaks, the county's most affluent town, while we lived in Sherman, a working-class section of Harrison that bordered I-13. Becca's father, Sinclair Brinley, was the managing partner at Brinley & LeReine, the largest law firm in Donn County, and her mother was a highly sought-after interior designer. But despite her parents' objections—or perhaps, given her rebellious nature, because of them—Becca decided I was the one for her.

For a few years, I made it work. But it's hard to describe to someone who isn't trans the internal struggle I went through every day. It's not like I didn't know I was trans when I married Becca—my birthday wish at age five was to wake up as the girl I knew I was supposed to be. I just thought that I'd be able to deal with it. After all, I wasn't like Sherry. Sherry always looked and acted like a girl. Sherry was attracted to guys. I could pass in the world of guys and had picked one of the most masculine professions, so no one suspected me of being trans. Plus, I liked girls and fell in love with Becca. And then when Nora came along, I adored her and thought I could never upend her life by coming out. But despite all the promises I made to myself that I could hide as a man for the rest of my life and that no one would ever know—I couldn't.

It wasn't that I loved Becca or Nora any less. It was just that my unhappiness about not being able to be who I knew I was kept growing, and suddenly the scales of my life no longer tipped in favor of staying in the closet. And when that happened there were only two possible solutions. I almost went with door number one, but I wound up here instead.

Ten years after we were married, I came out to Becca. We separated a year later and we divorced a year after that. I hadn't contested anything. By then Becca had left her job as a reporter at *The Harrison Gazette*, and her second novel was a *New York Times* bestseller. I always appreciated the fact that Becca and her lawyer were decent enough to just chalk up our issues to "irreconcilable differences." There was no mention of my transgender status in the divorce complaint, which had allowed me to stay in the closet for another two years after our divorce—two years when I teetered between solving my problem through either option A or option B.

"How's the new position?" she asked, bringing me back to the present.

I laughed and gave her the details, then shared the basics of my first case.

"Wait. You knew this person—the victim?" she asked.

"Yeah. We went to high school together."

"And she was out as trans back then?"

"That she was. Sherry was as out and proud a trans person as anyone I've ever known."

"Wasn't she bullied? I mean, when we were in high school no one was out as trans."

I paused. Sure, she was bullied. High school kids can be jerks. But not all of what she endured came from her classmates. It was probably toward the end of freshman year. Sherry had been out of school for a few days, and when she came back she had a black eye, a fat lip, and some bruising on her face. Our homeroom teacher, Ms. Webster, asked her what happened and she said she walked into a door in the middle of the night. No one believed her, but she refused to say anything else. I didn't know if it was true, but the rumor that later made the rounds was that her father had slapped around "his faggot son."

"Yeah, she certainly got picked on," I replied.

I could feel Becca studying me, wanting more. When I didn't give it, she asked, "So why don't you think the guy who was convicted did it?"

"While his conviction was on appeal, his public defender learned that potentially exculpatory evidence had been withheld by my office—evidence that showed that under Sherry's fingernails there were cells containing DNA that did not match his. Based on that, the appellate court reversed his conviction and remanded the case. My office retried him, but this time, he was acquitted."

"Maybe the second jury got it wrong," she said.

"Yeah, that's possible, but I don't think so. It just doesn't make sense that the boyfriend, who had been dating her for a couple of years, would kill and mutilate her."

"Men kill their wives, lovers, girlfriends all the time. The proverbial crime of passion."

"You're right, but there was almost no evidence against the guy. No witnesses, no murder weapon, and the only DNA found on her wasn't his. That, plus the fact she was mutilated after she was dead. I don't know. I guess it's just a gut feeling, but this guy doesn't strike me as that kind of sicko. I do feel like there's a connection to her being killed a week after she appeared on *The Michael Dobbs Show*. I just don't have a clue what it is."

"And you think that after twenty years whoever did this is still out there?"

I sipped my wine. "I don't know. But I need to try and find out who did it. If that person's dead, so be it." *But if they're alive, I'm going to find them.*

I had been on the job in Harrison about a year when Sherry was murdered. There was a lot of shit said about Sherry in the locker room. She was called every name I would be called years later and then some. And of course, the guy she had been dating was called a fag and a lot worse, folks assuming he was gay and ignoring the fact that Sherry was a beautiful woman that any straight man might be attracted to. The prevailing sentiment in the squad room was *One more dead pervert, who gives a fuck.* As painful as it was to recall, I had been complicit in my silence, just as I had been in high school.

I knew solving her murder wasn't going to undo my past mistakes, but I hoped I could assuage some of my guilt over having ignored the only other trans person I had known growing up and for not having had the courage to befriend her. For whatever reason I had been given a chance to try and make amends. So, "who gives a fuck?" Me. I gave a fuck.

"Was anything in the cold case files helpful?" Becca asked.

"No," I said. "But remember these are only Donn County cold cases. There's a whole state and country out there."

She didn't say anything, but I could tell from the look in her eyes that her journalist/author instincts were kicking in. Even though there was no one else assigned to the DCDAO Homicide Cold Case Unit, I now had a feeling I wouldn't be working this file alone.

CHAPTER 6

LIKE DOWNTOWN, THE RESIDENTIAL areas of Harrison also had distinct personalities—some better than others. My apartment was on North Eighth Street, in the College Hills section of the city, about a twenty-minute ride to the office. The three-story brick building was built in the 1940s, but it was well maintained and it was a nice neighborhood of mostly single-family homes. The décor of my third-floor walkup was definitely never going to make *Homes & Gardens*, it being a mishmash of things I got when Becca and I separated—primarily the bedroom set that Becca said went with me or to Goodwill. Yeah, she was a bit angry with me at the time. The rest were odds and ends that I got at secondhand stores or found on eBay. I had moved in before I transitioned and assumed I'd have to move again after I transitioned, but other than a few stares in the beginning, nobody gave me a hard time. It helped that a number of the apartments were rented by students who went to State, four blocks away, and so the makeup of my neighbors was both fairly young and constantly changing.

My commute was usually easy, and I could avoid most traffic from the interstates if I arrived at the DCDAO before eight in the morning. My routine was to get up around six thirty, shower, have breakfast, and head in. It got a little more involved after I transitioned with doing my makeup and hair, but I adjusted. Before I transitioned, when I had a lot of responsibilities, I liked coming in early, to get some work done before the office got crazy. I guess old habits die hard, because even after I was stripped of just about all responsibilities, I still showed up early.

Growing up, I hadn't envisioned law enforcement as a career path. But then again, unlike Brian, who always knew he wanted to be an actor, I can't remember having a "when I grow up, I want to be" moment. I was rudderless. Both my parents were gone, albeit in different ways, and when I went to State, I majored in criminal justice simply because I had lived with cop stuff all my life so a lot of the course work was second nature to me. Years later, when I finally went into therapy, I didn't need Freud to figure out that my desire to prove myself to my father—coupled with the desire to hide who I was by working in the most macho profession available—had influenced me in more ways than I cared to admit. Before I was confronted with the psychological elements of my career choice, I had always rationalized going to the police academy by convincing myself that I was motivated by the fact that with the resources available to me as a cop, I could track my mother down. I was twenty-two, and still hoped that I'd find her and fill that gaping hole in my life. It had only taken me about a year on the Harrison PD to realize I was on a fool's errand, and that my father had been right. "Sometimes people just want to stay gone."

The DCDAO was pretty much deserted as I made my way to my office. I placed my Yeti, half filled with my favorite Costa Rican Tarrazú from Ward's Coffee, next to my keyboard, powered up my computer and set about trying to find Joe Riccoli. From the original investigation, I knew that he had been an apprentice plumber, and I had his date of birth and social security number from the arrest reports. After a few searches, I had a hit—Joseph Riccoli, with the matching social and DOB, was employed by Perry Plumbing and had a home address in Pembrook City. I then checked the state database for plumbers and found Riccoli's license with his current headshot. Even from just the photo of his face, it was clear that the years hadn't been kind to him. The handsome, skinny kid who went on trial for capital murder had morphed into a mostly bald, puffy-faced forty-three-year-old who looked a decade older.

Having figured out where to look for Riccoli, I reached out to WQRE the station that aired *The Michael Dobbs Show*. I had the YouTube upload of the show, but if we ever needed to use it in court, I needed to try and find an authentic copy of the recording of Sherry's episode. When I finally spoke with the network archivist, not only was she sure they still had it, she thought they might be able to find an unedited recording of the show that she'd copy for me.

I made my way down the hallway from my office to the small kitchen. Four detectives from Major Crimes were chatting as I walked in to grab some coffee. When they saw me, they all turned and walked out before I even said "Good morning."

I stood there for a second, processing the bullshit. Being ostracized wasn't new—but I foolishly thought that with me now a lieutenant, the rank and file would at least fake being respectful. I figured wrong.

An occupational hazard of being a cop is a tendency to develop a myopic "us against them" mentality, where everyone who isn't in law enforcement just doesn't understand what the real world is like because they don't have to deal with all the crap cops deal with every day. The result is that cops become friends with other folks in law enforcement because they "understand" what the world is really like. I have to admit, before I transitioned, I had fallen into that trap. I had become friendly with a few civilians—primarily the husbands of Becca's friends—but most of my closest friends worked in law enforcement either in the DCDAO, Harrison PD, or in the highway patrol. Not surprisingly, given my desire to blend in, almost all were guys. Later, when I came out, it was as if I pulled a fire alarm, as all my friends in law enforcement ran for the exits. Until then, I never realized how alone you could feel in an office full of people. I had left the "us." I was now a "them."

It wasn't like I had any illusions that things would be easy. But I had taken pains to have a one-on-one conversation with each of my closest friends, trying to explain how I felt and what I was going through in hopes they'd understand. Most didn't.

The one that hurt the most—still hurt—was Sergeant Scott Ferguson. I had known Ferguson, Scotty to his friends, for the last thirteen years. I had already been a detective at the DCDAO for about a year when he came over from the Royal Oaks Police Department. Scotty and I had become friends—actually best friends. He and his wife, Mary, and Becca and I had spent a lot of time together as couples—vacations, family events, couples' nights out—and then I came out to him and Mary. After that, while Mary had remained friends with Becca, Scotty and I spoke only when he needed to speak to me for work, which he made sure was almost never. My therapist had warned me before I came out that it was impossible to predict how people would react to the news. But of all the people I knew, I would have bet good money that my friendship with Scotty would've survived—it was good I hadn't bet. The only positive thing I could say about our post-transition relationship was that he was one of the few people in the office who didn't hassle me. He just ignored me—which made perverse sense, given that, after I came out, he told me that the person he had been friends with no longer existed.

I refilled my Yeti with the slop the office called coffee. I needed the jolt of caffeine. My next step was to review the trial transcripts that were part of the appellate record from the first trial. Trials could be exciting, but reading trial transcripts was like watching paint dry.

One thing I discovered from reading the transcript of Vincent Chrystal's opening statement to the jury was that my office had argued Riccoli's motive for killing Sherry was he had been humiliated by some of the sexual innuendos Dobbs made concerning his sexual orientation after Sherry revealed she hadn't had gender-affirming surgery. While I suspected that her appearance on the show had something to do with her murder, since I didn't buy the premise that Riccoli had done it, the alleged motive Chrystal advanced didn't help me find the connection I was looking for.

Riccoli had been represented by a young public defender who, based on my reading of the transcripts, had done a decent job. I then pulled out the limited records in the file from the second trial. After his conviction was reversed, Riccoli was again represented by the PD's office, but before the start of the second trial, Raymond Ashley had taken over the case. *Strange.* Even twenty years ago, Ray Ashley was one of the preeminent criminal defense lawyers in the state. How and where did Riccoli get the money to retain him?

Knowing the chances of getting Ashley on the phone were slim, and the chances of him talking to me about the case were even slimmer, I decided to do a detective's tried and true method—show up unannounced.

ASHLEY'S OFFICE WAS LOCATED in one of the new towers on the river, a ten-minute ride from the DCDAO. I took the elevator up to the twelfth floor and approached the young woman sitting at the reception desk.

"Good morning. I'd like to speak with Mr. Ashley," I said, offering her my business card.

"Do you have an appointment?" she asked without taking my card.

"No, ma'am. I just need a few minutes of his time to discuss an old case he handled."

She took my card, looked down at it, then back up at me with renewed interest. I looked the part—black pantsuit, white tailored blouse, long brown hair pulled back in a high ponytail, a smidge of makeup, my gun and shield displayed prominently on my belt. When she finished studying me, she looked down at the phone, seemed to think better of it, and stood. "Let me check with Mr. Ashley's secretary," she said, taking a door out of the reception area.

A few minutes later she returned with a woman around my age, who proceeded to grill me. After answering her questions about the reason for my visit, this time in a little more detail, including the name of the case I wanted to discuss, the second woman told me to wait, and followed the same route out of the reception area.

Moments later, she stuck her head into the reception area and said, "Lieutenant Kelly. Follow me, please."

When I walked into Ashley's corner office, he was standing in front of his desk, his jacket off, the sleeves of his white dress shirt rolled up. Based on what I knew of his career, I figured him to be at least ten years older than me—late fifties perhaps. He was a physically imposing guy. I pegged him for about six foot four, with a close-cropped salt-and-pepper Afro and a neatly trimmed beard. We had only encountered each other once in a courtroom, when I was a witness on a motion to suppress evidence uncovered as a result of me going into his client's house and observing contraband in plain view. I had held my own under his cross, and the judge ultimately allowed the evidence to be admitted.

Ashley's office was huge, with a spectacular view of the riverfront. On the far side of the room, in front of three large windows, sat his glass desk, which was immaculate. Up against the interior side wall was a gray couch with a glass coffee table and, on the wall behind the couch, a painting that seemed to rival the size of *Guernica*.

"Lieutenant," he said, shaking my hand. "Have a seat."

He motioned me to sit in a gray club chair in front of his

desk. He took a seat opposite me in the matching chair as he studied my business card. "The Homicide Cold Case Unit," he said. "Can't say I've ever heard of this unit before," he offered, with a bit of a grin. Then his expression turned quizzical. "Lieutenant Kelly," he said slowly. "Have we met before?"

Sometimes I play my status close to the vest, but I had gamed this meeting out on the way over, and even though it was unlikely he'd give me what I wanted, I decided that my only hope was to play it straight with him. It's not like he couldn't figure out my backstory with a few quick keystrokes on the internet once I left.

"I guess it depends on how you define met," I replied. "You cross-examined me for over an hour on a motion to suppress in State v. Horvath." I paused for a beat. "Of course, that was before I transitioned."

He went to say something, but stopped himself with the slightest of nods. "Not polite to use a person's dead name," he said, referring to the term for a name a trans person had before they transitioned.

After that, he could've refused to talk to me and I would've still held him in high regard for that simple gesture of respect he had shown me.

He seemed to study me, then said, "You're the . . . person who walked into the house and saved my suicidal client from shooting himself—or from suicide by cop."

I nodded.

"That took—" He winced. "Guts. Then I tried to beat you up on the stand despite the fact that what you did probably saved my guy's life." He snorted and shook his head. "What a fucked-up profession."

There was no point in me telling him I was suicidal myself and being shot and killed by his client had a certain appeal. As for his cross-examination, I understood Ashley had just been doing his job. He had his role in the system, I had mine. Today, what I really wanted to know was whether or not he had any bend in him.

"So, what brings you here today, Lieutenant?"

"Joe Riccoli," I responded, "and the murder of Sherry Darling. I'm taking another look at the case."

He gave me a long hard look. "Look, Lieutenant. Joe was found not guilty almost twenty years ago. You can't go after him again."

"I'm not," I replied. "I don't think he did it. I'm trying to find out who did."

He stroked his beard and his eyes met mine. "Any particular reason you're looking at this case?"

"The first part should be easy. Sherry and I share being transgender. Second, I knew her—we went to school together. And . . ." I stopped.

"And?"

"And now that I've reviewed the file, some things just don't add up."

"So how do I fit in?" he asked.

"Joe Riccoli was represented by the public defender's office until his conviction was reversed. Then you came in and represented him as private counsel. Even twenty years ago, you were a well-known criminal defense attorney, commanding big legal fees. When he was arrested, Riccoli was a plumber's apprentice. Then he spent four years in jail, two on death row, yet somehow, he managed to retain you. Color me skeptical, but I don't think you took his case out of the goodness of your heart. So, where'd the money come from for your fees?"

Ashley chuckled. "Have you asked Joe?"

"No, but I plan to," I said.

"Good luck with that. Let me know what he says," Ashley said, a ring of sarcasm in his voice.

"Mr. Ashley, unless I'm misreading things, someone hired you to help Riccoli beat the rap the second time around. If I could find out who that was, it might help lead me to who was responsible for Sherry's murder."

"Look, Lieutenant, even if I knew and wanted to tell you— two huge assumptions—I don't think ethically I can. Seems to me it's privileged."

With a lesser lawyer, I might have tried to bluff and say I could ask for a hearing to determine the source of his legal fees. But this case was twenty years old and he had probably already figured out I'd never get authorization.

"Did you happen to order daily copy during the trial?" I asked, knowing that because Riccoli had been found not guilty there were no trial transcripts prepared for an appeal. Sometimes, however, one side or the other ordered daily transcripts to help prepare for what came next.

Ashley laughed. "No. I didn't have the money for that."

"Riccoli's conviction was reversed because of the failure to turn over the results of the DNA from under Sherry's fingernails, which it turned out didn't match Riccoli's. How did my office deal with that fact?"

His face twisted into scowl. "They argued that the victim was a prostitute and the DNA could have come from any of her 'customers.' Let me be clear, Lieutenant, it wasn't like your office made Sherry out to be a sympathetic victim. I think they had as much disdain for her as they did for Joe."

That wasn't a surprise. Given who Sherry was, I found it surprising that my office had even retried the case. "Was there anything else you had available that wasn't in the first trial?"

Ashley ran his index finger across his lips, appearing deep in thought. "It's been a long time and lots of trials ago, but if I remember correctly, your office had also failed to turn over photos of Riccoli."

"Photos?"

"Yeah. For some reason, someone in your office had taken photos of Riccoli standing in his underwear that weren't turned over to the PD who represented him in the first trial."

Photos of Riccoli in his underwear? "Sorry, you lost me. Why were they important?"

"There were no scratches or any other marks on his body that would indicate any kind of struggle," Ashley replied. "That, plus the fact she had defensive wounds indicative of her putting up a fight, let me argue to the jury it wasn't Riccoli who did it."

My father's mumbled "no scratches" danced forward, taking center stage in my consciousness.

"Yeah, but he was arrested weeks after the murder. Wouldn't any marks have faded by then?"

He smiled back at me. "They would have. But the photos weren't taken when he was arrested, they were taken the day her body was found and he was brought in for questioning."

Why wasn't any of this in the case files? "Do you know who took the photos?"

"Never had to get that far. Your office stipulated to the date they were taken and their authenticity. They didn't seem to care because it fit their theory that the victim had scratched some other client. So, I didn't need a witness."

"But didn't your client know who took the pictures?"

"I know for sure they weren't taken by then Detective Snyder. Riccoli hated that guy. When I asked Joe who took the pictures, all he said was he didn't know the guy who took them, but it wasn't Snyder."

If it wasn't Snyder, who took the pictures? Regardless, whoever took them certainly must have realized, at least eventually, that they were potentially exculpatory. None of this seemed to fit together.

"Snyder was the lead detective. Is that why your client hated him?" I asked.

Ashley folded his hands as if in prayer, appearing to be thinking carefully about his response. "Since you said you're going to be speaking with Joe, maybe ask him why he had such a low opinion of Detective—now Captain—Snyder. From my perspective as Joe's attorney, I think Snyder perjured himself concerning the statement he took from Joe. Snyder wasn't the first detective I've encountered who I believed lied to the jury, and he hasn't been the last, but he was one of the most blatant. You have to remember, Lieutenant, back when this happened, the law didn't require interrogations to be recorded. So, I'll never be able to prove what happened in the interrogation room, but . . . well, let's just say, I believe my client's version."

Wonderful. Based on Ashley's assessment, not only did I have to watch my back because Snyder was transphobic, he was a liar as well.

"Let me ask you this," I said. "Did you or your client have any theories on who might have killed Sherry?"

For a split second, his eyes seemed to flicker, but it quickly passed. "Look, Lieutenant. I don't have to tell you that sometimes straight guys flip out when they find out that the woman they're attracted to or who just performed some sex act on them has a little something extra. My guess is some dude like that discovered Sherry's secret."

Even I had to admit that was the most logical explanation, but I wasn't buying it, and from Ashley's expression there seemed to be more than what he was saying. I waited, letting the silence hang in the air for a beat, just to put an exclamation point on what I said next. "I really don't think you believe that's what happened any more than I do, Mr. Ashley."

"Sorry, Lieutenant. That's all I've got."

We both stood and we shook hands again. "Thank you for your time. I know how valuable it is." And then I pulled a Columbo. "One last thing. I assume that if Mr. Riccoli waives the privilege, you'll let me know who paid his fees."

Ashley did all he could do to keep from laughing, but he couldn't hide his amusement. "We'll see, Detective. We'll see." And then Ashley did my Columbo one better. "Years ago, I knew a Frank Kelly in the DA's office. Any relation?"

"My father," I replied.

"Give him my regards," he said, with a grin that would've done the Cheshire Cat proud.

CHAPTER 7

THE FOLLOWING AFTERNOON I drove the forty minutes out to Franklin and found Perry Plumbing in an industrial neighborhood not far from the Franklin Bears Stadium. The office looked like it had been pulled from a 1960s time capsule. There were two metal desks behind a wooden counter, the walls covered in cheap paneling that bulged, showing gaps at the seams. The computers on the desks were the only things ruining the '60s motif.

I introduced myself to Betty, who appeared to be around sixty, and had the rough-around-the-edges demeanor needed to be an office manager for a company employing hard-nosed plumbers.

After I showed Betty my credentials, I told her I was looking for Mr. Riccoli because he might have information on a cold case I was investigating. I took pains to make it clear that Joe hadn't done anything wrong, and my only interest in talking to him was to see if he had any information that might help me.

Betty studied me as she took a long drag from a cigarette, I presume trying to weigh whether I was on the level or not. "You sure Joe isn't in any trouble?" she asked in a voice that sounded gnarled by decades of smoking.

"I promise," I replied.

One of the advantages of me blending in as a woman was that I have tapped into the bond that exists between many women, especially those working in male-dominated professions. Betty turned, looked at the clock behind her—3:30 P.M.

"You can probably find him at O'Donnell's Pub. It's two blocks down on the corner of Harrison," she said, her tone making it sound like I could find Joe at O'Donnell's every day after work.

"Thanks, Betty. I appreciate the help."

"You wouldn't bullshit me about Joe not being in any trouble, would you?" she growled.

I smiled. "Pinky swear," I replied. "All I want is a chance to talk to him."

"Good luck with that," she said, raising an eyebrow. "I'm not sure I've heard Joe say more than twenty words in the ten years he's worked here."

IF THERE HAD BEEN music playing in O'Donnell's when I walked in, it would have come to a screeching halt. It was like a scene out of a classic Western. The room fell silent as all eyes turned to meet me. I'm not sure if it was because I was a woman, not a regular, or just that I was still in cop mode. But whatever it was, none of the men seemed happy to see me.

Thanks to the updated photo I had found, even in the dim light, Joe was easy to spot. He was at the far end of the bar, no one else within four barstools of him. I nodded to the bartender, whose unfriendly glare remained locked on me, and made my way to where Joe was sitting.

"Mr. Riccoli, my name is Lauren Kelly. Can I speak to you for a moment?"

Joe looked up from his beer and gave me the once over. "No."

"Let me try again," I said, sitting next to him. "My name is Lieutenant Lauren Kelly with the Donn County District Attorney's Office. I'd like to have a word with you."

If nothing else, that got his attention.

"About?" he asked, turning to face me. His look wasn't threatening, more wary. The look of a guy who had wound up on the wrong end of a police interrogation that had landed him on death row. I knew there was no way to force him to talk to me, so I needed to get him there even though I could imagine that every fiber of his being was screaming for him to ignore me. I had to connect on a personal level.

"Sherry Darling. I've reopened the investigation to try and uncover who really murdered her."

His shoulders slumped and he turned back, once again focusing on the beer in front of him. "Go away."

"Joe. I can't undo what happened to you twenty years ago, but I can try to do right by Sherry. It means a lot to me," I said, hoping my sincerity would overcome his reticence about talking to cops.

He gave me a sarcastic laugh. "Yeah, and why would it be so important to you?"

I leaned in so only he could hear me. "Because Sherry and I went to high school together. I was a cop in Harrison when she was murdered and," I paused for effect, "I'm also a trans-gender woman."

"Hey, Joe," the bartender called out. "Is she bothering you? You want me to call the cops?"

I turned, putting on my best annoyed-cop demeanor. "Relax. They're already here," I said, flashing my badge.

My bravado didn't seem to go over well with the regulars, who appeared to be growing a little restless—guys don't like it when a cop starts messing with one of their own, and Joe was so entrenched in O'Donnell's I wouldn't have been surprised if his name was engraved on his barstool. But before things got ugly, Joe intervened.

"Nah. I'm fine," he said with a wave of his hand. Then he looked me in the eyes, his face now defiant. "Look, whatever your name is, I talked to the cops years ago. I told 'em what I knew and then they jammed me up and said I murdered Sherry. I got nothing else to say."

"Kelly," I said. "My name is Lauren Kelly."

A confused look crossed his face, as if my name struck a chord. *Shit. Had my father done something to him?* I needed to do something or I was going to lose him. "Joe, like I told you, I knew Sherry. And someone should have said this to you twenty-one years ago, but I'm sorry for your loss. I know you were very much in love with Sherry, and you must have been devastated by her death."

I could tell by his face that he was trying to determine if I was genuine or not. And who could blame him for not believing me? He had trusted in the system once, and detectives just like me, maybe even my own father, had used that to screw him.

I turned and looked at a dingy wooden booth in the corner of the room behind us. "How about this? I'll buy us a couple of beers. We'll drink them, we'll talk, and when we're done, I'll leave you alone. Besides, nothing can happen to you. Double jeopardy—you've already been acquitted." I motioned to the booth. "What are you drinking?"

"Guinness," he finally replied.

I walked down the bar to where the bartender was standing, still eyeing me warily. "Two pints of Guinness."

I walked to the booth, placed the pint on the table in front of Joe and slid onto the bench opposite him.

"You knew Sherry?" he asked.

"I did. We were the same year in high school."

"Were you friends?"

"No. But I really admired her. I'd love to learn more about her. What her life was like after she left school."

I went slowly, trying to engage him around the edges, aware that I was dredging up shit from more than twenty years ago, shit that he had long ago tried to bury. It took a while, but eventually he slowly opened up about Sherry. She and her father never got along because she was so effeminate as a child. When she was twelve, she went to live with her grandmother in Harrison—primarily because her family didn't want anything to do with her. Sherry's grandmother adored her. She started hanging out with some drag queens when she was fourteen. Sherry's grandmother had been a huge fan of Frankie Valli and the Four Seasons, so when Sherry began doing drag shows, she had taken Sherry Baby as a stage name from the Four Seasons' song "Sherry." She later went with Darling as her last name in honor of Candy Darling. With the help of her grandmother, they found a doctor willing to give her female hormones and by sixteen, after she dropped out of high school, she had transitioned and was living full-time as Sherry.

As I listened to Joe, the Sherry I knew came into sharper focus—impish, fun loving. It was as if he was coloring in the outline of the person I had vaguely known.

After about forty minutes he stopped. "You said one beer."

He was on his third. I pointed to my half-full glass. "I'm still on my first."

Sensing he might be getting antsy, drunk, or both, I decided to start zeroing in on what was important to me. "In your statement and testimony, you said you argued with Sherry about her continuing to engage in sex work. Was her doing sex work new, or was that something she had done as long as you dated her?"

He dropped his head, his eyes staring at the table, and I was afraid he might shut down. But after a few seconds, he looked up. "She'd always done it. After her grandmother died, she was living on the street for a while. She needed to survive, so she did what she had to do. After we met, I tried to convince her to stop, but at the time, I was a twenty-two-year-old apprentice plumber. I wasn't making shit. She made next to nothing doing drag shows on the weekends, and even less working part-time at a temp agency run by a friend of her grandmother. She desperately wanted to have gender-affirming surgery, so the sex work was something she did to get the money."

"Okay, but if she had always done it, why'd you argue?"

He sighed. "I was jealous."

"I'm not trying to be insensitive, but why? Had something changed?"

His head nodded slowly. "Yeah, something had definitely changed in the three or four months before she was murdered." He drew in a deep breath before releasing it. "Before that she had a pretty random schedule. One week she might be out three nights, other weeks, maybe she wouldn't work at all. But then it all changed, and she worked every Thursday night, like clockwork. It was crazy. She'd leave at seven P.M. and be home before midnight. She was still making the same amount of money, but only working Thursday night. Look, maybe you won't understand this, but I loved Sherry because she was a beautiful woman and person, inside and out. Once those Thursdays started, I became convinced she was seeing someone else, someone who had big bucks. I was afraid I was going to lose her."

"How much was she getting?"

"Three to four hundred most weeks," he replied. "I mean, she brought home around two fifty to three because she had to share some of it with the guy who set this up."

I leaned back against the hard bench, trying to process what he was telling me. Three or four hundred cash for one night's work was serious money—real serious twenty years ago. "So, if I'm hearing you right, you argued because you accused her of having another boyfriend, a rich boyfriend, but not because she was involved in sex work."

"Yeah," he mumbled.

"But I read your statement. That's not what you told the detectives who interviewed you. Why?"

He looked at me like I was stupid. "Because they told me not to," he said, as if I was supposed to know that.

"What do you mean, they told you not to?"

"The detective said that made no sense that we argued over her having another guy when I knew she did sex work. He said that based on the way Sherry had been mutilated, I'd be better off saying I didn't know she was a sex worker and that she must've picked up someone who lost it when he found out she was trans. So, I said what they told me to say, and then based on my statement, they convinced the jury what really happened was that I flew into a rage when I found out she was doing sex work."

From reading the file I knew who had interrogated Joe, but I wanted to see how he'd react. "Do you remember the name of the detective who told you to say that?"

"You think I'd ever forget that son of a bitch? Detective Richard Fucking Snyder!" he spit out.

"Was he the same detective who took pictures of you the day you were originally questioned?"

"No. It was someone else. This guy just told me they needed some pictures. I'm not sure he even told me his name."

"You think you'd recognize a picture of him?"

His face looked skeptical. "It's been twenty years."

"When I told you my name was Kelly, you gave me a funny look. My father was a detective sergeant back then—Frank Kelly. Does his name ring a bell?"

"Yeah. I think he was a witness at my first trial. Not so much against me, just about where they found Sherry." His voice sounded suddenly far away, as if he was picturing Sherry, the beautiful woman he loved, thrown into a dumpster with the rotting garbage.

"Could he have been the one who took the pictures?"

"I don't know. My girlfriend was dead—murdered. The

cops had just questioned me for hours. Then someone said they needed pictures of me. I really wasn't thinking straight at that point."

I decided to move on. "Do you know where Sherry went on Thursday nights?"

"No. She wouldn't tell me. Even the night that she . . ." He stopped, and closed his eyes. I could tell he was reliving a scene that had probably played in his head countless times, thinking *If only I hadn't let her go*.

"Do you know how she got there and home?"

"Bus, I guess. I never asked."

"You mentioned she had to share the money. Did she have a pimp?"

"Not before this started. And I don't know whether the guy she shared the money with was actually a pimp, or just someone who had introduced her to this guy, so it was more like a finder's fee."

"What happened that day?"

"I came home from work. She was in a playful mood. We made love, had dinner, and then I begged her to stay home and not see whoever it was she was seeing. We argued. I accused her of being in love with someone else. She was hurt, but after a few minutes she came over, kissed me, and said something like, 'Joey, don't be jealous. You know I love you.' She then told me I had nothing to be jealous about because the other guy was a putz and she almost had all the money she needed. Then she'd stop and it would be just the two of us."

He reached up and with the back of his hand he wiped away a tear rolling down his cheek.

"I'm sorry," I said. "Again, I know this is insensitive, but she was a sex worker. Why didn't you use a condom? Weren't you afraid of getting an STD or HIV/AIDS?"

The kernel of a grin told me that the memory held some small joy for him, painful as it was.

"She told me that she made everyone else use a condom. I was her guy. I didn't have to wear a glove."

"What did you do when she didn't come home that night?"

"I didn't know what to do. I thought maybe she was just punishing me for being jealous, so I waited until I got home from work on Friday. Then I called the police. Of course, I didn't know it at the time, but her body had already been found."

I knew the rest. He was called in for questioning, he gave a statement, and then three weeks later, when the tests came back showing the semen stain was his, he was arrested.

He closed his eyes and bit down on his lip, his head moving slowly from side to side. "I don't know why whoever she was seeing would have done this to her. It's never made any sense. Why kill her?"

I knew better than most that bad shit happened to people all the time, sometimes with no rhyme or reason. A twelve-year-old kid sitting on his bed playing a video game, when someone a block away shoots at someone else, misses, and the bullet hits the kid in the side of the head, killing him instantly. Here one second, gone the next—just random bad luck. But that wasn't Sherry's case. There was a "why" for her murder. I didn't know what it was yet, but this wasn't just some random act of violence.

"That's what I'm trying to find out, Joe. Did anything change after Sherry appeared on *The Michael Dobbs Show*—any threats, stalkers, anything different for her?" I asked.

He thought for a moment. "Yeah, I think she regretted

doing the show. The only reason she did it was because they paid her twenty-five hundred under the table, but I know she was worried that whoever it was that she was seeing was going to get spooked by the fact that she had been on television. A few days before she was murdered, I got home from work and she was on the phone arguing with someone. After she hung up, I asked her who it was, and she just said some asshole. But I could tell she was upset."

"You know what they were arguing about?"

"No. As soon as I came in, she ended the call, and when I asked, she told me not to worry about it."

"Do you think it was related to what happened a few days later?"

"Honestly? I don't have a clue."

I needed to find out what Sherry was doing every Thursday—who she was seeing. She hadn't shared it with Joe, but girls talk to their friends. Surely, she must have told someone. "Did Sherry have any close friends? Someone she may have confided in?"

He shook his head. "No one that I knew."

"What about the folks at the club where she was in the drag shows? Did you meet any of them?"

"No, I never went to her shows." His voice was now a pained whisper. "I know how this makes me sound, but I didn't want to see a bunch of gay men looking at Sherry like she was another gay man." He looked up, anguish written on his face. "I know she did drag for the money, but I didn't want to be with people who thought she was pretending to be a woman—she wasn't pretending. She was a woman."

"Do you remember the name of the club?"

"Nah, I don't. It was the name of a bird. The Eagle . . . something like that. I'm sorry."

I knew from one brief conversation we had in school that Sherry didn't have a good relationship with her mother, a sore subject for both of us, but I decided to probe anyway. "I know you told me Sherry and her father didn't get along, but what about the rest of her family? Her mom? Any siblings?"

"She never saw her mom. I think she may have had a couple of brothers, maybe a sister, but she didn't talk about her family. All I know is that they considered her a freak and wanted nothing to do with her."

"Did you keep any of Sherry's personal belongings?" I asked, wondering if there might be any clues there.

"No," he said, his face twisted in pain. "I was in jail for four years. When I was released after the second trial, I had been evicted, our apartment had been relet and the landlord had gotten rid of everything in our apartment, both mine and Sherry's. I had nothing—literally nothing."

I wanted to scream. People in my office had fucked Joe over. Snyder told him to lie. Someone had hidden DNA results that were exculpatory—all to get him convicted and sent to death row. Why? They certainly hadn't done it out of a sense of justice for Sherry. To them she was just a piece of scum. Which meant there was someone else they were protecting. For my money, it had to be the Thursday night person.

I looked at Joe and could tell his tank was drained, but I had one more question. "When you were retried, you were represented by Ray Ashley. Even back then, Mr. Ashley was a high-priced criminal defense lawyer. Where'd you get the money to pay him?"

He gave me an *Are you serious?* look. "I didn't pay for Mr. Ashley. After the reversal, he visited me in jail and he told me he wanted to represent me. I had spent enough time inside by then to know who the good lawyers were, and he was at the top. When I told him 'I can't afford you,' he told me not to worry, everything would be taken care of. He never charged me a nickel. I have no idea who paid him."

It was the answer I expected, but who would hire one of the top lawyers in the state to represent Joe, and more importantly, why?

"I asked Mr. Ashley who paid him and he didn't want to disclose who it was. Do you care if he tells me?"

"Look, that's totally up to him."

Based on how Ashley had protected who paid his fee, I didn't see any point in revisiting it with him now.

"Here's my card," I said. "My cell number is on the back. Call me anytime if you think of anything or have any questions."

He took my card and studied it with glassy eyes.

"Can I have your cell number so I can reach out if I have any questions?" I asked.

He seemed to think it over, but then gave me his number. I pointed at his empty glass. "You want another?"

"Yeah," he mumbled.

I ordered him another and paid the tab. "Make sure he doesn't try to drive home," I said to the keep.

The bartender's eyes narrowed, as if to say "We take care of our own and don't need you telling us what to do," but he nodded.

When I got to my car, I took my work phone out of my

jacket pocket, turned off the recording app and did a quick check to make sure it had recorded our conversation. I had gotten a lot of information, but I was no closer to having a person of interest.

As I headed back to Harrison, I knew I needed to make two stops—the first at WQRE to pick up a copy of the unedited episode of *The Michael Dobbs Show*, and the second at my father's house to see if I could find a copy of my high school yearbook. I remembered Sherry had two good friends, a girl and a guy, that she hung out with at school—both of them were gay, but I couldn't remember their names. The three of them called themselves the three amigos, after the movie. West Harrison High was a tough place back then, and it was amazing the three of them survived. It was no secret that Sherry had been beaten up several times, but she never squealed. And maybe that's what saved her. That, and the rumor that she gave the best head in the school, and over time so many guys had gotten blow jobs from her, they stopped beating her up. Whatever it was, Sherry followed her own rules—the same rules that had probably gotten her killed.

CHAPTER 8

"THIS IS THE AUDITION of Sherry Darling for the 'I Have a Secret Life' episode of The Michael Dobbs Show.

Sherry, can I have your name please?"

"Sherry Darling."

"And Sherry, what's your real name?"

"Sherry Darling."

"I'm sorry. I mean that you were given at birth?"

"I don't use that name anymore."

"But we need it for legal purposes to be able to pay you for your appearance."

"No, you don't. I work for a temp agency and have a bank account in my name."

"Is there a reason why you don't want to give us your real name?"

"I have given you my real name—Sherry Darling."

"Look, I'm not trying to be difficult, but if we can't get your legal name, we can't have you on the show."

"That's fine." [Sound of mic being unclipped]

"Wait . . . Um, maybe we can work around it."

[. . .]

"Look into a crystal ball, Sherry, and tell us where you see yourself in five years?"

"I've had my surgery and I'm happily married to the guy I'm dating. I've gotten my GED and I have a good job, maybe as a legal secretary. Or maybe I get lucky and I'm a singer. Whatever I'm doing, I'm just enjoying being me."

"Do you see yourself as a mom—maybe you and your husband adopting children?"

"Gee, I don't know. It's not that I don't love children; I do. But it's something my husband and I would have to talk about because it's such a huge responsibility. And I guess because I had such a messed-up family life, there's part of me that worries whether I'd be a good mom. One thing I do know, I'd be better at it than my mom, because I'd love my child for whoever they were."

TWENTY MINUTES LATER, THE audition interview over, I pushed aside the last of the General Tso's chicken and ejected the thumb drive from my laptop. I folded my arms on my father's kitchen table, rested my head on my arms, and tried to digest not only what I had just eaten, but what I had just watched.

When I had arrived at WQRE around 5:45 P.M. the archivist couldn't have been more accommodating. Not only had she stayed late waiting for me to get there, but she had copied the unedited episode as well as the audition interview that Dobbs's staff had done with Sherry to see if she would make a good guest. Sherry was dressed casually for the audition— slacks and a sweater—and while she had run through some of the same details Riccoli had provided me, she refused to acknowledge to them that she did sex work. They tried, but she wasn't going there.

There were times during some investigations when you'd see that moment when if the victim had just done one thing differently, they wouldn't have wound up a murder statistic. When Sherry unclipped her mic and rose from the chair to leave the interview, I found myself wishing that I could find that alternate reality where she just left and never appeared on the show. Would she and Joe be a happy middle-aged couple at this point? How would Joe's life have changed if he hadn't spent four years in jail, two of them on death row, for a murder he hadn't committed?

I often wondered the same thing about my own life—the what ifs. What if my mother hadn't left when I was five; what if I had come out as trans the night my brother came out as gay in the middle of the argument with our father; what if my brother hadn't moved the knife out of my reach? All our lives are filled with the paths not chosen. Sometimes the paths we choose are deadly.

After I finished watching everything, it seemed like Sherry hadn't changed much since high school. She had remained fiercely independent and willing to do whatever she needed to get to where she wanted to go. Which, assuming Riccoli was telling the truth, included seeing someone willing to pay her hundreds of dollars every week for a few hours' work. The person or persons Sherry was seeing had money. And, if Sherry was to be believed—a tougher sell because she had been trying to calm a jealous boyfriend—the person, singular, was someone she considered a putz. In addition, some third party—a third party that even Riccoli didn't know—had paid Ashley's legal fees. Which raised the question, who benefited from Riccoli being found not guilty?

Added to the stew were my father's "no scratch marks" comment, and the fact that, according to Ashley, there were photos taken by someone at the DCDAO that showed no marks on Riccoli after Sherry's death. I hadn't gone down to the evidence vault yet, but I needed to see the photos and find out who the hell had taken them and why. I also knew from reading Snyder's investigative report that there was no mention of any photos, other than the ones I had already looked at of Sherry's body by the dumpster where she was discovered, and later, from the autopsy.

I sat back up, rolled my neck to work out the kinks and looked over at the West Harrison High School yearbook sitting on the table. To my surprise, it had been in the box in the basement where I had stored some of my things before I moved out of the house.

I opened the yearbook, catching sight of some of the guys with the bowl haircuts that were popular then, and turned to my senior picture. I took a look at my photo. Unlike some trans folks, seeing a pre-transition picture of me didn't upset me. I had a pretty good sense of self, and despite what I may have looked like in the past, I knew the present version of me was who I'd always been, even if no one else could see it.

I ran through the alphabet trying to recall the names of the other members of the three amigos. When I hit *M* one came to me—Marjorie . . . Marjorie Benson. I turned to the Bs, and there was Margie, as everyone called her in high school. Her hair was short, the top of her denim coveralls over a gray T-shirt, evident in the photo. Another pause as I tried to remember the guy's name—Tony, Anthony Russo—and when I flipped to the *R*s, I found him. I stared at Tony's baby face and wondered if he and Margie had stayed in touch with Sherry.

It wasn't like I had a lot of other leads, so I opened my laptop and started a search to try and track them down. It didn't take long to find a Margie Benson on Facebook who was the right age, working as an assistant manager at Tesh's, an upscale bar and restaurant in the heart of the gentrified section of Harrison. Looking at Margie's Facebook profile picture, I knew I had the right person. I then went looking for Anthony "Tony" Russo, but came up with nothing.

I thought about heading over to Tesh's, but it was late, and I had already had a long day. Besides, if I had any hope of talking to Margie, it would probably be best to wait until the place was empty, not at eight o'clock. My little high school reunion could wait until tomorrow. I decided to pack up my laptop and head back to my apartment. Even though I was going to have to start staying here from time to time, it could wait. There were still too many ghosts haunting this house. For now, the only ghost I needed to spend time with was Sherry.

BY THE TIME WE were halfway through our sophomore year, the first thing Sherry would do when she arrived at school was to go to the vice principal's office to receive her detention slip from Mr. Mann for wearing makeup. Every day she'd spend an hour after school in detention because she refused to remove it. Once she was suspended for two weeks for showing Mr.

Mann her breasts. She had been sent to the office for wearing a bra under her blouse, and when he confronted her about the violation of the dress code, she had pulled up her shirt and bra to reveal a developing pair of breasts. Apparently, Sherry had been able to secure female hormones. She had argued the suspension was unfair because if they were going to apply the boys' dress code to her, then she had the right to show her chest.

The only time I ever remember talking to her was one afternoon in detention. We were the only two in the room when Mr. Buckley, the teacher assigned detention duty, stepped out. Sherry looked at me and said, "What are you in for?" Her wording made it sound like we were in jail.

"I punched a kid," I replied.

"Why?" she asked.

I hesitated, not sure how much I wanted to say. "He made a comment about my mother."

She gave me a quizzical look, but she seemed to know better than to ask me what he said. "Sorry," she said, her eyes looking past me. "Mom is a tough subject for me too, especially since she doesn't want me the way I am."

I nodded. "Mine left when I was five. She didn't want me either."

"How about your dad?"

My eye roll must have given her the answer, because she said, "Yeah, mine's an asshole who hates me."

She reached out to me, and for the briefest moment her hand hung there, ready for me to take it, but I hesitated. Suddenly, the door swung open. "The two of you," Buckley barked as he reentered the room. "Silence! This is detention.

I hear another word from either of you and I'll see you here tomorrow."

With that, Sherry laughed out loud. "Oh, come on, Mr. Buckley. You know I'll be here tomorrow."

And that was how I remembered her—fiery, independent, and defiant.

CHAPTER 9

"ANYBODY HOME?"

The front door of Tesh's had been locked, so I walked down an alley and found an unlocked back door and called out, not wanting to surprise anyone.

"Who is it?" a disembodied voice finally replied from a room on the right side of the hallway.

"Lieutenant Kelly, Donn County District Attorney's Office."

I heard what sounded like a chair rolling across a floor and then a man stepped out into the corridor. He looked to be about my age, on the short side, his dark hair combed back, and a shirt unbuttoned enough that his chest hair was on full display.

"Is there a problem, Lieutenant?"

"I don't think so. Is there?" I replied with a crooked smile, wondering what problem he was worried about.

"Ah, no . . . What can I help you with?"

"I'm looking for a Marjorie Benson. Does she still work here?"

"She in trouble?"

"Not that I'm aware of," I said. "I'm just investigating a cold case that involves someone she knew back in high school."

"Oh," he said, the relief in his voice palpable. "Yeah. She's here. She's the assistant manager. She should be up front by the bar."

"Thanks. And your name is?"

"Peter Tesh—I'm the owner."

"Is it all right if I head up to talk to her, Mr. Tesh?"

"Sure. Sure, Lieutenant. And please, call me Peter," he said, now very accommodating.

"I appreciate your help, Peter. I'll have to come back another time when I'm off duty and have a drink," I said, doing my best to give him a sexy smile, something I had yet to master.

"You do that. Just let the bartender know it's on me," he said, giving me a look that bordered on a leer.

"Thanks."

All the lights were on in the main area and there was a person cleaning tables and another vacuuming. A woman behind the bar appeared to be taking inventory of the liquor. I recognized Margie in a heartbeat. Sure, she had changed. Everyone changed over the course of twenty-eight years. But the years had been kind to her—she just looked like a slightly older version of the yearbook picture I had seen last night. She always had a pretty face and that was without a hint of makeup. She had been a string bean of a teenager, but she had definitely filled out. A singlet from a local 5K race showed off her upper body, including tattoos on her left shoulder and on both arms. Her hair was short, blond, and spiky, with splashes of pink, and her ears sported multiple piercings.

"Excuse me, are you Ms. Benson?" I asked, even though I knew the answer.

She glanced over her shoulder. "Yeah."

"I was wondering if I could ask you a few questions."

This time she turned to face me. "And you are?"

"Lieutenant Kelly from the DA's office."

She threw her hands up in a mock surrender. "I didn't do it. If I did, it was self-defense, and if it wasn't self-defense, I was standing my ground," she said with a small chuckle. Her hazel eyes showed a mischievous gleam. "Sorry."

"No problem," I responded, trying to suppress my own grin.

"What can I do for you, Lieutenant?"

"I'm investigating a murder."

"Anyone I know?" she said flippantly.

"Actually, yes, but before you get upset, the murder occurred over twenty years ago. But it was someone you went to high school with."

The look on her face conveyed the question without her even having to ask.

"Sherry Darling," I offered.

A look of confusion wrinkled her brow. "I thought they caught the guy who killed her," she said, wiping her hands on a bar towel.

"The guy she was dating at the time was arrested and convicted, but it was reversed on appeal and when they retried him, he was found not guilty. No one else was ever charged with her murder so it's a cold case that I'm looking into."

"Why now?"

"Because it's my job," I responded, deciding at least for now to hide behind the badge. "And because what I've uncovered so far indicates that the boyfriend didn't kill her. So, I'm trying to find out who did."

"Interesting," she said, turning her head slightly as if to get a better look at me. "You want something to drink? Soda, water?" she clarified. "There's also coffee on the table over there," she said, pointing to a coffee pot on a warmer in the corner.

"Coffee sounds great. Thanks," I said.

She walked out from behind the bar, her eyes locked on me as she went to the table and poured two cups. "Milk, sugar?"

"Black, please," I replied as I watched her watching me.

She handed me a cup of coffee and motioned with a nod to a table near the bar. "I have a couple of minutes. Have a seat."

We sat down opposite each other, her eyes boring into mine. "I feel like I know you from somewhere. What did you say your name was?"

"Lauren Kelly." I wanted to get whatever information I could on Sherry before coming clean, and knew if I told her why she knew me, it would sidetrack things. I reached into my jacket and pulled out a small pad and a pen. "Mind if I take notes?"

"Whatever."

"You went to high school with Sherry, right?"

"Yeah, we were friends. We were kind of two misfits together. She was the first trans person I knew and I was the only out lesbian in that hellhole."

"What do you know about her family?"

"Not much. She and her father didn't get along. From what she told me, before she moved out, he used to smack her around, trying to make a man of her." She raised an eyebrow. "Obviously, that didn't work out too well. I saw him once when he came to her grandmother's. He was a scary-looking dude. When she was about twelve, she moved in with her grandmother. I forget where she was from originally—Sheldon, maybe. I hung out at her grandmother's house a lot. She was a great lady. She just loved Sherry for who she was."

"Sherry have any siblings?"

"If I remember right, she had two brothers and a sister. Her dad was from Ireland, and they all had Irish names. I think her oldest brother was Seamus—he was maybe seven years older or so. A sister—Fiona, maybe? She was about five years older than us. And a brother, Padraig, who was a couple of years older." She paused and frowned. "Sherry didn't really talk about any of them, but her grandmother would mention them from time to time. I got the feeling the oldest brother was rough on her—calling her names and shit."

"You stay in touch with her after graduation?" I asked, quickly realizing that my question was inartful.

"Actually, she never graduated," Margie said, picking up on my miscue. "Her grandmother passed away and she dropped out after her junior year. But we stayed in touch for a while—maybe for about two years after I graduated. And then we lost touch."

"A falling out?"

"No, nothing like that. After her grandmother died, Sherry survived doing sex work. Between that and the fact that she was staying with some trans women she had gotten to know, and I had become friends with some of the lesbians in

Harrison, we were just hanging with different crowds. That's all. I always thought she was cool."

"When was the last time you saw her?" I asked.

"When was she murdered?" Margie asked.

"April 12, 2001," I replied. "She appeared on *The Michael Dobbs Show* the week before that."

"Oh, shit. I forgot about her being on that show. That woman, I swear sometimes she was her own worst enemy."

"What do you mean?"

"Sherry was fearless, but sometimes she could be reckless." Margie closed her eyes and sighed. "When we were in high school, she was constantly getting bullied for being trans, although nobody even knew what trans was then, so most of the assholes in our class thought she was just an effeminate gay guy, and they gave her nothing but shit. But she didn't care. That was Sherry being fearless. But one day she tells me that she had just given half the guys on the football team blowjobs. I said, are you out of your mind? And she laughed and said it was fun. She loved triggering gay panic, making these guys wonder if they were gay because they just got their rocks off getting a blowjob from her. Besides, she said, there was safety in numbers. No one would do anything for fear someone else would rat them out. That was the reckless Sherry. Just like going on *The Michael Dobbs Show*—what was she thinking." Her eyes again studied me. "Do I know you?"

"Can you answer my question first? When was the last time you saw her?"

She took a sip from her coffee. "Ironically, it was probably about three months before her murder. I hadn't seen her in years, but one night I happened to go to the gay bar where she was in a drag show. We hung out at the bar and talked for a while after. She seemed like the same Sherry. She told me she was trying to save up enough money to have gender-affirming surgery, although that wasn't how we referred to it back in the day. She was in a good mood. She said she was dating a nice guy and had found a sugar daddy who paid her good money for sex. She was hoping he'd be her ticket to her surgery. Even though we talked about getting together again, we never connected after that. Next thing I knew I was reading about her murder in *The Harrison Gazette*." Her eyes suddenly went wide. "*The Gazette*. You were in *The Gazette* a couple of days ago. That's why I know you. Liam Kelly," she said, using my dead name. "We went to high school together."

"Good to see you again, Margie."

"Holy shit! Who the fuck would have ever guessed that you were trans? Oh, for fucks sake," she said, shaking her head in disbelief.

"We can reminisce later," I said. "Let me ask you, did she say anything about this guy—the sugar daddy?"

Margie placed her fist against her lips. "Not that I remember."

Shit. Another dead end. I took a mouthful of coffee, and tried to think of next steps.

"Wait!" she said. "I remember Sherry said something like, 'You thought I was crazy when I blew the football team, if you knew who this was, you'd know I was insane.'"

"Do you think she meant he was dangerous?"

"I'm not sure. But from the sound of things, he had money. So, I don't know if he was dangerous or just well connected. But I got the sense she knew she was playing with fire."

"It also sounds like she was suggesting you would've known who it was if she shared his name?"

"That was my impression too. Which is weird because twenty-something years ago, I didn't know anyone rich or well connected."

"Maybe it was someone famous?" I suggested.

She replied with a shrug.

This certainly didn't jibe with what Sherry had told Joe—the guy was a putz. Maybe Sherry had colored the truth because she didn't want her jealous boyfriend to get even more upset. Or maybe, if the guy was truly dangerous, she was trying to protect Joe.

"The gay bar where Sherry performed, does it still exist?"

"No. It's long gone. It was called The Hawk. Went out of business in the early 2000s. I think there's a CVS there now."

"Yeah, I remember it," I said.

She gave me a funny look.

"I was a Harrison cop before I went to the DA's office," I said.

She flashed me a snarky grin. "Just wondering."

"You know any of the other people in the drag show she was in?"

"Nah. Drag wasn't my thing. I just happened to go with some friends that night. Most of the time I hung out in Licious, a lesbian bar on the other side of town. But I guess you know that one too. From being a Harrison cop, I mean." The grin returned. "So, look at you *Ms.* Kelly. Aren't you one for keeping secrets," she said, putting extra emphasis on the Ms. "Tell me about yourself."

She sounded genuinely interested, so I spent about ten

minutes giving her the *Reader's Digest* version of my life. When I finished, she said, "Good for you. Too bad we didn't know about you back in the day. You could have joined our exclusive club."

I felt another pang of guilt for staying on the sidelines back then and never defending them—but this wasn't the right time for mea culpas, so I moved on. "Speaking of the three amigos, do you happen to know where Tony Russo is these days?"

Based on the change in her expression, it wasn't hard to guess bad news was coming next. "Tony passed away," she said. "Actually, before Sherry. After high school, he moved to Miami. I'd bump into his sister from time to time and she told me he died of complications from AIDS. He couldn't have been older than twenty." She shook her head. "We lost so many gay men, but no one gave a shit. I'm the only one of the amigos left."

"Sorry," I said.

"Yeah. Those two helped me survive high school. All we had was each other. Not sure I would have made it if it wasn't for them." She fell silent, seeming to lose herself for a moment in a flashback only she could see. Then, just as quickly, she was back.

"If I remember right, your mom was gone and your dad was a cop, right?"

"Yeah" was all I said.

"Yeah," she replied, with a nod.

I thanked her for the coffee and information, gave her my card, and shook her hand. "My business and personal cell numbers are on there. Give me a call if you remember anything else."

She grabbed a piece of paper by the cash register and wrote something on it. "That's my cell," she said, handing me the paper. "Stop by for dinner or a drink sometime, Lieutenant—when you're off duty," she added with a wink.

"I'll do that," I said.

When I got back to my car, I looked at the paper with Marjorie's phone number and found myself wondering what it would be like to go on a date again. I had carried a torch for Becca for so long, even the thought of going on a date with someone else seemed foreign. *No time for that now*, I thought, throwing her phone number into my briefcase.

AS I HEADED BACK to the office, I decided to call Becca. "I got the sense the other night that you might have an interest in helping me out on the Sherry Darling case," I said after opening pleasantries.

"What makes you think I'm not already helping?" There was a conspiratorial lilt in her voice.

"I didn't want to be presumptuous."

"Come on. You had to know that I'm into true crime. It's where I get my best book ideas."

"Find anything helpful—for me or your book?" I asked, realizing that I really should read her bestseller.

"Not yet, but still looking."

"Thanks. By the way, there used to be a gay bar over in the Highlawn section of the city called The Hawk. Do you remember it?"

"Vaguely. But I never went there. Did you?" she asked playfully. "Seriously, is it related to Sherry's murder?"

"Honestly, I don't know. At this point, all I know is that

on Saturday nights Sherry performed in the drag show there. I'm trying to find anyone who knew or worked with Sherry around the time of her murder, and other than the boyfriend, I haven't found anyone."

"If you want, I can check and see what I can find out."

"You sure?"

"Yeah. You know I love doing this stuff. Besides, it'll give me a break from looking at murdered Jane Does."

"Okay, thanks. Let me know what you find."

After we hung up, I felt an ache that I just couldn't push away. Co-opting Becca into helping me was nothing more than my desperate attempt to keep her in my life—I knew that. I could've looked up the information on The Hawk—I probably would when I had time. But even though I knew we'd never be a couple again, I clung to the tattered pieces of our relationship. I'd convinced myself I did it because I loved her, but there was another voice in my head telling me that my reluctance to let go was informed by the fear I'd never find someone else who I loved as much as Becca. I glanced at the closed briefcase holding Marjorie's number and considered that buried in my conflicting emotions was another conundrum—that just by trying to find a new relationship, I'd wind up losing the small part of Becca that I had managed to hold onto and, if that was gone, I'd once again find myself falling into the abyss of rejection.

WHEN I GOT BACK to the office, I grabbed my laptop and notes out of my briefcase and sat down to prepare the investigative reports of my interviews of Ashley, Riccoli, and Benson. I clicked on ProsDox, the DCDAO's secure document storage system, but as my fingers hovered over the keyboard, I froze. I could hear Snyder's secretary chatting on the phone down the hallway. If I saved my reports to my computer, they'd be on the system, meaning that anyone in the office my rank or higher—or their secretaries—would have access to them, including Snyder. There wasn't a single doubt in my mind that Snyder would review everything I entered in Sherry's case. I didn't know what Snyder would do when he saw Riccoli's allegation that he'd told Riccoli to lie in his statement to the police, or Ashley's allegations regarding perjury and the with-holding of evidence, but I knew it wouldn't be pretty. On the other hand, if I omitted that information from my reports, and we did eventually arrest a suspect, their attorney would have a field day with what I left out. On cross they'd be able to rip me a new one. And not only me—Riccoli and the others as well, arguing that if it wasn't in my report, the witnesses were making it up on the stand.

It took me a few minutes to come up with a work around, but it required someone in the office I could trust—and I could think of only one person.

CHAPTER 10

THE MISCONCEPTION MANY PEOPLE have about a DA's office is they think it's one cohesive office—it's not. It's divided between the sworn law enforcement officers, who investigate crimes, and assistant DAs, the lawyers tasked with providing legal advice to the investigators and then prosecuting the cases. Usually, it's a cooperative environment, but not always. Add to the mix the fact that, in this state, district attorneys are elected. Which means that the DA, Harrison Graham, who's been in office for just over ten years, is first and foremost a politician. In Donn County, that means he's as conservative as they come. Since he hired the majority of the assistant DAs and detectives, they're made in his image—mostly white, mostly male, and closely aligned with him politically. The one exception was Assistant State Attorney General Lisa Weiss.

Weiss had been assigned to the office three years ago as a result of a mini-scandal in the Narcotics Unit involving over-time being paid to detectives for hours they never worked. Facing some unexpected political blowback, Graham had agreed to bring in Weiss from the State Attorney General's Office to oversee the DCDAO's Internal Affairs and Professional Responsibility Unit. The unit, which was made up of Weiss, an assistant DA, and two detectives, not only handled IA complaints involving the DCDAO personnel, but they also investigated and prosecuted any cops in Donn County facing criminal charges. Tasked with investigating their own, IA was a thankless job. But when Weiss came to the office, she not only faced the usual enmity toward IA, she had to deal with outright stonewalling because she was going after the sacred cow—Narcotics, considered by the sworn side of the office to be the elite of the elite. Despite Weiss's best efforts, none of the superior officers involved in the overtime debacle were disciplined and only three of the seven detectives involved were punished, each receiving a two-week suspension—the proverbial slap on the wrist. No doubt the brass hoped Weiss would leave in frustration and go back to the AG's office—she didn't. A woman after my own heart.

In some respects, her background made her as much an outsider as I was. True there were other women in the office, but not only was she being paid by the state as an assistant attorney general, to the best of my knowledge she was the only Jewish person working at the DCDAO. The other reason I felt I could trust her was because she had reached out to me when I was going through my promotion ordeal to let me know that, in her opinion, she had the authority to investigate discrimination complaints if I wanted. I hadn't gone that route, but I nonetheless appreciated her willingness to get her hands dirty on my behalf.

Because of Weiss's unique status as an assistant state

attorney general embedded in our office, she had two email addresses—one linked to the DCDAO system, and the second a state email address that she monitored from her laptop and cell phone. Because emails to the state email address couldn't be monitored on the DCDAO computer system, it provided anyone wishing to file an IA complaint some level of confidentiality. I made my email short and sweet and sent it from my personal email account on my personal computer.

AAG Weiss, I need to speak with you about a matter of some importance. If possible, I'd prefer to meet in person, off-site. Lt. Kelly

Her response was almost instantaneous.

Heading out to a lunch meeting. How's the coffee shop in the back of BookTowne at 2pm?

Perfect. See you then, I replied.

BookTowne was in Cambria, about five miles outside of Harrison. I got there ten minutes early, bought a coffee, and took a seat at one of the tables. Right at 2 P.M., Weiss spotted me at the table and made her way over. I stood and we shook hands. We had met each other before at office events, but this was the first time we had met one-on-one. She was in her late forties, attractive, and just a couple inches shorter than me, with long black curly hair. She looked very much the lawyer in her heather gray Ralph Lauren suit.

"Thanks for meeting with me so quickly. Can I get you a cup of coffee?" I asked.

"Thanks," she said, taking a seat, "but I crossed my caffeine limit at lunch. Sit," she said in a voice that was both cordial and commanding. "Tell me, what's going on?"

Appreciating her directness, I explained what my new

position entailed and the background on the Sherry Darling case, and then I laid out the new information I had learned from Riccoli, Ashley, and Benson. "So, here's where I need your advice," I said. "I'm afraid if I put all of the information I've received into my investigation reports on ProsDox, Captain Snyder will read them and pull me from the case."

"Sounds like you don't trust Captain Snyder."

In for a penny, in for a pound, I thought. "I don't," I said. "If what Riccoli told me is accurate, Captain Snyder told him to lie, which turned out to be part of the reason he was convicted. And if Ashley is accurate, our office not only withheld exculpatory DNA evidence, but also photos of Riccoli that showed he had no marks on him. Captain Snyder was the lead detective. All of that lands on him."

"Are you suggesting he acted intentionally in trying to have Riccoli convicted?"

How else could I interpret what had happened? Damn straight I believed he had tried to get Riccoli convicted. But despite my own internal certainty, her incredulous tone caused me to hesitate. Was I basing my belief just on the fact that Snyder was a transphobic asshole? Or was I really convinced he was a lying transphobic asshole? I was about to waffle and give a "no one can be certain of someone else's intent" response, but instead, I fell back on my original condition. "If what I've learned from Riccoli and Ashley is accurate, then yes, I believe Captain Snyder's actions were done to try and convict Mr. Riccoli."

"But wasn't that his job—to convict Riccoli?"

"Of course, as long as we follow the law," I offered, trying to thread the needle. As the assistant attorney general who headed IA, she knew better than I did how to color inside the lines. There was also a part of me that felt like she was testing me.

For the first time since she sat down, I saw a smile behind her eyes. "So, what do you propose we do, Lauren?"

I had a solution in mind, but it involved her sticking her neck out for me. "My thought was I'd prepare a memo to you that details exactly what I'm doing and why. I'd then prepare two sets of reports, one with all the information I received. Those reports I'll prepare in Word on my personal computer and provide signed and dated copies to you at your state AG email address so you'll have copies with the metadata to confirm when they were created and edited. At the same time, I'll prepare a second set of reports, leaving out anything concerning Snyder's role, and enter them in ProsDox. If I ever come up with a suspect that we can prosecute, we have copies of my full reports for discovery. If I don't find anyone, or if the suspect is dead, then no harm, no foul."

She glanced down at her watch, then back at me. "I changed my mind. I need a cup of coffee," she said. "You want another?"

"Thanks. Costa Rican, black."

When she came back, she slid my coffee across the table and took a long drink from hers. "I needed a minute to think," she said. "Basically, you're suggesting that I endorse cutting your commanding officer out of an investigation. An investigation he has every right to know about. Do I have it right?"

"You do," I replied.

"You understand that if I go along with what you're proposing it has the potential to blow up in both of our faces. I'm sure I don't have to tell you that there are folks here that would like nothing better to get rid of me and you."

I inhaled and nodded. "All I'm looking to do is prevent Snyder from interfering in my current investigation. I promise I'll give you the full reports so you know what I'm doing every step of the way. That's all I need for now."

She rested a curled index finger on her lower lip, the red of her perfectly manicured fingernail matching the color of her lipstick, and I could almost see her mind turning the pieces over in her head. "I understand why you want to look into this case. The front office is trying to sideline you and put you in this position where you'll do your time and then go away. But you know about this cold case that involves the murder of a trans woman, a case that fits into your job description perfectly. And it also conveniently provides you with the opportunity to give your bosses the one-finger salute." She stopped and her eyes narrowed. "If I'm going to help you, I need to know everything you know. I don't want to be surprised."

"Fair enough," I said.

I proceeded to tell her about my father's involvement in the investigation, his Alzheimer's and his "no scratches" comment that came out of his tangled memories. And if I hadn't come to trust AAG Weiss as much as I had over the last forty minutes, I probably would have stopped there.

"There's one other thing. It's probably just coincidence, but I've been doing this job long enough that I have a hard time believing in coincidences. There were five people from the DCDAO involved in the Darling investigation. Lieutenant Clarke, my father, and then Detectives Snyder, Hammond, and

Reed. After Riccoli's conviction was reversed and before the retrial, my father and Clarke retired, Hammond died by suicide, and Reed, who was only twenty-six at the time, resigned. Add to that the fact that one of the DAs who tried both cases, Vincent Chrystal, also retired shortly after the second trial. Now, I don't know anything about Clarke or Chrystal, but I was shocked when my father retired. He lived for two things, and one of them was the job." *The other was drinking*, I thought. "Him walking away when he did never made any sense to me."

"Have you talked to your father about why he retired?"

I let out a small snort. "My father and I had a horrible relationship. The only thing we ever talked about was what pieces of shit my brother and I were, and that was before I transitioned, when he still spoke to me."

"Okay. But if he has Alzheimer's, why are you giving any credence to something he said about there being no scratches on Riccoli?"

"He talks to me because he doesn't even know who I am," I replied. "And every once in a while, he'll have a moment of lucidity and remember something from his distant past. Apparently, it's not unusual with Alzheimer's patients."

"You think the fact that all the detectives involved in the investigation except Snyder left the DCDAO is somehow connected to the Darling case?"

"I don't know. Maybe I'm seeing shadows, but it's certainly strange that everyone except Snyder, who was the lead on the case, is gone and now, twenty years later, he's a captain and in line to become the deputy chief."

I didn't add—I didn't think I had to—the possibility that he had survived and thrived by protecting someone.

Weiss looked down into the remnants of her coffee. "I hope you're wrong," she said. "And even if you're right, I doubt you'll ever be able to connect the dots. But, based on what you've told me, I'm willing to provide you with cover. I just don't want any surprises. Keep me updated, and if at some point I think you're going down a rabbit hole, I may change my mind. Fair?"

"Fair," I replied. "There's one more thing. Since you have access to all the old IA investigations, would you be willing to see if there were any IAs over the fact that the DNA and photos were not turned over in the original trial? That might provide a legitimate explanation for all the sudden retirements—retire or face discipline."

I can't say she looked happy; in fact, her look contained a bit of suspicion. "I'm not sure our records go back twenty years. Even if I find something, I'm not sure I'll share it. But let me see what's there."

We agreed I would email her the memo and reports from my personal email. I also gave her my personal cell phone so we could text each other if necessary.

After she left, I wandered over to the bookstore part of the shop and picked up a copy of *Knot Guilty*. It was time for me to read Becca's bestseller—maybe she'd even sign it for me.

CHAPTER 11

WHEN I GOT TO the office Monday morning, I was surprised to see the voicemail light blinking on my phone—it was only 8:30 A.M. I hit the button and listened to a message from Grace Coughlin at the state crime lab letting me know that she would be emailing me the lab analysis I had requested and asking me to call her. I booted up my computer. Already in my inbox was an email from Coughlin with the subject line *Barr, Owen—DCDAO File No. 01-0542-H* along with three attachments.

Three attachments?

I opened the first attachment. It was the original report used at the first trial that showed the only sample analyzed was Riccoli's semen. The second attachment was the one that had led the appellate court to reverse. In addition to the semen sample, it also had the scrapings from under the fingernails on Sherry's right hand.

Then I opened the third attachment. Like the others, it was a forensic biology unit laboratory report from the state

forensics lab. The opening paragraph gave the background of
the crime and the submitting agency. The next section listed
the evidence examined. I did a double take. There were six
samples analyzed. Six samples? There was nothing in the file
documenting six samples being submitted.

Samples analyzed—10245645A: Semen found in the
victim's rectum; 10245645B: Scrapings from under the victim's fingernails, right hand; 10245645C: Scrapings from
under the victim's fingernails, left hand; 10245645D: Swab
of the victim's mouth; 10245645E: Pubic hair located in the
victim's head hair; 10245645F: Blood on the victim's body.

I scrolled down to the report's conclusions.

The semen found in the victim's rectum was consistent
with a control DNA sample taken from Riccoli, Joseph. No
DNA matches found in CODIS. The scrapings from under
the fingernails of the victim's right hand were from a male.
Victim is excluded from being the primary source of the
DNA. No DNA matches found in CODIS. The scrapings
from under the fingernails of the victim's left hand were
from a female. No DNA matches found in CODIS.

I stopped and reread it—a female. Since this was done in
2001, and they weren't accounting for intersex conditions
in the reports back then, it meant that Sherry had scratched
someone with two X chromosomes, likely a cisgender woman,
either prior to or during her murder.

I pulled my hair tie out, let my hair hang loose, and then

redid it in a high bun as I tried to visualize what the DNA
results were telling me about how Sherry was murdered.
I couldn't rule out that Sherry had scratched people at different times during the day, meaning the two different sets of
DNA under her nails were unrelated to her death. But, given
the autopsy's finding of defensive wounds, the scene I saw
unfolding was Sherry clawing at people in a desperate effort to
defend herself—and there had been at least two people there,
a man and a woman.

I continued reading.

The DNA from the swab of the victim's mouth is a mixture of
DNA from at least two people. The mixture, which contains
traces of semen, is consistent with having a predominant
contributor and one minor contributor. The primary contributor is the victim, the secondary contributor is consistent
with the DNA found under the fingernails on the victim's
right hand, although the sample was insufficient to provide
a positive match. No DNA matches found in CODIS.

I paused, allowing this piece to work its way into the developing picture. While I was aware that DNA from sperm could
be detected for up to several hours after oral sex, the more
likely scenario was that it had occurred shortly before Sherry's
murder. It also appeared that Sherry hadn't been totally candid
when she told Riccoli she made her customers use a condom.
Apparently not when she performed oral sex.

The pubic hair is consistent with the DNA found under the
fingernails on the victim's right hand. No DNA matches

found in CODIS. The DNA from the blood on the victim's body is a mixture of DNA from at least two people. The mixture is consistent with having a predominant contributor and one other contributor. The primary contributor is the victim, the secondary contributor is consistent with the DNA found under the fingernails on the victim's right hand and the pubic hair. No DNA matches found in CODIS.

I felt my breath escape me like someone had punched me in the stomach. Two people had been bleeding when Sherry was killed and the second person wasn't Riccoli. Two people were scratched and neither was Riccoli, and Sherry had recently had oral sex with someone and it wasn't Riccoli. *What the fuck!* Why hadn't these results been turned over? They changed everything.

The chronology of the reports was also confusing. The first report chronologically was the one with Riccoli's semen sample. The second contained the analysis of all six DNA samples, which had never been disclosed to anyone, and based on the DCDAO file I had, didn't exist. The last one showed the same semen sample and scraping from under the fingernails on Sherry's right hand. All three reports were signed by Randall Forsythe, Assistant Analyst, Forensic Biology Unit.

I picked up the phone and punched in the number Coughlin had left. "Coughlin, state lab," she answered.

"Ms. Coughlin, this is Lieutenant Kelly at the Donn County District Attorney's Office. I'm calling on—"

"I know what you're calling on, Lieutenant," she interrupted before I could give her the file number. "Thanks for getting back to me so quickly."

"No, thank you. I got your email and I have some questions."

"Well, that makes two of us," she said.

"You go first," I offered, not wanting to contaminate her with my doubts. Better to let her go first and maybe she'd provide a logical explanation for all of this that somehow had escaped me.

There was a slight pause, then she cleared her throat. "I'm presuming you didn't work on the original investigation, since it's twenty-one years old, but . . . well, there's something odd here."

Once again there was a hesitation before she continued. "The two original samples submitted for DNA analysis came from the Donn County District Attorney's Crime Scene Forensic Unit on April 17, 2001, consisting of a semen sample from the victim's anal cavity and from the nails of the victim's right hand. They were logged in and properly stored. The same day, four more samples were received for testing. These were submitted by the Donn County Medical Examiner's Office. Two days later, there was an urgent request from Detective Richard Snyder at the DCDAO to expedite the analysis of just the semen sample. That was done, and sent back to the DCDAO on April 25, 2001, with a cover letter to Detective Snyder. The actual analysis of the remaining samples took place about two months later on June 25, 2001."

"Was that the normal turnaround time back then?"

"Yes. The report was generated and there's a copy of a transmittal letter to a Detective Barry Reed on June 26, 2001. But here's what's strange. Three days later, on the twenty-ninth, the third report was generated with only the semen sample and the scrapings from under the nails from the victim's right hand being shown as analyzed. There's also a transmittal letter dated the twenty-ninth, referencing the nails and the initial analysis of the semen sample, but there's no reference to the earlier analysis of the other four samples."

"That is strange," I said, stalling as I tried to figure out in my own head what it all meant. Why would a report examining six samples be replaced by one that only analyzed two, unless someone was trying to bury the results? A conclusion further supported by the fact that there were absolutely no records in the DCDAO file of anything being sent to the lab by the ME's office.

"Is Mr. Forsythe still at the lab?" I asked.

"No. That's the first thing I thought of. Unfortunately, he retired two years ago."

I considered that for a moment. "If he was doing analysis up until two years ago, there are samples he analyzed where those cases are coming to trial now. He must have left contact information so he could be contacted if his testimony was needed on samples he handled. Can you check for me?"

"Sure," she replied.

"Can you scan and send me copies of all three transmittal letters and let me see if I can make sense of it?"

"Of course," she replied. "Do you need me to do anything on this end? Should I be reaching out to a supervisor?"

I wasn't sure yet what any of this meant, but one thing I knew was that I didn't want anyone knowing exactly what I was looking at in Sherry's case, especially if it could lead to Snyder getting wind that I had gotten a complete set of the DNA results. "There's probably a simple explanation for this.

If after I check things out, there's anything I think you need to do, I'll let you know."

"All right," she said, doubt remaining in her tone. "But I want you to know that when I send my email it's going to be a CYA. I don't want anyone blaming me for anything."

"Fair enough," I replied, understanding her need to cover her ass. "Have you rerun all the samples through CODIS?"

"I have," she said. "Sorry. There were no matches."

"Thanks." I was disappointed, but not surprised.

After I hung up, I walked down to the office's kitchen and poured fresh coffee into my Yeti. I knew I drank too much coffee, but after the shit I'd just learned, I felt like today I was going to need an intravenous drip of caffeine. Coughlin's email with the attached documents was waiting for me by the time I got back to my desk. As I read her email, I let out a small laugh—she certainly had covered her ass. She had also provided the contact information for Randall Forsythe, who was now in Tucson, Arizona.

The first attachment was the transmittal letter of April 25, 2001. The letter was addressed to Detective Richard Snyder and enclosed the analysis of the first sample, Riccoli's semen, which had been done on an expedited basis. Interestingly, the letter was marked as being delivered via same-day courier service.

The second attachment was the letter of June 29, 2001, addressed to Detective Barry Reed. It was three sentences long. This was the letter and the attached results that led the appellate court to reverse Riccoli's conviction because it had never been turned over to the defense.

I then opened the June 26, 2001, letter, which was also

addressed to Reed. Its contents were similar, except this letter was written three days before the June 29 letter and referred to all six specimens. As far as I could tell, this letter had never been turned over to anyone. Which meant that since the letter had been addressed to Reed, he might hold the key to what had happened.

I got to the bottom and winced. Unlike the letter of the twenty-ninth, Randall Forsythe had sent a copy of his letter of June 26 and the initial report of June 25 analyzing all six specimens to one Detective Sergeant Francis Kelly, DCDAO.

CHAPTER 12

I STOOD ON THE corner of McCabe and Simpson, staring at 1622 McCabe Avenue, trying to stay focused and not force a conclusion onto what I knew so far. There was a letter purportedly sent to Reed and copied to my father with the results of the analysis of six DNA samples that was never turned over to the defense and wasn't even in the DCDAO's file. Two days later, a second letter was ostensibly sent to Reed that omitted the samples sent by the ME's office and contained the analysis of only two samples, which also wasn't turned over to the defense until after the first trial. The logical conclusion was that Reed and my father had hidden the results. But there were several dots to connect before I could pin it on them. First, I needed to establish the letters were sent and received. Then, if they were, the question became, what did Reed and my father do? Did they bury the results, or was that on someone else?

One conclusion was inescapable—someone had concealed evidence that almost certainly would've exonerated Riccoli.

Someone wanted Riccoli to take the fall—and not just take the fall, to be executed.

I wasn't naïve and I wasn't blind. I knew there were bad cops, crooked cops. More than a few were racist, misogynistic, homophobic, transphobic—you name it. But after more than twenty years on the job, my experience was that most cops were regular folks, just trying to do their best in a sometimes very shitty job. Up until an hour ago, even though he was a bastard at home, I would have put my father in that latter group. But now . . .

When I grew exhausted sitting at my desk, unable to make sense of it, I decided to head here—1622 McCabe Avenue—to where Sherry and Joe had lived. There was a small convenience store called One Stop on the ground level and three floors of apartments above. From Riccoli's file I knew that they had lived on the third floor in a one-bedroom apartment. The place was in the southeast corner of Harrison, in the Greenville section of town, which was about as far away from where Sherry lived with her grandmother as one could get and still be in the same city. Although the ethnic makeup had shifted from mostly Irish and Italian Americans to a large Mexican and Central American population, this was one section of town that physically hadn't changed much from my days back on Harrison PD. It was a mostly working-class neighborhood, the busy streets lined with three- and four-story buildings just like the one Sherry and Joe lived in.

There were four buses that stopped within a six-block radius of here, but I needed to check the routes that were here twenty years ago to see if that might help me pinpoint what area of town Sherry went to every Thursday night. I already knew that the 94 bus stopped two blocks from here and, after a twisty five-mile route, made a stop three blocks away from the CVS that used to house The Hawk.

I tried to picture Sherry's life here. A young, attractive woman trying hard just to fit in and lead a normal existence far away from the turmoil she had grown up with. Dreaming of something better—maybe even making it as a singer. Her and Joe struggling to make ends meet and save enough money for her surgery so they could get married. A hard-working woman—secretary by day and sex worker by night. Maybe not your typical American dream, but close enough. Then, as Margie put it, Sherry got reckless and went on *The Michael Dobbs Show*. Once again, "what if" came forward and took a bow.

There was an APARTMENT FOR RENT sign taped inside the door to the building with a phone number. I thought briefly about calling it and taking a look around one of the apartments, just to get a better sense of Sherry's day-to-day. But even if twenty years ago their apartment might have held some clues, as Joe had told me, there was literally nothing left of their life together.

No. The answers I was looking for lay elsewhere. As shitty as the letters from Forsythe were in terms of what my office had likely been complicit in, they did offer me something I hadn't had before—a lead. Someone—a guy—had bled on Sherry. There were countless possibilities: The person was murdered along with Sherry, their body dumped, but unlike Sherry's, never found; they were hurt, but not badly; or perhaps they were rich or powerful enough to avoid detection. More questions than answers, but at least I had something to go on.

I stood on the corner soaking in the sounds and smells of the neighborhood. I looked up at the third floor and I could almost hear Sherry's laugh as she and Joe made dinner together.

I still had to forward the lab results to Weiss, but it was getting late and I decided to head for home. I'd forward everything to her tomorrow. I turned and headed back to my car and for the first time since I started the investigation, I felt confident that I had picked up a scent that would lead me to Sherry's killer. Maybe tonight I'd finally get a good night's sleep.

I HAD JUST FINISHED dinner when I received a text from Becca asking me to call her.

"Hi," she answered, a hesitancy in her voice.

"Hi. Is everything okay?" I asked, sensing something was off.

"Not exactly."

"What's wrong? Are you and Nora okay?"

"Yeah. We're fine. No, I need to talk to you about something else."

"Sure. What's going on?"

"I just got a call from someone I know at *The Gazette*. They called to let me know there's going to be an article about you in tomorrow's edition."

"Me?" They ran something on Tuesday about my promotion. "What now?" I asked, wondering if it was related to me looking into Sherry's case.

"I haven't seen the article, but the way it was described to me was that it was a 'hit piece' designed to discredit you. It talks about the fact that you're transgender, and cites a confidential source in the county for the fact that when you came out, the office had such concerns about your mental competency that you were relieved of all your supervisory duties, sent for an evaluation and relegated to serving subpoenas. Apparently, this same unnamed source said people in the DA's office felt you shouldn't have been promoted and that the only reason you were was because you hired a lawyer who threatened to sue the county."

What the fuck. From the way Becca described the article, it certainly was an accurate version of how the office treated me when I transitioned, and honestly, if I hadn't hired a lawyer, I probably would've been fired or still serving subpoenas. The unnamed source clearly knew the office's perspective. What was more troubling was, who was the source and why now?

"Lauren, are you there?"

"Yeah. Sorry. I'm here. Just trying to put the pieces together."

"Do you think this has to do with your investigation of Sherry's case?" she asked.

It's always dangerous to jump to conclusions, especially for a cop, but I had to admit that was my first thought. "Don't know," I said. "Maybe. But it also might be someone in the county that wants to make my life miserable just because I'm trans. They certainly have done that before."

"You okay?"

"I'll let you know after I read the article," I quipped. "Actually, I'm more worried about the impact on you and Nora."

This time the silence was from her end. Finally, she said, "Hopefully, it won't be a big deal."

We both knew that Nora hated the publicity around me being transgender. Being a teenage girl was hard enough.

Having a transgender parent in this environment only added to her teenage angst. "I'll check in with you tomorrow after we both get to see the article."

I got up, cleared off the table and began washing the dishes. As much as I wanted to believe the article was unrelated to Sherry, it had only been a couple of days since I told Weiss that I had a hard time believing in coincidences. Obviously, I had no idea who the source was, but other than Becca and Brian, the only people who knew I was looking into Sherry's case and also knew my history at the DCDAO were Snyder and possibly his secretary. Then again, for all I knew Snyder was sharing my every move with the deputy chief and chief. I paused, realizing how paranoid I was beginning to get. *It's not paranoia if they're really out to get you*, I thought—which was both reassuring and not at the same time. There was also the possibility that this had nothing to do with Sherry and someone was just trying to humiliate me. If that was the case, given how well known my post-transition exile had been in the office, a whole world of possibilities opened up for the source behind the article, starting with the county executive, Ron Furst, and proceeding all the way through the chain of command, right down to the lowest secretary in the DA's office.

It's always baffled me why being transgender seems to cause people so much consternation. Folks in my area of the country are supposed to be nice. Sure, Harrison, Donn County, and the rest of the state are conservative, but where is the libertarian spirit of letting people choose for themselves? That's all I, or any trans person, ever wanted—to be left alone so we can be the best version of ourselves. Other than those closest to me, how is anyone else impacted if that version of me is female?

Because trans folks make up such a small segment of the population, most people don't know anyone who is transgender, which in turn makes it easy for politicians to paint us as the "other." I just wish people would keep an open mind before accepting some politician's bullshit.

I finished washing the dishes, and headed into the living room. I grabbed the copy of *Knot Guilty* and cracked it open, smiling at the dedication. *For Nora, the joy of my life.*

I was hooked from the opening line. Becca's years as a journalist had given her a unique perspective into the crime/mystery genre and her protagonist, FBI Special Agent Marsha Donahue—young, blond, and petite, with a photographic memory—clearly was not based on me. But there were certain aspects of her career that seemed loosely related to mine, especially that she was treated as an outsider by her colleagues, in her case because she was a lesbian. By around eleven, my need to try and get some sleep overcame my desire to find out how Marsha, who was tied to a support column in the basement, was going to get out of the burning house alive, and I headed to bed.

AFTER TOSSING AND TURNING all night, I crawled out of bed at six and fired up my laptop—so much for a good night's sleep. *The Harrison Gazette* had a decent website. It wasn't *The New York Times* or *The Washington Post*, but it was certainly the equal of *The Kansas City Star* or the *St. Louis Post-Dispatch*. The story about me wasn't at the top of the page, but I didn't have to scroll down too far before I found

it—QUESTIONS SURFACE OVER PROMOTION OF TRANSGENDER
DETECTIVE.

It was exactly what Becca had warned me it was going to
be—a hatchet job, designed to discredit me and question the
safety of the residents of Donn County with me as a lieutenant
in the DA's office. It referenced the fact that my weapon had
been taken away from me twice and that I was the subject of
two fitness for duty evaluations, making me sound like a nut
job who shouldn't be carrying a weapon. Whoever the source
was, they clearly had inside information and weren't afraid to
break the rules because the DCDAO policy was that, unless
you were found unfit for duty, fitness for duty evaluations were
confidential. Not surprisingly, the article left out the circumstances surrounding why I was sent for each of those exams.

The first time I was relieved of my weapon and sent for an
exam to determine if I was mentally fit to be a law enforcement
officer was the first day I came to work as Lauren. I had barely
settled into my office when Snyder, who was then my lieutenant, and Captain Davidson, my captain at the time, came
in, demanded my duty weapon, and handed me an order from
the chief that I was to see Dr. Seymour Lawrence immediately
for a fitness for duty exam. The chief's position was that the
mere fact that I was transgender made me mentally unfit to be
in law enforcement. Needless to say, they were all extremely
disappointed when two weeks later, Dr. Lawrence issued his
report finding me fit for duty.

We repeated the process a year later, after I had my gender-affirming surgery, except this time they sent me to Dr.
Valerie Spencer, who had a reputation for ending many a law
enforcement career. Unbeknownst to them, Dr. Spencer had

a transgender cousin, so she was very sympathetic, and once again, I was back within two weeks after her report cleared me for duty.

I wasn't happy about the article attacking my competence, but the part that bothered me the most was a single sentence. "Before Kelly decided he was a woman, he was married to a woman and they had a child together." It wasn't the fact that I was misgendered twice, it was that Becca and Nora had needlessly been brought into the mix. Sure, their names hadn't been used, but it wouldn't be hard for some kook to figure out the names of my ex and our child. The fact that the sentence was in the article, even though Becca's father was one of the best-connected lawyers in the state, also sent my antennae up. People didn't generally fuck around with Sinclair Brinley—or anyone close to him.

One thing I was sure of now, this article wasn't a trans-phobic screed—it was a warning. Someone was telling me to back off and if I didn't, not only could they make my life miserable, they'd do the same to anyone close to me. Message delivered. I suspected when Becca read the article, she'd get the same message.

CHAPTER 13

WHEN I GOT TO the office, I picked up where I left off the day before and forwarded the letters and forensic reports to my personal email, then sent everything to AAG Weiss along with a recap of my conversation with Coughlin. About an hour later, Weiss replied.

Received your email and attached reports. The implications are troubling and inexplicable. Please follow up with Forsythe ASAP. Regarding your inquiry on any IAs, after the conviction was reversed, an IA was opened against Reed for malfeasance. However, a deal was worked out allowing him to resign in good standing, with the further understanding that the DCDAO would not interfere with him pursuing other law enforcement positions. Let me know if you have time to meet for lunch and we can discuss Reed and what you found.

I emailed her back and we set up a late lunch at Harold's, a deli about fifteen minutes from the office. Then I called Randall Forsythe.

"Hello," a male voice answered on the third ring.

"Good morning. This is Lieutenant Lauren Kelly with the Donn County District Attorney's Office. I'm looking for Randall Forsythe."

"You found him," Forsythe responded, his voice friendly and confident.

"Hello, Mr. Forsythe—"

"Call me Randy," he interjected.

After I explained the case I was calling about and why, he asked if I could email him the information I had from the lab to see if it would help him remember the case. I gave him my direct line, and emailed everything to him. He called me back five minutes later.

"I remember the case," he said.

"How well?" I asked.

"Unfortunately, better than most of my cases, Lieutenant. In fact, maybe I should speak to a lawyer before I speak with you."

"Look, Randy, assuming for purposes of argument you did something that was questionable, it occurred over twenty years ago. The statute of limitations ran a long time ago on anything potentially criminal. Trust me, I'm not looking to jam you up. The only thing I'm looking to do is find out who murdered the victim."

There was a long silence before he spoke. "I spent close to forty years in that lab, and it's the only time in forty years I was asked to . . . How should I say this? Hide not only the results, but what was submitted as well. And you know what—it's stayed with me all these years later."

This was an unexpected gift. It sounded like I was dealing with an honest guy—well, at least honest enough to admit he had lied. "Who asked you to do that?"

"David Hudson. He was the executive director of the lab at the time. In other words, the head honcho."

"Do you know why he asked you to do it?"

"He just told me that I was better off if I didn't know. He said he'd take the fall if the shit hit the fan."

"You believed him—about taking the fall, I mean?"

"Yeah. For the most part I did. By that point, I had known David for about ten years, and he struck me as an honest guy."

Yet another honest guy willing to hide lab results, I thought. "Did you document his request in any way?"

"Nah, I believed him when he said he wouldn't let me take the fall. Besides, if the shit did hit the fan, a written record would probably have buried both of us."

"Can you tell me what happened?" I asked.

"If I remember it right, we got one evidence envelope from the forensic folks at the DCDAO that had two samples for analysis—a semen sample from the victim's rectum and one from under the fingernails. After we received it, I was told they needed the semen sample done on a rush basis, which I did. In addition to the fingernails that were in that evidence envelope, a second evidence envelope came from the ME's office that contained a number of other items to test in the normal course. Based on what you sent me, there were a total of six samples. After I did the analysis, I prepared a report and sent it out. That's when David came to see me. Initially, he wanted me to destroy everything because my report was causing problems, but I had already entered the results into CODIS. A couple of hours later, he came back and said he needed a report with just the semen sample, which had been done on the expedited report, and the results from the fingernails on one hand, which, if I remember correctly, were not consistent with the DNA from the semen sample. In other words, I was ordered to lose the report on the samples received from the ME's office. I put up a stink, and that's when he ordered me to do it and said he'd take the hit."

"So, I just want to make sure I have this right. You didn't destroy anything, you just created a new report?"

"Correct," he replied.

That answered why Grace Coughlin had been able to send me all the results.

"Do you know where David is?" I asked.

"Unless you can communicate with the dead, I'm afraid you're out of luck," he said.

"Did David ever ask you to do anything else like that, either before or after?"

"Never. This was it—the one and only time."

"Did he tell you who wanted it changed?"

"No. Like I said, he let me know the less I knew, the better."

"I know I'm asking you to speculate, but did you get the impression that whoever had asked David to take care of this had some clout?"

"As you said, Lieutenant, I'd be guessing. But knowing David, whoever asked him to do this was not someone he felt he could say no to, or he would have."

"Any idea what he would have done if you had said no?"

There was a laugh. "Yeah, I have a damn good idea. David told me that if I didn't, he'd go in and do it himself and sign my name to it."

"Have you ever spoken with anyone at my office—Detectives

Snyder or Reed, Sergeant Kelly, or anyone else, about the case?"

"Never. The only one I ever spoke with was David. And after I did what he ordered me to do, we never spoke about it again either."

I thought for a moment and decided there was nothing else I needed for now. "Randy, thanks for your help. I may need to reach out again and record our interview. Are you okay with that?"

"I suppose. Not sure I'd be eager to testify about this—but it has bothered me for twenty years. So, if I have to, I have to."

I prepared a memo of my call with Forsythe, and then reviewed the transcripts of the first trial to see if Forsythe had testified as to the results of the DNA testing. It turned out that the defense had stipulate to the results because the only sample introduced had been from Riccoli's semen. No witness was ever called concerning the testing by the lab.

WHEN I WALKED INTO Harold's at around 2 P.M., Weiss was already at a table in the back. We exchanged pleasantries and then she handed me a piece of paper.

"Here's Barry Reed's social and date of birth. I don't need to tell you that information is extremely confidential."

"Understood," I said. "Is there any other information you can give me concerning the circumstances of his IA and his resignation?"

"No," she said. "But not because I'm holding back on you. There are literally two pieces of paper in his IA file. A memo that says an internal affairs investigation was commenced against him for malfeasance. But, before the investigation was completed, he offered to resign, as long as he could resign in good standing. The memo notes that his request was agreed to by the chief of detectives and the DA. The other document is his letter of resignation."

"Does it indicate what the malfeasance was, or what case it involved?"

"Nothing," she said.

"Were there any other IAs involving Clarke, Hammond, Snyder, or my father?"

"None."

"So, we don't even know if Reed got jammed up on Sherry's case or something else?"

"Correct. We don't, although given the timing, that would be my guess."

"Shit," I mumbled. "Do you have access to their personnel files?"

"No. The chief's secretary keeps all the personnel records for the sworn side under lock and key."

The waitress came over. We each ordered a sandwich and a soda.

"I read what you sent over from the lab. Sounds like you had an interesting afternoon yesterday," she said, changing subjects.

"Yeah, but there's more," I said, filling her in on what I had learned from my conversation with Forsythe. "What's really troubling was that even at the second trial it was never disclosed that there were another four specimens submitted for analysis. At the very least, my father, Reed, Hudson, and Forsythe had to know there were other exculpatory DNA results floating around that were never disclosed to anyone. And one of those results came back to a woman."

She was quiet for a while. "Why would they risk another Brady violation after having already been reversed?" she asked, referring to Brady versus Maryland, the Supreme Court's decision that required prosecutors to turn over exculpatory evidence to the defense—a bright line rule known to everyone in the DA's office. "It had to be intentional."

I knew she was right, but I was still no closer to who had ordered the results buried, or why. Everything pointed to someone higher up the food chain than my father or Reed, but even if that was true, there was no getting around the fact that what they had done had almost cost Riccoli his life. They would have been complicit in what amounted to murder. For what?

Our sandwiches came and, as we ate, we discussed the possible reasons that Snyder would have been sent the first DNA results, but the next two sets were sent to Reed and my father, and then Reed. We agreed that I would track down Reed to try and meet with him to get some answers.

I had just gotten back to the office when my personal cell phone rang. I reached over and looked at the display—Becca.

"Hi," I said. "Did you read the article?"

"Yes, and I didn't like it." Her tone left no doubt that she was in protective mom mode.

"I know," I said. "Were any of your sources at *The Gazette* able to give you the lowdown on why the story ran?"

For several seconds she said nothing. "All I was told was that it came from the front office," she finally said.

"Is that unusual?"

"Unusual—yes. Unheard of—no. I've seen it happen when they're trying to curry favor with someone. Usually, it's a big advertiser or a politician. Whoever it is wants you gone."

I couldn't disagree, but the why and who still remained. "Yeah, I got it—loud and clear."

I thought Becca would return to the reference in the article to her and Nora, but she didn't. The silence hung in the air, giving space for us to dwell on our darker thoughts.

"I do have some news regarding the folks who performed in the drag show at The Hawk."

"Really. What'd you find?" I asked, anxious for some good news.

"I came across an article in the magazine *Out in Harrison* from December 2001, when The Hawk closed down. One of the performers interviewed was Wanna Dance. I did some digging and found that, as you would suspect, Wanna Dance was a stage name. Their given name is William Dash. I also found that William is now part owner of a gay bar in Sheldon called Eppie's."

"That's huge! Thank you."

"You're welcome." She paused. "And Lauren, please be careful." Her tone was so gentle it took me back to a different time and place in our relationship.

"I will," I said, hoping she hadn't heard the catch in my voice.

I HUNG UP AND did a search for Barry Reed. Since Weiss had given me his date of birth and social, it didn't take me long—Reed Investigative Services, 502 West Avenue in Highbury. The bio posted on the RIS website confirmed I had the right guy—four years with Newfield Police Department, then the DCDAO, before joining the Cartwright County Sheriff's Department. He had retired from the sheriff's department in

2019 to start RIS. When I checked the area in my Maps app, it showed that RIS was in the same building as the law firm of Spector & Phillips.

Next, I turned my attention to finding William Dash. I found Eppie's on Fourth Street in Sheldon, which was in Dawson County, about seventy miles from Harrison. I checked the state's online liquor licenses database, and confirmed that Eppie's was still owned by Dash and a Robert Eppie. I also found the old records for The Hawk, and the liquor license had also been in Eppie's name.

After I found Eppie's, I recalled Margie telling me that she thought Sherry was originally from Sheldon. I did a quick online search to see if I could find if she was buried nearby, but came up empty. Next time I spoke with Riccoli, I needed to ask him where Sherry was buried. I wasn't sure why it was important to me, but I wanted to pay my respects, despite knowing it wouldn't mean anything to anyone other than me.

It was too late to travel the hundred and fifty miles out to RIS in Highbury, but if I went the next morning, I could stop at Eppie's on my way back to the office.

It was time for a road trip.

CHAPTER 14

FOR THE ENTIRE TWO-HOUR ride out to Highbury, my mind had wandered between the facts of Sherry's case and the connection to the newspaper article about me. *No coincidences*, I reminded myself. Someone was trying to scare me off Sherry's case. As I got out of my car and headed for the offices of RIS, the refrain from Tom Petty's "I Won't Back Down" echoed in my head. I knew the song by heart; Brian and I had played it constantly as teenagers when our father wasn't around. I took a deep breath and focused on why I was here—to find out who killed Sherry.

Once I entered the building, two things were apparent—the law firm and RIS were the only offices in the building, and RIS's office was in the same space as the firm. I approached the receptionist and asked for Mr. Reed. When she asked who she could tell him was here to see him, I knew I had gotten lucky—I was now two for two on my unannounced visits.

"Lieutenant Kelly from the DA's office," I replied, leaving which DA's office I was with purposely vague.

She picked up her phone, and as she relayed the information, I turned on the recording app on my phone and placed it in my jacket pocket. Two minutes later a gentleman who I recognized from a picture on the RIS website strolled into the reception area. He was tall, probably around six two or three, and looked like he hit the gym regularly. He had wavy gray hair and a neatly trimmed salt-and-pepper goatee. His expression made it clear that he was taken aback at the sight of me, since I presumed he had been expecting a man. I nodded, purposely holding my hands behind my back so my badge and weapon were clearly visible.

"Lieutenant Kelly?"

"Yes sir. And hopefully you are Barry Reed," I said with a warm smile.

"I am." He returned the smile, but his was tempered, presumably by his curiosity over who the fuck I was. "Have we met, Lieutenant? Forgive me, but I don't remember any female lieutenants at the Cartwright County DA's Office."

"No sir. We've never met. And truthfully, I wouldn't know if there are any female lieutenants in Cartwright. I'm from Donn County."

The remaining portion of his smile evaporated. "How can I help you?" he said, his voice tight.

"I just need a couple of minutes of your time. Is there a place where we could sit and chat?"

He eyed me suspiciously, but turned to the receptionist. "Is there a conference room open, Morgan?"

"Three is open, Mr. Reed."

"Follow me," he said.

We walked down a hallway and entered a small, windowless

conference room with a round table surrounded by five chairs. He pointed me to a seat, closed the door, grabbed a legal pad off a credenza, and sat down opposite me.

"Can I see your credentials, please?" he demanded.

I handed them to him and he studied them before writing down my information on the legal pad.

"So, to what do I owe the honor?"

No sense beating around the bush, I thought. "I'm reinvestigating the murder of Owen Barr, a.k.a. Sherry Darling." Even though it pained me to use Sherry's birth name, this was not the time to stand on transgender etiquette. "You worked the original investigation."

His look hardened, then froze, as if a sudden paralysis had swept across his face. "Yeah, so?"

"Well, of the detectives assigned to the original investigation, you and Captain Snyder are the only ones left who I can speak with."

"Why? Where's Kelly?" he asked, tacitly acknowledging that he knew Clarke and Hammond were no longer on the green side.

"Alzheimer's," I replied, but I could sense that when he said "Kelly" it had pinged on his radar.

He looked down at the legal pad in front of him. "You related to him?"

"He's my father," I said.

"This conversation's over," he said.

"If it makes a difference, even before he got sick, we didn't talk."

"It doesn't," he said.

"Look," I said, still hoping to get something, "I know you

got jammed up with an IA. Did it have anything to do with hiding evidence in the Barr case?"

He stood up, pushing his chair back so fast it almost tipped over. He stood there, towering over me, his glare ratcheted up to lethal. "Get the fuck out of here," he hissed. "I don't like hitting a woman, but I'm always willing to make an exception."

I rose slowly from my seat, my eyes never leaving his. He had a good four inches and probably close to seventy-five pounds on me, but in the years since I transitioned, I had replaced four years of testosterone with four years of karate. I wasn't overconfident, but I wasn't intimidated either. I had to admit that a part of me hoped he'd try—because, in that moment, he represented all the macho bullshit that I had dealt with my entire life.

As we faced each other, a thought crossed my mind and I allowed myself a small grin. "I'll take that as a yes," I said, and walked toward the door.

"What the fuck is that supposed to mean?" he spit out.

I turned back to him when I reached the door. "You're a former detective. You figure it out. See you around, Mr. Reed."

I WAS ONLY TWENTY minutes outside of Highbury when my work cell rang. I looked at the display, and let it go to voicemail. If I was going to talk to Captain Snyder, I wanted my recording app on.

"Kelly, where are you?" he asked as soon as I called back.

"On my way to visit a witness," I replied. Which was true.

"Who?" he asked.

"His name is William Dash. He's located in Sheldon," I replied.

"Sheldon? What case is that on?"

"The Sherry Darling case."

"You're not listening, Kelly. I told you that wasn't an unsolved case. Riccoli was guilty. Find another fucking case." I could almost see his face turning beet red. "I want you in my office when you get back."

"I probably won't be back till around six, Cap. You still going to be there?" I asked, knowing he wouldn't be, which was why I picked six.

"Six? It's fucking twelve thirty. What the fuck are you doing until six?"

"Like I said, Cap, I'm on my way to Sheldon. When I get there, I'm entitled to my lunch break, and then I have a four o'clock witness interview," I lied. "Meaning I won't be done until around five and then have to battle rush-hour traffic to get back to the office."

I heard some type of angry grunt. "Nine tomorrow—in my office, Lieutenant."

"Yes, sir," I replied before disconnecting.

I thought about calling Weiss and filling her in, but in the end decided I didn't want to be the girl crying wolf. I'd wait to see what happened. Plus, I needed some time to piece together what the hell had just happened with Reed. The mere mention of my father had set him off. My gut reaction was that my father must have let him take the fall on the Brady violation when Riccoli's conviction was reversed. But I needed more than my gut to be sure.

Despite what I told Snyder, when I got to Sheldon, I didn't stop for lunch. I found Eppie's and decided to try my luck.

IT TOOK MY EYES a couple of seconds to adjust from the sunlight to the dim light inside the bar. When they did, I saw two older men sitting on stools at the bar, along with a bartender who looked to be in his twenties. As I approached the bar the three of them looked at me like I must be lost. "Can I help you?" the bartender asked.

"I hope so. I'm looking for Robert Eppie or William Dash."

"And you are?"

"Lieutenant Lauren Kelly, from the DA's office," I replied, once again conveniently forgetting to add which DA's office.

He gave me a questioning look, but asked me to wait and walked through a pair of swinging doors. When he came back out, he held the door open and said, "Make a left and the office is on the left."

I followed his directions to the doorway and peered inside. A Black man, late fifties, early sixties, with a quarter-moon of short gray hair at the back of his head, was sitting behind a desk. "How can I help you?" he asked, turning away from the computer monitor on the desk to look at me.

"I'm looking for William Dash," I said, in my best *Yes, I'm a cop, but you're not in trouble* tone.

"And you are?" he asked.

"Lieutenant Lauren Kelly, Donn County DA's Office," I said.

He rubbed his chin. "You're a long way from home, Lieutenant." He continued to eye me with apprehension. "Why you looking for William?"

"Would you be Robert Eppie?"

"Well, ma'am, I see you've done your homework," he said. "I'm Robert; Epps to my friends. Feel free to call me Robert." A sliver of a grin danced on his lips. "How can I help you?"

"I'm investigating a cold case. Twenty-one years ago, a transgender woman by the name of Sherry Darling was murdered. If the information I have is correct, Sherry performed in a drag show at The Hawk, where William also performed under the stage name Wanna Dance. I just want to talk to them to see if they have any information that might help find the person responsible for Sherry's murder."

He stared at me. "Come in and sit, Lieutenant," he said, motioning to an old wooden chair in front of the desk. "Billie hasn't used Wanna Dance in a good ten years. Not since he got the first cancer diagnosis."

"The first?"

"Yeah," he said, an unmistakable sadness in his voice. "But not for me to give you Billie's medical history." He dragged a phone closer to him and punched in some numbers. "Hey," he said. "I got a cop here from the Donn County DA's Office. She says she's investigating the murder of Sherry, from The Hawk." He listened for a bit, then looked up at me. "Yeah. She looks all right." After a brief pause, he said, "Okay," then hung up. "Look, Detective. I don't know how long Billie's got left on this earth, and I'm trying to make him as comfortable as possible. He doesn't need anyone getting in his face and getting him all upset. You hear me."

"Loud and clear," I replied, touched by his genuine care. "You have my word; I'm not here to harass Billie. They've done nothing wrong. I'm really just trying to find out all I can about Sherry."

"Go down to the end of the hallway and make a right. There's a door at the end that leads to an apartment on the second floor. That's where Billie is."

I followed the directions, and at the top of the stairs, I knocked on the apartment door. A hoarse whisper beckoned me in. The person sitting on the couch was wrapped in an afghan. It was impossible for me to tell their age or to take a guess at their height, weight, or physique, since the only things visible were their face and head. And even those were stripped of all distinguishing characteristics—no hair or eyebrows, and the brown skin was pulled tight, likely from either the ravages of the disease or the equally insidious ravages of an attempted cure.

"William Dash?"

"That would be me," they said.

"Good afternoon," I said, and then introduced myself. "Would you like me to refer to you as ma'am or by a different name?"

They smiled weakly. "Thank you. That's kind of you, but that time passed me by a while ago. Billie is fine."

"Pronouns?" I asked.

A momentary silence hung in the air before he said, "He and him are fine," even though his eyes seemed to suggest something different. "Robert tells me you're here because of Sherry. That true?"

"It is," I replied. "I'm reinvestigating her murder."

"Have a seat," he said, pointing to a chair opposite the couch. "That was—what—twenty years ago? Why now?" he asked, not even trying to hide his suspicion.

"Because I can . . . and because I knew her."

He tilted his head in a way that conveyed his next question.

"We went to school together," I offered.

"Were you friends?" he asked, his curiosity growing.

"No. We weren't. I was still in the closet back then."

"You're a lesbian?"

"I am now, but I didn't qualify until about four years ago."

He took a long look at me. "You're trans? You're one of us?" he said, confirming that even though he had deferred on using female pronouns, he was not a cis male drag queen, but trans.

"I am," I replied softly.

"Damn. Never thought I'd live to see a trans cop, and a lieutenant to boot," he said, his hoarse laugh quickly throwing him into a dry hacking coughing fit. He covered his mouth with the top of the afghan. When his coughing finally faded, I asked if he needed anything, and he pointed to a glass of water on the dark wood side table. I got up and handed him the water. He took a few small sips and handed the glass back to me. "Thank you," he said in a frayed voice.

I put the glass back on the table and returned to my seat.

"I thought about transitioning," he offered. "It would have been before The Hawk closed," he said, a bit of wistfulness invading his raspy voice. "Robert and I had been together for about ten years by then, and, well, let's just say that some folks in the Black community don't do gay real well. A lot of men don't even admit being gay. They're just men who sometimes have sex with men. To Robert's family, we were just two single friends, living together to share expenses. Everyone knew it was a lie, but it was much more convenient than the truth. We just let them hold on to the illusion we were roommates. I thought about transitioning, but realized that if I did, there would've been hell to pay. Besides, I'm not sure my relationship with Robert would have survived if I had done what you and Sherry did. Robert loved me this way. Not sure he could have loved the real me. So, I made myself happy being a part-time woman. But I'm not complaining," he added. "Robert's a good man and we've had a good life together, but that's a long story, for another time," he said, even though I think we both understood there was little chance of another time. "You're here to talk about Sherry."

I nodded, wishing that I could hear his long story because it was an experience so different from mine, even though the core was similar.

"What can you tell me about her?" I asked.

"That child," he said, shaking his head, the smile returning to his eyes. "I loved her like a daughter, but damn, that one had a mind of her own and there was no talking to her."

"How long did you know her?"

"Don't remember. I mean she was only a kid when she first started hanging around. Maybe fifteen. How old was she when she was murdered?"

"Twenty-three," I said.

"Yeah, that sounds about right. She began performing in the show when she was eighteen—at least, she told us she was eighteen," he added, his sunken cheeks disguising his grin. "Funny thing was, that girl actually had some talent. She had a good singing voice. So many queens, me included, lip-synched the songs, but she sang—yeah, she was pretty damn good."

I smiled, remembering Sherry telling the folks at *The Michael Dobbs Show* that maybe she'd be a singer. Apparently, it wasn't just a fantasy.

"You know she also did sex work, right?"

"Sure. A woman's gotta live." For the first time, he sounded offended.

"I'm not judging her," I said quickly, "but I think it's what led to her being killed."

He gave me a *No shit, Sherlock* look. "Woman winds up stabbed, mutilated, and thrown in a dumpster. I ain't no detective, but yeah, I'd say she made some john unhappy."

"That's just it," I said. "From what her boyfriend told me, she wasn't working the streets anymore. She had one steady customer every Thursday night. Did she ever say anything to you about having found a sugar daddy?"

He stroked the side of his hollowed-out face. "You're right. I do remember her saying she had found someone who was paying her good money."

"Did she tell you who it was?"

"Oh, please, honey. No. She didn't tell anyone."

"Her boyfriend also told me that she may have had a pimp, or at least someone she was splitting the money with. Do you know anything about that?"

He hesitated, then looked at his lap. "No. Don't remember nothing like that."

"You sure?" I asked, picking up on the telltale signs that he was holding back.

"Yeah, I'm sure," he said quickly.

"Did she seem nervous or scared—anything unusual?"

"If she was, I never saw it." He gave me a sad smile. "Look, Lieutenant, I'd love to help you, but it's not like Sherry, or anyone, would ever share who their daddy was. Some man is treating you nice, you protect him."

"Anything else you remember about her that might be helpful?"

"Like I told you, I loved her. She was fearless. And maybe

that's what got her killed. She didn't have the same sense of fear the rest of us girls had. What was she like when you knew her?"

"Basically, a younger version of the woman you've described."

I then told Dash the few stories I knew from when she was in high school, adding in the ones that Margie Benson had shared. Dash had his eyes closed as he listened. I wasn't sure if he had fallen asleep, but when I told him Margie's anecdote about Sherry giving blowjobs to most of the football team, he suddenly opened his eyes and leaned forward.

"Wait. The football team—say that again."

I proceeded to retell the story. Dash's eyes narrowed. "There was something—something about a football player. The guy she was seeing wasn't on the team, but there was a connection. A relative or something." He hung his head, before looking up at me. "I'm sorry. It's been a long time. And with all the drugs my brain just doesn't work as well as it used to."

"No worries," I said. "Um, can I ask you something else? I don't mean this to be too personal, but you mentioned it looked like it was an unhappy john because she was mutilated. Wouldn't anyone who had sex with Sherry know that she hadn't had gender-affirming surgery? I mean, that she still had male genitalia?"

Dash chuckled. "I'm guessing you've never been with a man, Lieutenant."

"You're guessing correctly," I replied.

He shook his head and smiled. "If a girl is doing straight guys and doesn't want them to know, there's a way to tuck where you move your balls back up into your abdomen, and then pull your penis back and tape it. It gives you a very flat look and when you have a man excited enough, they don't know where they're sticking their dick. All they want to do is get their rocks off. Between us, I was surprised when I heard Sherry had been mutilated, because she was very good at what she did."

"Thanks," I said, taking out my business card. I wrote my cell on the back and placed it on the table. "If you remember, please call or have Robert call me. Thanks for your help."

"Can I ask you a question before you go?"

"Sure," I replied.

He looked me up and down. "Regrets?"

"Does anyone get through life without regrets?" I asked rhetorically. I was going to leave it at that—after all, it wasn't like I owed it to him to bare my soul. But there was something about Dash. Maybe it was because he appeared so close to death, or maybe because I could sense that he really wanted to know what life was like for someone who chose the road he hadn't. "Sure," I said, assuming my expression matched my rueful feeling. "Like your concerns about what could've happened to you and Robert if you transitioned, my marriage ended, although I'm not sure it would have survived even if I hadn't transitioned. And I've made my daughter's life a lot more difficult—lots of guilt over that. But, if I had to do it all over again, I would."

He drew in a deep breath. "Yeah, I guess we're all just trying to muddle through." He gave me what passed for a smile on his drawn face. "I'm glad we met."

"I am too," I replied. I wanted to add more—wish him well or a speedy recovery—but I realized how hollow that would sound. Dash was measuring his life in weeks, not months.

"I hope you find whoever murdered Sherry." His eyes

found mine and despite the ravages of the disease, there was a fierceness there that I sensed was forged from surviving as a Black trans woman in a world that had tried to crush him at every turn.

"She deserves that," he added, his gaze lingering on me. "All of us—we all deserve that."

I STOPPED BY THE office on the way out and saw Robert still glued to the computer screen. "Thank you for your help."

"Was Billie able to help you?" he asked.

"A little. He had some trouble remembering things."

"Yeah," he said with a sigh. "Between the effects of the chemo and the pain meds, I'm a little surprised you could even carry on a normal conversation. Usually, he just fades in and out."

"I'm sorry. From what Billie said, the two of you have been together for a long time."

"That's true," he said, pursing his lips. "We met back in the late eighties. Height of AIDS. When we met, I was HIV positive. I really didn't think I was going to make it—HIV was a death sentence back then. But Billie took good care of me. Got me into a great clinic for treatment, and here I am." He brought his hand up to his mouth, his expression pained. "Fuck, it just ain't fair that I'm going to outlive him. It should be me going, not him. Then he coulda done what he wanted to do back when he was at The Hawk. He coulda become the woman he always was."

"When I checked the records, I saw the liquor license for The Hawk was in your name. Why'd you close down and come out here?"

He gave me a look to let me know that I was now asking

questions he didn't like. "Times change," he said stiffly. "People's attitudes change. I decided it was time to move on. If there's nothing else, Lieutenant, I have work to get back to."

His sudden desire to end our conversation left me wondering what the full story was behind his decision to close The Hawk, but I decided not to end on an antagonistic note. I left him my card and headed back to my car. I was parked two doors down from a sandwich place called Betty's. I looked at my watch—2:45 P.M. I was entitled to lunch, so Betty's was as good as any.

I grabbed my laptop out of the trunk and headed inside. I ordered a diet soda and a turkey club, then popped open my laptop and started my report. My guess was no matter what happened, I'd be the last person from the DCDAO who was ever going to interview William Dash. Knowing that, at least for this report, I could present her as who she knew she was—a woman.

At 1:45 on the above date, I met with Billie Dash, a transgender woman. Ms. Dash has a terminal cancer diagnosis. Ms. Dash was familiar with the victim from their time together working in a revue at The Hawk, a bar in downtown Harrison. Ms. Dash recounted that she had a close relationship with the victim . . .

By the time I finished my sandwich, my soda, and my report, it was four o'clock. As I headed back to my car, I mulled over the earlier call from Snyder. I knew my meeting with Reed had struck a nerve with him, and suddenly the possibility of him pulling me off Sherry's case in the morning loomed large. That meant I had to get to the office and copy as much of the file as I could before then. Because no matter what Snyder did, I wasn't ending my investigation.

CHAPTER 15

WHEN I GOT TO the office around eight the next morning, I headed straight to the kitchen to get another fix of caffeine to prepare me for my meeting with Snyder. A familiar voice greeted me.

"Hey, Lieutenant. I haven't seen you since your promotion. Congratulations!"

"Thanks, Stacy," I said, accepting a congratulatory hug from Detective Stacy Mills. Stacy was perhaps the only detective in the DA's office as hated as I was. The fact that she was the sole Black female detective in the office gave her two strikes with many of our coworkers right from the start, but the sin that had caused her excommunication was filing a sexual harassment complaint against her sergeant after he grabbed her breasts and quipped, "Don't these get in the way at the shooting range?" The chief had thought her failure to see the humor in the situation showed she wasn't a team player, which resulted in her being transferred from Sex Crimes to the Grand Jury Unit.

"How you holding up?" I asked.

She looked around to make sure we were alone. "Fucking assholes. They're sucking the life out of me."

"Anything I can do?"

She gave me a sardonic laugh. "You? Thanks, LT, but during the arson course at the academy, I learned that you never pour an accelerant on a fire because it may blow up in your face. Besides, I don't know that there's anything you can do to help." She hesitated. "Actually, maybe there is something," she said, glancing conspiratorially around the empty kitchen. "Mind if we talk in your office?"

"What's up?" I asked when we were settled behind closed doors.

"I've applied to become an FBI special agent."

"Hey, that's wonderful," I said. It was an unusual move. In my twenty-plus years of experience, I could count on one hand the number of cops that had joined the FBI. Most went to another state or local agency. I also knew that being a cop didn't make it any easier to get into the FBI Academy. "Congratulations. Where are you in the process?"

"Finished phase one, and passed the phase two written exam. Now they're doing the final background check."

"You worried about what the brass are gonna say about you?"

She snorted. "Worried isn't the right word. I know they're going to pan me. So, I told the feds what to expect and why."

"How can I help?"

"They saw my citation for heroism and when I explained what happened, they indicated they were going to contact you. And . . ."

"No worries, Stace. You were there for me, I'll be there for you. I haven't forgotten."

"Thanks, LT," she said as she stood. "You know, after you came out, everything that happened that day took on a slightly different meaning. Don't get me wrong, what you did was still incredibly brave, but . . . Well, I'm just glad it worked out the way it did."

"Me too."

She nodded slightly and headed out.

"Me too," I repeated in a whisper.

SOME MEMORIES NEVER FADE and can be played back at will. It was before I transitioned, shortly after I had been promoted to sergeant. I was working Homicide; Stacy was in Domestic Violence. We had just testified before the Sylvania County grand jury about a defendant who was wanted in a murder case I had investigated and a DV case Stacy had investigated. In Sylvania, the charges against him were for murdering a different girlfriend. I'm not sure why the DA felt he needed both of us to testify—maybe to show the defendant had long-term commitment issues—but we went. We were on our way back to the office when we saw a black and white with its overhead lights flashing parked in front of a house, the officer talking to a middle-aged woman by the curb. We pulled over to see if we could assist. We showed our IDs to the officer and listened as the woman frantically explained that she had gotten a text from her son, which simply said **Sorry. I love you. Goodbye.**

The officer looked at me expectantly, apparently assuming that since I was with the DA's office, I might have more experience. He was right, I did. Even though I was assigned to Homicide, I also served on the Donn County Emergency Response Unit, or the ERU as it was known. One of the things we were trained in was crisis negotiations. So, I took over.

"Have you tried calling him?" I asked Mom.

"Yeah. He doesn't answer."

"What's his name?"

"Kenneth Horvath. He goes by Ken. Don't call him Kenny."

I pulled out my cell. "What's his number?" I asked, and punched in the numbers as she called them out. It connected, but after four rings it went to voicemail. "Ken. This is Sergeant Kelly with the Donn County DA's Office. I'm talking to your mom and she's worried about you. Can you call me back at this number to let me know you're okay? Thanks."

"Any history of depression or attempts at hurting himself?" I asked.

"Yeah. He's been depressed since his dad died."

"When was that?"

"About six months ago."

"How'd Dad die?"

"He hung himself," she said, motioning toward an attached garage. "This was his house. Ken's dad and I were divorced and Ken lived here with him. Ken found him when he got home from work."

Shit. Like father, like son. As I continued talking to Mom, she told us that, like almost every adult male in this state, Ken owned several guns and had inherited even more from his father. I had her give us a description of the layout of the house, and although she didn't have a key, she explained that her ex used to keep a spare in a fake rock on the side of the front steps. Based on the layout, and hopefully access to a key, I began to sketch out a plan in my head. At some point, Ken called back and let us know in no uncertain terms that he was prepared to start shooting if anyone tried to enter the house. Then he texted a selfie of himself with a gun to his head—providing us with probable cause to believe that he was currently a danger to himself.

"You have a taser?" I asked the uniform.

He took it off his duty belt and handed it to me. "Call for backup," I told him. "No lights. No sirens. And when they get here, keep them back here on the street." I turned to Stacy. "Suicide by cop," I said. "He's begging us to come in so he can point his gun at us, we shoot him. He's just as dead, but it's not his fault."

I was confident I knew where Ken's head was, because mine was in a similar place. I had recently come out to Becca and we were talking about separating. I was struggling more than ever with my gender dysphoria and being dead seemed like a really good solution for everyone. Becca and Nora would get my life insurance and death benefits. I'd go out a hero, not as a suicide, and no one other than Becca would ever know I was trans—a win, win, win.

"Stay with the officer," I said to Mom. I looked at Stacy, her face wrinkled with uncertainty. "Come with me."

We walked up the walk, found the rock on the side of the steps, and I took out the key. I handed Stacy the taser and my weapon.

Her eyes went wide with concern. "What are you doing?"

"Stand over there," I said, pointing to the right side of the door frame. "The door is going to open inward to the left, and

according to Mom, chances are he'll be on the couch opposite the door. Stay here, out of sight. He doesn't know there's
someone with me. I'm going in with my hands up so he sees
I don't have a gun. If he doesn't shoot me when I walk in, I'll
try and talk him down. This taser has a range of about twenty
to twenty-five feet, so he should be in range. If he lowers his
gun, I'll say 'Thanks for lowering your gun.' At that point you
tase the shit out of him. If he shoots me, then do whatever
you got to do."

"Are you crazy?" she whispered.

"Probably," I said with a shrug.

I have to admit that even though death had seemed like a
good option when I walked through the front door, standing
there with my hands on my head, him ranting at me, and a
gun pointed at my face, I quickly found myself hoping I'd
come out of this alive. It seemed like he and I went back
and forth for an eternity, although Stacy later told me it was
around six minutes. At some point he lowered the gun, I said
the magic words, and Stacy came in and tased him. When it
was all over, he got arrested because he was high as a kite and
had left all kinds of drugs out in plain view. Charges that Ray
Ashley later represented him on.

Stacy and I received citations for our heroism. Becca was
the only one who questioned my motivation. When I finally
confessed the truth to her, she insisted I get help. I started
therapy a few weeks later.

"WHY'D YOU TRY TO interview Barry Reed?" Snyder
demanded.

"Because he was one of the detectives involved in the

original investigation of Sherry Darling's murder," I replied calmly.

"Stop with the Sherry Darling bullshit. His name was Owen Barr," Snyder fired back.

"Cap, the victim was a transgender woman. She had lived as a female since she was about thirteen. What's the harm in treating her with respect? After all, she was murdered, and it was probably because she was a trans woman."

He rolled his eyes. "Two fucking peas in a pod," he grumbled. "How'd you know there was an IA involving Reed?"

Sometimes manna does indeed fall from heaven. Now I knew that not only had Reed called Snyder after my visit, but he had filled Snyder in on the details of our very brief discussion. "I didn't," I replied. "I just took a guess based on the fact that, at the ripe old age of twenty-six, he resigned after the conviction was reversed. Looks like I guessed right." Which was partially true. I had guessed there was an IA before Weiss had confirmed it, but her involvement was one piece of information Snyder would never hear from me.

"If you're so fucking hot to trot to resolve this case, why haven't you interviewed me? I was the lead, you know." There was a challenge in his eyes.

The truth was, I really did have questions for Snyder. Why were the first DNA results sent to him, but the next two sets went to Reed and my father? Did he know about the other results? But just by asking the questions, I ran the risk of revealing what I already knew, and I didn't trust Snyder enough to do that. Better not to show my cards.

"Yes, sir. I know. And because you were the lead, I have all your reports from the initial investigation. And . . ." I paused. "Well, you haven't exactly kept it a secret that you still believe Riccoli was guilty. So, if I'm going to test out scenarios involving alternative suspects, I'm not sure speaking to you will advance the ball." I didn't want to push too many of his buttons, but I couldn't resist. "But, if you'd like me to interview you, I'd be more than happy to."

"Fuck you, Kelly. I don't need your sarcastic bullshit. Riccoli killed her and you're wasting everyone's time with this crap. I want your little dog and pony show finished."

We both knew that under the DCDAO's policies, he couldn't order me to close the file, but, as my commanding officer, he could order me to end this investigation and give me another case to work on. But given how little he thought of me, I was counting on him not having another case ready to throw my way. I also needed him to think that I understood the message *The Gazette* article had meant to convey, and I just needed some time to close the case so I could get out of the crosshairs. "Sir, if you end my investigation and I don't officially close the file, it'll stay on the books as a cold case, meaning probably in another two or three years someone else will have to look at it. Give me a month, Cap. I'm sure you saw the article in *The Gazette* about me. I want this case closed as much as you do. I just want to find some other cases that keep me out of the spotlight until I can retire. If you're right and it was Riccoli, I can do a memo saying the case was solved and permanently close it."

I watched his face and he seemed to be toying with the idea of telling me to "go fuck myself," but to my relief he didn't.

"You know I was in favor of firing your ass over you claiming you're a woman—it's bullshit. But the article—" He stopped, his look inscrutable. "A month, no longer. And if you know what's good for you, it'll be done sooner. Got it?" he said.

"Yes, sir. I appreciate it."

I SPENT THE REST of the day in the evidence vault. As I suspected, my inventory revealed that the only items missing were the four samples analyzed by the lab that had not been disclosed. Even the photos of Riccoli showing no marks on him were there, although there was no indication as to who took them—a clear violation of the office's rules concerning chain of custody.

I tried to put myself in the mind of a detective who knew that evidence had to disappear, but who also knew that the lab had a record of its existence. If there was ever an investigation, destroying the evidence would almost surely lead to termination and criminal charges for both obstruction and tampering with the evidence. The much safer route would be to make sure the evidence was simply misfiled—hopefully in a place where it would never be found. After four hours of searching files involving sexual assaults, I found the samples in the file of a serial rapist who had pled guilty to sexually assaulting over a dozen women between 1995 and 1998. Now all I had to do was find out who the DNA belonged to.

I WAS ON MY way home when my personal cell phone rang. It was somewhere in the bottom of my purse, so I let it go to voicemail. The ringing stopped and within seconds my work cell phone started to ring. I reached over to the cupholder where I had placed it, and looked at the display—Becca.

"Hi," I said.

"Where are you?" she asked, an urgency in her tone.

"On my way home. Why?"

"I need to talk to you about something I found when I was searching cold case files online."

"Okay, I can talk. What'd you find?"

"Laur, I need to talk to you in person. Please. It's important. Can you come now?"

"Yeah, I guess." I did a quick calculation of how long it would take me. "I can be there in about forty minutes."

"Good. It's about your mom."

CHAPTER 16

I PULLED UP IN front of Becca's four-bedroom brick colonial thirty minutes later, having spent the entire drive wondering what the hell my mother had to do with Becca's review of cold case files. The house sat on a quiet, tree-lined cul-de-sac in Brighton, which was in the northwest corner of the county. I was never sure if it was purchased with her father's largess or the royalties from *Knot Guilty*—it certainly was far more impressive than the two-bedroom Cape we had purchased shortly after we were married, which I had deeded over to her as part of the divorce. Guilt carried its own largess.

Becca must have been watching for me, because she opened the door before I had even started up the front steps.

I stopped in the foyer to allow her to close the front door. "What's going on?"

"Let's sit in the kitchen," she said, leading me down the hallway to her well-appointed kitchen, which was probably about the same square footage as my entire apartment. "You want something to eat?" she asked. "I made spaghetti and meatballs. I can reheat some for you."

Becca was a great cook, and even though she wasn't Italian, she made the best homemade sauce and meatballs. But I had no appetite. "Thanks, I'll pass."

"Coffee? It's fresh. Help yourself," she offered, pointing to her coffee maker, which was an imposing top-of-the-line model that did everything short of growing the plants and harvesting the beans.

"Thanks," I said, as I headed to the cabinet where I knew she kept her mugs. "What's going on, Becca? You had to know you were triggering me when you mentioned my mom," I said, pouring my coffee.

"Sit," she said, nodding to the kitchen table where her laptop sat open.

I pulled out a chair next to her and sat down. Even though I was sweating, I didn't take off my jacket because that would have exposed my weapon. Becca hated guns, the result of three colleagues having been shot in the newspaper office where she used to work. "Talk to me," I said, trying to remain calm.

"You know that I was searching to see what I could find out about the Darling case, and similar cases."

I nodded.

"First, I searched for information on Sherry Darling—and by the way, it would have been helpful if you had given me the name on her birth certificate. In 2001, none of the newspapers used Sherry Darling or even the right pronouns."

She was right. Even today, there was a fifty-fifty chance that in this state the press would get the name and pronouns of a victim wrong, especially if the information came from law enforcement. "Okay, you're right, but what does that have to do with my mother?" I asked, my impatience growing.

"I knew from my research on the book I'm working on that serial killers can go years, sometimes decades, without murdering anyone. Since Sherry's murder was in 2001, I went back to 1971 to look at cold cases that might be similar to hers. As I went through the years, I found a few that, at first blush, were intriguing, but nothing that seemed related to Sherry. When I got to 1983 . . ." She stopped, and drew in a deep breath. "When I got to 1983, I came across a case from Brisbane County that stopped me cold. It involved the badly decomposed body of a woman that had been discovered by a hunter on April 3, in a shallow grave, about a hundred yards off County Highway 516. The condition of the body made it hard to determine a precise date of death, but the coroner estimated she had been dead from two to six months, so a date of death possibly in 1982. The victim was a Caucasian female, estimated to be five foot two, and her weight was around a hundred and ten pounds. Both her ears were pierced, and she had given birth at least once. They couldn't determine her eye color, but she had red hair."

She turned to look at me, her face conveying a message that was a mixture of sadness and concern.

"Okay. But my mother's not dead, or at least she wasn't in 1982 or '83. I still have the birthday cards she sent."

Becca turned her laptop so I could see the photos on the cold case website she was looking at. There in the pictures, along with the remains of some tattered clothing, was a photo of a gold necklace with a gold Saint Christopher medal and a silver cross on the same necklace.

"I know it's not definitive, but every time I go into Nora's room, I see the picture you gave her of your mom, and in it, she's wearing the identical necklace. It's unique because it's a gold medal and a separate silver cross."

I couldn't tear my eyes away from the necklace on the screen. About two years ago, Nora had wanted to know about Nanny, my mother. I faked as best I could, trying not to make my mom out to be a total shit for leaving Brian and me. When Nora asked if I had any pictures, I had given her a copy of the one from Aunt Maeve, but I had cropped most of me out of the photo, so it was a picture of my mom leaning forward, her hand resting on my shoulder. Since I hadn't been in Nora's bedroom since the divorce, I had no idea that she had the copy of the photo in her room.

With a couple of clicks, Becca brought up on her computer the photo I had given Nora. When she zoomed in, the necklace dangled out over my mother's body as she leaned forward next to me.

Oh, Jesus, it can't be my mom. It just can't be her. Oh, please God, don't let it be her. She can't be—

My mind whirled before focusing on the picture of my mother forever locked in my memory—a young, beautiful woman, with a radiant smile and flaming red hair. Her leaving never made sense. She seemed so happy, and real or imagined, my memories of her were of us laughing together. Even the day she caught me in her clothes, she didn't seem angry, just bemused. All these years later, I clung to the hope that if she was still alive somewhere, someday we'd be reunited and she'd explain why she left and all my pain and guilt would vanish. But if she was dead—

"Look, I was five years old. Maybe it was popular to wear

the medal and cross together. For all we know, there were thousands of women doing it."

"You're right," she said. "But . . ." She hesitated. "Look at the cross. It's unique; it's filigree." She zoomed in on the cross in the crime scene photo. "It's identical to the one your mom's wearing in the picture." She split her screen so the photos of the crosses were side by side.

I tried to push back. "But the cards," I said. "Every year, Brian and I got cards." But as the words left my mouth, I realized just how foolish I sounded. Becca had already put together where my mind refused to go—that someone else had sent the cards to Brian and me. My eyes pleaded with her to give me an alternative theory, but she didn't. All I saw was the recognition that she had just torn my world apart. A muffled, involuntary moan escaped my lips.

I don't know how long it took, but at some point, my cop instincts kicked back in and began analyzing the information on the computer screen, trying to find holes in the conclusion that Jane Doe was my mother.

Victim: Caucasian female. Approximately 5'2", 110–120 lbs.; red hair; eye color, unknown; single piercing in each ear; evidence that the victim had given birth at least once.

Cause of death: Single gunshot wound in the area of the left temporal bone of the skull, no weapon found. Bullet recovered from brain tissue in autopsy—.38 caliber.

Date of death: Based on decomposition, impossible to determine with certainty, but estimate is sometime

between October 1982 and February 1983. Decomposition could have been slowed because of cold winter
weather.

Clothing: The victim was found wearing the remains of
blue jeans, a navy-blue sweater, winter coat, no shoes,
no rings, necklace around the neck.

Evidence of nail biting on both hands.

No evidence of sexual assault.

Toxicology: No evidence of drugs or alcohol in the victim's system.

Fingerprints not available because of the condition of the
body.

If this was my mother, she had been shot in the side of the
head.

Shot.

Who would shoot my mother, and why?

For a hot second, I considered whether suicide was a possibility—something new I could blame myself for? But that
didn't fit the evidence—she had been found in a shallow
grave with no weapon. Plus, how would she have gotten there
without leaving her car nearby? No. This was a murder.

"Your mom have any family?" Becca asked, her voice
sounding far away.

"None that I'm aware of," I replied.

I studied the screen. Brisbane County was about fifty miles due east of Donn County. Why would she have headed to Brisbane? Or maybe she didn't head there, maybe she was just dumped there.

Stop! But as hard as I tried to muffle the voice telling me it was her, there was another part of my brain beating me up for never having considered that she was dead. I had been a cop for over twenty years and seen more than my fair share of the crap people can inflict on one another. Why hadn't I ever considered the possibility that the reason she hadn't come back was because she was dead?

"There's no reference here to them having a DNA sample," Becca said.

"Yeah, they probably don't have one. They didn't start collecting DNA until the mid-eighties, and the FBI database didn't start until around 1990."

"How about matching dental records?" Becca asked. "They have a dental narrative here of fillings and extractions."

"I have no idea what dentist my mother went to. Besides, we're talking forty years ago. I'm pretty sure that's a dead end," I said. "The only sure way is to exhume the body and check the DNA."

"So, you're in the DA's office. Can't you do that?"

I closed my eyes and took a deep breath. No. I didn't want to do that. If it turned out that it was my mother, it meant she had been murdered forty years ago, and there was no way the higher-ups in the DA's office would let me investigate the cold case murder of my own mother. But there was no one else I trusted to do it. "I can't draw attention to this. I have to find another way," I said.

"Uncle Brian," I heard from over my shoulder.

Both Becca and I turned. Nora was standing in the kitchen doorway. At thirteen, she was a younger version of her mother. The only differences were that she hadn't filled out yet, her hair was blond, and instead of her mother's green eyes, she had inherited mine—robin's egg blue.

"How long have you been listening?" I asked.

"Long enough to know that Nanny might be dead," she said.

"Nora, we don't know anything yet," I lied. "There's still a lot to figure out."

"Uncle Brian's a celebrity. He could probably have people check without anyone knowing," Nora said, which, for a thirteen-year-old, was scarily perceptive.

I didn't give voice to it, but it was actually a good idea.

Nora walked across the kitchen and put her arms around my neck and gave me a hug. "I hope it's not your mom, Mads," she said, using the blend of "Mom" and "Dad" we had come up with for her to call me.

"Thanks, hon," I said, using every ounce of reserve I had left to avoid dissolving into a blubbering mess.

"Give Mads and me some time to talk?" Becca said, saving me.

"Okay," Nora said, her eyes not leaving mine.

"I'll let you know when I'm leaving," I assured her.

Nora nodded, before heading up to her room.

Once Nora was gone, Becca said, "It's not a bad idea."

I closed my eyes, lowered my head, and desperately tried to block out everything that had happened in the last thirty minutes. But it wouldn't fade. It was like I was looking at a split screen. Mom leaning over next to me, a beaming smile, and next to that, the image my mind conjured up after seeing pictures of too many dead bodies—a corpse, decaying and lifeless, and knowing in my heart we had found Maureen Margaret Kelly. I covered my face with my hands and cried, the uncontrollable sobs coming from some well of tears that had been stored untapped for decades. Becca pulled her chair next to mine and held me as my tears flowed.

When I finally stopped crying, I looked at her. "I have to talk to Brian—in person."

"Yeah" was all she managed to say.

The thought of having to share all of this with my brother made me nauseous.

"Maybe it's not her," Becca said, her attempt at optimism falling flat.

As much as I wanted that to be true, reality was setting in. "Look at the picture," I said, pointing to the cropped photo of my mom on the computer screen. I zoomed in on her hand, resting on the shoulder of five-year-old me. "She bit her nails."

CHAPTER 17

ALL THESE YEARS, I had clung to the belief that someday my mom would walk back into my life carrying an armful of regrets and a bundle of "I'm so sorrys." She'd give me a huge hug, explain to me why she had left, and we'd all live happily ever after. Even after I had grown up and happily ever after had left the building, I still believed we'd somehow find each other. Of course, once I got on the job, I tried to help that along by running her through every law enforcement database I could access, all without coming across a whiff of her. But even then, I hadn't focused on her being dead, simply that it had been easier to assume a new identity back in 1982 when she'd left, and that was what she must have done. "Sometimes people just want to stay gone."

I placed my laptop on the tray table, plugged my earphones in, and stared blankly at the screen, my mind focused on Brian and the shit I was about to dump in his lap. I didn't know what illusions he had constructed about our mother—we rarely talked about her—but whatever they were, I was about to destroy them.

I assumed whatever he had planned for a Friday night—him being a celebrity—was better than seeing me. But when I told him I had to discuss something with him and needed to do it in person because it was urgent, he hadn't hesitated. He hadn't even asked me why we couldn't discuss it over the phone. He simply bought me a first-class ticket and told me he'd have a driver pick me up at LAX.

The flight attendant offering me a drink roused me from my thoughts and despite a desire to drink myself into oblivion, I politely declined. I turned my attention back to my laptop, opened up my copy of *The Michael Dobbs Show*, and began rewatching it.

"So, Sherry, you told us that you lived with your grandmother until you were sixteen."

"That's right."

"What happened then?"

"My grandmother passed away. She had lung cancer."

"I'm so sorry."

"Thank you. It was hard. She was diagnosed in April and passed away in August. So, she didn't suffer long, but she was basically my mom, so I was lost without her."

"What happened after she died? Where did you go?"

"I had to drop out of school and for a while I lived in a homeless shelter in Harrison. Then some of the girls I knew from doing the drag shows took me in until I had enough money to get a room on my own."

I remembered that at the start of senior year I'd seen

Margie and Tony sitting in the cafeteria having lunch together as usual, but no Sherry. West Harrison High was a big place, just over two thousand students, so it took a while for me to figure out that she wasn't in school anymore, and even longer to hear the rumors about her living on the street. It wasn't like I had any plans on coming out, but it was a cautionary tale nonetheless—be trans, be alone. Even your family wouldn't want anything to do with you.

"And in addition to the shows, did you do anything else to make money?"

"I did. I worked for a temp agency as a secretary."

"That's all you did?"

"That's all, Mr. Dobbs."

"What do you do in the show?"

"I sing."

"You mean lip-synch to a recording?"

"No, I sing. Because I started hormones when I was young, my voice never changed. I have a nice singing voice."

"How old were you when you started performing?"

"Sixteen."

"That's awful young. Was that legal?"

"I don't know, Mr. Dobbs. I never asked and no one ever stopped me."

"We know that you now have a boyfriend. When did you meet him?"

"About two years ago."

"Did you meet at the club where you perform?"

"Oh no [giggles]. No. I met Joey at a bar. I was working a temp secretarial job and after work, I went out for a drink with some of the other girls and Joey was at the bar with some of the guys he *worked with. When I saw him, I thought he was really cute. So, I kept checking him out until he noticed me checking him out, and he actually blushed. Eventually, he got up the courage to come over and talk to me, we exchanged phone numbers and luckily, he called me and we started dating."*

"How long before you told him about your little problem?"

"First of all, Mr. Dobbs, I don't have a problem. But what and when Joey and I discussed things about me is nobody's business."

And there it was—"I don't have a problem." *Amen, Sherry.*

I turned off my laptop and stowed it in my carry-on, my thoughts ping-ponging between Sherry and my mother's cases.

If Jane Doe was in fact our mother, who had mailed the cards? The why seemed pretty obvious—to keep us, or anyone else, from suspecting she was dead. But they were postmarked from California and Arizona. Which meant someone in those states had to be mailing or forwarding them to us.

I put my seat back and closed my eyes, thinking about the very real possibility that my mother was dead, something that for forty years I had never really contemplated. Now, as I drifted off, it was all I could think about.

BRIAN'S NOT-SO-HUMBLE ABODE WAS situated on the iconic Mulholland Drive. At forty-three hundred square feet, Brian's five-bedroom, four-bath home was four times the size of my place. That said, the décor was stylish, but not opulent—understated would be the best way of describing it.

We each took a spot on his black sectional and I took a generous sip from the chardonnay Brian had poured for me, trying to steel myself before I began.

"I tried to think of things you couldn't talk to me about

over the phone, and the only thing I could come up with was Mom. Did you find her?"

"Yes, but unfortunately, it's more complicated than that." I put my wine glass down and rested my hand on his. "I wish there was an easy way to say this, but I don't think Mom abandoned us—I think Mom died forty years ago."

His eyes went round and he drew in a sharp breath. "Ahh, Jesus," he whispered, shaking his head. He slowly leaned forward on the couch, brought his hands together, closed his eyes and rested his forehead on his clenched hands. "Shit," he muttered to himself.

"I'm sorry," I said, rubbing his shoulder.

"How sure are you?" he asked, still trying to find a way out.

I took a file folder from my bag and proceeded to explain what Becca had found and the website she had found it on— unknown John/Jane Does. I removed the pictures of Mom and the photo of the necklace from the website and laid them side by side on the black lacquer coffee table. Next to them I put two more photos of screenshots I had taken where I had zoomed in on the necklace in each of the pictures.

He shook his head. "Yeah. Sure as hell looks like the same necklace."

"It does," I said. "But if that's all it was, I wouldn't have flown all the way out to see you. There's more." I then pointed out the fingernails and the fact that the description of the victim fit Mom, including the red hair.

After several minutes, he looked up at me, his face unable to hide the pain. "I hated her," he said slowly. "I was three years old and all I was ever told growing up was that my mother had left me—left us. I know you always longed to see her again, but all these years I believed she had abandoned me to save herself from having to deal with Dad, and I could never forgive her for that." His eyes began to fill with tears. "And now this . . . Fuck."

I listened, stunned. I always thought I had been the one that bore the brunt of our mother leaving. Me, full of guilt and shame. It was my fault she left. Easier to leave than deal with a son wearing your clothes. Yet, all this time my brother had harbored a seething rage at being abandoned. I thought I knew Brian better than anyone, but he had hidden it so well that I had never even known it was there.

"I'm sorry," I offered. "I should've . . . I feel bad that I never asked."

He waved his hand as if giving me absolution.

"Do you know how she died?" he asked.

I let out a breath, knowing I was about to kick him when he was down. "Jane Doe was murdered. Shot once in the side of the head."

"Shot? Are you serious? Why?"

"I have no idea. But if it's her, I intend to find out."

"What do you mean, if it's her? You sound pretty convinced it's her," he said.

"Yeah, I am. But I'm a cop. Pretty convinced isn't good enough. I need to be certain."

"How?"

"We need to have the body exhumed so they can do a DNA test. By comparing what they find with our DNA, they'll be able to tell if it's her."

He leaned forward. "So, do you need my consent to exhume her body? Is that why you're here?"

"That's one of the reasons I'm here. But I can't be the one to ask. I need you to do it on the down-low," I said.

"Me? Why?"

"Because I don't want anyone to know I'm investigating to see whether it's our mother who was murdered. And, if it does turn out to be her, that I'm investigating who killed her."

"I'm confused. You're a detective. Isn't that your job?"

I shook my head. "Brian, under no circumstances is a cop ever allowed to investigate a case in which they have a personal connection. Add to that the fact I'm persona non grata, and I'd be cut out immediately."

"Okay. So, you'd be out. What's the big deal?"

"If it's her—if it's Mom, I have to do this case."

"Why?"

Now it was my turn to lean forward. "Think about it."

I could feel Brian studying me. Then the realization of where I was going hit home and he blew out a long breath. "Oh shit. Dad!"

AT ELEVEN THE NEXT morning we were on a video call with Carla Heck, Brian's manager, and Edward Norwood, one of the attorneys from the firm that represented him. It was a testament to Brian's clout that he was able to get his manager and one of his lawyers to talk with us on a Saturday morning with almost no advance notice.

They initially pushed back on how I wanted to handle the exhumation request, afraid of the negative publicity. But when I assured them that the last thing I wanted was publicity and the best way to avoid it was with their help, they asked how. I suggested that people were usually willing to go out of their way to do things for celebrities, so if Brian and his team laid the groundwork, explaining to the Brisbane County District Attorney's Office that, given who Brian was, he'd like to keep this quiet, there was a greater chance Brisbane would cooperate. Ultimately, after some back and forth, Carla agreed to make the request on Brian's behalf.

I leaned back against the sofa so I could study him. "You okay?"

"I guess," he answered softly.

Growing up, we were all each other had. Nanny died when I was seven, and two years later, Uncle Steve died in a car accident at the age of thirty-five. He and our Aunt Maeve never had kids, and within a year of him passing, Aunt Maeve moved to Florida. I was never sure if her decision was motivated by her desire to stop taking care of us, but there I was as a ten-year-old, trying to take care of myself and a little brother. The reality was we felt safer when our father wasn't around. He had a nasty temper when he was sober, and when he was drunk, he was violent. Brian had the broken arm—and I had the concussion—to prove it. Now, I couldn't help but wonder if our mother had fared even worse.

"You see a therapist?" I asked.

He chuckled. "One of the advantages of being a celebrity is that everyone sees a therapist." Then he lowered his eyes, staring at his hands. "The truth is," he began, his tone now serious, "I've lived so long in this surreal world of make believe and pretense, that until recently, I never really tried to deal with the shit in my life. You came out. You dealt with your shit. That's one of the reasons I admire you," he said softly. "I wish I had your courage."

I knew he was referring to the fact that he had never come out publicly as a gay man. It was ironic, given how close we were growing up, that until the night Brian outed himself in the midst of a screaming match with our father, he had never told me he was gay.

"Don't beat yourself up," I said. "We're in two entirely different worlds. You're Brian Kelly, a big star. Besides, it's nobody's business who you're attracted to. In my case, it wasn't a matter of courage; it was survival. Unless I wanted to quit my job, move out of state, and never see Nora again, once I decided to transition, staying private wasn't an option."

He closed his eyes and drew in a deep breath. "Thanks for understanding," he said. "It's funny, it was really only after you came out that I started to deal with my own baggage."

"What did my coming out have to do with it?" I asked.

He stole a glance in my direction. "Forgive me for misgendering you, but you were my big brother—you were my idol. You were a badass dude. I looked up to you. I wanted to be just like you. I can't remember how many times you stood up to Dad and protected me. For all intents and purposes, you were my father figure." He hesitated. "And the night Dad threw me out, if you hadn't come between us, I think he would have killed me. I know he seemed to hate both of us, but for some reason it always seemed he hated me more."

I couldn't disagree with him. As bad as Dad treated me, he did seem to treat Brian worse.

"Anyway," he continued. "I guess I was shocked when you told me you were trans. I don't know. It didn't change any of those things you did for me, or the way I felt about you, but it forced me to take a hard look at myself. I mean, I thought I knew you so well, and on some level, I didn't know you at all. You hid who you were so well, even from me. And it made me realize that I had buried a lot of stuff too—not so much being gay, but the abuse from Dad, Mom leaving, the pressure to succeed that I put on myself. One thing my therapist said was that based on what we went through growing up, it's pretty remarkable that we both survived and turned out as well as we did." He caught my eye. "For me the answer is easy—you're the reason I survived."

CHAPTER 18

I HAD A FITFUL nap on the plane ride back. Brian had graciously invited me to stay and go to a party, but I was working on the assumption that the DNA would confirm Jane Doe was our mom. I wasn't sure how much of a head start I'd have before news got out. Whatever it was, I couldn't afford to squander a minute. I was now investigating the murders of two women who, in very different ways, had managed to etch their presence into my psyche. Even though I couldn't bring either of them back, I felt like solving their murders offered a chance at redemption, not only for me, but more importantly for them, by showing they were loved and that their lives had meaning.

Before I left, I let Brian know that I had decided to temporarily move into Dad's house. Things had changed. This was no longer about satisfying the homeowners insurance. Staying there would give me more time when I was off the clock to see if I could find anything that would help illuminate what had happened to our mother—starting with cracking open his safe. I'd just have to learn to cope with the nightmares living there would bring.

I DRAGGED MYSELF OUT of bed Sunday morning, exhausted from the trip and my late arrival home. This was my weekend for visitation with Nora, and while Becca understood why I needed to see Brian, I didn't want to pass on seeing Nora for the entire weekend. I knew how hard it was growing up believing that a parent didn't love you enough to want to be part of your life. I didn't want Nora to think that I wasn't there for her.

When I came out, I had really wanted to keep my transition on the down-low as much as possible, to spare Nora as much as I could. Unfortunately, when the local FOX affiliate had gotten wind of the tranny detective from an "anonymous source," things quickly fell apart. Becca let me know that a few of Nora's classmates had made fun of her, but the most infuriating part had been the attitude of Rebecca's parents. Not only had they not hesitated to badmouth me to my then nine-year-old daughter, but my father-in-law, the hotshot lawyer, had even attempted to sue me to prevent me from having visitation. Fortunately, even in Donn County, grand-parents had no legal rights to interfere with the custody and visitation arrangements parents had agreed to, and his case was thrown out.

I got to Becca's around nine, and quickly filled her in on what had happened in LA. Becca in turn warned me that Nora had been unusually quiet the last few days, refusing to talk about what was bothering her.

"Anything you really want to do today?" I asked Nora once we were on the road.

"No," Nora replied, with the disinterest only a teenager could convey with one word.

"I thought we'd stop at IHOP for some breakfast. That sound good?"

"Whatever," she said.

"How's school?"

"Fine."

I took a quick look in her direction. "What's up, hon? Seems like you're upset."

She said nothing, but with her arms folded across her chest, her body language confirmed something was eating at her.

"I hate when you do this to me," she finally snapped.

"Do what?" I asked, truly confused.

"Grill me like I'm a suspect in one of your cases."

I tried not to smile. "Sorry. I was just wondering how you were doing."

We rode in silence for another five minutes. Sometimes silence can be a very effective interrogation technique—it was.

"Why is it that anytime something happens to you, they always talk about the fact you're transgender? Why do they always bring that up?" she unloaded.

I presumed she was talking about last week's hit piece in *The Gazette*, but the cop in me wanted to hear it from her. "Can I ask specifically what we're talking about?"

"The news stories about you being promoted and then the one about you not deserving a promotion," she replied, in a tone that made it hard for me to know if she was upset with me, the media, or both.

"Honest, hon. I have nothing to do with what they say about me. There are people in the county who aren't real big fans of trans people, and sometimes they use my story to try and get people upset and angry."

"You don't know what it's like for me when that happens," she said, her voice cracking. "People make fun of me because my dad pretends to be a woman. Why can't I just have a mom and dad like everybody else?"

Pretends? Shit! Up ahead I saw a Marathon station and I turned in and parked far away from the other cars, then shifted in my seat so I could look at my daughter, who now had tears streaming down both cheeks.

"I'm sorry, Nora. I never want you to suffer because of me."

"Well, I *do* suffer."

This was a conversation I had hoped I'd never have to have, and now that it was here, I was woefully unprepared. Although, truth be told, even if I had weeks to think about it, I'm not sure I would have come up with anything that would make things better. There was simply no way for me to undo the past.

"Would you like me to take you home?"

"Why?" she asked through her tears. "So Mom can tell me I have to be strong and accept you as you are?"

Oh boy. This clearly had been percolating for a while and Becca must've tried to handle it without telling me. Thirteen was such a tough age—middle school, puberty, social media, mean girls, and then add a transgender parent into the mix. That was a tough brew for any kid to deal with. My heart was breaking—not for me—for her. This was the same child who only days earlier had given me a hug when she realized my mom might be dead.

"You're right, hon. I don't know what it's like for you. I don't have the experience of being a thirteen-year-old girl, and even if I had, it would've been very different because we didn't have social media back then. Obviously, you've been dealing with a lot. I really am sorry."

"I don't understand why you had to do this. You hurt Mom; you hurt me; it was totally selfish."

I wasn't sure if all of those were her feelings or ones that had been implanted from listening to her mom's family, but whatever well of resentment they had sprung from, there they were. "Well, if I hadn't done this, I might be dead."

"You're just saying that," she said defiantly.

"I don't know, hon. I guess none of us ever know what would have happened if we had taken a different road. All I know is that's how I felt at the time. I also knew that I wasn't being a good husband, father, or even just a good person, and part of the reason was because I wouldn't allow myself to be who I knew I was. So, I did what I thought I needed to do."

"Grandma and Grandpop said you're not a woman, and you have no right to pretend to be one."

I bit my lip, trying not to let my anger with my ex-in-laws come through. "Your grandparents are certainly entitled to their opinions." I paused. "But remember what you said earlier, about me not knowing what it's like to be you? Same thing holds true when it comes to me. Neither they, or even you, know what it's like to be me. I'm just trying to do the best I can and that means being honest with the world about who I am. And this is it," I said, holding my hands up in front of me.

Once more silence enveloped us. I reached into the center console and took out my personal cell phone. "I'm going to call your mom and make sure she's still home."

"She's going out," Nora offered without looking at me.

I went to say something, but stopped. "Sorry. I guess you're stuck with me for the day."

Her chin rested on her chest and her despair at spending the day with me cut like the jagged edge of a broken bottle. I tried to think what we could do, knowing the last thing she wanted was to be seen in public with me.

"How about we head to my apartment and I'll make us some breakfast and we can figure things out from there," I suggested.

She gave me a wary look. "What would you do if I wasn't here?"

"I guess I'd head over to Grandpop's house. I'm going to live there for a few weeks."

"Why?" she asked.

"Grandpop isn't well enough to leave the nursing home, and I just need to start sorting through things to get the house ready in case we sell it."

She looked at me, her mood seeming to shift, a veneer of suspicion slowly replacing the anger. "Does this have to do with Nanny?"

God, how to answer her question? I didn't want to plant the seeds of doubt about my father, despite the fact that I was swimming in a river of suspicion. But I had just emphasized my need to be honest and now my instinct was to lie to her.

I sucked in a deep breath. "Yeah, hon. It does. If the cold case your mom and I were talking about turns out to be Nanny, I want to look for anything that might help me understand what happened all those years ago."

"How many years is it?" she asked, her anger fading. "I mean, since Nanny has been gone."

I closed my eyes and sighed. "Forty-one years on December 6," I said.

"If I went to Grandpop's with you, maybe I could help sort through things."

"All right," I said, trying to hide my reluctance. The last thing I wanted was for Nora to discover just how dysfunctional life had been for Brian and me, but I didn't have any other plan. "I need to stop at the store to pick up some groceries. There's a Kroger on the way to my dad's. We can stop there and then I can make us breakfast. How's that sound?"

"Okay," she said, a hint of contrition in her voice.

MY FATHER'S HOUSE WAS situated two blocks from I-13, in a neighborhood that had sprung up after urban renewal claimed the mostly Black neighborhood to make way for the interstate. When I was growing up, most of the dads in the neighborhood worked in the manufacturing plants in the industrial area of Harrison, while most of the women were stay-at-home moms. There had been lots of kids our age, which sometimes provided my brother and me with a respite from life in this house that was often our own private hell. I can remember lying in bed on warm summer nights with the windows open, hearing the roar of the eighteen wheelers on I-13 headed off to parts of the country I only knew from television, and wondering if I'd ever make it out of Harrison—I didn't.

The house was a typical 1960s split-level. On the first floor was the living room, dining area, and kitchen. Down three steps there was a den and a half bath. Up six steps was the second floor, which had three bedrooms and the bathroom.

Beneath everything was a full basement, and off the den was an attached garage, where my father's 2012 Ford F-150 sat.

The kitchen, like everything else in the house, hadn't been updated since my parents bought the house in 1976, shortly after they were married. After Nora helped me carry the groceries in, I scrounged around to find what I needed to make breakfast, but when I went to make coffee, I realized that the only coffee maker was a Mr. Coffee that looked like it had been given to my father as a retirement gift in 2004. I can be a bit of a coffee snob, and I suspected that the Mr. Coffee hadn't been cleaned since he got it, leaving me the choice of risking botulism or dealing with caffeine withdrawal. To my surprise, the coffee actually turned out to be decent.

We ate mostly in silence, an awkward truce lingering in the air. I tried to imagine what it was like for Nora having me as a parent; would she have been better off if I had just stayed an angry divorced dad, miserable with myself and the hand life had dealt me? On more than a few occasions, I had wrestled with my own guilt over whether, in an attempt to save my own life, I had damaged the lives of the people I loved. *Let it go*, I thought.

After cleaning up, I went down to the basement and carried several boxes upstairs, placing them on the living room floor. Even before his dementia, my father had not been an orderly person, so I knew there would be no rhyme or reason to the way things were stored. But even if there had been, I had no idea what I was looking for. It's not like I expected to find a typed confession stored in a box labeled *I Killed Your Mother*.

"What are we looking for?" Nora asked, as if reading my mind.

"I really don't know, hon. I think first we have to get a handle on what's here. So maybe we start by sorting what's here by years, and then into categories, like old bills, any letters or cards or anything having to do with my mom."

We had been at it for a while, me making several trips down to the basement to bring up additional boxes, when I noticed Nora was looking at some old photos. "Whatcha got?"

She looked up, puzzled. "Pictures. Some are in a photo album; some are just loose. The loose ones are mostly of Grandpop. The ones in the album look like you as a baby."

"Probably some are Brian too," I said.

"That's what's strange," she said. "Some of the photos have been cut, and it looks like whoever cut them purposely cut Nanny and Brian out of the pictures."

I took the album from her. She was right. Someone, presumably my father, had cut my mother and Brian out of the photos.

"Why are there no pictures of Nanny or Uncle Brian?" she asked.

I had a guess for both, but I wasn't about to share either with my daughter. After all, she didn't even know her uncle was gay, and I wasn't about to out him. But it was a pretty good guess that after Brian had come out, Dad had gone out of his way to remove all traces of Brian from his life, including any photographic evidence. The reason for Mom's removal was less clear. Whether she walked out and disappeared, or he killed her, either could account for him literally cutting her out of his life.

I finally responded with an answer that hewed close to the truth. "I don't know why my mom has been cut out of the pictures. As for Uncle Brian, he and Grandpop had a huge argument and I suspect that's why Grandpop got rid of his pictures."

"What did they argue about?"

"Uncle Brian was dropping out of college to move to California because he had gotten a part in a movie."

"Wait. That sounds really cool." Her eyes brightened with the small detail from her uncle's life. "Why was Grandpop upset about that?"

"Grandpop was old-fashioned, and he didn't think acting was a good career choice."

"But Uncle Brian's a huge star. Didn't they make up?"

"No. Unfortunately, they never saw each other again after that night."

She studied me, her lips pursed, clearly unsatisfied. I could tell she sensed there was something I was leaving out. "Never? Why?"

"I'm not sure, hon. Just because people are older doesn't mean they always act like adults, and your Grandpop is as stubborn as they come."

She focused her blue eyes on me. "Mom told me that Grandpop was very angry after you told him you were going to transition."

"He was," I said. "He refused to see me."

"If he was as angry at you as he was Uncle Brian, how come he didn't destroy your baby pictures?" she asked.

Good question. Why hadn't he? "Probably because he forgot he had them," I replied with the only answer I could come up with.

"I'm sorry," she said, looking a little sheepish.

"Why?"

"You were right. I don't know what it's like to be you, and . . . and I guess it must bother you when people say things about you."

"It does," I replied. "Just like I know it bothers you when people make fun of you because of me. I'm sorry that happens to you," I said, hoping that maybe we had found our way back to our usual parent/child space—comfortably uncomfortable.

She picked up something by her hip. "I also found this on the kitchen table when we got here," she said, holding out my high school yearbook. "You were kind of cute back then. I mean, you know, in high school," she said hesitantly.

"Thanks," I said, allowing myself the faintest of grins.

"I still have pictures of us together when you were still Dad—is that okay?"

"Of course," I said, a spark of guilt flaring as I remembered the picture on her dresser of the three of us outside Cinderella's Castle when she was five. "I'm never embarrassed about being your parent."

I put the yearbook aside and we went back to sorting documents. Around 5 P.M., when we hadn't come up with anything else, I went out and picked up pizza for dinner, and then drove Nora back to her mom's.

"Please don't think I hate you, Mads," she said, looking concerned.

"No worries, love. I don't think that."

"I'm glad you didn't kill yourself," she said.

"Me too." I leaned over and gave her a hug. "I love you. I'll see you Tuesday after guitar."

I watched until she was safely inside, then headed back to my father's house. I had a safe to crack.

WHEN I GOT BACK to the house, I opened the trunk of my car and pulled out my things. I had packed enough clothes, toiletries, and cosmetics to last me a few days. I went in, put on another pot of coffee and, while the coffee dripped, trudged upstairs and put my clothes in the room Brian and I had shared. Despite living in a three-bedroom house, Brian and I had always shared a room. After Mom left, our father moved out of the master bedroom and into the remaining bedroom, leaving the one he and Mom had used empty the entire time I lived there.

My brother and I had spent countless nights in this room when we were young, terrified that our father would come home drunk and hit us for some reason only he knew. Then, when we were teenagers, we'd lay here at night planning what we'd do when we got out of this place and hopefully as far away from him as possible. Now, as I took in the room, I noticed all traces of Brian had been obliterated. Gone were his Little League trophies, the books from his bookshelves—Vonnegut, Heller, Stephen King—and his baseball varsity letter that he'd hung on the mirror over the dresser. There was no evidence that we had ever inhabited this space. In my case, it was because I had packed up my stuff before I left, but Brian had left in a hurry. After the fight, he had quickly grabbed some clothes, put them into two gym bags, and had never crossed the threshold again. At some point after I had moved out, my father must've erased any evidence of Brian's existence.

After grabbing my cup of coffee from downstairs, I headed

up to my father's bedroom and took a look at the safe in his closet. It was a two-foot-square steel safe, with a combination lock, and it appeared to be about forty years old. I knew a number of locksmiths from my years on the job, so I wasn't worried. Eventually, I'd get in. But knowing my father, I figured I might be able to guess the combination. My father's badge number when he was with the DA's office was 314 and he had joined the DCDAO in 1981 after being on the force in Harrison for five years. Cops generally like to keep things simple, but I didn't even know if it was a three-number combination or a four-number one. If I couldn't get it, I'd call a locksmith in the morning.

First, I tried 4-31-1, figuring even my father would mix things up a bit—nothing. Then, 1-31-4. Again, nothing. Then I decided to try four numbers. The numbers didn't go as high as 81, so I tried 8-1-3-14—bingo. I pushed down on the handle and was in.

The safe was divided into two levels separated by a middle shelf. Inside were two gun cases. The one sitting on the shelf was made of wood, probably walnut. The second one, sitting on the floor of the safe, was a standard metal gun case. The keys to the locks were in both. I presumed my father had decided that storing them in a locked safe was secure enough. On that point, I agreed.

I opened the wood box first. Inside was a 9mm Glock 17, a fully loaded magazine lying next to it. As I looked at it, I remembered that this box, along with the Glock, which had been my father's duty weapon, had been presented to him at his retirement party by the union.

I then removed the metal gun box and took it over to my

father's bed so that I could sit on the edge as I opened it. Inside was a Colt .38 Detective Special snub-nose revolver and a box of .38 cartridges. I hadn't seen one of them in years. It had wood grip panels, a steel frame, and a two-inch barrel. I presumed this was my father's original duty weapon when he started with the DA's office. He had probably purchased it when the office switched to Glocks sometime in the '90s. There were no cartridges in the cylinder, so I looked inside the cartridge box. There were about twelve cartridges, but in the back, I noticed something else. My stomach sank: two rings—one was a diamond engagement ring, the other a wedding band.

I stared at them, frozen, knowing what they were, yet trying hard to convince myself I was wrong. Perhaps they belonged to my father's mother or his mother's mother. There had to be another explanation.

I finally managed to command my hand to move and pulled the rings out of the box. When Becca and I were married, I had my initials and the date of our wedding engraved inside her ring and her initials and the date engraved inside mine. I clicked on the flashlight app on my phone and there on the inside of the wedding band were three initials and a date—F. L. K. 10.2.76. I wasn't sure of the date my parents were married, but I sure as hell knew my father's name—Francis Liam Kelly.

I desperately tried to convince myself that this didn't change anything. There was still at least one perfectly logical explanation for why he had them—she had left them before she had run off. Made sense. But my mind also insisted on offering me all the potentially incriminating explanations too.

I left the gun box on the bed and returned to the safe, kneeling down and running my hand along the inside to see if there was anything else. In the bottom rear corner, my hand encountered something. I grabbed it and pulled it out. It was a stack of one-hundred-dollar bills. I reached in and there was another, then two more. On the last stack, underneath a rubber band wrapped around the bills was a tattered yellowed piece of paper with a handwritten notation that said $50,000—2-27-04. I sat on the bed and counted the cash—fifty thousand dollars.

Where the hell did my father get fifty thousand dollars in cash? Innocent explanations were becoming harder and harder to come by.

As I stared at the cash lying on the bed, one thing was clear—I needed to find out what the hell had happened on February 27, 2004.

CHAPTER 19

I STOOD IN MY parents' empty bedroom staring out the curtainless window into the darkness. The houses beyond the backyard were shrouded in gray mist. The sun wasn't due for another hour and the pre-dawn quiet lingered. Even the noise from I-13 seemed to be on mute. The room smelled musty. It was totally bare, adding an eerie quality to it, enhanced by the fact that no one had lived in it for over forty years.

After things had settled down a bit from Mom leaving, and Brian and I stopped staying with Nanny or Aunt Maeve and moved back home with our father, we found the door to what had been their bedroom locked, and our father now ensconced in the spare bedroom. Once, when I was six or seven, I asked my father if I could go in the room. His reply had been a curt "no." Years later, Brian, who had always been more willing to break the rules than I was, had found the key. On a Saturday when Dad was working a homicide, Brian convinced me that we should go in and take a look around. We did. There was nothing—literally nothing. The room was bare. No furniture, no rugs, no clothes—it was as if no one had ever been in the room before. The emptiness had been a shock. I had expected to find remnants of our mom, but just like the pictures she had been cut out of, her presence had been erased. Standing in the empty room, I felt like I had lost her all over again. I had fought back the tears, not wanting to let my little brother see me cry—boys don't cry. But later that night, when I knew Brian was asleep, I cried until there were no tears left. Had she ever really existed? Or was she just a dream that I held onto as protection against the nightmare that I found myself living in?

Now, here I stood, holding the fifty thousand from my father's safe and wondering if I was standing in the middle of a crime scene. Had my father shot my mother in this room and, being a cop, had the smarts to create a story to keep people from looking for her and then destroy all the evidence from the murder scene?

I tried to remember what it had looked like the last time I was in here before Mom left. I'm sure there had been curtains on the windows, and furniture, but whether there had been carpet or rugs or pictures on the walls or how things were arranged—all of that was a blank. There had been clothes in her closet—that I still remembered.

I wasn't about to get a forensics team in here. Assuming something had happened here, the passage of time and the suspect, a detective well versed in the forensics of crime scene investigations, left me less than sanguine about the chances of uncovering any evidence. I could go online and get some luminol, the chemical the forensic folks would use to look for blood, to spread around. Even forty years later, if there had been blood on the floors or walls, there was a decent chance there'd be a reaction. But if this had been where my mother was shot, the smart thing to do would've been to sell the house years ago and, while my father was a prick, he wasn't stupid.

I walked back to my father's room, threw the money into the safe and locked it. I needed to shower and get to the office. The clock was ticking on how long I'd be able to keep Sherry's investigation going. On top of Snyder trying to shut me down, the article in *The Gazette* had set off alarm bells. Not only was someone coming after me, its ripples had reached Nora, and probably Becca too—a reminder to me that they were in the blast zone. One thing I had never fully appreciated when I came out was that I'd be the gift that kept on giving. Naïvely I had hoped that the three of us would manage to ride out the initial shockwave of shit that would come our way, but after that passed, we'd arrive at a new normal. I had misread that by a country mile. But I had misread a lot of things.

Following my near-death experience with Ashley's client, Becca had given me an ultimatum—get help or get out. Faced with her ultimatum, I went to see a therapist. Unfortunately, it hadn't turned out the way either of us expected. True, I had lots of issues with my parents to work out, but a lot of my anger was self-inflicted over the guilt and shame that had built up over the years of struggling to hide the woman I had always known I was. But even after months of therapy, transitioning was the furthest thing from my mind. At that point, I was a sergeant in the DCDAO and I'd been in law enforcement for over fourteen years. I was considered a guys' guy, and I still hoped that somehow I could put the genie back in the bottle. But when I finally confessed to Becca that the reason I was struggling was because I was transgender, things hadn't gone well. The irony was that coming out had cost me my marriage, but probably saved my life.

BEFORE I GOT TO the office, I gave Becca a quick call to check on Nora and fill her in on finding my mother's rings and the cash. There was dead silence when I finished.

"You there?" I asked.

"I'm here," she said.

"Can you do me a favor and check a date for me in *The Gazette*'s archive—February 27, 2004. I don't know what it means, but it was the date on the paper with the cash, and I'm trying to figure it out."

"Sure, I can do that. What are you going to do?" she asked.

"Pay my father a visit after work," I replied.

WHEN I PULLED INTO the parking lot of Rolling Knolls after work, my mom's rings were in a jeweler's box in the pocket of my jacket. I was still undecided on how I was going to play this with him—confront him head on, or show him the rings and see if he had any reaction? Either way, the overwhelming odds were I'd get nothing. Even if by some miracle it turned out Jane Doe wasn't my mom, he sure as hell had known more about what happened to her than he ever told us. *Fuck him. I need some answers.*

I checked in at the front desk and headed back to the Alzheimer's wing. I was buzzed in, and made my way to his room. He was sitting in the recliner, his snoring letting me know he was in a deep sleep. At least today he was clean shaven, and his hair had been combed. I shook him awake—I only had twenty minutes before his dinner arrived, and, given the mood I was in, it wasn't like I actually gave a shit if his sleep was disturbed.

"Mr. Kelly, it's time to get up." He stirred but didn't wake. "Mr. Kelly," I repeated, louder and with a harder shake of his arm. "Time to get up."

This time he opened his eyes. "Huh," he mumbled through the fog of confusion. "Who are you?"

I unclipped the badge from my belt and showed it to him. "I'm a detective with the Donn County District Attorney's Office." Then I went all in. "I'm investigating the murder of your wife, Maureen Kelly, and I'd like to question you about your involvement."

It was hard to tell how much had actually registered, but he was suddenly awake. "What? Murder?" he managed to get out.

"Yes, Mr. Kelly, we have probable cause to believe that you were involved in the murder of your wife. We've found her body." I paused, taking the jewelry box out and snapping it open. "And we found her rings in an ammunition box in your safe. Care to explain?" I said, trying to use every word I could to trigger him, unconcerned about any negative impact it might have on his health or mental state.

He pushed down on the recliner's leg rest until he was sitting upright. "Wife . . . . rings?" he said, his eyes now wide, taking in the box in my hand.

"Yes, Mr. Kelly. Your wife was shot once in the head and we believe you were involved." I watched his eyes, looking for some reaction, anything to show that my words accusing him of murdering his wife had registered. "Can you explain why her engagement and wedding rings were in your safe?"

He tried to clumsily snatch the box from my hand, but my reflexes were quicker and I took a few steps back. "Why did you have these rings, Mr. Kelly?"

His eyes narrowed. "I should have killed both of them," he spit out, rage suddenly gripping his face.

"What did you do?" I demanded, stepping closer and leaning in so we were face-to-face. And in that instant, I saw a flash of recognition in his eyes.

"You!" he said, his mouth curling in anger. "You pervert. Get out. GET OUT!" he screamed at the top of his lungs.

Before I could do anything, there was a commotion in the hallway and a nurse's aide came through the door. "Mr. Kelly, is everything all right?" She stopped suddenly when she saw me, but her attention immediately shifted back onto my father.

"Get him out," he said, his rage still burning.

"I'm sorry," she said, looking around the room before turning to me with a look of bewilderment, probably hoping for me to clarify who my father was referring to.

When our eyes met, her expression shifted. Fear suddenly spilled across her face and she froze. When I saw her face, I realized that my hand was resting on my gun. I quickly moved it away and rubbed my hands together as if I was warming them against the cold.

"I probably should go," I said. I turned back to face my father, intent on warning him that we'd continue this conversation another time, wondering if he'd retain any memory of what had just happened. But when I did, I saw something I had never seen in my entire life. My father had his face in his hands and he was sobbing. Dumbstruck, I quickly walked past the nurse's aide out into the hallway, where I stood trying to process what had just happened. His brutal words and then tears. *Tears! Why tears? Guilt? Remorse? Grief?* Or simply the dementia wreaking havoc on his emotions? And then there was me. My hand on my weapon. What would've happened if the aide hadn't come in when she did?

Once in my car, I sat there shaking. *Focus*, I thought. I needed to process what had just happened, finding myself torn between the personal and the professional. There was me, the daughter, who when she confronted her father about her mother's death heard him say, "I should have killed both of them." Then there was me, the cop, who knew that if a suspect said that during an interrogation, it wasn't an admission he had killed anyone. Maybe he meant that she had run off with another guy and he wished he had killed her and her lover. I took a deep breath. I had screwed up. I had let my personal feelings take over. It's why you're not supposed to investigate a case that's too close to home. I hadn't even asked him about the fifty thousand dollars. I needed to fall back on my training. I had to have more. But what? What more could I get? I began to run through options. DNA would confirm if Jane Doe was Mom. According to the information on the cold case website, they had recovered the bullet that killed her. If they still had the bullet, I could have forensics check it against the .38 in my father's safe. But I needed someone to talk to. Someone who was around when all of this went down forty years ago. The only person that came to mind was Aunt Maeve, who I hadn't seen since before I transitioned.

When I came out, I had sent Aunt Maeve an email explaining that I was transgender, what it meant, and that she was welcome to reach out if she wanted to talk to me. Aunt Maeve, being a good Catholic, emailed back suggesting that I should pray and ask God to heal me. Our only conversation after that was about two years ago, to let her know that we were putting our father in a nursing home. She had listened, thanked me for the call, and hung up. Not exactly an encouraging prelude to a constructive conversation about my mother and father.

I thought about calling Brian to tell him everything, but realized it was only mid-afternoon on the West Coast, so I sent him a text asking him to call me later tonight. On my way home, I stopped at the Freshy Mart and picked up a premade Caesar salad with grilled chicken and a bottle of Kendall Jackson chardonnay. After the last twenty-four hours, I needed a drink.

WHEN BRIAN CALLED AROUND nine, I had already gone through half the bottle. I wouldn't say I was wasted, but I was feeling no pain.

"What do you make of the fifty thousand—a bribe?" he asked after I brought him up to date, giving voice to a question I had been wrestling with since last night.

"Not a clue. But here's the part that doesn't fit that he was on the take—the date on the money is after he retired. Unless he was getting money for something he had done while he was still on the job, or had some kind of side hustle, I'm stumped."

"You okay?" he asked.

"No."

"Anything I can do to help?"

"Me personally, no. But in terms of next steps, yes."

"What can I do? Just name it."

"I still have a small window while Brisbane considers your request and then, assuming they agree, while they get the paperwork together to exhume the body. Which will give me time to pay our Aunt Maeve a visit."

"Aunt Maeve? Are you serious?"

"Yeah. Unless you can think of another option, she's the only person I know who was around forty years ago when this went down."

"When you plan on going?"

"Assuming she's available, as soon as possible—either Wednesday or Thursday of this week."

Neither of us had seen Aunt Maeve in seven years—the last time was for the funeral of her younger sister, our Aunt Jackie. Five years younger than our father, Jackie just never seemed to find her footing in life. Married and divorced twice, she had a son from her first marriage, but we never really knew him because Jackie lost custody when she and her ex divorced. Back in the day, you really had to be a bad mom in this state to lose custody—based on the stories, Jackie was that and then some. Dad told us she died of a heart attack, but I saw the police report. She OD'd.

"Do you ever hear from Aunt Maeve?" I asked Brian.

"Once, a few years back. She was out in LA with a friend and I got her passes to visit me at the studio. We had lunch in the commissary and that was it."

Brian was aware of Aunt Maeve's pray-the-trans-away response to me, so he knew that I wasn't on Aunt Maeve's Christmas card list. "Okay, this is where I need your help."

"How?"

"I don't want to fly down to Florida to find out she's away. And I suspect that if I email her to ask if we can meet, she'll leave town before I get there. Could you email her and say you're in town to shoot a scene and you'd love to stop by for a few minutes to say hello?"

He chuckled. "Sure. And it'll be your fault if she never speaks to me again."

"You're welcome to join me," I replied.

"Thanks, but we're shooting a new episode this week. Guess I'll have to take a rain check, but let me know how it goes."

"Will do. And don't worry, I'll cover for you."

"You always have," he replied.

CHAPTER 20

I WAS SITTING AT Becca's kitchen counter, sipping my coffee, my pounding head a taunting reminder of my stupidity for having finished the bottle of wine. Nora had just left for school, and I was trying my best to concentrate on Becca as she scrolled through an Excel spreadsheet containing the list of names I had asked her to put together for me.

"I took what you gave me—that Sherry allegedly had oral sex with X number of members of the West Harrison High football team sometime during high school."

"She wasn't there senior year," I interjected.

"Yeah, but she was still in the area. So better to include them. When you take into account that there were guys on the team for multiple years, there are a total of eighty-two guys."

"Shit! Eighty-two?" I said.

"Yep. Sorry."

"Go ahead."

She gave me a half smile. "Then I tried to track down their

fathers, and what they were doing back then. So far, I've been able to find thirty-one." She gave me a quizzical look. "How confident are you that Dash's comment meant that Sherry's sugar daddy was a relative of someone on the football team?" she asked. "You're assuming it was someone's father. Maybe that's not what Dash meant, or given what you told me about Dash's condition, maybe he simply got it wrong," Becca said, adding more variables to the mix.

But there was something there. "Benson said Sherry hinted that if she told Benson who she was seeing, Benson would know the person. So, if all our information is correct, we're looking for someone who could shell out four hundred in cash every week, with good name recognition. Somebody, who, even if you didn't know them, you'd recognize their name. I think I can safely ignore the fifty-one fathers you didn't find— they're not well known enough," I offered. "If our parameters are correct, my suspect is one of the thirty-one you found."

"Sounds like you're feeling optimistic," she said.

"Yeah, maybe I am," I replied, knowing the DNA results had given me some new puzzle pieces that I hadn't shared with Becca. Results that led me to believe Sherry had engaged in oral sex with the man near the time she was killed, and that there was also a chance that a female had been present. It was a guess, but I could think of one scenario that fit—a wife or significant other catching their man in flagrante delicto with Sherry. They lost it, cut the guy, and killed Sherry. If that was the way it played out, it meant my murderer might be a woman.

"You want me to do some further checking?" Becca asked.

"Thanks, but I think I need to run this down on my own. I

have an idea of what I'm looking for. If I find it, and if it leads to a suspect, I think it's better if I've actually done it myself."

"Works for me," she said. "By the way, I ran down February 27, 2004, and I can't find anything of significance. I mean nothing."

"Okay. I appreciate you trying, and for all your help on this."

"You know I enjoy this stuff. It's the journalist in me," she said. She pointed to her screen. "You want me to email or print the spreadsheet for you?"

"If you don't mind, could you do both?"

She hit a few keys on her laptop. "Done. The copy printed in my office. Don't forget to grab it when you're leaving."

"Thanks," I said.

"You haven't told me about your conversation with your father."

I hadn't. I was still trying to process it—both his reaction and mine. I wasn't sure if I'd be able to forget the look of terror in the nurse's aide's eyes when she saw my hand on my gun. The scary part was that I hadn't even realized that's where my hand was. Even scarier was I didn't know what would've happened if she hadn't materialized.

Over the course of my career, I had dealt with all kinds of people who had broken the law. Some were truly evil, and others were just unlucky. Maybe they were in the wrong place at the wrong time, or they just snapped. I had almost snapped. There was a guy I interrogated who was accused of murdering his wife. They had three kids ages twelve through four, and after he confessed, he broke down in tears and said, "There's nobody who can piss you off more than the person you love the most."

I certainly couldn't say my father was the person I loved the most. That honor fell to Nora, followed closely by Becca. But I knew what he meant. My father was someone I was supposed to love. Despite what a miserable person he was, he had provided for me until I graduated college. I owed him. But in that moment, the thought that he had killed my mother . . . I wasn't sure what I could have done to him. And I knew the only other time I had come that close to crossing the line had also been with him.

When I finished telling Becca what had happened, she was stunned. She came around to where I was sitting and we embraced and shed a few tears. "I'm sorry," she said. "What are you going to do now?" she asked, grabbing a tissue and blowing her nose.

"Brian and I spoke. At this point while we're waiting to have the body exhumed, I'm flying down to Florida tomorrow to talk to my Aunt Maeve and see if she knows anything. I probably have a week or so before word gets out."

"I didn't think your Aunt Maeve talked to you anymore."

"She doesn't. She thinks Brian is coming to visit. We're going to do the old bait and switch."

"What if she won't talk to you?"

"Don't know. I haven't gotten that far yet."

I told Becca I wouldn't be able to make our weekly wine and dine, promising to make it up to her and Nora next week. After we chatted a little about Nora, I took the Excel spreadsheet and we said our goodbyes.

IT WAS EARLY AFTERNOON when I headed to Snyder's office. He was sitting behind his desk, a pair of reading glasses sitting on his head as he squinted at his computer monitor. I knocked on the doorframe and when he looked up, I asked if he had a minute to talk. When he nodded, my first inclination was to suggest the glasses on his head might help him see the screen better, but I held my tongue.

"What is it, Kelly?"

"Cap, sorry for the short notice, but I'd like authorization to take a couple of days of PTO. I have to fly down to Florida to see my aunt, my father's sister, about his condition, so I want to take a few personal days." I didn't expect a hard time. After all, from Snyder's perspective, any day he didn't have to look at my happy, smiling face was a good day.

"Everything okay with your father?" he asked, showing a human side I didn't know existed.

"His Alzheimer's is getting worse, and I just need to talk to my aunt about whether we need to move him to a different facility," I said, granting myself absolution for the lies based on the fact that a detective was always permitted to be deceptive when interrogating a suspect.

"Sure. Put in your request for PTO and I'll approve it."

"Thanks, Cap," I said, standing and heading toward the door.

"And Kelly."

"Yes, sir."

"I still want that investigation closed."

"Roger that," I said.

I LOOKED AT MY Fitbit—5:30 P.M. I had a 7:55 A.M. flight the next day, so I began to pack up a few files to read on the plane and during the layover. As I stuffed things into my briefcase, I saw a piece of paper with a phone number and smiled—Margie Benson. It's not like I'd had a thing for Margie in high school. She was an out lesbian and, back then, I didn't play for the same team. But when I saw her the other day, there was something about her that intrigued me. And, unless I had totally misread things, she seemed curious as well—she had suggested that I come by for a drink when I was off duty. Becca had moved on. Maybe it was time for me to try and let go of the torch that I still carried for her. *Why not? I'm off duty.*

IT WAS A LITTLE after six when I walked into Tesh's. The place was packed. I managed to find a seat at the bar and ordered a diet soda. "By any chance is Margie Benson working tonight?" I asked the bartender.

"Well, she's not working, but she's over at the table in the back corner if you want to say hello," she said, pointing me toward the dining area.

"Thanks."

I grabbed my soda and headed toward the back, only to see that Margie was sitting with three other women. I was never good at socializing, and joining a table with three complete strangers didn't check the box for having a good time. I turned and was about to head back to the bar to finish my drink when a voice called out, "Kelly. Yo, Kelly. Over here!"

I looked back over my shoulder to see Margie waving me over. Reluctantly, I headed over to the table.

"Join us," Margie said. "We can make room."

I glanced at the three other women at the table. The two dressed in business suits both looked younger than Margie while the third, in a flannel shirt, looked to be close to seventy.

I tried a polite smile. "I didn't mean to interrupt. I just stopped by and thought I'd say hi if you were around." I gave an animated wave. "Hi," I offered, probably making a total ass of myself.

"You sure you don't want to join us?" Margie asked.

"Yeah, thanks. I have to go to Florida tomorrow, so I have an early flight. Maybe next time." I raised my glass in a salute, and headed back to the bar to finish my drink and get out of Dodge.

I found a seat at the bar and began the process of self-flagellation. For fuck's sake, what had I been thinking? I didn't know the first thing about Margie Benson except she was a lesbian and we went to high school together. But before my self-recrimination could continue, Margie slid onto the stool on my right.

"Hey, nice of you to stop by." Her look was somehow both genuine and mischievous. "I honestly didn't expect to see you again. I thought you were just being polite when you said you'd come in for a drink."

I found myself tongue-tied in a way that I hadn't experienced since trying to ask Sarah Gittins to the senior prom—and that had turned out to be a disaster. Putting aside my own gender identity issues, I think part of my social awkwardness around women was there weren't any women I was close to growing up. My mom was gone; Nanny died; and Aunt Maeve moved to Florida. And as much as I felt I was a girl when I was growing up, I avoided girls because I didn't want anyone to suspect my secret.

"Um, no," I stuttered. "It was good to see you. Just thought it'd be nice to catch up when I wasn't on duty."

"That would be nice," she said. "I have to get back to my friends, and you have to pack for a flight. You have my number. Give me a call when you get back from Florida. We could go on a date." She appeared to consider something. "Or maybe I'll call you, since you're a little more girly than I am," she said, her mischievous grin having spread to her eyes. "Safe travels, Lieutenant. Let me know when you're back in town."

"Will do," I said, watching her walk away and wondering what the hell had just happened.

CHAPTER 21

THE BLANK LOOK ON Aunt Maeve's face when she opened the door to her townhome let me know that she didn't recognize me. In spite of her vacant stare, Aunt Maeve was an attractive and stylish woman, the counterpoint to my father. Where he could easily pass for ten years older than his sixty-eight years, Aunt Maeve at seventy looked ten years younger. Her auburn hair was cut in a chin-length bob with sideswept bangs, and it looked like she had dressed to meet her movie star nephew—white slacks, a gray silk blouse, and classic black flats.

"Can I help you?" she asked.

"Hi, Aunt Maeve."

I assumed that my salutation would have given her a pretty good clue as to who I was. After all, other than me, there were only Brian and Aunt Jackie's son, who might call her aunt. Yet her face remained devoid of recognition.

"It's me, Aunt Maeve—Lauren Kelly."

"Lauren?" Then the light bulb went on. "Liam?"

"That's what my name used to be. It's now Lauren."

She looked past me, scanning the immediate area. "Where's Brian?"

"Unfortunately, the studio needed him to head back sooner than expected, so he won't be able to make it. He asked me to let you know how sorry he is, but he's scheduled to be back in Florida soon, so he'll reach out to reschedule," I said in an effort to avoid throwing my brother under the bus.

"Why are *you* here?"

"Can I come in, Aunt Maeve?" I asked, my concern growing that she just might shut the door in my face. "And I'll explain what's going on and why I'm here. It has to do with my father," I finished, deciding to leave *and my mother* until after I got in the door.

She hesitated for a moment as if weighing her options, but she finally stepped aside so I could walk in.

"Nice to see you," I said.

I had to admit, I had mostly warm feelings toward Aunt Maeve. Despite not wanting anything to do with me post transition, she had taken care of Brian and me for several years after Mom left, often providing a respite from the storm that was our father. I really couldn't blame her for heading south after first Nanny and then her husband had passed. After all, she hadn't signed on to raising two kids. We used to see her once a year around Christmas, and when I was twelve and Brian was ten, Dad put us on a plane to spend a week with her. She had even driven the two hours to Orlando so that we got to visit Disney World. All in all, I still had a soft spot in my heart for Maeve.

We stood awkwardly in the foyer until I said, "Can we sit somewhere? There are some things I need to talk to you about."

"Would you like coffee?" she finally asked. "I only have instant."

She could have offered me warmed-over dog piss and I would've said yes. She was giving me a chance to talk to her.

I stepped aside so she could lead the way to her kitchen, which was modest, but still a great deal better than mine. I took a seat at her kitchen table while she ran water into a cup and put it into the microwave.

"Is Frank okay?" she asked.

"His dementia is getting worse," I said, and then proceeded to fill her in on his condition. "How are you?" I asked in the hopes of putting her at ease. The one good thing about asking a seventy-year-old how they're doing is that, chances are, they'll tell you in detail—and she did. And seriously, I could only hope that I would be doing as well as she was when I hit seventy. Of course, that assumed I'd make it to seventy.

She put my coffee in front of me, and took the seat opposite. "Aunt Maeve," I began, "the other reason Brian and I wanted to talk to you has to do with our mother."

"Your mother?" she repeated, her face tensing.

"Have you heard from our mom since the day she left?"

"No. But . . . well, given the circumstances of her leaving, it sort of made sense."

I took a deep breath and told her about Jane Doe being discovered in 1983. I studied her, hoping to see if she knew what was coming, but if she did, there were no tells. She just sat and listened. "I don't know if you remember, but when I was about eight, you gave me a picture of my mom, from my birthday party when I was five."

"I remember," she said, sadness in her voice.

I removed three pictures out of my laptop bag and laid them on the table. "This is the original picture you gave me," I said, pointing to the picture, and for the first time, Maeve reacted with a sad smile and a sigh. "This," I said, pointing to the second picture, "is an enlarged photo of the necklace Mom was wearing in the picture. And this," I said, tapping the third picture, "is a copy of the necklace found on the body of Jane Doe."

She looked up at me. "It . . . it looks like the same necklace," she said. "But . . . but, it can't be Maureen's."

"Why?" I asked.

"Because she's not dead. She left your father for another man."

"How do you know that?" I asked.

Her eyes locked onto mine. "Are you trying to tell me your mother died in 1983?" Her voice was suddenly unsteady.

I inhaled. "We're not a hundred percent certain yet. But, even though the body was found in 1983, the date of death was probably late 1982, right around when my mom left. We're going to have the body of Jane Doe exhumed so they can get DNA to make a positive identification. But there are other things that lead us to believe it's our mom." I then filled her in on the other pieces. "There's one other thing, Aunt Maeve. The woman, whoever she was, didn't just die. She was murdered. She was shot once in the side of the head with a .38 caliber handgun."

Her eyes went wide. If I read them right, they betrayed a feeling of terror.

"The same kind of gun my father carried at the time."

She shook her head. "No. It can't be."

A look of defiance took shape. I'd seen that look before,

usually from a parent when we were arresting their kid. It's a look that mixes denial and disdain and says *Why are you trying to frame my son, daughter*—fill in the blank—*for something they didn't do?*

"Aunt Maeve, I won't know for sure until we have the DNA, but I wouldn't be here unless I was almost certain that my mother was murdered in 1982."

She folded her arms on the table and then bent over and began to weep into them. When she finally looked up, the defiance was gone. Instead, her face, blotchy and wet from her tears, begged to go back thirty minutes, before I arrived, before I shook her illusions of what happened forty years ago.

"He would never kill her," she offered in a weak protest. "Frank might not have been the best father or husband, but a killer—never!"

My mind went back to the confrontation the night our father threw Brian out. Up until that moment, I would have protested that I would never kill anyone. But I knew better. All of us were capable of doing unspeakable things.

I didn't want her to close down on me, so I eased off. "I didn't say he killed her, Aunt Maeve. As I told you, we're not even a hundred percent sure it's Mom. But when did my father tell you she ran off with another man?"

"The day after—the day after she didn't come back to pick you and Brian up. I asked him what was going on and he said she left him a note and her engagement and wedding rings on the kitchen table. The note said she had found someone else."

How I wished I could get him in an interrogation room and grill him. The rings left on the table explained why he had them, but he was an experienced cop by then; he would've known how to cover his tracks. "Did he show you the letter?"

"No. No, he said he was so angry that he ripped it up and threw it away."

Of course, he did, I thought. "Did he tell you who it was she ran off with?"

Her eyes pleaded with me to stop. But I had to know what happened. "Did he, Aunt Maeve?"

"No. Why would he tell me that?"

I took a second to lower the temperature in the room. "Aunt Maeve, didn't it strike you as strange that my mother would abandon Brian and me and never contact you? I know I was only five, but I have nothing but good memories of my mom. Well, good memories until she never came back. Some part of me has always despised her because she left me—us," I added, correcting myself.

"No, don't feel that way. Your mother's a good woman."

I took note of Aunt Maeve's use of the present tense for my mother, lending credibility to her belief she thought Mom was still alive. "But how did you square that with the fact she left with another man—and abandoned her two young children?"

Her eyes met the photos of Mom, her necklace, medal and cross, spread across the table. "Oh God, Liam . . . I mean Lauren," she said, "I didn't know what to think. You're right. It made no sense. She adored you and Brian. But my brother—well, I don't have to tell you. I don't think he was as nasty before she left, but if he treated her like he treated the rest of us after she left, I guess I thought she must have been so afraid of him that she got out to save herself and hoped my mom and I would protect the two of you." A part of Maeve seemed to deflate. Like her cocoon had suddenly been shattered and she was looking at the truth she always knew was right in front of her. "I hope it's not her," she said weakly.

I wanted to say "me too," but I had lost hope. My mother hadn't come back because she was dead. Did she die fleeing in the arms of another man? Was she the victim of a robbery gone bad? Or had my jealous father killed her in a fit of rage?

"Did she ever say anything to you about my father physically abusing her, or being afraid of him?"

"No, never. I mean, don't get me wrong, my brother had a temper, always did, and was used to getting his own way, but she seemed happy and if she was afraid of him, she never said anything. Sometimes your mom would complain about the fact that your father always seemed to be working and, with two young kids, she never had any time to herself. Remember, when she had you, she was only like . . ."

"Twenty," I said.

"So, she was only twenty-five when she—"

There was no need for Aunt Maeve to finish the sentence. A week ago, both of us would have finished the sentence with "left." Now it was more ambiguous.

"Did she have any close friends? Anyone you might have met when you visited us?"

"That was more than forty years ago. I'm lucky if I remember what I did last week."

She was right. I was grasping at straws.

"When will you know? If it's her, I mean," she asked.

"It depends on how long it takes for us to get them to exhume the body. Once that's done, we're hoping the DNA doesn't take too long.

"There's something else I have to ask, Aunt Maeve. Did my father ever say anything about coming into a large amount of cash?"

She looked at me quizzically. "Large amount of cash? What are you talking about?"

"I found fifty thousand dollars in cash in my father's safe, with a note that, if I'm reading it right, indicates that he got it on February 27 2004."

Her face scrunched. "Frank never had that kind of cash. Are you suggesting Frank was doing something illegal?"

"Honest, Aunt Maeve, I have no idea what it means. But it was sitting in his safe in hundred-dollar bills."

"No," she said. "Frank never said anything to me about coming into any money—not that he would have. We weren't particularly close after I moved down here. We'd talk maybe once or twice a year. I'd call him on his birthday. He'd usually call me two weeks after mine to wish me a belated birthday. He never knew when it was," she said with a shrug. She looked at me, and for the first time since I arrived, I saw a sympathetic face looking at me. "I'm going to make myself a cup of tea. Would you like another cup of coffee?"

"That would be nice," I said.

We made small talk as she boiled some water, and I told her about Nora, who Maeve had met just the one time, when she had been up for Jackie's funeral. And I told her about Brian and how he was doing.

Finally, she placed our cups on the table and sat down. "Why did you do this?" she asked, gesturing to me with her hands.

"Because this is who I am, and who I've always been. I just hid it from everyone."

"I don't believe that. Did you pray like I told you to? I told you; God doesn't make mistakes. He made you a man and you just needed him to help you battle your delusions."

"I'm not a mistake, Aunt Maeve, and I'm not delusional. I didn't wake up one morning and say, 'Oh, I think I'm a woman.' I've always known this is who I am. I'm not smart enough to know why, but I certainly didn't choose to be this way. So, assuming you're right and God doesn't make mistakes, this is the way God made me."

She gave me a skeptical look. "But what you did wasn't fair to your father or your daughter or your former wife. Don't you feel bad?"

"Of course, I feel bad for how this impacted them, but I was miserable—not with Becca or Nora—but with myself. I don't know where my father's anger came from. I always assumed it was because his wife left him with two kids. But at some point, I found myself becoming just like him. In my case, I knew where my anger came from. It came from the fact that I couldn't be myself. I was trapped living as someone I hated. One of the most important things I've tried to teach Nora is to be honest. People should always be able to take you at your word. And at some point, I realized I was a huge hypocrite because I was living a lie every day."

"But I saw you as a baby. I know you were born a boy. You fathered a child, for crying out loud. How can you sit there and tell me you're a woman just like I am? That's wrong," she said.

"I know it's hard for someone like you to understand what it's like for me, but just like you always knew you were a woman—something inside told you that you were a woman—something inside me always told me I was a woman."

"That's crazy," she snapped. "I knew I was a woman because I had a vagina and a uterus."

"So, it purely comes down to sex organs, is that it?" I asked.

"Yes," she answered without hesitation.

"Do you really think that if my father lost his penis and testicles in a horrible accident, he'd wake up the next morning and say, 'Well I guess I'm a woman now?' Of course not. No matter what's between his legs, there's a knowledge between his ears that he's a guy. You can't change that. For me, the knowledge between my ears was always that I was a woman, and it didn't matter what was between my legs."

"Did you ever wonder if you felt this way because your mother left?" she asked. "You know, some deep-seated need to replace the mother in your life."

I actually laughed. "No, Aunt Maeve. Never."

She looked unconvinced.

I pointed to the picture of me blowing out the candles on my fifth birthday that was sitting on the table. "Back then, when I was five, I believed birthday wishes could come true." I let out a slow sigh. "The wish I made that day was that when I woke up in the morning, I'd be the little girl I knew I was." I paused, trying to keep my emotions in check. "For years I blamed myself for Mom leaving because I wasn't the little boy she wanted me to be. After she left, even when I no longer believed in birthday wishes, I still prayed that I could be the boy my mom wanted, so she'd come back to me," I said, wiping a tear away with the back of my hand, the reality that me wanting to be a girl never had anything to do with my mom leaving now staring me in the face. All these years, I had carried that around like an anchor.

She looked into her tea and shook her head. When she finally looked up, she asked, "Are you happy . . . Lauren?"

"Yes, Aunt Maeve. I am. I know I haven't made it easy for everyone else in my life, but I think I would have wound up making it harder on everyone if I hadn't done this."

There was a long silence. "Tell me about my mom," I finally asked, and in that moment, I realized it was the first time I had ever asked anyone that question.

Maeve sighed. "She was a beautiful woman—her red hair and blue eyes. She was a stunner. And oh, how she could light up a room when she walked in. She had this full-throated laugh that was infectious, and when she smiled it seemed to start in her eyes . . ." She paused, staring at me. "You have her eyes, Lauren. In fact, I can tell you're her . . . daughter." Maeve closed her eyes and a small smile graced her lips. "She wasn't afraid of having some fun and she could be a bit of an imp, in a good-natured way of course. I remember she loved to bowl. There used to be a women's bowling league in town and your mom was good—one of the best. She was a good woman. I missed her after she was gone," she said wistfully.

After we chatted for a while about her, Dad, and Brian, there was one last thing I needed to do—really one of the main reasons I had come. I also knew that if I got the response I expected, it would shatter both of us.

"Can I ask you one last thing, Aunt Maeve?"

"Of course," she said.

"Every year until I was fourteen and Brian was twelve, we received birthday cards from our mom."

Her face told me the answer. As she dissolved into tears, my last ray of hope disappeared behind the clouds.

"I didn't know, Lauren. Frank told me he didn't want the two of you to think your mother had forgotten you. I thought I was helping. I had a friend who lived in San Diego and I'd mail her the cards, and she'd mail them to you. Oh God, I'm so sorry."

I went over and crouched next to her chair. "It's okay, Aunt Maeve. You didn't know."

I embraced her, knowing that I had just made her feel complicit in hiding the truth. I didn't blame her—she didn't know the truth. But I understood that, despite the best of intentions, some part of her would never be the same again.

CHAPTER 22

I STARED AT MY laptop trying to assess just how truly fucked I was. I had stayed for dinner with Aunt Maeve and hadn't gotten back from Florida until late yesterday afternoon. Fortunately, Captain Snyder was lingering under the impression I was still visiting with my aunt. Instead, I had spent most of today at my kitchen table combing the internet for backgrounds on the thirty-one men on Becca's Excel spreadsheet. Turns out the list included the county executive, the assistant superintendent of the Harrison School District, six lawyers, three doctors, three teachers, assorted insurance brokers, financial analysts, and corporate executives. Five of the people had passed away. That didn't eliminate them as potentially being Sherry's sugar daddy, it just dropped them to the end of the list, because if it turned out that it had been one of them, it probably meant that I had just hit a dead end, literally and figuratively.

In 2001, the county had two major newspapers, *The Harrison Gazette* and *The Oxford Herald*. *The Gazette* still existed, but the *Herald* had gone out of business in 2003. Fortunately, with my library card, both were accessible online going back to 1998. I had guessed that what I was looking for would have appeared between Friday, April 13, the date Sherry's body was found, and Friday, April 20, 2001. The only problem was I didn't know what I was looking for, I just had hoped I'd know it when I saw it. Fortunately, or unfortunately, I found it.

As I studied the grainy copy of the newspaper article on my screen, I realized I had come up with the worst possible result, and the one that also made the most sense—at least the most sense in the tinfoil-hat world of conspiracies I seemed to have waltzed into—County Executive Ronald Furst.

On April 15, 2001, the Sunday after Sherry's murder, there was a two-inch article on page eight of *The Oxford Herald* that County Executive Ronald Furst had been hospitalized as a result of injuries he sustained while using a power saw in his basement. The article stated he had suffered severe lacerations, requiring him to be hospitalized for another day or so, but he was expected to make a complete recovery.

Of all people, why him? A lot of folks had wound up as bugs on the windshield when they crossed Ron Furst. And here he was as the leading candidate to have been Sherry's sugar daddy—the damn county executive and chair of the state Republican Party. As county exec, he ran the county. And while technically the DCDAO was supposed to be independent of the county executive, anyone who believed that was a fool. But there he was, checking all the boxes, including having a son on the football team—Sam, a classmate of mine—and I cringed thinking that during high school I had wanted to be part of his social circle.

Senior year I had gone to a party Sam had thrown, trying desperately to fit in as one of the cool guys. His parents were out of town and word had spread that he was having a bash. There was lots of beer and booze and at some point, Sam unlocked his father's gun cabinet that held every kind of gun imaginable, including several antique Colt revolvers, a World War II–era German Luger, a snub-nose .38 revolver, and a few 9mm handguns, along with several hunting rifles and military-style semiautomatic rifles. My father may have been an asshole, but he had drilled into Brian and me the danger of guns, and when I saw what was happening, I made my exit. Fortunately, a neighbor had called the cops about the rowdy party, and they showed up before anyone got hurt. Of course, given who Sam's father was, the whole thing was quietly swept under the rug. Like a lot of people who paid no consequences for their bad behavior, Sam had been an arrogant bully. In that regard, apparently, the apple hadn't fallen far from the tree.

I hated to keep dragging Becca back into my quixotic hunt, but I desperately needed another voice—a voice I could trust—to tell me I was crazy or fucked, or perhaps both. Besides, having spent close to twelve years at *The Gazette*, she would know better than anyone the dirt on Furst that never made it into the newspaper.

"Good morning. You have a couple of minutes to chat?" I asked Becca when she answered her phone.

"Sure," she replied. "Did you meet with your aunt?"

"Yeah, I did."

"How'd it go?"

"I know where my birthday cards came from."

Her painful sigh matched mine. "I'm sorry, Lauren."

"Me too."

We walked through the rest of my conversation with Aunt Maeve, but then I shifted to the real reason for my call—Sherry.

"I think I've narrowed the search of the thirty-one names on your spreadsheet to one," I said.

"Really! Who?"

I took a deep breath, steeling myself for her reaction. "Ron Furst."

"Are you out of your mind?" Becca said, her reaction exactly what I expected. "Lauren, you can't be serious. I mean, I remember seeing his name on the list, but you'd have to be crazy to investigate Ron Furst. He's untouchable. Even the US Attorney's Office hasn't been able to nail him."

I already knew she was right. It wasn't like I wanted to go after the top dog in the county, and maybe even the state. But I also didn't want Sherry's case to fall by the wayside. As much as I was doing this for her, part of it was for me. My own private penance for not being there when it counted.

"You covered politics when you were at *The Gazette*. What's the inside story on him?"

"You're serious," she replied.

"Becca, I know who Furst is—everyone knows who he is. Just like everyone knows he has a reputation as a ruthless SOB, who'll do whatever he has to in order to hold onto power."

"He's dangerous," Becca interrupted. "There are things about him—things you don't know."

"Here's what I do know," I said. "He's sixty-five, and he's been the Donn County executive for the last thirty-one years, having been the youngest person ever elected to that position.

He's married to Elizabeth Furst, nee Millington. They have one son, forty-five-year-old Samuel, who played football at West Harrison High during the time Sherry was there. Ron's father, Otto Furst, is a self-made multimillionaire who made his fortune in real estate. Otto served eight terms as a Donn County councilman and his reputation for ruthlessness is only exceeded by his reputation for making money through shady financial deals. Like Ron, Otto has been a frequent target of the feds, but never indicted. Although he did settle several civil lawsuits. Since taking over as Republican state chair, Ron's considered politically untouchable. How am I doing?"

"You haven't scratched the surface," she replied.

"That's why I called you, Becca. You were at *The Gazette* for almost a dozen years, I need all the news that wasn't fit to print. The one thing that doesn't fit is that Sherry told Riccoli that the guy she was seeing was a 'putz.' I've met Furst, and even in his sixties, he's a handsome man."

She was quiet for a long time, as if weighing what she wanted to tell me. "First off, if I had been Sherry and my boyfriend was jealous of my relationship with a very rich man, of course I'd tell my boyfriend that the other guy was a putz. He's jealous, so the best way to calm him down is to make him feel like he's the one and the other guy's a loser. As for Mr. Furst, you're right; he is a very handsome man, and he's a notorious lothario, whose numerous affairs are an open secret. It's a shame the Me Too movement never caught on here, because he would have been a prime target."

"What do you mean?" I asked.

"He generally hires young, attractive women, many of whom are also bright and ambitious. From what I hear, any woman who goes to work for him has three options—either sleep with him, resign very quickly, or ignore his bullshit until they have to pick option one or two."

"I presume no one has ever gone after him because they're afraid of him."

"That and he has good lawyers," she said.

"Your father's firm," I offered, already knowing that from my threats to sue the county.

"Yep, specifically, my dad."

"Here's the dot that I find hardest to connect," I said. "If he's such a womanizer, why would he pay for sex, and, on top of that, why potentially risk his reputation by having sex with a trans sex worker?"

"I know a lot of men who think with their small heads. Maybe he didn't know. I've seen pictures of Sherry. She was a very attractive woman."

"That's a lot of money to get your rocks off," I said.

"Trust me; money isn't an issue. He's loaded, mostly as a result of his real estate holdings."

"What about his wife, Elizabeth?" I asked, knowing that if Furst was the sugar daddy, and if my theory about how the various DNA samples fit into the picture was accurate, it turned Elizabeth into a person of interest. The question then became, was she capable of murder, or had Furst pissed off some other jealous mistress?

"What about her?"

"How does she fit into the picture?"

"Eliza—which is what everyone calls her—is tough to read," she said. "Her family had money, but her dad died by suicide when she was about thirteen and her mother never left the house after that. She's generally not known for being warm and fuzzy."

"Any rumors about her being fed up with his affairs?"

"Nothing that I know about, but I've been out of the loop for a while now."

"They're still married, right?"

"As far as I know," she said.

"So—it's just a marriage of convenience?" I asked.

Becca chuckled. "I don't know, Laur. Eliza and I haven't chatted about her personal life recently," she said sarcastically. "But if I had to guess, yeah. He's one of the most powerful men in the state. I'm sure people are always trying to do things for her to curry favor with her husband. She gets to hobnob with the rich and powerful. She's probably around his age, so why give all that up?"

"That's pretty transactional?" I offered.

"You're surprised that people have transactional marriages?"

She was right. Why was I surprised? Was it any less transactional when folks stayed together for the kids?

"Even though I don't know her, I've heard rumors she's having some health issues," Becca said.

I made a note to see what I could find out about Elizabeth.

"I don't like you tangling with Furst," Becca said. "When I was at *The Gazette*, I wanted to do a story exposing him for the corrupt, misogynistic sexual predator that he is. I had several women who, as long as we maintained their anonymity, were willing to go on record that he'd sexually assaulted them. When I ran the initial draft of the story by my editors, they killed it. It's one of the reasons I left the paper and became a novelist."

I could hear her draw in a deep breath.

"My editors told me it was for my own good. There are rumors, Lauren. Rumors about people whose careers were ruined, or worse. I know I'm probably being melodramatic here, but all I can think of is Putin's opponents or critics who happen to fall out of windows or commit suicide."

"I have no windows in my office."

"Lauren, I'm serious," she fired back.

"Sorry. I'll be careful. Trust me, I'm not suicidal." *At least not anymore*, I thought. "Besides, Furst already hates me for hiring a lawyer and threatening to sue the county for my promotion, so you don't have to worry about my career being ruined. Not to mention that if anyone here got wind of what I'm doing, I'd be fired in a heartbeat."

"Um, please don't take this the wrong way, but I wasn't necessarily just worried about you. Think about Nora. Even though we weren't mentioned by name, the article last week in *The Gazette* referenced me and Nora. Furst has been known to unleash his minions to harass the family members of people he's pissed off at. Nora's already dealing with shit because of who you are. I don't want her to be the target of much worse."

In my twenty-plus years on the job, I'd never felt like I was putting anyone but myself at risk. And the reality was that, since I had left Harrison PD and joined the DCDAO, leaving aside the time I waltzed into Horvath's house unarmed, I could probably count on one hand the number of times I had felt I was putting myself in danger. But the article last week in *The Gazette* had certainly hinted that whoever was behind it wasn't afraid to drag my family into the mix.

"Is Sherry worth that?" Becca asked.

Nora was the most important person in the world to me. I'd die for her. Even if Becca was being melodramatic, why risk it? I still had nothing solid linking Ron Furst to Sherry's death. Besides, Sherry had been gone for twenty-one years. No one's life was going to change if I never found out who killed her. If I stopped now, I could justify it. But I'd taken an oath. Sherry was no different from any other victim. Why didn't she deserve to have her murderer brought to justice? And what about Joe Riccoli? Wasn't he entitled to know who killed the woman he loved?

Then there was me. If I walked away, I'd have to live with the fact that in the face of evil, I'd backed down. And that's why the Ron Fursts of the world existed, because people refused to stand up and say "No, we won't accept this."

"No, Becca. Sherry isn't worth that," I said.

But finding the truth is, I thought.

CHAPTER 23

DESPITE ALL MY BRAVADO, Becca probably didn't have to worry about Furst exacting revenge. The only way to confirm that Furst was at the scene of Sherry's stabbing was to obtain a DNA sample from him and compare it to what the lab had. And how exactly was I going to get a DNA sample? Waltz into his office and ask him to spit into a cup? Drive up to his house and collect his garbage? Follow him around and hope he threw away a coffee cup? Yeah, good luck with that. And even if I could somehow magically obtain a sample, even if I could get it to the lab without raising a red flag, it would take months to get the results back. By then, with Snyder breathing down my neck, the investigation would be long over. I had run into a wall.

My personal cell phone chirped and I looked down to see that Brian was calling. I would have preferred to tell him about the birthday cards yesterday over the phone, but he had texted me last night that he was going to be tied up, and wanted to know what happened, so I had emailed him. "Hey, what's up?" I answered.

"I got your email," he said.

"Yeah," I responded. "Sorry."

"I guess we both knew what was coming with the cards," he said. "But even though I knew it was coming, I have to admit it sucked some piece of my soul out of me."

"Yeah, that was basically my reaction too. I knew it was coming and I still couldn't duck out of the way," I replied.

"It is what it is," he said. "Listen, the reason I'm calling is that, believe it or not, my manager and my lawyer had a long video conference with some folks in the Brisbane DA's office yesterday, and they've agreed to try on Monday to get a court order allowing the exhumation. They're optimistic that since it's a Jane Doe, they won't have any problems. I know this sounds a bit obnoxious, but, because it's me, the DA's office is going to expedite things and see if they can get the DNA results in a week to ten days."

"A week to ten days? Holy shit. That's insanely fast. It usually takes months. What did you promise them— starring roles in next season's episodes?"

"Almost," Brian chuckled. "Actually, I have a week-long break in my schedule coming up, so I promised that if they could get the results by then, and it turned out to be Mom, I'd come in and appear at the news conference and hang out and sign some autographs."

"Must be nice to be famous," I said.

"It doesn't suck," my brother responded dryly. "Until it does," he added. "Listen, this is where I need your help. My people . . ." He paused. "God, does that sound obnoxious enough? *My people*." I heard him exhale. "Sorry," he said. "Anyway, my people don't want some law enforcement agency putting my DNA into a law enforcement database, so they're going to have my DNA tested here, and Brisbane is going to send Jane Doe's DNA results to the lab out here. But, there's a catch."

"Let me guess. The lab *your people* are going to use isn't part of the FBI's National DNA Index System, meaning your DNA won't be accessible to law enforcement. But it also means that the Brisbane DA can't 'officially' use it."

Brian laughed. "See, that's the difference between a fake cop like me and a real cop like you—you actually know this shit."

"You realize that even if you let Brisbane run it, your DNA will go in as a reference sample and won't be part of the CODIS database. In other words, your DNA wouldn't be in the suspect database searchable by law enforcement," I said.

"Yeah, well, color me skeptical. On this one, I agree with my people. Better safe than sorry."

It was kind of hard for me to argue with him or "his people." If I were him, I wouldn't trust anyone in law enforcement to safeguard his information either. "I guess that means your people would like me to submit my DNA to the DA's office."

"Yeah, that's the ask," Brian said.

"Stupid question, but if I'm submitting my DNA, why are you even bothering with a lab out there?"

"Come on, Laur. I'm in California. Californians are by nature obnoxious snobs. You think anyone out here is actually going to trust the results coming from some lab in Podunk County in your flyover state? Besides, I already gave a sample this morning. It's in the works."

I knew that the Brisbane DA was going to use the state forensics lab, just like every law enforcement agency in the state did. And if we were having this conversation a week ago, I would have said the state lab's reputation was impeccable. But now, after my recent encounter in Sherry's case, I wasn't so sure. I wasn't worried about my DNA floating around in some database, but I did worry that Brisbane might call my office and tip them off about my possible connection to the Jane Doe case, making it impossible for me to keep digging around. But as I thought about it, I realized my worries were probably meaningless. The only wall harder than the one I had run into in Sherry's case was the one I was banging my head against in my mom's case.

At this point, I assumed Jane Doe was my mom, and yet I knew that when it was confirmed, it would still knock me over as if I'd been hit with a sledgehammer. It was one thing to know something in your gut, it was quite another to be certain of something. As long as that one percent of uncertainty remained, some part of my brain could cling to the belief she was alive. It was like I had one hand desperately grasping the ledge of the cliff. But once the DNA came back and pried my fingers away, I'd be in freefall, and when I hit the ground, I'd be flattened.

"Sure. Who at the DA's office should I reach out to?" I asked.

"First Assistant Paul Morocco. You know him?" Brian asked.

"No, not really."

"He seemed like a decent enough guy. He understood why we didn't want to submit my DNA and was happy to learn I had a sister who was in law enforcement who would come in and give a sample for their official use."

Of course, this would mean outing myself, because my DNA would reveal that I had been assigned male at birth. Still, while I was fairly certain I wasn't well known in the Brisbane County DA's Office, it wasn't like my status elsewhere was a secret. Out was out—such was my life.

"You better confirm with the company that's going to analyze your DNA that they don't share DNA with law enforcement," I said. "You've probably heard about the case out in California involving the Golden State Killer. The cops used forensic genetic genealogy to track down a suspect. It's pretty amazing. Some relatives put their DNA into a consumer DNA database, and the cops used it to help identify a suspect."

"Good point," he said. "No reason to use a private company if it's going to wind up in the hands of law enforcement anyway."

Suddenly, something clicked—a private company. A shot in the dark, perhaps, but maybe . . . maybe if someone in the Furst family had used one of these companies, I could identify him that way. I needed to run this by Weiss, but what did I have to lose?

"Everything okay?" Brian asked, snapping me back to the present.

"Yeah, sorry. I was just thinking about how a private DNA company might help me with Sherry's case. But listen, I'll reach out to Morocco tomorrow and try and get there ASAP."

"Tomorrow's Saturday," Brian reminded me.

Damn. I checked my watch. Four P.M.

"Been a long week. I'll try him now," I said, "and I'll get back to you."

BRIAN HAD GIVEN ME Morocco's direct line—of course Morocco had been eager to share his private number with Brian—but I wasn't sure how he'd feel about me having it.

He answered on the second ring, which told me two things—he was at his desk on a Friday afternoon, and he answered his own phone. Two check marks in the plus column for Mr. Morocco. I told him who I was and why I was calling and he couldn't have been nicer, insisting on being on a first name basis.

He quickly went over the status of their application to exhume the body and we agreed I'd come to his office on Monday to have my sample taken, which was perfect. Snyder wouldn't be expecting me in the office until Tuesday and it would give me the weekend to research genealogy companies. We made an appointment for 1:30 P.M. and as soon as I hung up, I texted Weiss to see if she had time to meet for coffee first thing Monday morning. I told her I had a person of interest, but I wanted to talk to her face-to-face because when I told her who it was, she'd wish I didn't have anyone. To my surprise, she texted back and suggested her house at seven thirty. I agreed and she sent me her address.

As I started doing more research, my enthusiasm began to wane. Even if I was lucky enough that a genealogical search pointed to relatives of Furst, I'd still need to come up with Furst's DNA to prove or disprove it was him.

I glanced at the clock on my computer and it confirmed what my stomach was already telling me—dinner time. I was contemplating my options when my personal cell rang. I never answer a call on my personal cell when the caller isn't in my contacts, and all that showed on the display was the number, so I let it go unanswered. Within a minute, my work phone rang and the same number showed on the display. "Kelly," I said.

"Hi, Lieutenant," a familiar voice said.

"Margie?" I asked.

"I told you I'd call you for a date." I could hear the smile in her voice. "Are you back in town and have you had dinner yet? I have to go to work at nine, but was wondering if you wanted to join me at Ric's for a pizza?"

Ric's was two blocks from Tesh's and famous for its New York–style pizza. Since I had never been to New York City, I had to take their word for it.

I guess I hesitated longer than I thought because she spoke again before I said anything. "Don't worry. I'm not one of those lesbians who moves into your place on the second date, but even if I were, this won't count as an official date," she said with a bit of whimsy in her voice.

I laughed in spite of myself. Then it hit me—a date! The thought of a *date* with a woman other than Becca felt almost like a betrayal. I still loved Becca. Yet, in spite of that, for the first time since our separation, I found myself intrigued by the thought of spending time with another woman. So why was I hesitating? It was pizza for crying out loud. It wasn't like I was going to have a romantic interlude.

I swallowed the lump in my throat. "Sure," I said. "What time?"

"How far are you from Ric's?" she asked.

"Twenty minutes, give or take."

"Then how's twenty minutes—give or take?" she asked.

"Um, but I worked from home today. I need to get dressed."

She laughed. "As long as you didn't work in your PJs, come as you are." She paused. "Actually, even if you are in your PJs, come as you are. I've seen you all dressed up, Lieutenant. Now it's time for me to see the other side."

"I only have one side, Margie. You're going to be disappointed."

"We'll see," she said. "And, by the way, my friends call me Gee. I hate Margie. What the fuck were my parents thinking naming me Marjorie? Anyway, see you in twenty. I'm in a booth in the back."

"Okay," I said.

"Hey, wait. What kind of pizza do you like? And if you tell me veggie lovers' or vegan, stay home."

I couldn't help but smile. "What am I allowed to like?"

"Plain, sausage, pepperoni, meatball, and if you're partial to mushrooms, I can pick those off," she offered.

"Sounds like you don't like vegetables," I replied.

"They're against my religion," she said.

Twenty-five minutes later, the hostess showed me to Gee's booth. She had half a glass of beer sitting in front of her, and she was texting. She looked up when I slid into the booth across from her.

"You showed," she said, sounding genuinely surprised. "And, it didn't take you a half hour to do your makeup. Good for you. Want a beer?"

"Sure," I replied. "What's that?" I said, motioning to the beer in front of her.

"Kickers IPA," she said. "And it does have a bit of a kick."

She called over the waitress and I ordered a Kickers.

"I was thinking of something on the way over," I began. "I'm happy to have pizza and beer with you, but for reasons I'll explain, this can't be a date, formal or informal."

She side-eyed me, and I was trying to decide whether she was insulted or just curious.

"Okay, but you didn't have to show up to dis me. You could've just said no on the phone," she said.

"It's nothing like that. The simple fact is that I don't know if anything will ever happen in Sherry's case, but if it does, you're theoretically a witness. And so, I wouldn't want to prejudice the case in anyway by . . ." I hesitated.

"Having a relationship with a witness," she finished.

"Yeah, basically," I said.

"How come you didn't think of that before you came to the bar the other night?"

"Things changed," I said.

She tilted her head.

"Please don't take it personally," I said, hoping my tone conveyed that I was disappointed too.

The waitress brought my beer and asked Gee if she wanted another. "No thanks," she said. "Have to work tonight." She turned her attention back to me, her index finger curled around her mouth. "So, there's something new in Sherry's case?"

That was another question I had thought about on my way over. I didn't know her well enough to be sure that whatever I said would remain just between us. In the end, I decided I could use exactly what she gave me and see if it led anywhere. "Based on what you told me about Sherry, I began to wonder if the football team and her sugar daddy might be connected.

So, I put together a list of rich and well-known people who had sons on the football team when we were in high school."

Gee laughed. "Well that probably covered at least half of the football team."

"Not quite, but close," I replied. "I came up with thirty-one out of eighty-two guys."

"Anyone I might know?" she asked.

Before I could answer, the waitress put a pizza stand in the middle of our table, placed a flat pan with the meat lovers' pizza on it—sausage, meatball, pepperoni, and bacon—then laid a few paper plates and a stack of napkins on the table. "Anything else, ladies?" the waitress asked.

"A root beer, please," Gee said.

I smiled. "Nothing else for me, thanks."

The short delay had given me time to think about how I wanted to approach this with her. I went through the list, throwing out names, and watching to see if she had any reaction. I had started with the financial and insurance people, figuring those were least likely to get a reaction. As I moved through the teachers and doctors, there was nothing. I went with the superintendent of schools next, but got no response. Finally, I put Furst's name in amongst the six lawyers. Then I grabbed a slice of pizza and waited.

"That last group, I know two of the names from Tesh's. Charles Saunders, I know he's a big-shot lawyer, and the Furst guy," she said between bites, "I know he's a bigwig politician in the county. He and a group of guys take over a private room at Tesh's once a month."

"You think either of them could have been Sherry's sugar daddy?" I ventured.

"They both have money. Although with Furst, Pete basically gives him everything on the house. Pete fawns over him like a dog waiting for a bone—it's disgusting."

"You're the assistant manager—you ever talk to Furst?"

"A couple of times. But the dude is always flirting and I wear my sapphic pride proudly." She studied me. "If you're asking me if I think it's possible that twenty years ago Sherry was practicing her oral skills on Furst, sure, it's possible. But it's just as possible that it was any one of the other names you threw out."

"You ever see Furst's son, Sam?" I asked, hoping for a potential family DNA link.

"Unfortunately," she replied. "He's a regular. Still as big a dick as he was in high school. Come by around eleven tonight and he'll probably be holding court at the bar."

"No thanks," I said. "I have no desire to have a high school reunion. But let me ask you, do you ever get pressed into bartending?"

"Just about every Thursday, Friday, and Saturday after we stop serving food at ten. Why?"

"Next time he comes in, you think you could grab a glass or bottle Sam drank out of, put it aside and make sure it doesn't get washed or thrown out?"

Her eyes narrowed. "What the fuck are you doing, Kelly?"

"An investigation into the murder of your friend," I said.

"You think Sam did it?"

"No." I was going to add more, but stopped. "All I need is his glass or bottle. Can you do that for me? If you get it, I can pick it up from you tomorrow."

She sighed. "Are you always a cop?"

"Yep," I said flatly.

"No wonder your ex dumped you," she said.

I laughed. "Not sure that was the tipping point," I said, turning my palms up to indicate that perhaps there was a bigger issue.

"How long have you been a cop?"

"Almost twenty-two years. Ten years in Harrison PD. Then moved over to the DA's office, just about twelve years ago."

"I have to admit, I'm kind of surprised that in Donn County you made it to lieutenant as a trans woman."

"Having a lawyer with a good reputation helped. Plus, I only came out four years ago. Before that I was so far in the closet that even my closet had closets," I said with a weak grin. "I was promoted to sergeant before I came out. At that point, the chief considered me a rising star in the office, and he saw a great future for me." I shrugged. "Guess his crystal ball wasn't working because three years after becoming a sergeant, I came out. Definitely not a good career move, especially not in Donn County."

"So, what were you like before you came out?"

"I don't know. I guess I was like a lot of cops. Probably a bit of a jerk."

"I don't remember you being a macho asshole in high school."

"I don't think I was then. It was only later."

"Trying to man up?" she said with a snarky grin.

"Yeah. Something like that."

We both took another slice and munched away.

"So, tell me, you still have the hots for the ex?" she asked.

I coughed, almost choking on my partially chewed pizza. "What makes you ask that?"

"I don't know. Just a hunch. I can tell you're interested, but you're using your cop alias to keep me at bay. Plus, based on your ineptitude at being around other lesbians, I figure you're a baby lesbian, probably haven't even been out on a date or made love to a woman since you and your wife divorced." She allowed herself a snarky grin. "How am I doing?"

I could only hope my face wasn't as flushed as it felt. "One more reason for us to keep things professional," I said after I regained my composure. "That way, I don't have to answer personal questions."

"Right," she said, a sly smile slowly forming. "Got it."

CHAPTER 24

I HONESTLY HAD NO intention of ever seeing my father again, but by Sunday I had changed my mind. My meeting the next morning with Lisa had taken on added significance: Gee had been successful in securing a bottle that Sam Furst had been drinking from. Now I needed something from my father.

Today he was clean shaven, wearing a DCDAO polo shirt along with a pair of gray pants. His half-eaten lunch sat on a tray on a corner table. The television was off, but there was something new—music. Sitting on his dresser was a Bose all-in-one speaker system and docking station with a vintage iPod in it. My father was sitting in his usual chair with his eyes closed. I would have assumed he was asleep except his lips were moving and he appeared to be silently singing along to Johnny Cash's "Folsom Prison Blues." My father always liked country music and Johnny Cash in particular. That's probably the reason why Brian and I listened to anything but country. I tended toward a mix of the classics—The Beatles, Stones, The

Who—with some '90s stuff like Guster, Dave Matthews, and Tom Petty. My brother, on the other hand, got into the heavier stuff, Nirvana, Guns N' Roses, Poison, and then, when he was about fifteen, N.W.A. Whenever our father wasn't around, he'd play "Fuck tha Police" as loud as our ears could take. We were rebellious, but not stupid, so when our father was home, my music catalogue was our playlist. He still considered my music "shit," but he tolerated it.

When my father was first diagnosed with Alzheimer's, I had done a fair amount of research trying to get a handle on how things would progress, and selfishly trying to figure out my chances of winding up in the same boat. Now, as I watched him lip-synching to the music, I remembered reading about how music might help slow the progress of the disease, or even be able to open a small window of memory for the afflicted.

"Folsom Prison Blues" folded into "Ring of Fire," and once again, my father sang silently along.

I wasn't sure who set this up for him—a staff member or an old law enforcement buddy—but whoever had done it had it set to play continuously until manually stopped, so I went over, took his spoon out of the empty Jell-O container, wrapped it in the paper napkin and put it in my pocket. Then I brought a chair over, placed it in front of him, hit pause on the iPod, and sat down.

He opened his eyes and his stare was once again vacant. "Do I know you?"

"Yes sir," I replied. I had no patience today for our usual dance and simply wanted to see if I could quickly score some information and get out—the music had given me a sliver of hope. I leaned forward in my chair. "Detective Lauren,

DCDAO. You're my sergeant. We're working the Owen Barr murder file together," I said, using Sherry's dead name to avoid provoking his transphobia.

A confused look slowly took over his face, but he nodded.

"Sarge, I have information that County Exec Ronald Furst might have been present when Barr was stabbed." I paused, hoping for a reaction—any reaction.

"Furst," he mumbled.

"Yeah, Sarge. The county exec. I'm thinking we should bring him in for questioning."

His eyes widened. "No! Can't touch him," he responded, his confusion replaced by something else. What was it? Fear?

"Why not, Sarge? My information is that he was there," I tried again.

"Dangerous," he said, before a noise behind me startled us both. I swiveled my head and standing in the doorway was the nurse's aide from my last visit, along with a security guard.

"What's going on?" the guard asked. He was a big guy—looked like he could also work as a bouncer at any nightclub in the area.

"I'm talking to my father," I said, not wanting to go into cop mode.

"Look," he said. "From what Patty saw the last time you were here, we're a little worried for Mr. Kelly's safety. You seem to agitate him and he seems to irritate you."

"I can't argue with that," I replied. "I agitated him before he had dementia. It's like that in some parent-child relationships."

"I don't want to have to call the police," he said, as if this was supposed to scare me.

"For what?" I replied innocently.

"For causing a disturbance," he replied, looking down at the nurse's aide standing next to him.

"I've been coming to see my father for the last two years, and the only incident we ever had was when I was here last time," I said, suspecting that Patty had informally said something, but hadn't filed a formal complaint. If she had, I would have been confronted long before I got to my father's room. Still, I appreciated that she cared enough about him to be on the lookout for his maniacal daughter who had appeared like she was ready to shoot him. At this point, I wasn't worried about getting thrown out; I had probably gotten all I was going to get from him anyway. I was more concerned with what they had heard, and more importantly, what they would do with anything they might have heard.

I looked back at my father. Whatever window of recollection I had opened was now closed tight. I hit play on the iPod, moved the chair back to where it had been, and weighed my options.

I was off duty and wasn't wearing my gun or badge. Instead, I was carrying a small purse, which I unzipped, then removed my DCDAO credentials. "I'm a lieutenant with the Donn County District Attorney's Office," I said, showing them my ID. "My dad also worked there, so sometimes I try to talk to him about his 'good old days.' Last time I was here," I said, making eye contact with Patty, "I apparently touched on a trigger for my dad, and that's why he went ballistic. Sorry if I caused any trouble. As you saw, things were much better today."

The security guard scowled, not taking my explanation at

face value. Patty, on the other hand, seemed to relax a little. Perhaps the story made more sense to her, having witnessed my father screaming about getting "him" out of his room, when to her, there was no "him" there.

"Thanks for your concern," I said. "I was just leaving anyway."

I took another step forward and they parted like swinging doors as I walked out. *Damn, I wish I knew what they had heard*, I thought as I headed to my car.

LISA WEISS'S KITCHEN WAS everything you'd expect from a thirty-five-hundred-square-foot home in one of the most exclusive areas of Donn County. It was stark white with gray granite countertops, a gray-and-white tile backsplash, and all JennAir appliances. By all appearances, she and her husband, John, who was a corporate attorney at one of the largest law firms in the country, were doing very well. Their two children, ages twenty and eighteen, were at Dartmouth and MIT, respectively, and my guess was that Lisa drove a Volvo instead of a Mercedes for reasons other than cost.

"Coffee?" she asked.

"Thanks," I said.

"So, are you going to ruin my day or my week?" she inquired, handing me a mug.

"If it goes nowhere, I'll probably only ruin your week. If it turns out to be what I think, it'll probably ruin our careers."

That got her attention. I explained why Furst and his wife were persons of interest. I ran through my initial thoughts about using forensic genetic genealogy like the investigators in California had done in the Golden State Killer case.

"You're just going to take a shot in the dark and submit the state lab results to some DNA genealogy company?" she asked.

"I was," I said. "But I now have a better alternative."

She gave me a quizzical look.

I reached down into the canvas tote that I had brought in with me, and produced a Budweiser bottle in a clear evidence bag. "This is a bottle that Ron Furst's son drank out of Friday night. A helpful bartender gave it to me Saturday afternoon. I've had it since then."

Her face scrunched like she just got a whiff of rotten eggs. "What are you suggesting, Lauren? Sending this to the state lab?"

"The state lab—God no! What I'm suggesting is that we give a copy of the DNA results from the crime scene to a DNA genealogy company along with this bottle and see if there are any genealogical matches between the DNA from the crime scene and what's on the bottle. If there isn't, there's two possibilities. Sam is adopted, or the DNA from the crime scene can't be Ron Furst's. If there is a genealogical match . . ." I stopped.

"Then we're well and truly fucked," she said, both her words and tone taking me by surprise.

"Well, basically, yeah," I replied. "Then we'll need to get a sample directly from Furst, but I may have a way to do that."

I then told Lisa about Marjorie Benson and my hope that I might be able to get Ron Furst's glass the next time he and his bros got together at Tesh's. If that was a match, then we could work on getting a sample from Elizabeth.

When I was done, she refilled my cup without even asking. "I don't know what to hope for."

"Sure you do. We run Sam's DNA and find no genetic connections to the crime scene DNA. Nowhere to go from there, and the case gets closed," I said.

"That's certainly the easiest," she said. "But I suspect that's not what we're hoping for." She looked at the evidence bag sitting on her countertop. "And how do you propose we get this analyzed?"

"I've done some research and there are a few places that I could reach out to, but I wanted to talk to you first," I said. "We also have to discuss how to pay for it, because obviously, we can't go through normal channels."

She picked up the evidence bag. "Leave it with me for now. I have an idea. I'll get back to you by tomorrow. As for the cost, I can put it through my budget with the State Attorney General's Office. No worries."

"Thanks," I said. It wasn't the result I expected, but it was one less thing for me to worry about. It also provided me with some official cover.

Next, I told her about the possibility that I had been overheard trying to get information from my father about Furst.

"From what you've told me, your father's Alzheimer's is pretty far along. Why were you trying to get information from him? You'd never be able to use it."

I nodded. "You're right. But like many people suffering from dementia, he has rare moments when the fog seems to momentarily lift. I know nothing he says will be admissible, but that doesn't mean it's not potentially helpful to my investigation."

"Okay. Keep me posted on whether you think anyone has been tipped off," she said.

She gave me a look that conveyed she hoped we were done, but I had to let Lisa in on Jane Doe and the fact that this afternoon I'd be driving out to the Brisbane County District Attorney's Office to provide a DNA sample to see if Jane Doe was in fact my mother. If Brisbane wanted to contact anyone, I wanted it to be Lisa, not Snyder, or potentially worse, the chief. Halfway through my explanation, she poured herself a second cup of coffee and me a third. When I was done, she came around the island and gave me a hug.

"I'm so sorry, Lauren."

"Thanks," I managed.

I could see her mind sorting through what I had just told her. She was, after all, an experienced DA.

"There's more, isn't there?" she asked. "Your father," she said slowly, somewhere between a question and a statement.

"Maybe" was all I could get out.

I reached down and pulled out another clear evidence bag from my tote. "We need to have this run too," I said.

Her curious look conveyed the question—why?

"It's from my father's lunch tray."

Her brow furrowed. "I don't understand. If Jane Doe turns out to be your mother, forty years later, the chance of Brisbane getting any usable DNA in terms of murder suspects is remote."

"I know. But it's not just for Brisbane."

"Surely you don't think your father is connected to Sherry's murder," she said.

"He was part of the investigative team. In fact, the first DCDAO person on the scene. So, I . . . I just need to know."

AFTER BRINGING ME UP to his office, First Assistant District Attorney Paul Morocco let me know that earlier that morning, the court had signed the order permitting them to exhume the body. His office had already scheduled it for tomorrow and he remained cautiously optimistic that they could get the DNA results back within a week. Apparently, Morocco had promised the people at the lab a special invite to the office if my brother came to visit.

"Have you run Jane Doe's clothing and personal items for DNA?" I asked.

"We did. After your brother and his representatives spoke with us, we pulled the evidence from storage. I'm not sure what the condition of the items was when they were recovered, but the techniques for storing evidence have evolved a lot in the last forty years, so I assume a lot of the decay was just from the way they've been stored. The bottom line is there was nothing. Sorry."

"I saw online that a bullet was recovered during the autopsy. Do you know if it's in good enough shape to do ballistics on?"

"Actually, it might be. But after forty years, not sure that we'd ever be able to trace the gun," he replied.

I said nothing. No sense in offering up my father's .38 unless the remains were my mom's.

We were about to head to the DA's lab for them to take a swab, when I asked the obvious question. "I presume you've researched my background?"

"Yeah, I did," he replied. "I'll alert our people that they can submit your sample for both mitochondrial DNA and Y chromosome markers."

Puzzled, I said, "Well, no reason to do the Y chromosome

markers since the DNA from Jane Doe will be from a woman and only mitochondrial."

"Yeah, I hear you. But Brian's people asked for both," he offered with a shrug.

Fifteen minutes later, I was on my way home when my work cell buzzed. It was Snyder.

"Hello, Cap," I answered.

"I thought you were in Florida," he said.

"I finished up early with my aunt and since I had put in for a couple of personal days, I've been trying to take care of some issues involving my dad."

"What happened at the nursing home yesterday?" he asked.

"Nothing," I said honestly. "The last time I was there, my dad flipped out on me because—well, you know how he feels about me being transgender. But nothing happened yesterday."

"The chief got a call from a security guard. He said it sounded like you were questioning your dad about a case."

"Cap, my dad has Alzheimer's. Why would I ask him about a case? Ninety-nine percent of the time he doesn't even know who I am."

"You were asking him about the Barr case, weren't you?"

"Like I said, he doesn't even recognize me. What could he remember about a twenty-year-old case?"

"I gave you a break, Kelly, when you came in and gave me a song and a dance, but folks are tired of this bullshit. I want the investigation finished this week. This fucking week. Got it?"

"You gave me a month, Cap."

"I changed my mind. I don't give a shit if it remains a cold case. End your investigation. That's an order!" he bellowed before hanging up.

Folks are tired of this bullshit, I repeated to myself—folks, plural. And the security guard had called the chief. *It's not paranoia if they're really out to get you,* I reminded myself.

I called Weiss on my personal cell. It went to voicemail. "Lisa, this is Lauren. I just got a call from Snyder. He's ordered me to end my investigation into Sherry's case this week. I'm not anxious to lose my job. Let me know if you have any suggestions."

Fifteen minutes later, my phone rang.

"I got your message. My husband's firm represents one of the biggest private DNA testing companies, DNAhit. They're going to get the bottle and spoon tested for us in the next forty-eight hours. Let's see what the results are. Like you said earlier, if they come back and find that there's no match, you've hit a dead end. No point losing your job over that. If it comes back with a hit, we'll figure it out."

"Thanks," I said.

Now all I had to do was figure out why my brother's *people* wanted the Y chromosome markers. There was only one logical explanation that I could think of, but could that really be what my brother was thinking?

CHAPTER 25

"YOU SEEM UPSET," BECCA said, taking a sip of her wine as we waited in McBride's for Nora to finish her guitar lesson. "Is everything all right?"

"Not really," I said, before quickly updating her on the status of Jane Doe and that we might have the DNA results by next week. I didn't mention Snyder's ultimatum, which was also eating at me, but since I knew Becca didn't want me working on Sherry's case, I was hoping she wouldn't bring it up.

Her eyes were forgiving. "Sorry," she said. "I didn't realize things were moving that quickly."

"No. Totally my fault for not letting you know what was going on."

"Speaking of not sharing things, I forgot to tell you that Nora and I went to visit your father on Saturday."

Now it was my turn to be caught off guard. "Why?"

She sighed. "Nora was curious. She hadn't seen her grandfather since he went into the nursing home, and I guess with everything going on with Jane Doe and with you at your father's house, she wanted to see him."

"How was he?" I asked.

"He had no clue who I was. He kept asking me if I worked at the DA's office."

"And with Nora?"

"It was different. For the longest time, he had no clue. But . . . well, Nora wanted to bring him something. I remembered that your father liked country music. So, I picked up an iPod and a Bose docking station on eBay, then I downloaded some country music onto it. Anyway, when the music started playing, Laur, he seemed to change. After the first song, he looked up at Nora and smiled. Then he said to her, 'Give me a hug.' And when she did, I could see the tears running down the side of his face. It was like, even though he didn't know her, he knew she was family. I know what you think of your father and what he did, but I have to admit that it was very emotional."

Now I knew where the iPod had come from. Maybe if I had played more country music as a kid, my father wouldn't have been such a monster—music soothes the savage beast, I mused, then quickly dismissed that as wishful thinking. Maybe age and dementia had mellowed him, but my memories of his rages were too vivid to think Johnny Cash could've saved Brian and me. "That was very kind of both of you," I said. "How'd Nora react to seeing my father?"

"A bit sad, a bit confused. I know you've tried to hide your feelings toward your father, but she's a perceptive kid, and she doesn't understand your relationship with him."

"In other words, she blames me for that too," I said, my frustration a little more evident than intended.

Becca looked down at the table, a sure sign I had nailed it.

"She still upset with me?"

"I wouldn't say upset, it's more that she's struggling to understand you. She's a teenager—she's struggling to understand herself."

"I know. Plus, people give her shit about me. I get it."

"Do you, Lauren? Do you know what your transition was like for us? I lost my husband; she lost her father—or at least the man she knew as her father. I know it hasn't been easy for you either. But in the end, you got to be the person you knew you were, while Nora and I lost the person we loved."

I went to defend myself, but she held up her hand.

"It was hard for us," she said. "I don't blame you for what you did, but even though some part of me will always love you, you're also the person who took away the man I loved. But I'm an adult. I can move on—build another relationship. Nora can't. You're her father; sorry, her parent. But to her, you'll always be her father and she's still coming to terms with that. Give her time. Be patient. She'll get there." Becca reached across the table and touched my hand. "She loves you. She really does."

I had a lump in my throat. I knew everything Becca said was true. It was why I had wrestled so hard with coming out and transitioning. My therapist had warned me, "You never transition alone. Everyone who loves you will have to make a transition too"—and she was right.

I picked up my wine glass, took a sip, then set it back on the table and stared into it.

"Are you still working on Sherry's case?" Becca asked, dashing my hopes she wouldn't raise it.

I looked up from my wine glass. "My captain has ordered me to end the investigation this week," I replied, avoiding answering her question. I returned my gaze to my wine, but I could feel her eyes measuring me.

"I'm sorry. I know it must be hard for you to walk away."

"Whatever," I said. I was usually a better liar, but I was still trying to recover from the emotional beating I had just taken over the impact of my transition on her and Nora, and I couldn't take another one for not walking away from Sherry's case.

"Um, look, I know my timing on this really sucks, but I wanted you to hear it from me before word gets out or Nora tells you."

I looked up, not sure what was coming.

"Roger has asked me to marry him, and I've said yes."

I felt like a boxer who, after taking a couple of body blows, had dropped their arms only to take a right hook square on the jaw. If I had been standing, I probably would have staggered aimlessly around the room. When my synapses started to work again, I managed to say "Congratulations." I think I also managed the obligatory "I'm happy for you," but I wouldn't swear to it.

"Thanks," she said, with an inscrutable expression.

"Have you set a date?" I managed to ask.

"Actually, that's one of the reasons I needed to talk to you. I know over the last few years you've had Nora for dinner on Christmas Eve and you bring her home so she has Christmas with me, but we're getting married on Friday the twenty-first."

"So, you want Nora to spend Christmas with me?"

"Actually, we're having a destination wedding in St. Croix, and I'd like Nora to be with us," she said.

Damn, I was getting tired of being punched. "What am I going to say? No, Nora, you can't go to your mother's wedding in St. Croix because I demand you have Christmas Eve dinner with me. If she didn't hate me before that, she certainly would after." I threw up my hands in mock surrender. "Guess I'm not invited."

"Do you want to come?" she asked.

I raised an eyebrow. "No, Becca. Probably better for both of us if I miss it."

After I paid the bill, we headed out to pick up Nora. "What's Nora's reaction to the whole getting remarried thing?" I asked as we waited.

Going by the expression on Becca's face, I think she actually felt guilty about being honest, and she probably tempered her response. "She's happy for me," she replied. "Um, we're going to live in my place until the end of the school year, but then we'll move to Roger's place in Beverly Heights, which means Nora can start high school at Far Meadows."

I was glad it was dark so Becca couldn't see me wince. Far Meadows was a private school, considered by most to be the best high school in the state. *Elite* didn't do it justice. All I could think was that Becca's father, Sinclair Brinley, must be ecstatic. Becca had attended Far Meadows before going to Amherst, only to disappoint him by marrying me. With Becca marrying Roger and Nora attending Far Meadows, it looked like all his sheep had returned home to the flock.

I thought I was saved from any further calamities when Nora came through the door of the studio with her guitar case in hand. I gave her a hug and asked, "Where to—Giger's?"

"Can we go to Tesh's?" Nora asked. "All my friends say it's a cool place."

"What do you think?" Becca asked.

"I've never eaten there," I managed to get out, which was the truth.

"So, let's give it a try," Becca said.

It was a Tuesday night and Gee would be working. All I could hope was that if we bumped into each other, she'd be discreet—although my ex had just finished telling me about her upcoming wedding plans. What was I worried about? I hadn't even had an official date.

As it had been last week, Tesh's was crowded, but we got a table far away from the bar and things were fine. But then, as the waitress was clearing our plates, I saw Gee making the rounds, asking folks how they were doing. Tonight, she was in assistant manager mode. She had on tight black jeans, and a form-fitting gray blazer over a white blouse. She saw me and headed toward our table. "Lieutenant," she said with a broad smile, "nice to see you." She looked down at Becca and Nora. "How was dinner, ladies?"

"Everything was great," Nora said.

"Good to hear," Gee replied.

"Marjorie, this is my daughter Nora and this is Rebecca Brinley. Marjorie is the assistant manager."

They all exchanged pleasantries and then Gee said, "Nice to meet everyone. Thanks for coming in. Please order coffee and dessert. It's on the house." She gave everyone a big smile and went off to say hello to folks at another table.

"I thought you hadn't eaten here," Becca said somewhat accusingly after Gee had moved on.

"I haven't. I know Marjorie from high school and as a potential witness in an investigation I'm involved in," I said, watching a look of recognition cross Becca's face. "What are we going to get for dessert?" I asked with a wry smile.

It was around nine thirty by the time I got back to my father's place. I put my weapon away, washed my face, moisturized, threw on my PJs, and was about to collapse on the couch when my personal cell vibrated with two messages. The first was from Gee.

Nice family. I understand why you're still in love.

The second was from Lisa.

They should have the results Thursday.

What a fucking night.

CHAPTER 26

I WOKE UP AT five, in the middle of a night sweat. It seemed like since I transitioned, I was either too cold or too hot. I chalked it up to what I chalked most things up to over the last four years—hormones—even though it was probably stress. I crawled out of bed, grabbed a fresh pair of pajamas from my dresser, and made my way to the bathroom. I peed, changed, and made my way back to the bedroom, crawling under the covers. I don't know why I bothered getting back in bed. My mind was on overdrive now, and sleep would be impossible.

I lay there, staring at the ceiling much like I had when I was a kid. Back then, I was trying to figure out why my mother had left, or wondering why I wasn't the girl I was supposed to be, or praying that my father was passed out or asleep. Now, my concerns were different. In the next couple of days, I would know if my mom was Jane Doe. Strange how before this, I thought I knew death—I worked in Homicide for years. Death had been my constant companion. But this was different. This was personal. For the first time I was experiencing what it was like for all those people I had met with over the years and started the conversation with, "I'm very sorry to have to tell you this, but . . ." Now it seemed likely that I was going to be on the receiving end of that news.

I had spent my entire life chasing a ghost, believing that my mom was somewhere out there, alive and happy, and it was my fault she had left. Yet, as much as I knew that if Jane Doe turned out to be my mother it should absolve me from any responsibility for her leaving, I could never wish that my mother was dead. No, I wanted her alive and happy with a new family in Vegas or Arizona, somewhere, even if it meant she left because she couldn't love me.

Unfortunately, the ceiling held no answers. It was 5:45 A.M. when I finally dragged myself out of bed and decided to go for a run. I ran now more than I did when I was married, since there was no one to be upset with me when I went for a run at 7 P.M. and ate dinner at eight thirty. But today was a morning run. I hated to run in the morning. Whenever I did, I expected Dorothy to come by on her way to see the Wizard and oil my joints because I was so creaky and stiff. But today I made an exception, given that my only alternative was to head to the office at 6:30 A.M.

I changed into my running gear and, since it was brisk, threw on a running jacket. I stuck my keys and phone in one pocket and my pepper spray in the other. That was another thing that had changed post-transition. Before, I'd go for a run anywhere, at any time, and not think twice about it— not now. Even after four years of karate, there was a sense of vulnerability I carried with me that I hadn't experienced before I transitioned. I struggled through four miles at a nine-and-a-half-minute mile pace, and was back just after seven. An hour later, I had showered, dressed, applied some makeup and was out the door.

On my way to the office, I decided I needed to cover my ass and let Snyder think I was moving on to a different file. In less than thirty-six hours he was shutting me down.

The warehouse opened at eight, so I stopped in on the way to the office. "Moving on to a new case?" Stan Kaminski asked as he directed me to the cold case file that I had asked him for.

"Yeah." I nodded, trying to look defeated, unsure if Stan might be keeping tabs on me for someone at the DCDAO.

"Good luck," he said.

"Thanks, Stan," I said. Ten minutes later I had signed the file out, and I got to the office before nine.

UP UNTIL NOW, I hadn't spoken with James Barry, the one surviving assistant DA involved in both trials of Riccoli. I knew Jimmy, as everyone called him. I'd actually been lead detective on several cases he tried. He was a decent lawyer with lots of street smarts, although his personality outside the courtroom was aging frat boy. Most of the women in the office had considered him a misogynistic jerk. Despite that, or maybe because of that, he had quickly risen through the ranks on the DA side, at various points being head of Major Crimes, then the Political/White Collar Crime Unit and finally serving as the executive assistant DA, the number three in the office. There were those that thought he might run against Graham for DA in the last election, but instead, five years ago, right before I came out, he left the office and went into private practice. Given what I knew of Jimmy's political leanings, I didn't think he'd welcome me with open arms.

Jimmy had been in the office for six years when they tried Riccoli the first time, meaning he was no longer a baby district attorney, but not ready to head the trial team in a capital murder case. He sat second chair, his role to assist Vincent Chrystal, who, at that point, was a grizzled trial veteran, having already sent a number of defendants off to meet the executioner.

When I called Jimmy's office, his secretary let me know that he was at a sentencing before Judge Payne, whose courtroom was two floors above me. I decided to walk up and see if I could talk to him after his client was sentenced.

I quietly took a seat in the back of the courtroom as Jimmy was making his sentencing pitch. His client, a twenty-year-old college student named Connor Walsh, had pled guilty to sexually assaulting a woman who had passed out at a frat party. I expected his sentence to be somewhere between eight and ten years, the presumption range under the statute. But to my surprise, Payne put on the record how both the victim and defendant had been drinking and under the circumstances, he felt that the young man, who came from a good family and had his entire life in front of him, wasn't entirely to blame for his conduct. Even though Payne didn't say it out loud, the subtext was that the attractive victim had been responsible for leading the poor young man astray. Payne then sentenced Jimmy's client to twelve months in the county jail, suspending six months, meaning he'd be out in about ninety days. It was times like this that made me want to turn in my badge. I stood up while Payne was still lecturing the defendant about second chances and headed for the door. A young woman was raped and the DA, judge, and defense attorney essentially gave the rapist a free pass while shitting on the victim in the process. Anyone who said heterosexual white male privilege didn't exist had to be a heterosexual white male.

I moved out into the hallway to wait for Jimmy. He walked out a few minutes later with a couple, who I presumed were his client's parents, the woman sobbing about the horror of her son going to jail. Wanting to avoid overhearing their conversation, I positioned myself so I could see Jimmy's face. Eventually, I caught his eye and held up my badge, gesturing that I'd like to speak with him. He gave me a puzzled look followed by a slight nod. With that, I moved down the hallway to give him space to talk to the bereft couple—probably about what strings they could pull to get Connor out even sooner.

Ten minutes later, Jimmy sauntered in my direction, his gaze fixed on me, trying to figure out who the hell I was. He was around my height, and well north of two hundred pounds. He was broad-shouldered, but his lack of exercise was catching up with him, his paunch noticeable over his belt. His gray-black hair was slicked back, exposing thinning on top. Still, he carried himself well. His bespoke black pinstriped suit conveyed the impression that private practice was agreeing with him.

"Hello, Jimmy," I said, extending my hand. "Lieutenant Lauren Kelly from the DA's office."

A look of recognition slowly emerged, I assume because just like almost everyone else in the county, he had seen the articles about me in *The Harrison Gazette*, including the one with both my before and after pictures prominently displayed.

He took my hand, his grip tighter than it needed to be just in case I decided to give him a dead fish. "Look at you," he said, shaking his head. "Aren't you the picture of femininity." His expression was a mixture of curiosity and disdain. "Congratulations on your promotion, *Lieutenant*."

I nodded.

"So, still serving subpoenas?" he asked.

I did a quick calculation and decided to hold my fire to see where this was going, if anywhere. "No, Jimmy. I'm running a homicide cold case unit now. That's why I wanted to chat with you. I'm looking at one of the cases you were involved in—twice."

"Which case?" he asked.

"The defendant was Joseph Riccoli. You were second chair. Vinny Chrystal was lead on both trials."

His sneer was telling. "Doesn't take a rocket scientist to figure out why you're looking at that case. But Kelly, if you want my advice, find another case to waste your time on."

"Why's that?"

"You're close to the magic number, right?"

"Yeah. Why?"

"If you want to make it to retirement, leave it alone," he said in a tone that left me wondering if it was a threat or a warning. It was almost as if he was telling me not to touch a hot stove.

He glanced around the hallway, then motioned with his head to a row of tables and chairs that lined the window side of the hallway. We each took a seat.

"Look, Kelly, I'm not going to pretend to understand you or what you did," he said, gesturing to my body. "But this case is jinxed. Snyder and I are the only ones in the office who touched this case whose careers weren't destroyed. Clarke and your father retired. Hammond offed himself. Reed left the office. And as soon as the second trial was over, Chrystal was told to leave."

"How'd you not only survive, but thrive?" I asked, trying to keep any hint of an accusation out of my voice.

He gave a sarcastic laugh. "I was far enough down the food chain that I had no clue what was going on at the top. So, when the shit hit the fan, I wasn't in the line of fire."

"Where was the fire coming from?"

"Don't know," he said. "Clearly someone with enough clout to shake up the office."

"You must have an educated guess," I said.

"I don't, but even if I did, I wouldn't tell you."

I was torn. I wanted to throw out Furst's name, but I couldn't trust Jimmy. One call to Snyder and I was toast. I decided to move on. "I understand that in addition to the DNA not being turned over, there were also photos of Riccoli taken when he was initially interrogated that showed no marks of any kind on him. Do you know who took the photos?"

"Jesus, that was a cluster fuck. Your father said it was Reed, and Reed said it had to be your father or Hammond. It was like magic. Somehow those pictures just suddenly appeared out of nowhere."

"Why weren't they turned over in discovery before the first trial?"

"Because we didn't know about the DNA under his fingernails," he said, misgendering Sherry. "I don't even remember seeing them before the first trial. But even if I had, I wouldn't have understood the significance of the photos. They were just some photos of the suspect."

"Now I'm confused," I said. "When did you find out about the DNA under the fingernails?"

"When the fucking public defender waltzed in and laid it on Chrystal's desk right before he filed the appeal. All we had for the first trial was the DNA from Riccoli's semen. How the PD got it, we never knew. But the lab confirmed it was accurate."

"Do you remember who confirmed it with the lab?"

"Give me a break, Kelly. This was twenty fucking years ago. Maybe Reed or Hammond. I don't remember."

"How come Snyder, who was the lead, survived?" I asked.

He shook his head. "I don't know, ask him. Reed took the hit for the Brady violation and Chrystal took the fall for losing the second trial. What Snyder did right and what everyone else did wrong, I don't have a clue."

"You ever ask anyone?"

"Not me. I wanted to survive. Why should I stick my neck out?"

"Your career didn't suffer either. What'd you do right?"

"I learned not to ask too many questions." He paused. "A good lesson to learn, Kelly."

"What about Hammond? You think what he did was related to this case?"

He gave me an unexpected icy stare. "Tom was a good cop. Unfortunately, he took everything to heart. He blamed himself . . ." He hesitated, then finally said, "I don't know why he did what he did."

Based on his scowl, there was something about Tom Hammond that had stayed with him.

"Is it possible someone else took him out?" I asked.

He looked at me for a long time and then stood up. "His gun, his car—give me a break, Kelly, you're starting to sound a little conspiratorial."

He turned to walk away. "Jimmy," I said, reaching out and grabbing his arm before he could walk away. "Who killed Barr?"

He gave me a long, hard stare. "You're not listening—leave it alone, Kelly. I hate going to cops' funerals." Then he looked me up and down. "Although yours I'd probably skip."

He started down the hallway.

"Hey, Jimmy!" I called after him.

He hesitated, then stopped. I could see his shoulders rise as he drew in a deep breath. He turned and glared back over his shoulder at me.

"Kind of ironic that I have more balls than you do," I said.

He gave me the finger, and disappeared down the hallway.

CHAPTER 27

I MADE MY WAY up the walk to the front door of the white clapboard Cape. It sat on what looked like a fifty-by-fifty lot in a neighborhood filled with houses that all looked like they were stamped out of the same mold. The grass had recently been mowed, and despite the trees shedding their leaves in earnest, the front lawn was immaculate. I rang the bell and an attractive woman who looked to be around sixty answered the door. She was petite, around five foot one, maybe a hundred pounds. Her blond hair was cut in a curly bob, and her makeup was understated.

"Mrs. Hammond?" I asked.

"Yes," she said.

"Lieutenant Lauren Kelly," I said, showing her my credentials. "I appreciate you making the time to talk to me."

After my talk with Jimmy Barry the day before, I had called Hammond to ask if we could meet. I wasn't sure that she could provide me with anything useful, but something struck me as off in Barry's response when I asked about Tom Hammond.

Barry had hinted that Hammond took his own life because he blamed himself for Riccoli's conviction being reversed. But that just didn't square with what I knew. Tom Hammond had nothing to do with the DNA not being turned over. So why would he blame himself? Chances were his wife wouldn't know, but it was worth checking out.

"Of course. Please come in, Lieutenant," she said, stepping aside to let me enter. "And please call me Joan."

We walked through the foyer and back to the kitchen. She offered me a seat at the kitchen table and took her seat opposite me.

"Joan, I apologize in advance for what I'm here to discuss with you; I'm sure it's not pleasant for you."

She nodded, her face resolute.

"As I told you on the phone, I'm reinvestigating a murder that your husband worked on. The victim was a transgender woman by the name of—"

"Sherry Darling," she said before I finished.

"Yes," I said, struck by her use of Sherry's correct name. "I guess I'm a little surprised you remembered the case."

"Why wouldn't I recall the case that cost my husband his life?" she said, her face remaining placid.

I tried not to show my surprise at her answer. "Can I ask why you believe that case cost Tom his life?"

Her eyes, now filled with certainty, locked onto mine. "When Tommy caught the Sherry Darling case, it wasn't a big deal. I don't mean to make it sound like he was a callous guy, he wasn't, but to him it was just another murder case. That is, it was until *The Michael Dobbs Show* started running with the story of her murder. Then all hell broke loose."

"What happened?" I asked.

"I'm not sure. Tommy tried not to bring his work home with him, so we never talked specifics, but I could tell they were under a lot of pressure to make an arrest. Specifically to arrest the boyfriend. Tommy was a good cop. I don't think he ever felt comfortable with the case against the boyfriend. I remember that even after the guilty verdict, Tommy didn't go to the party to celebrate; he came home, and seemed upset. I asked him what was bothering him, and he just said the stress from the trial. Which, truthfully, Lieutenant, made no sense to me, because Tommy wasn't the lead on the case and by that point in his career, he had been part of dozens of murder cases."

If he was upset with the conviction, why would he be blaming himself if it was reversed? "Someone told me he was depressed because the conviction was reversed. But that doesn't seem to square with what you're saying. Was he depressed after the reversal?"

For the first time, her face hardened. "No! Absolutely not! And he definitely wasn't suicidal." She paused, inhaling. "Lieutenant, please understand something. At the time of Tommy's death, we had two boys, ages eighteen and sixteen. He adored our sons. We had a good marriage. He was within four years of hitting the magic twenty-five years on the job. The boys would go off to college, he'd retire and . . . we talked about moving to Colorado. Things were good. Tommy did not kill himself, if that's what you want to know."

"Okay, but did something happen after the conviction was reversed?" I asked as gently as I could.

She looked down at the kitchen table before looking back

up at me. "Lieutenant, I presume you weren't in the DA's office twenty years ago, when the first trial occurred."

"No ma'am, I wasn't," I replied.

"I saw the newspaper article about your promotion—your father is Frank Kelly, correct?"

"He is," I said.

"Your father was Tom's sergeant and he and Tommy went back a ways. Tommy joined Harrison PD a couple of years after your father started there, and then went over to the DA's office, a few years behind your father." A sadness seemed to sweep across her face like the morning mist making its way across a field. "A couple of days after the conviction was reversed, Tommy was called to a meeting."

"Did he tell you what the meeting was about?"

She shook her head no. "All I know was that he was upset. I asked him what was wrong, and—" She hesitated. "He said he thought your father had said things that were going to cause a problem. That's why he had to go to this meeting."

My heartbeat picked up. "Did he tell you what my father had said?"

"No."

There was something in her denial and the way she looked away that left me thinking there was more there than she was telling me. For the first time, I felt like she was holding back. I weighed pressing her, but decided if I pushed too hard, she might shut down.

"Do you know who else was at the meeting?"

"No."

"Did you tell the folks who investigated his death that you didn't believe Tommy tried to take his own life?"

"Of course I did. I told them exactly what I'm telling you."
She closed her eyes, as if allowing a pain to pass. "They said
that at the meeting he went to, Tommy was beating himself
up about the DNA not being turned over and blamed himself
for the conviction being reversed. They said he apparently had
gone to his car, put the barrel of the gun to the side of his head
. . ." She stopped. She couldn't go any further.

Why should she trust me? She had already told detectives
from my office and no one listened to her. Why should she
expect me to be any different?

"I'm sorry, Joan."

She got up, grabbed some tissues out of a box on the kitchen
counter and blew her nose. "I swore I wasn't going to get emotional," she said, then looked at me accusingly. "Someone in
your office murdered my husband."

I was stunned by the certainty of her accusation. It seemed
like she wanted to say more, but she fell silent.

"Do you think it was my father?" I asked point-blank.

She looked at me for a long time, sadness growing behind
her eyes. "I . . . I don't know. All I know is that Tom didn't
shoot himself."

I wondered if there was any way I could pull the file on the
DCDAO's investigation of Tom's shooting without drawing
attention. Who was I kidding? Assuming Joan was right, I was
sure there'd be no hint of foul play in the reports. But maybe
they'd tell me who was at the meeting.

"One last thing," I said. "Do you happen to have a photo of
your husband from around the time of his death?"

She walked into the living room and came back with her
phone. "What's your number?"

I gave her my number and my phone vibrated with her text and a picture of Tom. "Thank you, Joan. I know this hasn't been easy for you."

I went to stand when she said, "Can I ask you a question? I mean, a personal question," she added quickly.

"Sure," I said, figuring it was the least I owed her for forcing her to relive the worst period of her life. I assumed she was going to ask me something about being transgender.

"Do you ever hear from your mother?"

I dropped back onto my seat as if I had been punched, and in a way, I felt like I had been. The breath was knocked out of me. I was stunned. *What?*

"I'm sorry," she said. "I didn't mean to pry. It's just that your mom and I knew each other and . . . well, I liked your mom. We were friends. And when she left, I felt terrible."

I heard her words, but I don't think I was processing them. *She knew my mom? They were friends?* "I don't understand," I managed to squeak. "You knew my mother?"

"I did," she said. "We were about the same age. And we both worked for the county for a couple of years, your mom in personnel, me in insurance. We were just down the hall from one another. Sometimes we had lunch together. Plus, our husbands had both been on the police force together. She stopped working there when you were born. Your brother, Brian, and my son Eric are the same age. We had a lot in common."

The thought of my mom as a young twentysomething with friends ripped at me. I went to say something, but I couldn't find my voice.

"No. I don't hear from her," I finally whispered.

"I'm so sorry," Joan offered. "I feel awful for asking. I didn't mean to upset you."

A spark of hope suddenly forced me to ask, "Have you heard from her?"

She hesitated. "I . . . I received a few Christmas cards from her. They were postmarked from California, but there was no return address and I haven't gotten one in years."

I'm sure she could see me deflate like a burst balloon. I had so many questions, but I couldn't ask them now. Not yet. First, I had to know if she was dead.

"Would it be okay if I came back some time to talk?" I let out a sigh. "I'd really love to know more about her. The only people I know who knew her were my aunt, who moved to Florida when I was ten, and my father, who never spoke about her. I never knew my mother had friends." I looked down at the table, embarrassed. "I guess I should have known, but it just never occurred to me."

She reached across the kitchen table and took my hand. "I'd be happy to talk to you about her. Whenever you'd like."

I pursed my lips, and nodded. "Thanks."

I WAS ON MY way back to the office when my personal cell rang.

"Where are you?" Weiss asked.

"Heading back to the office."

"I have the results. We need to talk. Can you swing by my house?"

"On my way," I replied, certain now that we hadn't hit a dead end.

She was dressed for the office when she opened the front

door for me—red jacket over a black dress, hair and makeup done, a strand of pearls around her neck and pearl studs in her ears. Which, juxtaposed with me—gray slacks, black jacket, a smidge of makeup—qualified as haute couture.

"I'm guessing you didn't invite me here to tell me we struck out," I said when we were settled in the kitchen.

She gave a small snort. "Oh, you didn't strike out. You hit a home run."

"What do you mean? Did Sam's DNA provide a lead?"

"It did more than that. It provided a probable match."

"What?" I said, mystified. "Sam's DNA was at the scene?"

"Not Sam's DNA," she said. "His parents' DNA."

I squinted, trying to make sense of what she just said. "Sam's parents'—plural, as in Ron and Elizabeth Furst."

"You hit the jackpot—well, let me qualify that. Assuming the DNA we tested was Sam Furst's, all the male DNA recovered from the scene, the blood, fingernail scrapings, and the pubic hair, all likely belong to Ron Furst. The female DNA found in the scrapings from the other hand probably belong to Elizabeth Furst."

They were both at the scene? I tried to piece together likely scenarios—a three-way gone bad? Elizabeth walked in on him having a good time with Sherry and flipped out? Sherry went after Elizabeth and Ron defended his wife?

"But, before you get too excited, we have a problem," Lisa said, interrupting my train of thought.

Several, I thought. "I'm listening."

"The DNA you got—we'll never be able to get that into evidence. A bartender takes a beer bottle that Sam allegedly drank out of and gives it to you? We can't establish the chain of custody of the bottle. And if we can't show it's Sam's DNA on the bottle, we can't show it's his parents' DNA that was found on the victim. Think about it. Let's say that in addition to Sam Furst, John Doe was also at the bar and he was drinking with Sam. And maybe John Doe took a swig of Sam's beer; or maybe the bartender grabbed John Doe's bottle instead of Sam's. That means John Doe's parents are the ones whose DNA was recovered, not the Fursts."

She was right. Even a mediocre defense attorney would have a field day with how the DNA sample had been obtained, and the Fursts would definitely not have mediocre attorneys. Somehow, we had to get a sample from Sam, Ron, or Elizabeth that would also be admissible and put them at the scene. If this were a normal investigation, I'd go up the chain of command, and they'd assign detectives to follow the three of them until we had secured an admissible sample. But this wasn't a normal investigation. If I walked into Snyder's office and suggested we follow Ron Furst, I'd be fired before I finished saying "DNA."

On top of that, this was an investigation that I was supposed to close by tomorrow. Damn it! Every time I seemed to take a step forward, I quickly took two steps back.

Then, something else occurred to me. "So, if all the male DNA was likely from Ron Furst, that means my father's didn't match any DNA from the scene, correct?" I asked.

"Correct."

Well, at least it appeared he wasn't directly involved in Sherry's murder. What role he played in the investigation remained unknown.

"You know anything about Elizabeth Furst?" I asked. "I was told by a source that she may be having some health issues."

"We don't exactly run in the same social circles, but I can check with some people who know her. But let's assume she is having serious health issues, so what? What are you hoping for, a deathbed confession?" Her tone showed how little she thought of the possibility.

"Confession is good for the soul," I suggested with a shrug.

"Yeah, unless it's to a cop," she rejoined.

"Snyder wants me to end the investigation tomorrow. I need time."

"What if you were out sick?" she suggested.

That would at least buy me the weekend. Then something else came to me. "I think I have a better idea," I said. It left me feeling a bit uneasy, but it was the truth and it might throw Snyder off stride. It would also allow me to give him a heads up on the news that might be coming out of Brisbane.

CHAPTER 28

IT WAS A LITTLE after four when I knocked on Snyder's door. He looked up from whatever he was reading, unable to hide his disappointment at seeing me. "Yeah," he said, looking back down at what was in front of him.

"Can I speak to you for a moment, Cap?"

His shoulders tensed. "What is it, Kelly?"

"Can we speak privately, sir?"

He seemed to momentarily contemplate saying no. But after a few seconds, he motioned me in with a wave of his hand. I stepped in, closed the door, and took a seat opposite him in one of the standard county-issued metal chairs with a green vinyl seat and backrest. "Sir, I need to share something with you that, at least for now, I'd ask you to keep confidential."

I swear in that moment he must have thought that I was resigning. He actually relaxed, a look of anticipation on his face.

"Of course," he said. "What's on your mind?"

"The Brisbane County DA's Office has exhumed the body of a Jane Doe, and they've asked me to provide a DNA sample," I began, watching his expression dissolve from hope to confusion. "The Jane Doe that they exhumed is a woman who was murdered approximately forty years ago, right around the time my mother left." I paused to let that sink in. "They have reason to believe that Jane Doe may be my mother. They're running DNA on the body now."

"Wait, you said this woman, this Jane Doe, she was murdered?"

"Yes, sir. Single gunshot wound to the left temple. The murder weapon was a .38."

"Okay, but I thought . . . I mean what your father said was that she ran off . . . ah, sorry, you know, she left for another guy."

"That's what he always told me as well, Cap. And look, I asked you to keep this between us because obviously I'm hoping it's not my mother."

"All right, but you know as well as I do that it will take the lab six to nine months to run the DNA."

"That's true—if this were a normal case."

He gave me a quizzical look.

"This is all happening because my brother Brian brought this to Brisbane's attention and they are moving on it like there's no tomorrow. I was told by Paul Morocco, the first assistant DA, that they could have the results by sometime next week."

"Next week? That's insane. What did your brother promise them?"

"That if it did turn out to be our mother, he'd come out and do the press conference and sign autographs."

"Must be nice having a famous brother," he said, coating his words in sarcasm.

"Not always," I replied, "but he can get things done." I paused for a beat. "I wanted to give you a heads up because, if it does turn out to be my mother, and given who my brother is, I think it's safe to assume that there will be reporters nosing around asking a lot of questions and I wanted you prepared so you could brief the front office. And candidly, sir, between you and me, it's looking more and more like it's my mom."

Up until now, he had been in boss mode, but he suddenly shifted into cop mode. "Any evidence of who murdered this Jane Doe—fingerprints, DNA?"

"They didn't get any from the victim, but the bullet that killed her was recovered during the autopsy and might be in good enough shape to do ballistics on."

"Kelly, for Christ's sake, it's been forty years, you're never going to find the murder weapon." But as he spoke, his years in Homicide surfaced and it seemed as if the picture had suddenly come into sharper focus. "You're not thinking your father, are you?"

"Don't know, Cap. He does own a .38," I said, leaving it hanging.

"You mean 'owned.' By the time your father retired, everyone had switched to nine millimeters."

"You're right, they had switched. But you were here then. I was told that folks were given the opportunity to purchase their old duty weapon. Apparently, my father did."

"You have his .38?" he said, surprised.

"I do, and if Jane Doe turns out to be my mother, I plan on turning it over to the Brisbane DA's office for testing."

"Why? From what you tell me your father could never stand trial."

I'm sure my face betrayed a momentary flash of disbelief—how could I not want to know?—but I quickly regained my focus. I needed him on my side, or at least, not adversarial. "With all due respect, sir, if Jane Doe turns out to be my mom, and she was shot with my father's gun, I absolutely need to know that. Whether he can stand trial or not doesn't matter. Cap, I was five years old when my mom disappeared. I need to know what happened to her," I said, letting my pain infect my words.

For one of the few times in my career, I actually saw Snyder get flustered. "Um, yeah, of course. I understand. Sure, you'd want to know. I just meant, maybe for your own . . . I don't know, mental health, it would be better not to know. That's all I meant."

Keep him off balance—more flies with honey, I reasoned. "I appreciate that, Cap. I know you're only trying to look out for my well-being, but I need closure." *Whatever that is*, I thought.

"Of course, I understand." He stopped and appeared to consider his options. "Do what you need to do. All I ask is two things. Please keep me advised of the results, so that if it does turn out to be your mother, I can pass the news up the chain of command before they hear it from the press."

"Of course," I replied.

"And," he continued, "if it is your mom, you go through official channels to turn over your father's weapon for Brisbane to run ballistics on."

His request caught me off guard. My paranoia kicked in.

What if I gave them my father's gun and then they turned over a different gun to Brisbane? Luckily, before I gave voice to my concerns, I realized that I could easily compare the serial number on my father's gun to any ballistics report Brisbane did. Then, even if Snyder or the higher-ups turned over a different .38 to avoid the embarrassment of having a former sergeant in the DCDAO linked to a murder, I'd be able to figure it out without breaking a sweat. Of course, given what I knew from Sherry's case, there was always the possibility that my office would *lose* my father's gun.

"I guess that's the right thing to do," I said, hoping I had managed to mask my reluctance.

He studied me, and for a moment I thought he was going to order me to turn over the gun now. "We'll revisit this if and when we need to," he finally said. "Let's hope it's not your mother."

"Amen to that," I said. "Thanks for your consideration, Cap. I really appreciate it." I stood, preparing to leave. "In light of all this, I hope it's okay if I take a few more days to end the Barr investigation. I'm barely functioning right now."

His stare was so cold it sent a chill up my backside. "I heard you've already picked up your next case," he said, confirming my suspicion that Stan was helping Snyder keep tabs on me.

"I did," I said. "But . . . well, this stuff with my mom has really messed me up. I just need to find out if it's her and go from there," I replied, the ache in my words coming from a very real stew of emotions that were simmering just beneath the surface.

Snyder seemed genuinely taken aback by the anguish in my voice. "Keep me posted."

I nodded and got out of his office as quickly as I could. True, he had never specifically said yes to giving me more time to end the investigation, but we had left it murky enough that I had the cover I needed. I also realized that I needed to make sure that the .38 in my father's safe was the same one he had in 1982 when my mom disappeared. Hopefully that would be easy, since the DCDAO would have the serial number of my father's old weapon on file. *No time like the present*, I thought.

JULIE PALMER HAD BEEN the secretary for the chief of detectives at the DA's office since before I arrived. Her tenure covered three different men who served as chief. Not surprisingly, she had more institutional knowledge than anyone else in the office, and probably knew more secrets than anyone else as well. She was quick to smile, but getting information from her was like trying to pry the foil off the covering on an aspirin bottle—next to impossible.

"Hi, Julie," I said, knowing she wasn't one to stand on formality. "It's Lauren Kelly."

"Hello, Lauren. How are you?"

"I'm good. Julie, as you know, my dad has Alzheimer's and isn't doing well. My brother Brian and I," I said, dropping my brother's name because Julie was a huge fan of his show, "are going through his things and we came across an old Colt .38 revolver. I'm trying to figure out if that was his duty weapon when he was here and thought you might have the serial numbers of the weapons he was issued while at the DCDAO."

There seemed to be a moment's hesitation, but then she said, "Your father's full name and date of birth?"

"Francis Liam Kelly—June 1, 1956."

"Hold on," she said. I heard a shuffling noise and then the sound of a metal file drawer being opened. Another minute or so passed before she picked up the receiver and said, "On March 15, 1981, when he first joined the office, your father was issued a Colt .38 Detective Special snub-nose revolver, serial number 1589R. On December 7, 1982, he reported his weapon stolen and was issued a second Colt .38 Detective Special snub-nose revolver, serial number 8486R. In 1995, he was issued a nine-millimeter Glock 17, and he purchased the Colt .38. Does that help?"

"That's great, Julie. Thank you so much. I'm sorry I made you go digging through files. I thought everything would be computerized."

"Oh, it is now, but we didn't start computerizing everything until 2007."

"Got it," I said. "Thanks again, Julie."

Stolen gun—what a crock of shit, I thought after I hung up. My father got a second weapon the day after my mother disappeared. That meant that even if Jane Doe turned out to be my mom, the weapon in the safe probably wouldn't be the weapon used to shoot her. It also meant that he may have had a reason to "lose" his original weapon. Shit. Even if Jane Doe was my mom, I'd never be able to prove he did it.

Realizing I needed to move on, I made a quick call to Gee, but the call went right to voicemail. Hoping that she was one of those people who actually listened to their voicemails, I left her a message indicating there was a problem with the beer bottle, so if she could let me know the next time our football friend was in, it would be appreciated.

On the way home, I debated whether at some point I

should've explained to Gee that there was no longer a romantic relationship between Becca and me. But why? Any relationship with Gee was off limits anyway. What was the point? Besides, Gee and I were like night and day. She was a gold star, a term in the lesbian lexicon that meant she had never been with a man. And me, I hadn't even dated another woman since transitioning. No, we were definitely not a match made in heaven. But I felt something with her that I hadn't felt since I met Becca—a curiosity, an attraction, a desire to get to know her better.

Let it go, I said to no one. *Just let it go.*

WHEN I ARRIVED AT my father's house, I headed up to his bedroom and opened the safe. As I suspected, the serial number on the .38 was the second one Julie had given me—which also meant I was shit out of luck.

I put the gun back in the case, grabbed one of the stacks of hundreds, and stared at it, hoping that somehow I might magically discern the reason why my father had it. February 27, 2004, wasn't even remotely connected to my mother. It was closer to my father's retirement after Riccoli's conviction had been reversed. Was it a payoff to get him to retire? But why?

I threw the money back in the safe. *Don't force a connection, let the connection come to you.* Out of nowhere, I could hear my brother's impression of Obi-Wan echoing in my head. *Be the force, Lauren.* And for a brief moment, despite my frustration, I found myself smiling.

I made dinner and, as I ate, I contemplated Joan Hammond's accusation that someone at the DCDAO had killed her husband. Somehow, even for a cynic like me, that was hard to fathom. Sure, I was convinced that not only had people covered up for whoever had murdered Sherry, they had also let an innocent man be sentenced to death. And I was also trying to determine if my own father, a sworn law enforcement officer, might have murdered my mother. Still—the idea that one detective might murder another in cold blood seemed beyond the pale. But Joan's certainty was hard for me to shake.

It was around ten and I was curled up on the couch reading Becca's novel when my personal cell phone chimed with a new text. It was from Gee.

Sam and his buddies just walked in - drinking at the bar

CHAPTER 29

TESH'S WAS PACKED. INSTEAD of my usual jeans and top, I'd put on my one and only push-up bra, found a top I disliked because it was too tight and cut too low, threw on a skirt with my black boots and reapplied my makeup. As I headed to the bar, it occurred to me that I hadn't seen Sam Furst since our tenth high school reunion about seventeen years ago. I had skipped our recent twenty-fifth, not wanting to explain the new me to my old classmates. I was counting on him not recognizing me; I hadn't counted on not being able to recognize him.

Gee was working behind the bar. I made my way down to the far end and found a space where I could squeeze in and catch her attention. It took about five minutes, and when she caught my eye, she did a double take. She gave me a wistful smile, and eventually headed to where I was standing.

"You clean up nicely," she said with a wink. "What can I get you?"

"Where is he?" I asked.

"Far end. He's the heavy-set dude with the thinning blond hair wearing the Lynyrd Skynyrd T-shirt and leaning up against the bar. He's with the two guys who look like they just came from a Klan meeting and the two twentysomethings fawning over them."

Sam Furst's six foot, two-hundred=pound linebacker's body was now that of a middle-aged overweight dude. He held a bottle of Bud in his right hand, giving me a hint that he was right-handed.

I turned my attention back to Gee. "Thanks. Chardonnay."

"You have a plan?" she asked.

I don't know why, but just seeing her again emboldened me. "Solve the case so I can have that date," I offered, enjoying being a bit flirtatious.

Gee struck me as someone who didn't fluster easily, so I was a little surprised when the color rose in her cheeks. "Chardonnay," she repeated, quickly composing herself.

A minute later she came back and handed me my wine.

"How much?"

"This one's on Tesh, remember?"

"No. Take my card," I said, barely audible over the noise in the bar, handing her my credit card. "I'm going to forget that I left it with you. When I get to the other end, near him, call my name to give me my card back."

She took the card and nodded.

"Gee," I said as she went to walk away. "Do me one other favor; alert the bouncer to keep an eye on Sam. I may need help."

This time she gave me a quizzical look. "Be careful."

"Thanks," I offered with a warm smile. I took my wine and

headed toward the other end of the bar, where Sam Furst and his companions were holding court.

I stood a few feet from Furst, my back to him, facing the dining area as if looking for someone. Suddenly, I heard from behind me, "Hey, Kelly! Lauren Kelly."

I turned to see Gee behind the bar right on the other side from where Furst was standing, waving my credit card along with a receipt.

I headed back to the bar. "Excuse me," I said as I tried to reach around Furst for Gee's outstretched hand. As I did, I followed her eyes to a very imposing gentleman, who I took to be a bouncer, positioned a few feet from where Furst was.

Furst looked over his right shoulder and reluctantly scrunched over to make room.

"Thanks, Gee," I said, taking the card and receipt from her, the familiarity of my tone causing Furst to take another look at me.

"Do I know you?" he asked, turning so he was facing me, our legs touching we were so close to one another, his eyes going up and down my body, stopping on my chest.

"Yes and no," I replied, trying my best to give him a coy smile, but since I was woefully uneducated in coyness, I had no idea what it looked like to him.

"What's that supposed to mean?" His tone was more belligerent than expected. *So much for my coy look.*

"We went to high school together. My name is Lauren Kelly, but I had a different name back then."

His eyes narrowed. "You're the fucking detective who just got promoted," he said with a slight Budweiser-induced slur. Then he snorted. "I saw your before and after pictures in the paper. Jesus Christ, they'll promote anything these days. Fucking faggot."

When I walked into the bar, I really didn't have a plan—I was just going to see how things developed. Now, I knew. I was going to goad him. I cringed a little thinking about what I was about to say, but I took solace in the fact that my goal was provocation, not accuracy. "I think you meant anyone can get promoted, not anything. And I'm transgender, not a faggot." I placed my wine glass on the bar just in case I needed two hands. *Here goes.* "A faggot might be someone who enjoyed getting blowjobs from someone like me. You know, like maybe when we were back in high school."

We were so close to each other I knew he'd either have to go for a quick left jab, which would have been the smart thing to try, or reach back with his right hand that was still clutching his beer and attempt to smash the bottle over my head. He went with the second option.

As soon as I saw Furst start to raise his arm, I prepared to break it, but fortunately, the bouncer grabbed his arm before he could begin its downward trajectory, bottle in hand, toward my skull. The bouncer then skillfully turned Furst so that he was face-to-face with the bouncer's snarl. I was hoping that the beer bottle would fall to the floor, where I could scoop it up and make my exit—but it appeared glued to Furst's hand.

The two guys who had been drinking with Furst were suddenly energized and the one closest to the bouncer screamed, "Hey! What the fuck are you doing? Let him go."

Once again, I prepared to intervene, when the cavalry arrived in the form of a second bouncer who, while not as physically imposing as the first, wore a security shirt that let you know the body underneath was as hard as granite.

"Back off, guys," he said in a voice that commanded respect, and to their credit, it looked like they quickly realized that even at two against one, the odds weren't in their favor.

The first bouncer had walked Furst a few feet away, and while I couldn't hear what the bouncer was saying, I assumed it amounted to something akin to, "Settle down or I'll have to throw your ass out of here." Furst, who was now all fired up, was screaming, "Do you have any idea who the fuck I am? If I call the cops, you'll be arrested. No one's going to listen to you, you overgrown gorilla."

The bouncer, who was a Black man, drew in a sharp breath. I could see his shoulders and neck tighten. Fortunately, his self-restraint held. He turned Furst around so they were no longer face to face, but kept his arms wrapped around Furst, pinning his arms to his side. I decided that, discretion being the better part of valor, it was time for me to go. I didn't need either of the bouncers getting into a free-for-all over me. Reaching into the inside pocket of my leather jacket, I took out my credentials and a business card, approached the bouncer and flashed my badge. "Thanks for your help. If he tries to file a complaint against you, let me know. Happy to be a witness. Here's my business card," I said, stuffing it in his shirt pocket. "Just hold onto him until I can get to my car." Then I tossed out, "Nice seeing you again, Sammy."

As the bouncer held him, Furst pulled his head back as if he was going to try and headbutt me, but instead, as he threw his head forward, I heard a gurgle sound and he proceeded to spit in my face. The bouncer immediately spun him around and pressed him up against the nearest wall. There was a collective intake of air as those nearby gasped.

Nonplussed, I reached into my jacket pocket and removed a tissue. Slowly and meticulously, I wiped the spittle from my face. I then folded the tissue, placed it back in my jacket pocket, and continued heading for the door. Gee stopped me before I got outside. "God, Kelly. I'm sorry. Are you all right?"

I'm sure my sly grin confused her. "Yeah. I'm good. I got what I came for," I said, patting my jacket pocket. "Thanks for your help. You were great."

Her eyes narrowed as she took my measure. "I can't figure you out, Kelly," she said. "But I hope you solve the case."

"Me too, Gee. Me too."

I walked out and inhaled as much of the cool night air as my lungs would hold. The adrenaline rush that had fortified me inside the bar was slowly fading, my heart rate returning to normal. And once again, I saw Sherry sitting across from me in detention, her hand reaching out between our desks. I should've said more. I should've taken her hand. I should have befriended her.

"I'm sorry, Sherry," I mumbled into the cool breeze. "I won't let you down this time."

CHAPTER 30

I RESTED THE LAPTOP on my thighs, slipping the flash drive into the USB port. After my encounter with Sam, I needed to see Sherry again. I found the segment I was looking for and hit play.

[Unedited recording—Episode 127—"I Have a Secret Life."]

"What? Karen, are you telling me you're a dude?"
"No, Jay. I'm telling you that I'm a transgender woman."
"What the fuck!"

[Voiceover—Bleep the word "fuck." Edit by removing 32:07 to 48:06 where Jay turns and hits Karen Mosley three times in the face. Security guards come onstage and restrain Jay from landing additional punches. Karen is taken offstage for medical treatment. Resume at 48:10 with Dobbs speaking to the television audience.]

"For the audience at home, we had an incident on stage. On learning that his girlfriend Karen was transgender, her boyfriend Jay assaulted her. We have called the police and Karen is on her way to the emergency room.

"Sherry, let me ask you this. You saw Jay's reaction when he found out Karen was transgender, is that something trans women have to be concerned about, being assaulted by men when they find out?"

"Mr. Dobbs, I think you should start with the fact that men being violent toward women isn't unique to trans women. Many women have to be concerned about being assaulted, both physically and sexually. But you're right. The dangers can be higher for trans women when the man they're intimate with doesn't know they're trans, or sometimes even when the man does know, he'll become violent just to prove his manhood to his friends when they find out he's been with a trans woman. And it's not just boyfriends—trans people are often the victims of violence just because we're trans, and it's even worse for trans women of color."

"Is a man becoming violent something you worry about?"

"Why would I worry about that, Mr. Dobbs? I have a wonderful boyfriend who loves me just the way I am."

Sherry was looking out at the audience with a playful smile, mischief in her eyes. And even though I knew that she engaged in sex work to make money, I couldn't help but feel that her response to Dobbs was truly the way she felt—she wasn't worried. Another one of those *what ifs*. A week later, she was dead, thrown away in a dumpster.

I hit pause. It was late. Unfortunately, the smiling image of

Sherry now frozen on my screen couldn't erase the crime scene montage of her mutilated body that had haunted me since I left Tesh's. The need to know what happened the night she was murdered surfaced again. I had just experienced firsthand how quickly some men could turn violent. I had been prepared— my guess was Sherry never saw it coming.

Still, I tried to find solace in the fact that my gut told me I was closing in. Tonight, I had gotten a good DNA sample from Sam. Even though we couldn't use the DNA sample from the beer bottle at a trial, in my mind it confirmed that Sam Furst's parents were both at the scene when Sherry was stabbed. It didn't prove that they stabbed her, but their cells under her fingernails were pretty damning.

But for Ron and Elizabeth Furst, I needed more than pretty damning. Even proof beyond a reasonable doubt probably wouldn't be enough to convince the DCDAO to go after them. I needed to meet an even higher standard—certainty.

If this was any other investigation, once the DNA was confirmed, I'd haul both suspects in for questioning. But with them, it would result in quick calls to lawyers, assertions of the Fifth, and, before you knew it, the investigation would be over, and I'd be out of a job.

One step at a time, I reminded myself. Confirm the DNA and figure out next steps from there.

I headed up to bed. As I passed the master bedroom, I stopped and stared into the dark, empty room. For now, Mom was like Schrödinger's cat—both alive and dead. No matter how remote, there was still a chance Jane Doe wasn't my mother. There was a part of me that wondered if I had been better off not knowing—at least then there had been a hope

I'd see her again. But hope could morph from an elixir to a poison—one I feared I'd soon taste.

I WAS UP AND dressed by 7 A.M. I texted Lisa to let her know that I had a new sample from Sam Furst. She called me within five minutes and I explained what had happened at Tesh's. Thirty minutes later, I had delivered the evidence bag with the tissue that had Furst's spittle on it to Lisa. I wasn't an expert, but I knew that the sample on the tissue could be amplified by various methods to get millions of copies of his DNA. I also knew that there were witnesses to Furst spitting on me. This was a good sample—this would be admissible as evidence.

Once in my office, I called Riccoli, but it went straight to voicemail. I left a message that I was sending three photos and asking that he call me back. The first photo was of my father taken at my graduation from the police academy— just about a year before Sherry was murdered. The second was the one Joan Hammond had sent me of Tom, and the third was of Barry Reed that I had gotten off his website. I wasn't sure Riccoli would get back to me, but one thing I was confident of, he wouldn't confuse my father, Tom, or Reed. The picture of my father showed a man whose buzz cut was still mostly black, although it had grayed around the temples. He had a long, angular face with a prominent jaw. Tom had a round face with blond hair parted on the side. Reed, with his goatee and salt-and-pepper hair, looked nothing like either of them.

Next on my checklist was scouring the file from Riccoli's second trial for anything useful. Without transcripts it was impossible to tell what had happened during the actual trial, but I needed to know why my office had even bothered to retry him. They had DNA from under Sherry's fingernails that didn't match his. There were photos of him with no marks indicative of a struggle, and at least Reed and my father knew there was even more DNA evidence that hadn't been turned over to the defense, a failure that would have provided the groundwork for yet another successful appeal had Riccoli been convicted. Someone was pushing for a retrial, and someone had the clout to get the lab to try and doctor the DNA results. The possibility that it had been Ron Furst trying to protect his wife no longer seemed farfetched—it seemed likely.

As I flipped through the file, I noticed that after Riccoli's conviction had been reversed, he wasn't represented by the same PD that had represented him in the first trial. The second time around, his attorney was a lawyer from the PD's office by the name of Seymour Leonard. There was an order entered on Monday, February 23, 2004, denying some motions Leonard had filed. The next paper in the folder was a filed substitution of attorney, where Ray Ashley had taken over as Riccoli's attorney. The date on the substitution jumped off the page—February 27, 2004. The day my father came into fifty grand, Ray Ashley took over as Riccoli's attorney. *What the fuck!* Was the universe just screwing with me, or were they related in some way?

I had been at it for a half hour trying without success to come up with a connection when my work cell rang.

"Hi, Joe. Thanks for getting back to me."

"Yeah, I got your text with the pictures. What's this about?" he said, an edge in his voice.

"I was wondering if you recognize any of the men in the photos I sent you?"

"Hold on," he said, and I could almost see him pull the phone from his face, open my text, and stare at the photos.

"Listen, I'm not looking to get myself jammed up. I don't want to be accused of lying as part of an investigation. I can't be sure about anything that happened more than twenty years ago. I'm looking at three pictures on my phone. Maybe they're the cops who were involved in the investigation of Sherry's case, but I don't know."

"Joe, I promise you I'm not trying to jam you up," I said, realizing as the words left my mouth that Snyder had probably said the same thing to him. "You're right. All of these guys were at the DA's office and were part of the investigation," I offered. "I was just wondering if any of them looks like the person who took the photos of you the day you were initially questioned?"

I heard a sigh. "I can't remember who took the pictures, but I think all of these guys spoke with me."

"Joe, the pictures of the two clean-shaven guys are from twenty years ago. The picture of the guy with the goatee is a current photo, so you'd have to try and picture what he would have looked like twenty years ago. Let me know if you recognize him."

"Yeah, I think this is the guy who hung out with Snyder. Again, I can't be certain, but I remember the guy who was with Snyder was younger. This could be him, but I'd have to see a picture from twenty years ago. The guy who took the pictures of me was probably mid- to late forties at the time."

I knew from the investigation reports that Reed had sat in when Snyder interrogated Joe, so Joe's memory was good.

It also meant that if the guy who took the photos was in his forties, it wasn't Reed, meaning it was my father or Hammond—another dead end.

"You . . . you getting anywhere with your investigation?" Joe asked, sounding reluctant to get his hopes up.

"I am," I said, buoyed by last night, but knowing I couldn't say too much, both out of fear of compromising the investigation, as well as not wanting to build up what little hope he had.

I knew my next question was going to sound strange to him because it had no real connection to the investigation, but instead came from my desire to visit Sherry's grave.

"Joe, I did a quick check online trying to locate Sherry's grave. I've looked under her birth name, as well as under Sherry Darling and Sherry Barr, but I haven't been able to locate it. Where's she buried?"

Joe let out a short but unmistakable groan. I waited several beats before saying, "Joe?"

"I don't know," he finally said in a whisper.

"I'm sorry, Joe. I'm not trying to pry, but didn't you go to her funeral?"

"Ah geez," Joe moaned before continuing. "As far as I know there was no funeral. I contacted the coroner's office and asked to be notified when I could pick up her body so I could arrange one. They told me that since we weren't married or related, they couldn't release the body to me without permission from the family. I didn't know what to do, so I wrote a letter explaining who I was, how they could reach me and that I'd like their permission to bury Sherry. I drove out to their house in Sheldon and left it in their mailbox. About six hours later, two guys paid me a visit. They told me they were her brothers and made it clear that I should go away and not come back. That's all I know."

"Her brothers?"

"That's what they told me. But I didn't ask for ID. Like I said, it wasn't a friendly conversation."

This was a bit of a curveball. Assuming these guys were her brothers, why did they even care?

"Did Sherry ever talk to you about her family?"

"No, not really. She mentioned running into one of her brothers once in a bar. But you have to understand, her family disowned her. She was dead to them after she came out. There just wasn't much for her to talk about. That's why I was so surprised when these guys showed up."

There still was nothing that suggested her family had been involved in her murder, but I needed to check them out. On top of the visit that Joe got, there was the rumor from back in high school that Sherry's father had slapped her around, and Gee's description of him as a "scary-looking dude"—yeah, they definitely deserved a look.

"What about her father? Did Sherry ever say anything about him?"

"Nothing specific. I know Sherry hated him. That's why we lived in Harrison, to be as far away from him as possible."

"Thanks, Joe. I know this is hard for you, but this has been helpful. I appreciate you taking the time to talk to me."

I had just started to research Sherry's family when my concentration was broken by a ding on my personal cell with an incoming text from Gee.

Just wanted to give you a heads up that Harrison PD
was here asking questions about what happened last
night. They took the video from the security camera. I
made a copy.

Great. Just what I need.

Can you see or hear me say anything to him? I responded.

No audio & the camera is from the ceiling above the
bar. U can c sam looks angry. But when you turn to face
him, all U c is the back of your head.

Well, at least I didn't have to concern myself with lip readers.

Thanks. Keep it safe in case I need it.

Seems like these dudes are coming after you.

They are. A message is being sent.

Watch your ass. I want it in one piece when this case
is over.

Roger that.

This is not what I need, I thought. I should have been content to lurk in the shadows until I had another sample. Instead, I was out there now. No good was going to come if people suspected I was sniffing around Sam.

Not ten minutes later, I received an email from Snyder demanding that I respond to allegations made by the chief at Harrison PD that I had called Sam Furst a faggot and had almost provoked a fight in Tesh's.

I replied with what had happened—mostly—and thanks to the heads up from Gee, I urged Snyder to obtain the videos from the security cameras, videos I told him I was confident would back up everything in my report.

Of course, now I had to hope that if Harrison PD or Snyder looked at the video and saw Sam spit on me, they wouldn't understand the significance of it. Regardless, I was definitely in someone's crosshairs.

After I responded to Snyder, I returned to looking at Sherry's family. I knew from Sherry's death certificate that her father's name was Declan Barr. His rap sheet on the NCIC database was impressive. It went back forty-five years, with a number of gambling and extortion convictions and one murder conviction for which he did ten years. Last time he had been a guest of the state was ten years ago, when he did three years on an extortion charge. None of the charges had originated out of Donn County, but I wondered why there hadn't been anything in any of the investigation reports in Sherry's file looking into her father's criminal background.

When I finished with her father, I decided to see what I could find out about the rest of the family. Gee had given me their names, so I had started with her oldest brother, Seamus, and ran his through NCIC. He was clean—no record at all. I checked the Department of Motor Vehicles to get an address and struck out, leading me to think he moved out of state or he was dead. After exhausting every official and unofficial database at my disposal, I had come up with nothing. Had he been wiped? Not an easy feat, but possible if it had been done in a pre-9/11 world. Or maybe he had gone into the witness protection program. If that was the case, I'd probably never find him.

Fiona seemed to have had a fairly sedate life—mother of two, no involvement with law enforcement and living on the same street as her parents. Then I did an NCIC check on Sherry's other brother, Padraig. Bingo! While I hadn't found anything on Seamus, it looked like Padraig had joined his father in business. A number of arrests for drugs, bookmaking, promoting prostitution, extortion, a couple of aggravated assaults, and one attempted murder for which he had done five years. And then I saw it under aliases—Padraig Barr a.k.a. Patrick Barry. He had anglicized Padraig to Patrick and added a *y* to Barr to become Patrick Barry. *Ah shit.* If I did the same thing with Seamus Barr—

James Barry.

As in Assistant DA Jimmy Barry.

CHAPTER 31

SUNDAY WAS A GRAY overcast day, providing a fitting back-drop to my two-hour drive to the Dawson County Cemetery, located in Carney, twenty miles north of Sheldon. Unlike Donn County, with sprawling suburban communities sur-rounding the city of Harrison, Dawson County, like most of the state, was rural, and I had no traffic on I-13 as I rolled through the wheat and soybean fields that lined the inter-state. The drive, along with its lack of distractions, provided me with far too much time to think about the women in my life—both living and dead.

As if my thoughts had summoned her, Becca called. I could tell immediately from her tone—a mixture of frustration and anger—there was more in play than our usual chat about Nora.

"You're still working on Sherry's case, aren't you?" she asked, when she finally got to the real reason for her call.

"I am," I replied, remembering the first two rules of being cross-examined—answer only the question asked and don't volunteer.

"Why? You told me nothing was more important than Nora. Nothing. I thought you were going to walk away. But that's you—always doing whatever you want regardless of the consequences to us." I heard the agitation in her voice growing.

Ouch. It had been a while since I had heard Becca this upset, and the thought had crossed my mind that perhaps she was doing her father's bidding—another approach to shutting down my investigation. But her anger seemed far too genuine for that, so I decided to probe and see how she reacted.

"Bec, it's my job to try and solve crimes and, if I don't see this through, no one else will."

"You're only doing this because she was trans," she interrupted.

"Does her being trans make her murder less important?"

I waited, and when she didn't respond, I felt she may have realized that what she said hadn't landed well—even if she wasn't entirely wrong.

"I know you're worried for Nora," I said. "I get that. But for now, I'm confident that you and Nora are safe. If it turns out Ron Furst is somehow involved, remember, he's represented by your father. As ruthless as Furst is, I suspect even he wouldn't go after Sinclair Brinley's daughter and granddaughter." I wasn't totally convinced I was right, last week's article in *The Gazette* being Exhibit A. But I needed something—something that would fire up Becca's own sense of righteous indignation and lay to rest my own doubts about her motivation.

"Remember when you were a journalist. You were so incensed by *The Gazette*'s refusal to run the story you did on Ron Furst, you quit. You know who Furst is and we both know that if no one stands up to the rich and powerful because of fear of retribution, we'll cease having a democracy."

"You really think our democracy is going to crumble if Lauren Kelly doesn't go after Ron Furst?" she asked, her anger fading into sarcasm.

"No, Bec. I don't think that. But he's emblematic of a much larger problem."

"You know that even if my father protects Nora and me, he won't protect you."

I laughed. "I assume he'll not only throw me under the bus, he'll offer to drive the bus."

Becca let out a long sigh. "If anything happens . . ."

"It won't," I said, sounding surer than I was. I waited, weighing if we were back on solid ground.

"Be careful," she finally said, allowing my paranoia to evaporate.

"I will."

"Call me if you need anything," she added, reassuring me that she still had the beating heart of a journalist, even if tempered by her role as momma bear protecting her cub.

WHEN I ARRIVED AT the cemetery, I stopped at the gatehouse. It had taken me a couple of hours Saturday night, doing an online search of every cemetery in Dawson and Donn Counties, to find Sherry's grave. Since I had already searched under her birth name, I searched using her date of birth and date of death and came up with two hits: one in Donn County, one in Dawson. When I had checked the name on the one in Dawson, I knew I had found her. Sherry had been buried under the name R. Barr, Ryan being her middle name at birth.

Since I was out of my jurisdiction, I decided not to come on as law enforcement doing an investigation. Instead, I opted for a made-up tale of woe, which, enhanced by some fake tears, ultimately persuaded the man at the counter to check the records and confirm that the number on the cemetery plot I had given him had been purchased by Padraig Barr.

After getting direction from him, I made my way through the headstones until I stood looking down at the grave located in section 52, grave number 1019.

I stared down at the starkness of the grave. No headstone, no name, no marker except the cemetery designation of location. It offended every fiber of my being. Her dead body had been discarded in a dumpster, and then, her family made it worse by hiding her in an unmarked grave. Over the last few weeks, I felt I had come to know Sherry just a little better, especially from watching the recordings of the Dobbs show and audition. She was young, vibrant, confident, with her whole life ahead of her, and then she was gone. As the tears slowly snaked down my cheeks, the irony that I knew Sherry better than my own mother wasn't lost on me. I reached into the bag that I carried with me, and took out a framed photo of Sherry. I had captured her image in a screenshot from a video of the Dobbs show, printed it, and framed it. I squatted down next to the small stone marker and propped the photo up next to it. Then I made a promise.

"I know you've waited over twenty years for justice, but I think I'm on the right track. Just be patient with me." With the memory of us being in detention together all those years ago, I reached down and laid my hand on the grass, and made a silent vow—*I got you this time and I'm not letting go.*

CHAPTER 32

AS I HEADED TO the office on Tuesday, the temperature had already broken seventy degrees and there wasn't a cloud in the sky. It was one of those gorgeous fall days that hinted at the summer just past, and not the impending winter. It was also the day my gut told me I'd get the news about Jane Doe.

As I pulled up to the traffic light on Market Street, I made an impulsive decision. Instead of turning right toward the office, I continued straight until I got to River Street and then made a left. I found a parking space across the street from Shaky Grounds, grabbed a large Kona coffee, crossed back over River Street and began strolling the path that ran along the Dagda River. I found a bench about a quarter of a mile upriver and took a seat, sharing the company of about six Canadian geese pecking at the grass, three mallards floating along on the current, and the ever-present joggers running on the path along the river. The leaves on the cottonwood trees that were scattered along the riverbank had begun turning vibrant yellow, their reflection adding a splash of color to the dark river water. Behind me was one of the former warehouses that had been turned into luxury riverfront condos.

As I sat there, I tried to make sense of all that was going on. Assuming Jane Doe was my mom, how could I mourn the loss of a woman who had been nothing more than a specter that I had chased for more than forty years? The only history I had with her was the history of longing for her and wondering why she had abandoned me. And now I'd have to rewrite that history. Sure, I could do it intellectually, but how could I do it emotionally? Those scars were so deeply embedded, I wasn't sure they could ever be erased.

On top of that, the person I loved most in the world, my daughter, was struggling to come to terms with who I was. My fear was that, with Becca getting married to a handsome local celebrity, my daughter's desire to distance herself from me would only grow.

There was one thing I agreed with Nora on: Why was I always a "transgender woman"? I remembered Sherry's frustration with being labeled as a trans woman. Why couldn't people just see us as women? Didn't being a woman carry enough of a burden? Did we always need an adjective in front of our womanhood to make it even harder?

Before my thoughts devoured me, I forced myself back into thinking about Sherry's investigation.

Yesterday, when I had tried digging into the history of James Barry, Esq., I had come up with plenty of articles on the cases he'd tried both when at the DA's office and in private practice, but nothing that gave me his background information. I needed to get his whole story.

The fact that Padraig had anglicized his name didn't mean

that Seamus had done the same. No question, James Barry was a common name. And even if it turned out that Seamus was former Assistant DA James Barry, it didn't mean there was a nefarious reason behind him changing his name. It was just as likely that he had done it to distance himself from his family history for career purposes.

Yet, it was incomprehensible that, if Jimmy was Seamus, he had prosecuted the man accused of killing his sister and said nothing—or at least hadn't said anything about Sherry being his sibling. I wasn't a lawyer, but even I knew that an assistant DA had a conflict of interest and wasn't ethically allowed to handle a case in which they had a personal interest—and the victim being your sister certainly qualified. I knew I was guilty of doing something similar, because for over a week I had been clandestinely investigating my mother's murder and told no one—at least no one in a position to stop me. But there was something different about prosecuting the alleged murderer of your sibling—something that didn't pass the smell test.

Right in the middle of my research yesterday, I had to leave for court to testify at a hearing on one of my old cases. Frustrated that I hadn't found what I wanted, I had called Becca on my way home and asked her to see what she could find on James Barry, Esq., a.k.a. Seamus Barr—and then I told her why I needed it.

I looked at my Fitbit—9:05. I needed to get to the office. When I stood, the geese defiantly held their ground. I slowly walked back down the path toward my car, soaking in the musky smell of the river. I stopped at Shaky Grounds and picked up another coffee. This way I wouldn't have to deal with the stares in the office kitchen. I only had a few more years to go until I could walk out the door for good. But for the first time in a long time, I began to wonder if I'd be able to make it that long.

I TRIED TO STAY busy throughout the day. Around 3 p.m., I began thinking that I should leave work early, a kind of magical thinking taking hold that if I wasn't in the office, it would prevent bad news from arriving. My thoughts were broken by the buzz of my office phone. "Kelly," I answered.

"Lieutenant, First Assistant Paul Morocco for you."

I looked at my phone, but there were no incoming calls on hold. "Which line?"

"No, Lieutenant. He's here. He'd like to come to your office."

Oh shit. I drew in a deep breath, releasing it slowly. "Sure."

I took a moment, trying to mentally prepare myself for what I knew was coming, then walked out into the hallway so Morocco would see me when he was buzzed in. I didn't know Morocco's background, but as he walked down the hallway, there was something in his bearing that suggested he was experienced in delivering bad news.

I extended my hand as he approached and he took it in both of his. "You could have called," I said, choking on my words.

"No, Lauren. That's not the way we do things."

"Come in," I said, leading him into my office and letting him sit in one of my guest chairs before taking my seat.

We both knew there was only one reason he was here in person, yet when he said "I'm so sorry, Lauren," it still took my breath away. "We have the DNA results back and they confirm that Jane Doe is your mother."

I closed my eyes, a wheezy sob escaping involuntarily.

"Obviously, I wish I had better news for you, but I hope in some small way, after all these years, knowing what happened to your mom will help."

"I hope it will too," I said, unsure that it would.

"We're sending the results out to the company your brother has retained to confirm them, but before we do that, I wasn't sure if you'd want to be the one to tell him the news, or if you'd prefer I do it?"

I swallowed and tried to steady my shaking hands. "Thanks, Paul. I appreciate that courtesy," I said, hearing the quiver in my voice. "I'll let him know. And, thank you. I appreciate you coming to let me know . . . and everything your office has done for my brother and me."

"No need to thank us."

"I know he promised to come for the press conference, so I'll let him arrange that with you."

"Thanks, but honestly, Lauren, that's not a top priority. I can't imagine how hard this is for you, and will be for Brian. Don't worry about us."

Somehow, I managed to tap into some part of my cop psyche. "No, that's important. If the person responsible for our mom's death is still out there, I want them to know you're looking for them."

"Okay," he said. "We'll figure it out after we hear from your brother. And Lauren, my sincerest condolences."

"Thanks, Paul. I appreciate it."

We both stood, but when I came around my desk, instead of reaching out to shake my hand, he embraced me in a hug.

After he left, I folded my arms on my desk, rested my head

in my arms, and started crying. I don't know how long I cried after he left, but all I could see in my head was that young, beautiful woman, leaning over next to me as I blew out my birthday candles. And now I knew that within weeks of my party, she was dead, and just like Sherry, had been dumped to rot.

CHAPTER 33

"LT, ARE YOU OKAY?"

I looked up to see Detective Stacy Mills standing in my doorway. Suddenly, I was lost in trying to figure out how to explain that I just learned that my mother died forty-one years ago. The temptation was to say nothing. But I knew sooner rather than later it was going to be on the news. "It's a long story, Stace, but I just learned that a Jane Doe that was discovered forty-something years ago up in Brisbane has been ID'd as my mom."

"Oh my God. I'm so sorry, Lauren. Can I get you anything—water, anything?"

"No. Thanks. I'm still trying to process it."

"You want to talk?" she asked.

"Thanks. Maybe later. Right now, I need to call my brother with the news," I said, the burden of telling Brian suddenly weighing on me.

"I'm here if you need me," she offered, walking into my office and giving me a hug. "I mean it. I'm here for you."

"I know you are. Thanks."

After she left, I looked at my watch and wondered if Brian would be on the set. Closing the door, I tried to steel myself for what was to follow. I grabbed my cell, punched in his number, and held my breath.

"Hey," he answered. "I thought I might hear from you today. It's Mom, right?"

I appreciated that he had just spared me the pain of breaking it to him. I was only confirming what he'd already guessed. "Yeah," I said. "It's Mom." I bit down on my lower lip, determined not to fall apart again.

"Fuck." There was a sigh followed by a long silence. "I spent the last week trying to figure out what would be worse, to know she was gone, or to find out that maybe she was still out there somewhere. Obviously, I'll never know how I'd be feeling right now if you had told me it wasn't her, but this sure as hell sucks." He fell silent for a moment. "Damn, dead for forty-one years and no one ever knew," he finally offered.

I spoke before I could censor myself. "Oh, someone knew. Just not you or me."

"You don't know that," he said.

"You're right. But there's more."

I explained that our father had been issued a new weapon the day after our mother disappeared.

"Ah, shit. That sure as hell makes him look guilty as sin, but without the murder weapon, we'll never be able to prove it was him."

"Unfortunately, you're right on both counts," I said.

He said something to someone else, but his words were unintelligible. He then returned to our conversation. "I'll probably fly in on Thursday and do the press conference on Friday. Does that work for you?"

"Yeah, that's fine."

"You okay?" he asked.

I sighed. "No. I'm still trying to wrap my head around it. It really hasn't sunk in yet, if that makes any sense. I mean, it's not like I didn't expect that this was coming. But now that it's here, it's just so hard to accept. I mean our mother was murdered and dumped. How could that have happened?"

"I hear you."

"By the way, before I forget, the results are being sent to the lab that you picked to confirm them."

"Got it. I'll call you later with my travel plans."

"Thanks." I sighed. "Hey, Bri?"

"Yeah."

"I love you."

"I love you too, Sis. Talk soon."

I knew there were two more people I had to tell. The first was Becca.

"Hi," she answered, apprehension in her voice.

"Hi. I just met with someone from the Brisbane's DA's office." I paused, the words caught in my throat. "It's my mom," I finally managed to get out.

"Oh, Lauren, I'm so sorry."

"I know. But I also wanted to thank you. If it wasn't for you, we might never have known what happened to her. As hard as it is to know, maybe at some point it will help me forgive myself for her disappearing." I swallowed hard. "Now I need to find out if it was him."

"Do you?" she asked. "Will that really help? Maybe it's better not to know?"

"No. I have to know. Or, even if I can never be certain, I need to do all that I can for my mom. I owe her that."

"Just don't do anything you'll regret," she cautioned.

I knew what she meant, but, at least for now, my desire for retribution had passed. This wasn't about letting my mother rest in peace. I had no belief in an afterlife, so it wasn't as if I felt my mother was watching from above, calling for justice. No, it was more so I could look myself in the mirror and know I had done all that I could to solve her murder. It was the same way I felt about Sherry. "I won't," I finally responded. "And Becca, one of us needs to tell Nora."

"Do you want me to?" she asked.

"Please," I said. "I think it would just be easier for her to hear it from you. I might get too emotional. Plus, if she's going to ask questions, I prefer she asks you."

"Sure. I'll talk to her." She hesitated. "There's one other thing, but I know this isn't the right time. It's about James Barry."

"Is James Barry Seamus Barr?" I asked.

"Yes. But there's more," she said.

As curious as I was, I just couldn't go there right now. "Okay. Thanks. Can you email me what you found? Right now, I have to report what's going on to my captain."

"Sure. I know you're overwhelmed, but I think what I found will help."

We said our goodbyes. I went to see Snyder. Fortunately, Snyder kept it short, extending his condolences and asking what I needed. I thanked him, told him that I hadn't figured

out yet if I was going to take some time off, and I let him know
that the Brisbane DA's news conference would most likely be
on Friday, so he could pass word up through the chain of
command. He asked if I still had my father's .38 and I told
him I did and I'd be happy to let our office do the turnover.
Why not? I thought. I already knew it wasn't going to be the
murder weapon. It was like giving someone ice in the winter.
I left without him saying anything further about Tesh's, so I
hoped that for now that crisis had been averted.

WHEN I ARRIVED AT Rolling Knolls, I locked my weapon
in the lockbox in the trunk of my car, placed my phone in my
pocket, then checked in at the front desk. Since I didn't want
any problems, I showed them my credentials when I checked
in. The woman looked at her computer screen and told me
that since my father was easily upset there was a notation that,
when visiting, I had to keep the door to his room open. I
nodded and headed toward his room, carrying a file folder
with an enlargement of the picture of my mom at my birthday
along with the picture of Tom Hammond. I also had my old
iPod where I had downloaded a song I wanted to play.

　　When I got to his room, my father was sitting in his chair,
his eyes fixed on a pastoral scene. Had he been looking out
the window, I would have understood his focus, but instead
he was staring at a painting on the wall of his windowless room. There was no music playing, and unlike the last
two times, he was unshaven, his thinning hair looking like
someone had dumped the remnants of a bowl of spaghetti on
his head, strands flying this way and that. As I looked at him,
it dawned on me that Patty, the nurse's aide, probably wasn't

on duty today. When she was, he was clean shaven with his hair combed.

I went over to where the iPod was plugged into the Bose docking station. I pulled his iPod out, plugged mine in, scrolled to the song I wanted, and hit play. I adjusted the volume so it was loud enough to be heard during the conversation I needed to have.

I pulled up the other chair next to his. It seemed like it took all the will he had to pry his attention away from the painting on the wall. "Do I know you?" he asked.

"You do," I said calmly. "You're my father." I handed him the picture of my mother. "And this is a picture of my mother—your wife."

He looked at the picture, and then up at me with a blank expression.

"Dad, the Brisbane DA's office has just confirmed that Mom was murdered forty-one years ago. She was shot once in the head." *Keep it simple*, I thought—*yes or no answers*. "Did you know she was murdered?"

His eyes left me and returned to the picture. His hand began to tremble. "My wife," he said in a tone that left it unclear if it was a question or a statement.

"Yes, Dad, your wife. Did you know she was murdered?"

This time, when he looked away from the picture, his eyes found mine. As he took me in, he seemed to hear the song playing in the background for the first time—"Maureen" by Jim Reeves.

"Your wife, Maureen," I said, almost in a whisper.

"I knew," he mumbled.

"Did you do it?" I asked as gently as I could.

"Do it?" he questioned. "Who are you?"

I needed to be patient. I had set the iPod to play "Maureen" on a loop, so I tried again.

"You're my father," I said slowly, enunciating each word. "Your wife, Maureen, was murdered forty years ago. Did you murder her?"

I wished I could understand what was going through his head. Sometimes it appeared as if he was looking through a fog, trying to see something in the distance, something he knew was there, but was shrouded by the mist—a shroud that distorted everything.

"*Maureen*," Reeves sang in the background.

He raised the picture in his hand, his eyes now fixed on it. "It wasn't her fault," he said. "I was wrong." He let the picture fall from his hand. "Oh God. Forgive me." His head dropped into his chest, and he clasped his hands together.

I closed my eyes and sighed, frustration taking hold. That was the best I was going to get. I already knew that when I played back the recording of the conversation I was making on my phone, I'd get no more clarity as to what he meant. I didn't know if I had the strength to stay and continue. My mother was dead and I felt like I was talking to the Greek Sphinx, his answers nothing but riddles. I got up, took my iPod out of the docking station, and put the one that Becca had bought for him back in. I found a Johnny Cash playlist, pushed play and plopped down in the chair.

It was several minutes before he looked up. "Do I know you?"

I felt like I owed it to Joan Hammond to at least try. "Yes, sir. I'm Detective Jones from the DA's office. We're working together on a case." I pulled the photo of Tom Hammond out of the folder and handed it to him. "Someone shot Tom and I'm looking for information. Were you at a meeting with Tom before he was shot?"

As he had done with my mother's photo, he turned his attention to the picture. "Tom?"

"Yes, sir. You were at a meeting together before he was shot," I said.

"Don't remember," he said, his eyes never leaving the image clutched in his hand.

"Did you shoot him?"

His head snapped up. "No! Not me."

"Who then?" I asked, and for the first time I allowed my voice to demand an answer.

His face was blank and it looked like I had lost him. In the background Johnny Cash was singing his version of the old gospel song "Ain't No Grave Gonna Hold My Body Down."

He put his finger to his lip. "Barry."

I startled. "Barry Reed shot Tom?"

I thought I heard a noise behind me and I turned quickly— nothing. I went to the doorway and looked down the hallway, but the only person I saw was Michelle, sitting at the reception desk, guarding the door to the world on the other side.

"Was anyone just here?" I asked.

"Just Vinny, the security guard," she replied. "He just likes to check because we know your father sometimes gets agitated when you visit."

Shit. Vinny had called the chief last time. If Vinny overheard today's conversation and passed it along, Snyder would lose his shit. And if Snyder passed the information along to

Barry Reed, God knows what would happen. The clock was running, and as much as I wanted to just curl up and mourn my mother, I knew I didn't have that luxury any more.

I turned back and watched my father from the doorway, his head bowed, Johnny Cash a musical backdrop. There was a part of me that hated him. Some of the things he had done to us were seared into my memory and no matter how hard I tried to forget them, they'd resurface. The night he threw Brian out being at the top of the list. That night, I had almost crossed the line. "Get out! Get out of my house you fucking nancy. You queer piece of shit. You're no son of mine," he had screamed, and in his rage threw a punch that glanced off Brian's head. I had jumped between them, grabbed my father by the collar, and shoved him up against the wall in the kitchen as hard as I could. I tried desperately to get my hand on the butcher knife on the counter, and if I had, all our lives would have been different. But Brian pushed the knife away from my outstretched hand. He always says I saved his life that night by coming between him and my father, but I'm not sure he appreciates that he saved mine as well.

As Johnny Cash belted out "A Boy Named Sue," my father silently sang along. *How fucking ironic.* Despite what he had done to me, and despite my efforts to man up, neither he, nor I, could change who I was—or, for that matter, who Brian was. Somehow, we had managed to live our truths. Yeah, there were some parts of me that could never forgive him, but he was my father. I wouldn't exist but for him. And, even though there was the very real possibility he had killed my mother, the fury that I had experienced only a week ago was spent. There was something almost pitiful about him. Clearly, he no longer was the person he had been all those years ago. His dementia had robbed him of so many things, but in a strange way, it robbed me too. How could I hate someone who no longer existed?

CHAPTER 34

I DIDN'T HAVE THE energy to even start my car. Instead, I watched through the windshield as the sun set over the wheat fields that stretched out beyond the parking lot. I had no idea how they came up with the name Rolling Knolls—there wasn't so much as a small rise in sight, just acres of fields waiting for the first frost. As hard as I had tried to prepare myself for the news about my mother, when it came, the finality had unmoored me. There were certain truths I had grown up with that seemed as fixed as the North Star. And now I had discovered that my compass had been pointing in the wrong direction my whole life. I had grown up believing that no one could ever love me for who I was. If my own mother couldn't love me, how could anyone else? I had gone so far down the road of self-loathing, turning around at this point to course correct seemed impossible. It had been a few years since I had pondered if it was worth going on, but, as I watched the darkness beginning to settle over the fields, I felt the seeds of despair sprouting in me much like the winter wheat was in those fields.

My cell phone startled me. *Ignore it*, I thought. But, as if by some Pavlovian response, my eyes found their way to the cupholder where the phone sat. Joan Hammond.

"Kelly," I answered instinctively.

"Lieutenant, it's Joan Hammond. I need to speak with you."

"It's actually not a good time right now, Joan."

"Please, Lieutenant. It's important. I wasn't entirely honest with you when we spoke. There's something about your mother that I need to tell you."

AN HOUR LATER, I sat across from Joan at her kitchen table. "Thank you for coming. I know you said it wasn't a good time and you sounded upset on the phone, but there are some things I thought you'd want to know."

I shook my head and took a sip from the water she'd given me. "Okay. That's why I came."

Joan rubbed her hands together, her eyes downcast, avoiding mine. "When I asked you about your mom, your reaction . . . you seemed hopeful that I might have heard from her."

I waited, deciding not to give her the news, always the cop—gather, don't give. "I was."

"I don't think she ran off with another man," she blurted out.

My muted reaction was probably a tell, but she didn't seem to pick up on it. "Why do you think that?" I asked, my voice level.

"We were friends. We shared . . . secrets, our dreams. I

would've known and she wouldn't have left and not contacted me. Plus, she adored you and your brother. She would never have abandoned you."

There was more, I could feel it—more that I didn't know yet. "So, you think something happened to her?"

She nodded. "The day your mom left," she began, then hesitated. "That day, she called me in a panic. She said that Frank—I'm sorry, your father—had just discovered something and she was terrified about what he might do."

"What was it?" My interest was piqued.

She swallowed, trying to wade through her thoughts. "He found out that your mother had been raped."

I leaned back, my breathing momentarily interrupted. My mother—raped! I reached up and cupped my hands over my mouth, trying not to scream.

"Who raped my mother?" I somehow managed to ask.

"I . . . I don't know. She didn't tell me who it was," Joan said, but her eyes told a different story.

My head was spinning, questions blurring together.

"She . . . she told me after . . . after it happened. She had gone to the county Christmas party—that's what it was called back then. She had left the Personnel Department when you were born, and she wanted to see people. You were young, a little over a year old. Your dad was working late and your grandmother had come over to babysit. She had gotten all dressed up and was feeling pretty. She had a few drinks and then someone tricked her into going to his office, and . . . She was blaming herself for what happened. She needed to talk to someone who would understand."

Joan's last sentence reverberated—it wasn't just about my

mom. It was about Joan too. Maybe I would've understood even if I hadn't transitioned, but maybe not. "You're a survivor too," I said.

She nodded. "Yes," she mumbled.

"I'm so sorry, Joan."

We sat in silence, neither of us knowing what to say.

"It happened to you before my mom?" I finally asked.

She lowered her head. "Yes."

"You had told her about what happened to you?"

"It was when we worked together. I needed to warn her never to be alone with this person."

"Was it the same person who assaulted you?" I asked.

"I told you, I don't know who assaulted her, but I don't think so. She would never have been alone with him."

"Who assaulted you?" I asked.

"No, Lieutenant," she said, leaving no room for debate. "I won't go there with you. That's for me, and me alone."

"Did you report what happened to you?"

She shook her head. "No one would have believed me, and even if they did, I was afraid that it would ruin Tom's career. Maybe things are better now, but it was different back then. The police didn't believe you. You were blamed for wearing a short skirt, or being attractive. It was always our fault. We tempted the poor men who couldn't help themselves," she spit out.

My mind flashed back to Jimmy Barry's client and wondered if things really were different. Maybe now the police paid lip service, but the system still blamed the victim.

I let it drop—for now. "How did my father find out she was assaulted?"

"She told him."

"Why?"

"I don't know," she said, and for the second time I sensed she wasn't being totally honest.

Every detective, especially in a homicide, looks for three things—means, motive, and opportunity. My father now owned the complete package. Time to zero in.

"Joan, the reason I didn't want to see you when you called was that, a few hours ago, I learned that the remains of a Jane Doe discovered over forty years ago in Brisbane County are those of my mother." I closed my eyes and sighed. "My mom was murdered. Shot once in the head."

Her head drooped, more in sorrow than surprise. Ask, don't tell, I reminded myself. "Do you think my father murdered my mother?"

She looked up quickly, surprise flooding her face. "No. No, it wasn't your father."

Her certainty took me aback. "But you said that when my mom called, she was in a panic because she didn't know what my father was going to do. Maybe he blamed her and killed her in a fit of rage over the fact that she was raped?"

Her eyes conveyed a sadness that words couldn't. "She wasn't panicked over what he'd do to her. When she called me, he had already left. She was sure he was going to kill the man who had raped her and she didn't want your father to go to jail for the rest of his life."

I wasn't convinced, his .38 "stolen" the day after my mother disappeared lurking in my thoughts. "Joan, I lived a long time with my father. He's got a violent temper. He may have changed his mind and come back."

Again, she shook her head. "I know your father had a reputation for having a nasty temper, and guys in the office either
loved him or hated him. But Lieutenant, you have to trust me
when I tell you that your father wasn't always like that. It was
only after your mom was gone that he changed."

Her words struck a chord. Aunt Maeve had said almost the
same thing—he wasn't a bad guy until my mom was gone.

She pursed her lips. "A few years after your mom disappeared, Tommy had moved over to the DA's office and was
working in Homicide with your father. One night, Tommy
got a call from a Harrison cop he knew. They had just pulled
your father over, stinking drunk. The cop didn't want to jam
him up by giving him a DUI, so Tommy agreed to come drive
him home. When Tommy got back, he was rattled—and he
was hard to rattle. I mean, by that point in his life, Tommy
had been in the military and in law enforcement for about
eight years. He'd seen a lot, and I never saw him like he was
when he got home that night."

"Why? What happened?"

"Tommy said that when he was driving your father home,
your father was alternating between screaming, cursing, and
crying. He said that it was the fifth anniversary of the day your
mother died and he wanted to kill himself, but then there'd be
no one to take care of you and your brother."

I quickly did the math. That would have been around the
time that Uncle Steve died and Aunt Maeve moved to Florida.

"Did Tom report what my father told him?"

She hesitated, seeming to see the road not traveled. "No.
First thing the next day, your father cornered Tommy and
told him to ignore anything he said. He was just drunk

and babbling and he didn't want Tom getting into trouble for making a false report. Tommy was torn as to what to do, but he didn't know who he could trust, so he didn't say anything. I know it was something he regretted, because he wondered sometimes what would have happened if he had reported it."

We both sat in silence. Joan hadn't completely exonerated my father, but she had created a reasonable doubt. Even assuming my father had gone off to kill the person who raped my mother, why was he alive and she was dead? Why did he report his .38 stolen? There were still too many unanswered questions.

"Is there anything else you can think of that might help?"

She sighed. "I also didn't tell you everything Tommy said about the Riccoli case when you were here the other day. I guess because I really didn't know you and . . ."

"And?" I asked.

"I wasn't sure if I could trust you."

"Okay," I said softly. "Hopefully you trust me now."

She brushed the hair off her face. "The night Tommy was shot, he told me your father had come to his office that afternoon and was bitching because they were going to retry Riccoli. Your father said something like, if Barry would stop hiding the DNA evidence everyone would know who did it. Tommy said at that point he looked up and saw Snyder standing in his doorway and said, 'Hey Rich, what's up?' And Snyder just said he'd talk to him later and walked away. About an hour later, Tommy got a call that there was going to be a meeting that night to talk about the retrial and he needed to be there."

I struggled to connect the pieces. "So, you think there's a connection between what my father said and the meeting being called?"

She leaned forward. "Tommy believed your father knew who had killed Sherry and that there was DNA evidence that would prove it."

"Did Tom tell you who he thought it was?"

"No," she said, leaning back in her chair, her voice barely above a whisper. "I don't think Tommy knew who it was your father was referring to."

"Who called Tom about the meeting?"

"One of the DAs. Tom didn't say who. He figured the meeting was because of what Snyder overheard your father say. Tom felt like they decided to take the meeting out of the main office at night to have a private discussion."

"Where was the meeting?"

"I don't know if you'd remember it because they closed it shortly after Tommy was shot, but twenty years ago, the DA's office had a 'secret,'" she said, putting "secret" in air quotes, "building the Narcotics Unit worked out of. That's where he went that night."

"Did they tell you where Tom was found?" I asked.

"I was told that they had all agreed to go have a drink at the Elks after the meeting. He was found in his car in the Elks' parking lot." The pain slowly enveloped her face, and she began to sob.

"I'm sorry, Joan," I said, knowing that she had given me almost everything—everything but the name of the person who had raped my mom, and why my mother told my father.

LATER, SITTING ON THE couch in my father's living room, I replayed the timeline—it all seemed to fit. Riccoli's conviction was reversed as a result of his public defender getting DNA results not previously turned over. Based on the copy of the letter my father had received from the state forensics lab, he and Barry Reed knew that there were even more DNA results that hadn't been turned over, so him bitching to Hammond about Barry hiding other DNA results made sense. Snyder overheard his conversation with Hammond, and that night, Hammond was shot. Shortly after that, my father and Clarke retired and Reed resigned—leaving Snyder as the only one who may have known about all the DNA results.

But why kill Hammond? My father and Reed knew about the other DNA results, and they were still alive. I felt like I was wandering in a maze, and I kept getting lost—each turn sending me farther from the exit.

I turned off the light and, as I sat in the darkness, I finally allowed my mind to find its way back to my mother. I wondered what that last day was like for her. Getting up and making breakfast for Brian and me. Doing what moms do—dishes, laundry, worrying about what to make for dinner. And then for some reason her day changed, and, if Joan was right, suddenly she was in a panic that her husband was going to murder someone—not just someone, the person who had raped her. But even then, I couldn't imagine that she ever thought for one second that this was the last day of her life. That when she dropped us off at Nanny's, she'd never see us again, hold us, kiss us, tuck us into bed. Does anyone ever allow themselves to consider that this is the day that it all ends?

I wasn't sure how long I sat there in the dark, trying to understand how tenuous and fortuitous life was, but at some point, I realized it was getting late. Get up, wash your face, and go to bed, I said to myself. *Five more minutes*, I thought, closing my eyes—just five minutes to decompress.

I woke with a start, still on the couch. I flipped my wrist and my Fitbit displayed 3:07 A.M. I heard a noise. It sounded like the door from the garage into the den—and I knew in that instant that I was no longer alone in the house.

CHAPTER 35

I GRABBED MY CELL in the dark and gently slid off the sofa, crouching behind its raised arm. Adrenaline churned through my veins as I desperately tried to piece together what was happening. Someone must have picked the lock on the back door to the garage, and then from there, the lock on the door between the garage and the den would've taken anyone with a modicum of experience about fifteen seconds to pick. Was it just a random breaking and entry because they thought the house was empty, or was someone coming for me? *Too much of a coincidence*, I thought, cursing myself for leaving my gun in my bedroom. But I was at my father's house. Who the hell even knew I was here?

As my eyes adjusted to the darkness, I spotted the decorative mirror that hung on the wall behind me. I couldn't remember a time when it wasn't there, and yet I couldn't remember a time I had really paid attention to it. Now it was the most important furnishing in the house. The mirror hung high enough on the wall that it showed the stairway leading up from the den. I didn't think it reflected any part of me, but I scrunched up even more, trying to be sure I remained unseen. Then I waited.

I watched in the mirror as the figure appeared at the base of the three steps that led up to the living room. Slowly, stealthily, they started up the steps. The person was tall and solidly built, dressed entirely in black, wearing night vision goggles and holding a handgun with a suppressor in their hands, both arms extended out in front of them. It was a man and this was definitely not a random B&E.

When he reached the top step, his head pivoted as he did a visual sweep of the room. I held my breath, knowing that if he spotted me the couch wouldn't even slow the bullet down, much less provide cover.

He took a few steps into the room, then checked the dining room and kitchen. It was as if he knew the layout and expected his target to be up the six steps to the second floor where the three bedrooms and bathroom were. My heart was pounding so hard, I was sure he'd be able to hear it. I had to do something, but what? And when? Once he completed his upstairs search and found no one in the bedrooms, he'd come back, turn on the lights, and I'd be dead. *Fuck!*

I quietly inhaled, trying to calm myself and focus. I ran through my options. When he got up the stairs, I could make a break for the den and try to get out the same way he came in, through the garage. I had my phone. I could hit 911 once I was outside. But chances were that I'd either never make it out of the house, or with his night vision goggles, he'd be able to hunt me down before the cops had even answered my frantic call.

If I could get to the kitchen, there were knives there—at least I'd have a weapon. No. A knife in a gunfight—not a good idea.

Fuck it, I was going to die anyway, might as well die trying. He was on the second step, moving cautiously toward the second floor.

In sheer desperation, I came up with a plan. It was about fifteen feet from me to the light switches on the dining room wall. One switch illuminated the dining room, the second, the light the hallway at the top of the stairs. Light suddenly became my ally.

I squatted and silently eased myself out, moving toward the dining room. He was now at the third of six steps, focused on the doorways at the top of the stairs. I had to make my move now. Once he reached the high ground of the hallway, my plan, such as it was, would be useless.

When I was about six feet away from the wall, I tossed my phone to my right in the direction of the front door and dashed toward the light switches. When he heard my phone clatter against the door, he turned and fired at the noise. I made it to the wall and flicked on both light switches simultaneously. With his night vision goggles on, the sudden burst of light blinded him. He staggered down one step, trying to rip the goggles off, and when he did, he put himself at the perfect height. It was like the first time I broke a board with my foot in karate class—same principle, different target.

My first kick broke his left leg at the kneecap, causing him to tumble down the remaining two stairs screaming in pain. As he fell, he squeezed off several rounds that fortunately weren't in my direction. When he landed at the bottom, his goggles were askew, part resting on the top of his head, the other covering his right eye. My second kick, actually more of a stomp, was squarely to his face, breaking his nose and spewing blood. He howled, his hands flying to his face, and as he did, I kicked the gun from his hand, then quickly scampered to retrieve it. As he lay writhing on the floor, I bolted up to my room, threw his weapon on my bed, and retrieved my own weapon, cuffs, and work phone. When I got back down the stairs he was attempting to get up, his left leg unable to support any weight.

"On the floor, motherfucker!" I screamed at the top of my lungs. "On the floor—now!" I placed the barrel of my Smith & Wesson 9mm against the back of his head. "I won't say it again, because I would love nothing more than to blow the back of your head off."

He dropped to the floor and moaned as he tried to move his leg.

"Turn your head to the side and put your hands behind your back." I placed my right foot on his buttock. "You so much as flinch and I will stomp on your knee and then shoot you to put you out of your misery."

I took my cuffs and held them against the pistol grip, which was still in my right hand, then with my left locked the cuff on his right hand. I then repeated the process with his left hand so that his hands were secured behind his back. I patted him down—he had nothing. Not even a set of keys. Everything must have been stashed outside or in his car.

I walked over and retrieved my personal cell phone, then walked over to take a look at my would-be assassin who was moaning on the floor. Barry fucking Reed—son of a bitch.

I put my gun against the back of his head. "Is there anyone

else with you?" He said nothing. "He's the deal, Reed. You better be alone, because if I so much as hear a tree branch scrape against the house, I'll shoot you and wait and see if it was the wind or a buddy of yours. So, you may want to calm my jittery nerves."

"I'm alone," he groaned.

I ran upstairs and put my personal cell in my underwear drawer. After grabbing my badge, I headed back downstairs. "So, Mr. Reed, you have anything you'd like to tell me before I call the cavalry?"

"Go to hell," he snapped.

I raised my leg as if to stand on his broken left leg. His eyes went wide with fear.

"Perhaps you didn't hear me. You want to tell me who sent you?" I asked, my leg dangling above his.

"Fuck you, you miserable fuck," he spit out.

I took a breath and stepped back. "I'll give you credit for two things, Reed—your loyalty and stupidity," I said, walking over to one of the club chairs and taking a seat. I placed my gun on the chair next to my thigh and watched him.

He tried to look in my direction, although with the blood splattered across his face, I wasn't sure how much he could see. "Aren't you going to call 911?"

"At some point," I said. "Or maybe I'll just watch you writhe in agony for a few hours. I'm in no rush."

"You're full of shit, Kelly."

"Maybe. But here's the thing. If I call 911, who shows up? First, Harrison PD, and then because I'm part of the DA's office, folks from my office. The problem for both of us is that I don't know who in my office you're working with, but as soon as you're in custody, I figure one of two things happens—you get off easy, based on who you're working with, and they owe you for your loyalty, or . . ." I paused for effect. "Or, whoever you're working with decides you're too big a risk because you know too much, and some scumbag in the county jail takes you out. So, I'm thinking that maybe I should just cut to the chase and save us all a lot of time and aggravation and finish you now—consider it payback for taking out Tom Hammond," I said, throwing Tom into the mix to see his reaction.

He tried to sit up, but as he did, he screamed in pain. He laid back down, taking deep breaths and moaning. "I didn't kill Hammond. He offed himself with his own fucking gun."

"You're a lying sack of shit, Reed," I shot back. "You were willing to take me out, so we know you have no allegiance to cops."

"You're not a cop. Don't you ever put yourself on the right side of the blue line. You're nothing but a fucking crazy ass tranny piece of shit, trying to figure out who killed some other crazy ass tranny fuck."

"I know you killed Hammond," I said, picking up my 9mm and racking the slide, ejecting a round and chambering a new one. "How about that," I said as the bullet landed on the floor near his head. "I had a round chambered all this time."

"I'm telling you, I didn't kill Hammond," he said.

"Who did?" I screamed.

"Fuck you!" he screamed back.

"Who was at the meeting the night he died?" I demanded.

"I want a lawyer, I ain't saying shit."

"You're an idiot, Reed. After what happened tonight, do you really think they're going to protect you? You ever hear of the expression 'the leopard doesn't change its spots'?" I paused to consider how much I should put out there, and decided that there was still the chance that Snyder or Furst didn't know I had all the DNA results. No reason to tip them off yet. But there was one card I could play. "They sold you out before, I'm willing to bet that they're going to sell you out again. But what do I know? Maybe I'll help things along by lying a little and suggesting to Jimmy Barry that you were the one who told me he's a member of the Barr family—Seamus Barr. I gotta admit, it takes brass balls to prosecute a guy you know is innocent for killing a family member—just so you can protect the real killer."

He did his best to conceal it, but his eyes revealed that I had touched a nerve.

"Remember the scene from *The Godfather* when they come to the hospital to take out Don Corleone? That's how I figure you'll get it. Who do you think it will be, Reed? Padraig, maybe the old man, or maybe Jimmy himself will deal with you? Whoever it is, I'll be able to sleep at night knowing I gave you a chance to save yourself."

Reed stayed silent. I called 911, explaining who I was, where I was, and what had happened. I also told them that the situation was under control so no one had to burst in ready to have the gunfight at the O.K. Corral. When I finished the call, I unlocked the front door, turned on the porch light, and cracked open the door. I walked back to one of the club chairs and took a seat. Then I hung my badge around my neck and placed my gun behind me, trying to ensure that none of my trigger-happy compadres burst in and took a shot at me by mistake.

The squeal of sirens was getting closer. "If you ever change your mind and feel like unburdening your soul, give me a call," I said. "You may want to keep in mind that screw-ups, like the one you made tonight, aren't looked on too kindly by the people pulling the strings. Seems to me things are starting to unravel a bit, and your visit tonight tells me someone is getting nervous." I nodded toward his leg. "You're going to be immobile for a while. Tough to put up a fight when you're flat on your back—just saying."

For the first time, instead of cursing me, his expression wasn't one of anger or pain. No, if I read him right, it was a look of concern.

Harrison PD were the first ones through the door, and I wish I had a picture of the surprise on their faces when they saw me lounging in the chair with the black-clad Mr. Reed moaning on the floor with his hands cuffed behind his back, blood covering his face. Of course, part of my nonchalance was an act; the rest was because I was still on an adrenaline rush.

Bill Gibson and Fred Carr from the DCDAO Major Crimes Unit showed up about ten minutes later. By then, Harrison PD had called for an ambulance. I provided the locals, and then Gibson and Carr, with a quick narrative so they could charge Reed with B&E, attempted murder, and assault with a deadly weapon. That way, they could get a telephonic arrest warrant so they could place him under arrest when they got to the hospital and hold him under armed guard. I told them where his gun was, and that they were going to need a forensics unit to dig the bullets out of the wall and ceiling.

The EMTs were wheeling Reed out of the living room

when Snyder waltzed in. Snyder looked down at Reed, but said nothing. My first reaction on seeing Snyder was surprise that he was here. I mean, there was no question that he should've been here. He was my fucking captain and someone had broken in and tried to kill me.

"You okay, Lauren?" Snyder asked.

So, he did know my first name.

"Yeah, Cap. No injuries."

"Good," he said, and surprisingly it sounded like he meant it.

CHAPTER 36

BY THE TIME I finished giving my formal statement, it was 5 A.M. Despite the hour, I called Weiss. Unlike those of us on the investigative side, unless you were an assistant DA in charge of either Homicide or Narcotics, which she wasn't, it was likely she wasn't used to phone calls before dawn.

"Hello," she answered, her voice a bit groggy. From the generic hello, I was guessing she hadn't checked who was calling.

"Lisa, it's Lauren Kelly. I'm sorry to bother you so early, but Barry Reed broke into my father's house tonight and tried to kill me."

"What!" she hollered. "Are you alright?"

I explained what happened and that, although shaken, I was fine.

"Where are you?"

"Forensics is still crawling all over my father's place so I'm on my way to my apartment," I explained. "But when you have time, we really need to talk. I have new information from my father and from Joan Hammond, Detective Tom Hammond's widow."

"What are you doing now?"

"Hopefully driving to your house."

Thirty minutes later, I was sitting at Lisa's kitchen counter as she poured me a cup of coffee. As she listened and took notes, I caught her up on everything.

"You had a pretty shitty day yesterday," she said.

"Yeah, I did."

She took a sip of her coffee and shook her head ruefully. "I didn't want to tell you this yesterday, what with the news about your mom and all, but I have some information on Elizabeth Furst."

"And?" I replied.

"I have it from a very reliable source that she has stage four breast cancer, and has a terrible prognosis."

Shit. "Terminal?"

"No one is saying that, but that's certainly the impression I got."

"You happen to know where she is?"

"I'm told she had been at Sloan Kettering in New York, but came back last week and is currently at Holy Name," she said, referencing the hospital in downtown Harrison.

"I need to question her," I said. "I'm confident enough in the initial DNA results to confront her."

"You'll be fired before you get back to the office," she warned.

"Not if I go with the approval of an assistant attorney general who's been authorized to oversee the investigation."

It took her a minute, but then it seemed to click. "What are you suggesting?"

"Talk to whoever you need to speak to at the State Attorney General's Office. Explain that you think my investigation falls within your mandate to handle Professional Responsibility investigations because it potentially involves the murder of a DCDAO detective by another detective, and you want to authorize me to interview Elizabeth Furst and whoever else we decide is necessary to the investigation. What do we have to lose?" I asked.

"Based on what just happened to you? Our lives," she replied.

"You're right. You're a lawyer, not a cop. I shouldn't be asking you to put your life in jeopardy."

She looked insulted. "I didn't say I wouldn't do it, only that, just because they didn't kill you this time, doesn't mean they won't try again," she offered, raising an eyebrow. "If . . . or rather *when* this blows up, both of us will be in the cross-hairs—literally and professionally." She swept her arm around the kitchen as if she were a game show host displaying the grand prize. "I can afford to lose my job, what about you? You're only a few years from the promised land. If you get fired, you're going to lose a lot of money, as well as lifetime medical benefits. That'll hurt."

"Yeah, it will. But not as much as giving in to these bastards. Besides, I know a good employment lawyer."

She gave me a sad smile. "Okay. I'll see what I can do, but from an investigative standpoint you shouldn't go it alone. Is there anyone in the office you trust to take with you?"

I immediately thought of Stacy, but decided to wait. "Let me think about it. But even if there was someone I could trust, I'd be playing craps with their career."

"Give it some thought," she said. "If you think of someone, let me know."

IT WAS ALMOST SEVEN when I crawled under the covers. I had set the alarm on my phone for ten, which would give me enough time to shower and get ready to be at the office before noon.

I woke up to the sound of my phone chirping. Confused, I glanced at the old clock radio that sat on my night table—8:36 A.M. I was sure I had set the alarm on my phone for ten. Then it hit me, it wasn't the alarm, it was my phone ringing. I grabbed it, saw the display, and grew even more confused—it was only around six thirty where Brian was. "Brian?" I answered, the gurgle of sleep in my voice.

"It sounds like I woke you," he said. "Everything okay?"

"No," I said. "But you go first."

"I'm at the airport. I have a flight out in an hour. I'm going to be staying at the Marriott in Middletown. I figured I needed to be closer to the Brisbane DA's office for the press conference. I need to speak to you—in person. Can you meet me there this afternoon?"

"Sure. Are you okay? I thought you were coming in tomorrow."

"Yeah, I'm fine. But I found out something that explains a lot—something we need to discuss in person. That's why I'm coming in today. What's going on with you? What's wrong?"

I proceeded to give my brother a condensed version of what happened. When I was done, we agreed to meet at his room around 3 P.M.

Despite desperately craving sleep, I let my old Homicide

days, when we might go for forty-eight hours straight, take over. I got up, showered, and got ready for work.

On the way down the hallway to my office, I ran into Snyder, who let me know that Reed was in surgery because I had really fucked up his leg. When I suggested that I'd send Reed a get well card, I got the idea that he was unimpressed with my sarcasm.

Later, I was proofreading my report when Stacy knocked on my door. "Word has it that you had an interesting night, LT. You okay?"

"Yeah, I think so. It'll probably take a while to hit me."

"You have a minute?" she asked.

"Sure. What's up?"

She closed the door behind her. "I've been accepted at the FBI Academy. I'm starting in February."

I walked over to where she was standing and gave her a hug. "Congratulations."

"Thanks," she said. "And thanks, for the recommendation."

"When's your last day here?" I asked.

"I haven't given my notice yet. I'll probably make it around the end of the year. I have a couple of weeks of paid time off that I'll use in January."

The thought leapt out of my mouth before my better angels could shut it down. "Would you consider taking on one last assignment before you leave? An assignment that could get you killed or otherwise cause your career here to end sooner than you're anticipating."

She looked at me like maybe I was a little off-kilter. "I'm assigned to Grand Jury. You have a subpoena you need served on someone dangerous?"

"No, it's on a cold case investigation I'm working on."

"The chief would never assign me to a real case."

"The chief wouldn't be making the call. If it comes, it'll come from somewhere else," I said, watching her once again give me the "what have you been smoking" look.

"So, let me see if I have this right—it's dangerous, and the chances are, even if I don't get killed or maimed, I'll probably be fired in a New York second when the brass finds out," she said with a smug smile.

I nodded. "Yeah. That's about right."

"Count me in," she said. "Sounds like what I signed up for when I joined this shit show."

"Um, one last thing to consider. If this blows up, I don't want this to jeopardize you going to the FBI. It's one thing to ruin a career you've already decided you're leaving, it's quite another to ruin the career you haven't even started yet."

She thought for a moment. "Like I told you, I disclosed everything and they still wanted me, so I don't think this will rock the boat," she said with a shrug.

THREE HOURS LATER, AS I was driving to meet my brother, I called Lisa and relayed my conversation with Stacy, leaving out the part that she was leaving to go to the FBI, since I didn't want that to inadvertently get back to anyone. Although she didn't say it, I could tell Lisa had a mixed reaction—relieved I had found someone, while concerned that the someone I'd found was the complainant in an ongoing IA investigation.

"One last thing, Lisa. Can I send another DNA sample out for review?"

"You have more of Sam's DNA?"

"No. This is personal. I'll pay for this out of my own pocket. Assuming my brother gives me authorization, I'm looking for a company to do a forensic genetic genealogy on his sample," I said, going on to explain what I thought I would need. She agreed to text me the email for the person at the company to send the results to, and, if it was what I expected, she thought we'd have the results in short order.

I CHECKED IN AT the front desk of the hotel, my brother having warned me that I would need to get a pass card to allow the elevator to go to his floor. Apparently, it was a good thing that the president wasn't in town because Brian had the presidential suite in the penthouse. The elevator opened to a foyer with only one door, the door to my brother's suite. Standing outside the door was a man who looked like he had just retired from the World Wrestling Federation. He seemed almost as wide as he was tall, and if he had a neck, it was lost in the expanse of his shoulders and his arms. The sports coat he was wearing had to be a 4XL.

"Would you be Lauren Kelly?" he asked in a voice that was somehow as deep as a standup bass and as smooth as a Coltrane solo.

"I am," I said, handing him my credentials.

He looked at them, then me, before handing them back. "Your brother is expecting you, ma'am."

His hand engulfed the doorknob as he swung the door open for me. I walked into a suite that appeared to have more square footage than most homes. Not ostentatious enough for certain presidents, I thought, but pretty damn impressive for us normal folks.

Brian slid out from behind a granite bar and gave me a hug. "Good to see you," he said.

"Good to be seen," I replied, my most recent travails still fresh in my mind. "And good to see you," I added. "And by the way, if they ever do a remake of *The Princess Bride*, your bodyguard would make a perfect Fezzik."

He smiled. "Ben's actually had a few walk-on roles. He's a good guy. I don't usually bring him along, but figured things might get crazy after the news conference on Friday. You want a drink?" he asked, nodding to the bar.

"Thanks. Just a diet soda, if you have any."

"Are you kidding? The bar in this room is as well stocked as the one downstairs in the hotel restaurant—maybe better."

We both walked over to the bar, where he pulled a diet cola out of a fridge situated under the counter and poured some in a glass. Then he proceeded to mix himself something, which based on the sweet vermouth he used, I assumed was a Manhattan.

He walked us over to a couch facing a window with a panoramic view of Middletown and drew in a deep breath. "I wanted to do this in person because—well, I hope it doesn't upset you too much." He looked at me with those puppy dog eyes that had helped make him famous. "The company we used to run the DNA confirmed that Jane Doe was Mom. No surprise there. They did, however, confirm something else." He sighed. "I honestly don't know how to tell you this, but . . . well, um . . ."

I felt bad watching him struggle. "Bri, if it will make it any easier for you, I know and it doesn't change anything."

His head jerked back and he looked at me with wide-eyed surprise. "You know about me—about us?"

I nodded. "Yeah. When your people asked for my DNA to be analyzed for both mitochondrial DNA and Y chromosome markers, I knew you were looking for more than our link to Jane Doe. The Y chromosome would show if we had the same father. I guess I'm taking a bit of a leap here, but based on the fact that you came here a day early and wanted to meet in person, it kind of made me feel like you've discovered what I had begun to suspect—you're my half brother. We have different fathers."

His head dropped. "Yeah," he mumbled. "That doesn't upset you?"

"No. Why should it bother me? You're still my brother and I still love you. But how do you feel about it?"

"As long as we're okay," he said, gesturing back and forth between us, "I'm okay. I guess it also explains why Dad . . . sorry, I don't know what he is to me. It explains why the person who raised me hated me so much. Maybe that also explains why he killed Mom. He found out she had an affair." He took a heavy sip from his drink and sat back.

"Actually, I've discovered a few more things since we last spoke, and some of this will upset you."

My brother once again gave me a wide-eyed stare, walked over to the bar, refreshed his drink, and returned to the couch.

I began by telling him what Joan Hammond had shared about her friendship with our mom and what Tom had disclosed to her about the night he picked up a very drunk Frank Kelly on the anniversary of our mom's disappearance. I explained that while I was still uncertain as to what happened, I was no longer certain that my father had murdered our mother.

"What about the fact that Mom cheated on him?" Brian asked. "I'm not saying that it would give anyone the right to kill her, but it's kind of weird to find out in the same week that my mom is dead and she was also unfaithful."

I steepled my hands over my nose and closed my eyes, struggling to find the right words. "Actually, I wish it were that simple," I said.

"Meaning?" he asked.

"The day she disappeared, Mom had called Joan in a panic because Dad—sorry, my dad—had found out that Mom had been raped, and she was convinced he was on his way over to kill the person who had raped her."

"What?" he mumbled, clasping his hands behind his head. "Raped? Sweet Jesus. Can things get any more fucked up?" And then I saw the gears starting to turn. "Wait," he said. "When was she raped?"

"According to Joan, it was the Christmas party the year I turned one."

The gears meshed. "Oh shit," he muttered. "So, nine months before I was born." He snorted. "No wonder Dad hated me so much. Not only wasn't I his kid, I was the product of rape."

"You realize, you had nothing to do with any of that," I said. "Don't start blaming yourself for Dad's behavior. Instead of manning up, and doing the right thing, he became an abusive drunk. I understand that what happened sucked, but he still doesn't get a free pass. He was a piece of shit as a father. And I'm still not certain what happened. He leaves to murder someone and Mom winds up dead. There are missing pieces and I'm not letting him off the hook yet."

A droll smile creased Brian's face. "Don't sugarcoat it. Tell me how you really feel."

I slid over on the couch so I was next to him and leaned over and gave him a hug. "Listen to me. This changes nothing between us. We still have a blood bond, but we also have a bond that was forged by a lot of crap, and that bond will never break." I reached into my purse and took out a picture and handed it to him. It was a picture of our mom, lying on her back on the floor, her arms outstretched, holding Brian, who was about nine months old, above her and both of them laughing. "I thought you might like this, to let you know just how much you were loved."

"Where did you get this?" he asked.

"Aunt Maeve. When she thought you were the one coming to visit, she had dug it out to give to you. She asked me to pass it along."

He pulled me in even closer and squeezed me. "Thanks, Sis," he whispered in my ear. When we separated, he looked at the picture, a sad smile forming. "I'll have to go visit Aunt Maeve."

"I'll come with you. She was very good to both of us after Mom disappeared."

He nodded. "Yeah, you're right. She was." He closed his eyes, as if hitting pause before changing subjects. "We need to plan a funeral for Mom. I want the focus to be on her. For once, I want people to remember her, not as some piece of shit who took off on her husband and kids, never to be heard from again, but as a loving and caring woman and mom who was murdered before she ever had a chance to live her life."

"Are you thinking a big public funeral—a funeral befitting the mother of a celebrity?"

He sipped his drink. "I don't know. What do you think?"

My mind instantly turned to Nora and all the publicity that kind of funeral would likely generate—publicity in which I was sure to figure prominently. "Um, I was thinking perhaps a more low-key affair. You know, just immediate family and friends . . ." I paused, the realization of who my brother was suddenly sinking in—for him, just a few friends probably meant half of Hollywood. "I sometimes forget who you are," I said apologetically. "How many of your closest friends do you think would make their way to Harrison for the funeral?"

He shrugged. "Couple hundred, maybe."

"Is that what you want?" I asked.

"No," he snorted. "But let me explain what my life is like. Once I stand next to the DA on Friday and they announce our mom was murdered, all hell will break loose. We could try to do a small funeral with just us, Becca, Nora—but it would never happen. The press will want to be there. The folks in the biz who want to kiss my ass will want to be there. My fear is that it would be a fiasco. I really do think it'll be easier to face it head on and get it over with." He sighed. "I know it's not what you want, because suddenly you'll be all over the news as the transgender sister of Brian Kelly. I really am sorry about that."

He was right; it wasn't what I wanted. But it wasn't about me—I didn't give a shit about me anymore. I was worried for Nora. I explained to Brian how the publicity surrounding me was impacting Nora's life and my concerns this would only add to her angst. "When do you want to do this?" I asked.

"How soon before they release the body to us?"

"I assume now that the DNA testing is complete, whenever we want."

He picked up his phone and scrolled through his calendar. "How's a week from Saturday?"

"Yeah, that works," I said, knowing my social calendar was empty.

Then a sly grin formed on his lips. "I have an idea on how I can make this easier on Nora. Is she a Charlene Fox fan?" he asked, referring to the star of *Madison Rules*, the hottest series on Netflix.

"What thirteen-year-old girl isn't?"

"Char will come if I ask her. I'm sure you don't read the gossip columns, but we're a thing." Seeing my questioning look, he added, "We're friends. Let's just say we're opposite sides of the same coin. We provide each other cover from inquiring minds."

"Okay," I said.

"We just put Nora next to Char for all the public events, and so if there's any pictures of her, Nora's friends will be insanely jealous and forget all about you."

I could already sense that our mother's funeral was going to be an emotional roller coaster for me, so whatever I could do to make it easier for Nora would help. "Thanks. I hope you're right."

He looked at the picture from Aunt Maeve again and then at me. "Do you know who my father is?"

"No. I think Joan knows, but she told me she didn't. But there's a shot we might be able to find out without Joan's help."

"How?"

"Forensic genetic genealogy," I said. "If you remember, I'm working on the Sherry Darling case. The company we hired also does forensic genetic genealogy. Which means they can take your DNA profile and run it through their databases to see if they can find relatives, which might ultimately lead to your father."

"Can't my company out in California do the same thing?"

"Probably," I responded. "But if your profile is related to the searches I've already had done, we won't have to wait months for a result. If you're worried about confidentiality, you can have your DNA profile sent to me anonymously so that your name is never entered in any of the databases."

"You think they'll find who my father is?"

"Yeah, I think there's a good chance."

He stared at me, trying to pierce my façade. "I think you know."

"Honest, I don't. But I do have a hunch. So, have your company send me your results and if I'm right, I'll know within a few days."

He appeared momentarily lost in thought. "Okay, but if it's who you suspect, don't tell me. I'm not sure I want to know until I get through the funeral. It's not like it's going to change anything."

"No problem. When you're ready, just let me know," I said, once again staring into his puppy dog eyes, wondering how much it was going to hurt him if my hunch turned out to be correct.

CHAPTER 37

IT WAS LATE, AND there was almost no traffic on I-46 as I headed back to my apartment from Middletown. Despite my brother's claims that he was fine, in the last forty-eight hours he had learned his mother had been raped, murdered, and that the rapist was his father. That was a lot for anyone to digest. We had ordered room service, and while I stuck with my diet cola, he had gone through several more Manhattans. I knew I couldn't take the place of his therapist, but, after many years as a detective, I had learned the art of listening—so I listened and let him unwind his pain. I'd like to think he was in better shape emotionally when I left, but whether his improved state of mind was from my love or the booze was anyone's guess.

Strangely, I found myself in a better place as well. There was something about people wanting to end my life that tended to refocus me and make me want to keep going. Like Ken Horvath before him, Barry Reed's desire to send me to my grave had shoved my darkest thoughts to the background and motivated me to work harder. There were still missing pieces in both Sherry's and my mother's cases, but things were starting to come together. Because even though their murders were almost twenty years apart, I now saw the possibility that my father was a thread that ran between my mother's death and Sherry's.

Assuming he hadn't killed my mother, my guess was he knew who did. All these years, he had certainly known she was dead. Yet, as best I could tell, he never did anything about it—worse, he had helped cover it up. He had done the same with Sherry. He knew there was DNA that exonerated Riccoli and implicated someone else, yet he never said anything. Perhaps he was just a corrupt cop, but I couldn't help wondering if there was someone or something that had forced him to keep his mouth shut—another link connecting the two cases. Hopefully, I'd have my answers soon.

THURSDAY MORNING, LISA CALLED me to her office and handed me both the DNA results from Sam's spit and the ones that showed who my brother's father was—and there was my common denominator.

"That was fast," I said.

"With the spit they just ran it against what we had already provided from the beer bottle, and there was a match. With your brother's, your hunch was right, so it was just comparing it to what they already had."

I glanced down at the results. *Shit. Sometimes it sucks being right.*

When I looked up, Lisa was staring at me with an expression that was somewhere between a wince and a tight smile. "I know it's been a rough few days for you, but I do have a little good news. The AG's office has approved me taking over both the reopening of the investigation of Detective Hammond's death and the cold case involving Sherry Darling."

"Sherry, too?" I said, surprised. "I didn't even know you were going to ask for Sherry's case."

"They're related," she said. "And this way you don't have to worry about Snyder pulling the plug on you."

"Thanks."

"They also approved Stacy working with you," she added.

"Oh boy. I hope she doesn't regret it."

"I also notified DA Graham that I have an investigation going on that's IA related, but per AG policy, I didn't make him aware of the details or where this may be heading. All he knows is that it's related to your cold case investigation. For now, this is a DCDAO IA investigation. But depending on what happens, the AG's office may step in."

"Got it," I said, grateful she'd been able to pull this off.

Lisa removed her reading glasses and sat them on top of her head. "What did you say to Reed the other night?"

"Why?" I said, puzzled.

"I got a call from his attorney. He'd like to meet with us this afternoon at Reed's hospital room to talk about working out a plea deal."

"Really?" I said, raising an eyebrow.

"Reed may be willing to cooperate. He'll give us a proffer of what his testimony would be, with the usual caveats. We can't use anything he says against him, except on cross should there ever be a trial. He'll give a full taped statement if we're satisfied with the proffer and no deal if his proffer doesn't check out."

"What's he looking for?"

She took a deep breath. "No attempted murder charges. He'll plead to a breaking and entering charge instead. Once we talk to him today, whether we accept the proffer or not, he gets transferred to Highbury University Medical Center—in custody of course, but he recovers from his surgery there, not here. And once he's discharged from the hospital, assuming he hasn't been released on his own recognizance or can't make bail, he'll be held at the Cartwright County Jail."

"So, on his home turf," I said.

"Yeah. For some reason he doesn't feel safe in Donn County," she replied, giving me a knowing look.

"Smart man," I said.

"What do you think?" Lisa asked. "After all, you're the person he tried to kill."

The proffer would give us a preview of what Reed would say if he testified under oath, giving us a chance to check out his version of the events before striking a deal with him. I quickly ran his conditions through my bullshit detector and they didn't pass. I'd only had two interactions with Reed and neither left me convinced he'd be a reliable witness. But, as much as I didn't trust him, he should be able to tell us who sent him after me, and more importantly, he'd have the skinny on what happened in Sherry's case. That, plus the fact that if he lied to us on the proffer, the deal would be off, tipped the scales.

"Here's my thoughts. In return for dropping the attempted murder, he has to plead to burglary. At least with burglary he'd have to worry about getting jail time. With a B&E, since he has no priors, he'll definitely walk. And rather than letting him go to Cartwright County, we offer Memorial Hospital in

Brisbane County and after he's discharged, if he doesn't make bail, he's held at the Brisbane County Jail."

Lisa nodded. "Works for me. If they agree, we'll bring Detective Mills. You can question Reed on the Darling case and she can handle his attack on you. I'll call Ray and give him our counter."

"Ray?" I said. "Who's his attorney?" I asked.

"Ray Ashley."

I shook my head. *You can't make this shit up.*

ASHLEY GREETED US WARMLY when Lisa, Stacy, and I approached Reed's hospital room. He quickly agreed to our counter offer and our insistence that because Reed was still on major painkillers following his surgery, assuming his proffer checked out, we wouldn't do a formal recorded statement until he was off the pain meds. Ashley was so anxious to get Reed out of Harrison General that Lisa wrote out the terms of the proffer letter on a legal pad and she and Ashley signed it.

Two and a half hours later, we walked out into the hallway. Waiting there were sheriff's officers from both Donn County and Brisbane County. Lisa made sure all the transfer paperwork was in order, and signed off on moving Reed to Brisbane County. When that was taken care of, Ashley looked at Lisa. "Could I have your permission to speak privately with Lieutenant Kelly?"

She gave me a wary glance to assess my reaction. I nodded.

Ashley and I walked down the hallway until we were out of earshot. "Look, Lieutenant. I understand that after hearing what my client said he saw your father do, you'd probably like to go to whatever nursing home your father's in and wring his neck."

"Only if I believe your client," I said, trying to mask my disgust.

"Do you?" he asked.

"Frankly, Mr. Ashley, I don't know. We'll need to check and see what we can verify. But if it turns out that what he said about my father is accurate, then you're right about what my reaction will be. But for now, I'll take a wait-and-see approach."

"Fair enough," he said. He paused, tilting his head as if measuring what he wanted to do next. "I remember when we first met, I told you that I thought the information about who paid me to represent Riccoli was privileged. But now that I've had some time to think about it, I've come to the conclusion that it's not. Meaning, I believe I'm ethically free to share what I'm about to tell you because it isn't covered by the attorney–client privilege, or any other privilege that I'm aware of."

He paused.

"In addition to asking me who had paid Riccoli's legal fees, you also asked if I knew who had taken the photos of Riccoli showing that he had no marks on him. I know your father never wanted this information to be public knowledge, but the answer to both questions is your father. On February 27, 2004, your father paid me fifty thousand dollars in cash to represent Riccoli."

My brain momentarily froze. *My father? What?* Somehow, I managed to ask, "Why in God's name would my father pay you to represent Riccoli?"

"From what he told me, because he knew the guy had

been railroaded and he didn't want to be part of seeing him convicted a second time and perhaps executed. That's why he also gave me the pictures of Riccoli." He paused. "And why, after Riccoli was convicted the first time, he had anonymously provided the second set of DNA results to the PD who handled Riccoli's initial appeal. Your father was the one who was instrumental in getting Riccoli's conviction reversed."

Where had my father come up with fifty thousand dollars in cash? No, where the hell had my father gotten a hundred thousand? After all, there was still fifty thousand in his safe. And on top of that, he had turned over the DNA and the photos. My father?

"You look perplexed, Lieutenant."

"I passed perplexed a while ago. I'm having a hard time imagining how my father came up with that kind of money, and that he was responsible for helping Riccoli."

"Where the money came from, I can't help you with. I just wanted you to know what he did. Perhaps it will help . . ." He stopped and rubbed his chin. "I don't know what the right word is—maybe it will help ameliorate your reaction to what Reed said he saw your father do."

I was trying to reconcile these two conflicting portraits of my father, one brutal, the other trying to protect an innocent man.

"Are you saying he took the pictures of Riccoli to protect him?"

"That's what he told me. Obviously, it hadn't worked, because Riccoli had been convicted and the pictures had apparently been," he paused, "*lost*. But he had another copy of them and he gave them to me."

"Why didn't he just come forward and testify then? Based on what Reed just told us, Reed, my father, Snyder, any one of them could have prevented Riccoli from even being indicted."

"I asked him that," Ashley said.

"And?"

"And he gave me a sarcastic laugh. Then he said that the last guy who thought about doing that had allegedly taken his own life. When he said it, he gave me a look indicating it really wasn't a suicide. I assumed he was talking about Detective Hammond," Ashley said.

"Yeah" was all I managed to get out.

When I finished with Ashley, I walked back to where Lisa and Stacy were waiting.

"Everything okay?" Lisa asked.

"No. But Ashley just gave me some information that at least has calmed me down." I explained what he told me about my father. Needless to say, they were both as shocked as I had been.

"Leaving aside your father, do you believe what Reed said?" Lisa asked.

"I have my doubts."

"Why?" Lisa asked.

"Start with his claim that he decided on his own to take me out because he didn't like me sniffing around Sherry's case. According to him, no one else was involved. Sorry, but that just doesn't ring true. Remember, he attacked me when I was staying at my father's house. The fact that I was there had to come from our office because I had provided it to Snyder per office policy. The other thing is Reed claims that Padraig Barr murdered Sherry. Remember Sherry's birth surname was Barr. Padraig was her brother."

"Her brother?" Lisa said.

"Yeah, and Declan Barr is their father," I added. "There's no question that Sherry was disowned by her family, but Padraig killing her feels like a stretch."

I let them digest that for a moment before I laid the final piece of the Barr genealogy on them. "You should also know that there's another Barr brother, Seamus Barr."

"Does he have anything to do with this?" Stacy asked.

"He does, but I don't have a complete picture yet on what his role was. He also changed his name decades ago. We know him as James Barry."

"James Barry?" Lisa said, her face scrunched. "Not our James Barry, the former assistant DA?"

"The one and only," I said. "The former assistant DA who twice was part of the trial team that tried Joseph Riccoli for murder."

"Oh, sweet lord," Lisa said, looking up at the ceiling. "If Padraig did do it, Jimmy prosecuting Riccoli could have been part of a coverup."

We all stood in silence, lost in our own thoughts.

I had to admit, Reed had put together a pretty good story. He gave us a murder case against Padraig, implicated Ron in a conspiracy with one breath and then tried to exculpate him with the next, and handed us an attempted murder case against Elizabeth, knowing that she'd never be charged because of who she was and the fact that she was likely terminally ill. It all felt too easy, too convenient. Or had I become so blinded by trying to take down Furst that I refused to see what was right in front of me? Sherry, like so many other murder victims, was killed by a family member.

Lisa's face told me that she was wondering the same thing—was I not seeing the forest for the trees? I needed to reassure her, and myself, that finding Sherry's killer, even if it was her brother, was my only priority. "Assuming Reed is telling the truth, we still need corroboration."

The doubt in Lisa's eyes faded. "Okay. Who do you want to talk to next? Sam, Ron, Elizabeth, Captain Snyder, or Jimmy Barry?" she asked, laying out our options.

"Elizabeth," I said without hesitation. "If Reed is telling us the truth, and she didn't kill Sherry, maybe she'll confirm it was Padraig. But if Reed is protecting her, or Ron . . . well, let's hope that, faced with her own mortality, she'll want to unburden herself and let us know what really happened."

"When?" Lisa asked.

"Tomorrow, right after they announce that Jane Doe is my mom."

Stacy winced. "Are you sure you're going to be in the right frame of mind to interrogate someone tomorrow?"

I nodded. "I'll be in the perfect state of mind—pissed off."

I looked at Lisa and drew in a deep breath. Ashley's recounting of my father's comment about Tom Hammond, together with Joan's certainty that Tom had been murdered, had suddenly raised a question. "Could I ask you to do one thing this afternoon?"

"What's that?"

"Can you inspect the inventory records for the serial numbers for the weapons issued to Tom Hammond, Barry Reed, Francis Kelly, and Captain Snyder in 2004 when Hammond was shot?"

"Okay. I should be able to get that info from Julie Palmer."

I shook my head. "No. You need to look at the paperwork. The office switched to nine-millimeter Glocks in around 1995. That was before the records of the serial numbers for everyone's weapons were computerized in 2007. Before then, the records were typed. I need you to see if any of the serial numbers were changed. If they were, they probably would have used Wite-Out back in those days. You know, cover over the number and then type over it."

She gave me a quizzical look. "What are you thinking?"

"That maybe the gun used to shoot Hammond wasn't his, but someone changed the serial number on the records so that it looked like it was Hammond's gun."

"You think someone murdered him?"

"Someone tried to kill me—why not Hammond?"

The doubt I had when Joan first told me was gone.

I HEADED BACK TO the office. A few details in Reed's statement had set off alarm bells, but the first thing I did was pull up Padraig Barr's rap sheet. I thought I had seen something when I looked at it the other day that was relevant to Reed's statement. A quick check confirmed something was off. Next, I turned my focus to the conversation Reed claimed he'd had with Sam Furst about what happened the night Sherry was murdered. I took out my notes of the interview and read through them.

According to Reed, he had known Sam Furst since they were kids. Sam told Reed that when his dad (Ron Furst) learned that Sherry appeared on The Michael Dobbs Show, he panicked because Sherry was a whore.

He was convinced she was going to blackmail him because he didn't know she was trans. According to Sam, his father called Declan Barr, who he had a long-standing relationship with. The plan was that Barr would have his son Padraig and Sam wait for Sherry outside the condo and when she was leaving, they'd snatch her and Barr would "deal with her." Because Reed was both a longtime friend and a detective at the DCDAO, Sam asked him to keep an eye on the place when everything went down to make sure nothing went wrong. According to Reed, he had no idea that Barr planned on killing Sherry. If he had known, he would never have agreed. He thought they were just going to put the fear of God into her. Unbeknownst to everyone, Elizabeth Furst had hired a PI to follow Ron and he had determined that Ron was meeting a woman at the condo every Thursday night while she was at bridge. The night they were going to snatch Sherry, Elizabeth showed up at the condo. Since they already were waiting outside the condo, Sam and Barr saw Elizabeth go in and they quickly went in after her. When Reed saw what was happening, he also ran into the condo. By the time they got to the bedroom, Elizabeth had already stabbed Ron. Reed and Sam managed to pull Elizabeth off Ron and they took her into an adjoining room. Ron was freaking out because he was bleeding like a stuck pig. Sherry had some defensive wounds, but wasn't in bad shape. Sam decided to get his mother out of there. As Sam was leaving, they heard Padraig calling Sherry a

*faggot whore and just losing his shit on her. Reed said
when he turned around, he saw Padraig grab Sherry
and cut her throat.*

I locked my notes in my desk, still unconvinced Barr would
be so furious with his own sibling that he'd kill her. Even more
troubling was that according to Padraig Barr's rap sheet he was
locked up the night Sherry was murdered. So, either the rap
sheet was wrong—or Reed was lying.

Before I left to meet Brian for dinner, I opened Becca's
email from Tuesday to see what she had learned about James
Barry. When I finished, I knew Barry's legal career was over.
What I needed to figure out now was how to use the information she had found to my advantage.

CHAPTER 38

I WATCHED THE NEWS conference alone, and quietly wept for the woman I had barely known. Brian stood stoically as the DA from Brisbane County announced that a body discovered forty years ago had been identified as Maureen Kelly, the wife of former Donn County Detective Sergeant Francis Kelly and the mother of Brian Kelly and Lieutenant Lauren Kelly of the Donn County DA's office. Morocco then described how the body had been found in a shallow grave in a wooded area of Brisbane County and that his office was working closely on some promising leads with detectives from Donn County, where Maureen had lived and was last seen alive.

Brian spoke after Morocco finished and, with the cameras flashing, he thanked everyone from Brisbane County for their efforts in bringing his family some closure after all these years.

After the news conference, Stacy, Lisa, and I gathered in Lisa's office before heading out. "You sure you want to do this?" Lisa asked. "We don't have to do this today."

I nodded. "I'm fine," I lied.

Lisa took a manila file folder out of her briefcase. "Your hunch was right. The serial numbers for the guns for two detectives had been Wited-Out and new numbers typed in."

I looked at her. "Hammond and . . ."

"Reed," she said. "He lied to us yesterday. I spoke with Paul Morocco before the press conference. I'm having the AG's office put some plainclothes folks on the floor Reed's on at Memorial Hospital to keep an eye on him. I also alerted Ashley that we suspect his client lied, but I didn't give him the specifics."

It was time to go visit Elizabeth Furst.

WHEN THE ELEVATOR DOORS opened on the fourth floor, I was struck by the odor that seemed to permeate all hospitals—disinfectant mixing with the smells of disease and decay. Stacy and I made our way to the nurses' station, showed our credentials, and were directed to Elizabeth Furst's room. If my hunch was correct, our checking in had just started the clock running. Assuming she'd even talk to us, we'd have approximately ten to fifteen minutes until either a lawyer, a cop, or both showed up to shut down any discussion with Ms. Furst.

As one would expect of the county executive's wife, Elizabeth had a private room far from the noise and chaos around the nurses' station. I knocked on the open door. "Ms. Furst?"

"Yes?" a voice called out in a timbre stronger than I expected.

I motioned to Stacy and we entered the room, closing the door behind us. A woman was reclining in a hospital bed, the back of the bed raised so she was in a sitting position. It took me a moment to recognize Elizabeth. In all the pictures I had seen of her, she had beautiful, long blond hair that hung to her shoulders and her makeup always looked like it was professionally done. Today she wore no makeup, and her skin tone resembled the hue of old paste—a color that probably didn't exist on any makeup chart. Her once-glorious tresses now consisted of spiky gray hair that looked like she was auditioning for a punk band.

"Can I help you?" she asked.

"Good morning, ma'am. My name is Lieutenant Lauren Kelly and this is Detective Stacy Mills," I said as we both held our IDs out in front of us. "We're from the Donn County DA's Office and we'd like to ask you some questions."

"About?"

"It's about the murder of Sherry Darling. Although when the case was brought, she was referred to as Owen Barr. But before I ask you anything, I want to provide you with your rights."

"My rights!" she said, clearly taken aback. "Do you have any idea of who I am?"

"I do, ma'am. You're the wife of County Executive Ronald Furst, and you're a suspect in the murder of Sherry Darling."

I expected the next words out of her mouth to be "I want a lawyer," but instead her eyes narrowed and she said, "Let me see your ID again."

I approached the bed and handed her my credentials. When she finished, she peered back at me with an expression I couldn't place. It was no longer anger or indignation—it appeared to be a look of recognition, like seeing someone for the first time in years. "Frank Kelly's your father," she said. "I saw your brother on the news this morning."

"Half brother," I corrected.

Her eyes went wide. There are times in this profession when you know you've totally sucker punched a suspect—this was one of those times.

"Yes, Ms. Furst. I know who my brother's father is, and while at the present time you are not a suspect in the murder of my mother, Maureen Kelly, you may be a witness who can provide valuable information. So, we'll be questioning you on that as well."

The air seemed to come out of her, and her defiance slipped away. "I don't . . . I-I-," she stammered.

Stacy handed me a portable digital recorder, which I placed on the hospital table next to the bed and hit record. "Ms. Furst, as you can see, we are recording this conversation. You have the right to remain silent," I began, running through the rights that had become ubiquitous to anyone who watched any crime drama on television. "Do you understand these rights?" I asked when I finished.

"Yes," she said, her voice barely above a whisper. "Do you know I have terminal cancer?"

"I'm truly sorry to hear that, Ms. Furst. Does your medical condition, or any medication you're on, impact in any way your ability to understand or answer my questions or to tell the truth?"

"No," she said.

"Do you wish to waive the rights I just read to you and answer our questions?" I asked, holding my breath as she pondered her response.

"What do you want to know?"

"I need you to sign this," I said, taking a waiver form from Stacy, placing it on the hospital table and rolling it over. "I need you to initial that you've been given your rights, and then sign here to indicate you're waiving your rights."

I handed her a pen and watched as she initialed and signed the form. I took the form from her and handed it back to Stacy.

"Ms. Furst, for the record, do you acknowledge that you've voluntarily waived your right to remain silent and have agreed to answer our questions?"

"Yes."

"So that we're clear about who we're talking about, I am going to refer to the victim as Sherry Darling. Do you understand that Sherry Darling was also referred to as Owen Barr?"

"I do," she said, her eyes focused on the table across her lap.

"Let me start by telling you that our investigation has determined that when the victim's body was discovered on the morning of April 13, 2001, your DNA was found in skin cells that were under the fingernails of the victim. The coroner estimated that the victim was murdered the night before, April 12, 2001." I watched for changes in her body language, but she had no reaction. "Do you have an explanation for how your cells wound up under the victim's fingernails?"

"She scratched me," she answered, without emotion and using the correct pronouns.

"Where were you when she scratched you?"

Her eyes searched mine, but again, to my surprise, she didn't say the magic words—"I want a lawyer." "We were . . . it was in the bedroom of a condo my husband and I owned in Harrison," she said, a quiver in her voice.

"Why did she scratch you?"

"Because . . . because she was trying to get away from the knife I was wielding to try and kill my husband."

"And why were you trying to kill him?"

"Because I was fed up with him cheating on me, and this time I caught him red-handed with this—this Sherry person."

"Where were you before you found them in the condo?"

Suddenly, the door to her room flew open. Both Stacy and I spun around. Two Harrison police officers hurried into the room—followed by Ronald Furst.

"What the fuck do you think you're doing?" a red-faced Furst screamed.

"Sir," I said to Furst. "I know who you are, and right now you are interfering with an official investigation of the Donn County District Attorney's Office—an investigation in which you are a target. I am advising you, and the officers, to leave the room immediately or face charges for obstructing an official investigation."

"Who the hell do you think you're talking to?" he spit out, taking a step in my direction.

"I think I'm talking to a suspect in a murder investigation, and if you come any closer, I will have no alternative but to arrest you for interfering with that investigation."

I turned to face the two officers. "I am ordering you to escort Mr. Furst out into the hallway. If you don't, I will call for backup and I will have you charged with disobeying a lawful order."

The cops looked at each other, unsure what to do.

"Now! That's an order," I demanded as forcefully as I could.

After several seconds, one of the officers stepped forward. "Mr. Furst, sir," he said haltingly. "Let's go out in the hallway, and I'll call the watch commander for advice. The lieutenant is the ranking officer in the room, sir," he said with a nod in my direction.

Furst glared at me, a flash of recognition crossing his face. "You," he spit out. "We should have fired your ass years ago." His mouth tightened. "I don't give a shit who your brother is, you're going to rue the day you fucked with me."

This time I took a step toward him, my eyes fixed on his. "Do what you gotta do, Mr. Furst. Just be aware that I know you raped my mother, and you're my half brother's father."

He inhaled sharply and his body stiffened.

"I'll be interviewing you very shortly, Mr. Furst, and I promise to show you the DNA evidence establishing paternity. But for now, either get out of the room or I will place you under arrest."

Furst staggered a few steps backward as if he had been pushed. The officer next to him grabbed his arm to steady him. For the first time, he seemed to see his wife in the hospital bed. "You keep your mouth shut. You hear me, Eliza? Tell her nothing. Your lawyer is on his way."

As I pulled my jacket back and reached for the handcuffs on my belt, I sensed Stacy moving into position behind me in case things became physical.

"Mr. Furst, let's go out into the hallway. Please, sir," the officer who had him by the arm said.

Furst's eyes locked onto mine. "You're done," he said. "You fucked with the wrong person."

"We'll see," I said, watching as the officer turned him around and escorted him out of the room.

When I turned back to Elizabeth, I wasn't sure what to expect after her husband's outburst. "Are you okay?"

"Yes," she said, her eyes on the door.

"You ready to continue?"

"I . . . I think I better wait for my lawyer."

Shit. She had been right there. I was finally about to hear what happened to Sherry—what *really* happened to her—and now I had to stop. "That's your right," I replied, my frustration evident.

I was just about to start packing up, when she said, "I knew your mother."

"I'm sorry?" I said, caught off guard.

"Your mother—we knew each other."

"Ms. Furst, you've asked to see your lawyer. I can't talk to you anymore."

"But this isn't about Sherry whoever, it's about your mom."

"I understand, but we still shouldn't talk about it because that's also the subject of an ongoing investigation and I don't know what role, if any, you had."

"I saw the press conference. Don't you want to know what happened to her?"

I did a quick review of what they had taught us about Miranda rights. Although I thought I was safe questioning her because, at least at this point, she wasn't a suspect, I decided the safer course was to re-Mirandize her and protect any statement she might give from being suppressed.

"Of course, I do," I said.

I probably set a record for how quickly I redelivered her rights to her and the speed of having her waive. My heart was pounding, hoping her lawyer wasn't going to burst through the door and end the interview.

"You said you knew my mother."

"I did. I met her several times when she worked for the county. She worked in the same office as my husband, so I'd see her when I went to his office. And then . . . well, after he assaulted her at the Christmas party, and she found out she was pregnant, she came to me and told me what had happened." Elizabeth's calm and candor stunned me. Without any prompting, she was giving me everything. "Your mother wanted to go to the police, but she was afraid of my husband—as she should have been. Even then, my husband was powerful, but it was his father, Otto, that I truly feared. I . . . I told her that I'd help her get an abortion, but that I didn't think it was smart for her to go to the police because they'd never believe her." Elizabeth paused, pulled a tissue from a box, and blew her nose. "Your mother thanked me, but said that because she was Catholic, she didn't think she could get an abortion."

I momentarily considered if I should let Stacy take over—this was after all about the murder of my mother. I didn't want to do anything to jeopardize the investigation. But what was building had the feel of an intimate conversation between the two of us rather than an interrogation, and I needed her to finish. "What happened after that?" I asked.

"I hadn't seen your mother for a while, but the day she di . . . was murdered, she called me. She was hysterical. She had come home from the grocery store, and Frank was waiting for her. He had found out that Brian wasn't his child. When he confronted her, she . . . she told him that she had been raped at a Christmas party by my husband." Elizabeth stopped, her face contorting with anguish. "Frank had then stormed out of the house and his parting words were 'I'm going to kill that son of a bitch.' Your mother didn't care about Ron—she probably would've been happy if he was dead, but she didn't want Frank to spend the rest of his life in jail, or be executed, for murder." Elizabeth hesitated, took a sip of water, and drew in a deep breath. "At the time, Ron was working for his father's real estate company, Furst Realty." She stopped and looked up at me, her eyes filled with remorse. "I made several mistakes that day, Lieutenant," she said softly. "The first was telling your mother where the offices were. The second was calling Ron and warning him Frank was on his way to kill him."

There was a knock on the door and a man entered. When he saw me, he stopped. "I'm P. Jamison Coffler, Mrs. Furst's attorney, and I demand that this questioning cease immediately."

I looked from Coffler to Furst, wondering what she was going to do.

"Jay, you're not a criminal lawyer. Be quiet and take a seat. It'll do you good to hear this," she said, her tone as dismissive as her words.

Coffler seemed stunned by his client's rebuff, but dutifully made his way to a chair at the side of the bed.

Elizabeth turned her attention back to me. "After I called Ron, I decided to go to the offices, hoping to head your mother off and send her home. When I got there, Frank, Ron, Ron's father Otto, and Declan Barr were in the office. At the time Declan was Otto's muscle, and he had a gun trained on Frank." She hesitated, shaking her head. "Oh God, that's when I made my worst mistake." She closed her eyes, folded her hands, and placed them on the tray in front of her. "I wish I could redo things."

"Eliza, take a break," Coffler interjected, rising from his chair.

"No," she whispered. "She's waited forty years for answers. She has a right to know."

I'm sure Coffler had no idea what was going on, but he sat back down.

"I told them that your mother was on her way." Elizabeth's eyes locked onto mine and I saw the tears gathering. "I was young, naïve, and at that point, even though I knew he was evil, I truly had no idea what my father-in-law was capable of. But when he heard what I said, he nodded to Barr, and said 'Take care of it.' Barr walked over to your father, still pointing the gun at him, and took your father's weapon from his holster. Barr then walked back to Otto and handed him his gun, keeping your father's gun, and walked out of the room." Elizabeth sobbed, and choked out, "Oh God, I'm so sorry."

Declan—the gun—my father—Otto and Ron—it all made heartbreaking sense now.

"It's okay," I said, barely keeping my own roiling emotions in check. "What happened next?" I managed to ask.

She took a sip of water from the cup on the hospital table. "I . . . I don't know how long passed. Maybe it was five or ten minutes, but the four of us in the room were just looking at each other. Then—then we heard a muffled noise. At first, I didn't know what it was," she said, her hands gripping the sides of the hospital table as if she was holding on for support. "But a few minutes later Barr walked back in, nodded to Otto, handed him Frank's gun, and put something else in Otto's hand. That's when I realized that the sound had been a gun. And I knew . . ." She sniffled as she struggled to hold her emotions in check.

"Eliza, as your lawyer I'm telling you to stop," Coffler said.

"No!" she said, turning toward her attorney. "I'm dying, Jay. I need to finish. I've lived with this long enough. I need to do this for me too."

She drew in a deep breath, trying to compose herself. "Otto handed Barr's gun back to him and Barr left. Otto then turned to your father and told him that even though it was Ron who had screwed up, he couldn't trust your mother to keep her mouth shut and, if she talked, she could've ruined not only Ron's life, but his as well. He then looked at your father and said something like 'Here's the deal. Tomorrow, you report your gun missing, but we all know where it is. Should you try to report what happened to your wife, ballistics will show she was shot with your gun. Husband finds out his wife had a child fathered by another man, becomes incensed and murders his wife. Everyone in this room will testify you were crazy with rage at your wife's infidelity.'"

She paused, grabbing a tissue and wiping her eyes. "Otto then walked behind his desk and opened one of the drawers, took out several stacks of cash, put them in a bag, and walked back over to your father. I can still hear Otto; he was so matter-of-fact. He looked your father right in the eyes and said, 'Infidelity, Frank. It's terrible, but it happens every day.' He then suggested that if your father was smart, the story he was going to tell was that his wife ran off with another man, leaving him to raise two young boys. As an incentive for Frank to keep his mouth shut, Otto said he was giving your father money to cover child support for the child who wasn't his, and as compensation for his loss. He told your father there was a hundred thousand dollars in the bag, and handed it to your father." She paused, and gave a moan like a wounded animal.

"Eliza," Coffler said in a whisper.

She shook her head. "Otto then warned your father that if he didn't go along, Otto would see to it that not only would he be convicted of murdering his wife, but he would make sure that you and your brother suffered horrible deaths. He then told your father to put his hand out, and he dropped your mother's wedding and engagement rings into his palm." She took another drink from her water cup, then her shoulders drooped. "Since then, first Otto, then Ron, used that gun to blackmail your father into silence and doing whatever they needed. It sits in my husband's gun cabinet to this day."

"You never told anyone about the rape or the murder?" I asked.

She looked up at me. "My son was the same age as you. I . . . I didn't know what to do. I had just seen him order the murder of your mother. I was terrified, Lieutenant. So no, I never told anyone—until now."

The room fell silent. I suddenly felt Stacy's hand gently rubbing my back, unseen by Elizabeth and Coffler. So many things now made sense. The money my father had; his anger and resentment at the world, and specifically toward Brian; his drinking; and his silence about the truth—a silence forged, at least in his mind, in a desire to protect us. It didn't excuse him, but it did explain him.

"I've carried this with me for forty years, Lieutenant," she said, her voice catching. "I know nothing can change what happened, but—your mother was a good woman, who didn't deserve what happened. I don't know if I'll live long enough, but if by telling the truth about what happened that day, I can help undo any of the harm I've caused to you and your family, I will."

"Thank you, Ms. Furst, I truly appreciate that."

I turned to Coffler. "Mr. Coffler, before you arrived, I was questioning Ms. Furst about the murder twenty years ago of Sherry Darling, whose birth name was Owen Barr. At some point during that questioning, she invoked her right to counsel. I'd like to continue that questioning, but obviously must respect her right to counsel. What I would suggest is that you take whatever time you need to speak with your client. In the meantime, we'll head to the cafeteria for a cup of coffee." I retrieved a business card from my pocket and handed it to him. "My cell number is on the card. When Ms. Furst decides what she wants to do, call me or text me. If she wants to give a statement, we'll come back up and resume. If she wants to continue with her right to remain silent, we'll leave."

When Stacy and I walked out into the hallway, Lisa, who had followed us to the hospital, was standing there. She took one look at me and asked if I was okay. Emotionally, I felt like I had been run over by a truck, but there wasn't a doubt in my mind that everything Elizabeth Furst had said was the God's honest truth. It hurt like hell, but at least now I knew.

"Yeah. I'm okay," I managed. "Stacy and I can fill you in."

"And I'll fill you in on the fireworks you missed," Lisa said.

When Stacy and I gave her a blank look, she continued. "A little while ago, Ron Furst came back with the DA, the chief, and the deputy chief. They were about to go into the room when I stopped them. DA Graham was pretty bent out of shape, until I reminded him this was part of my investigation, authorized by the attorney general."

"Sorry I missed it," I said.

"Don't worry, you get a chance. As soon as we're done here, Harrison wants us in his office with a tape of Elizabeth's interview."

We headed down to the hospital cafeteria and grabbed a table in the corner. Stacy and I then filled Lisa in on what Elizabeth had told us about my mother's murder. Within minutes, Lisa had Morocco and Assistant Attorney General Wanda Black on the line, explaining what we learned from Elizabeth and discussing the jurisdictional issues, the murder having taken place in Donn County, while the body had been disposed of in Brisbane County. Given the political implications of an investigation focused on Otto and Ron Furst, Black deputized Morocco to proceed on behalf of the state. Morocco then conferenced Stacy in with a detective from his office so that Stacy could provide the information needed for a judge to grant a very limited search warrant on the Furst residence for the weapon allegedly used to murder my mother. Lisa then had one of the detectives assigned to her IA unit go to Furst's house to ensure no one entered until the detectives from the Brisbane DA's office showed up with the search warrant.

When everything was done, Stacy turned to me and said, "How you doing, LT?"

My head was swimming, and I was desperately trying to refocus. "I don't know, Stace. I don't think it's all really sunk in yet. I feel like everything is happening so fast, I can't process it."

"Maybe you should call it a day, Lauren," Lisa said, her concern etched in her furrowed brow.

I closed my eyes and did some deep breathing I had learned in therapy. I needed to see this through.

"I'll be okay," I said after a few minutes. "Besides, there's some things I haven't had time to share with either of you yet."

"Like?" Lisa asked.

"Yesterday after we interviewed Reed, I double-checked Padraig Barr's rap sheet. If those records are accurate, he couldn't have murdered Sherry. He had been arrested on April 11, 2001, and was still being held at the Donn County Jail the night of April 12, 2001. He was bailed out by his mother the afternoon of April 13. So, either Reed lied to us or the jail records are incorrect. Regardless, I still have serious doubts about Padraig Barr killing his sister."

"Interesting," Stacy said. "What was he locked up for?"

I shook my head. "Promoting prostitution. He later pled guilty to pimping out of a gay bar in Harrison called The Hawk—a club where Sherry performed in a drag show on weekends." I hesitated. "This last part is a bit of speculation on my part, but Riccoli told me that Sherry was splitting what Furst paid her with someone. I'm wondering if maybe Padraig was the one who had set Sherry up with Furst."

My cell phone vibrated and I saw it was a text from Coffler. "Interview's over," I said. "They want time to speak with a criminal attorney since Coffler's specialty is family law."

"Family law?" Lisa said.

"That's what he said," I replied, turning my hands palms up. "Maybe she and Ron are having matrimonial issues?"

No one said anything for several seconds. "We need to go see DA Graham," Lisa reminded me.

"Yeah. And after that, I want a crack at Captain Snyder," I offered, still convinced Barry Reed hadn't lied about everything.

CHAPTER 39

I DIDN'T KNOW WHAT to expect from Harrison Graham. He could be a bit of a dick, and he was as conservative as anyone in Donn County, but he never struck me as stupid. After he listened to the recording of the interrogation of Elizabeth Furst, and we filled him in on what we had on Reed, Graham proved me right. He knew the shit was going to hit the fan and he wanted to be standing behind the fan with Lisa and me, and not in front of it. Just as the recording ended, his secretary buzzed him to let him know that Ron Furst was on the line.

"Harrison," Lisa said, "before you pick up, you should know that the Brisbane County DA's Office has obtained a search warrant for Mr. Furst's home."

Having just heard the part of the recording where Elizabeth volunteered that my father's Colt .38 Detective Special snub-nose revolver was in the display of unique handguns located in Ron's study, he didn't need Lisa to say more.

As further proof that Graham knew where things were

headed, he answered with the speaker on so Lisa and I could hear it.

"Harrison, I got a call from my housekeeper telling me that there were cops at my house, so I headed there immediately. When I got here, I was told I couldn't go in because the DA's office was going to be executing a search warrant. What the hell are you doing?"

"Ron, it's not my office that has the search warrant. It's Brisbane County, in connection with the murder of Maureen Kelly. It was on the news this morning."

The silence from the other end was deafening.

"I have to go," Furst finally said. "My lawyer just arrived."

Graham then called his secretary. "Call Captain Snyder and tell him I need him in my office. Also get hold of Lieutenant Larry Conover, I'm going to need a union rep here."

When Larry Conover arrived, Graham directed him to a seat opposite me. Five minutes later there was a knock.

Snyder froze as soon as he saw Conover, Lisa, and me at the table. "Come in, Rich, and have a seat," Graham said, motioning to a chair opposite Lisa.

"Captain," Lisa began, "you are the subject of a criminal investigation. This meeting is being recorded," she said with a nod to the recorder in the middle of the table. "Accordingly, Lieutenant Kelly is going to provide you with your Miranda rights."

After I read him his rights and he acknowledged receiving them, Snyder looked at Lisa and me. "What am I being investigated for?" he asked.

"Criminally, conspiracy to murder Detective Thomas Hammond and conspiracy to murder Lieutenant Kelly. Internally, obstruction of justice in the investigation of the murder of Owen Barr, a.k.a. Sherry Darling," Lisa said.

"Oh, for God's sake, no," he said, shaking his head. "You can't be serious. You've got this all wrong."

"Captain," Lisa interrupted. "Before you make any statements, sitting next to you is Lieutenant Conover, who is here as your union representative for the superior officers' union. Should you decide to invoke your Fifth Amendment right to remain silent, which you have a constitutional right to do, I am advising you that in addition to the criminal investigation, you are the subject of an internal affairs investigation. As you are aware, under the law you are obligated to answer questions in connection with the IA investigation even if you invoke your Fifth Amendment privilege against self-incrimination. However, any statement you give in connection with the IA cannot be used against you in the criminal investigation."

Snyder was smart, and after almost thirty years in law enforcement he knew the drill. Take the Fifth, but answer the IA questions. That way you got the benefit of getting your story out, while knowing it couldn't be used to prosecute you. Plus, they couldn't fire you for refusing to cooperate with the IA. And that's what Snyder did.

With the preliminaries out of the way, Lisa asked, "You said we have it all wrong. What do we have wrong, Captain?"

"Tommy Hammond was a great guy, and a friend. I don't know why he took his own life, but murder—I don't know what the hell you're talking about."

"Let me see if this helps your recollection." I proceeded to lay out what Tom Hammond had told his wife about the conversation in his office with my father. "Is it accurate that you heard my father talking to Tommy about the DNA in the Riccoli case?"

"It is."

"What did you do after that?"

Snyder sighed. "The first thing I did was go to find the file. Nothing was computerized back then and Jimmy Barry had it in his office to work it up for retrial. I asked him if I could look through it. He asked me what I was looking for and I told him I had overheard Kelly telling Hammond about additional DNA results. I looked through the file and didn't see anything that hadn't been turned over. Then I went to see Reed and asked him if he knew what Kelly was talking about. He said no, and suggested that Kelly had probably been drinking at lunch again. That was it."

"When you overheard my father bitching to Tom Hammond about Barry hiding the DNA evidence, did you make any assumptions about who my father was referring to?"

Snyder gave me a puzzled look. "Yeah, since the DNA results had been sent back to Barry Reed, I assumed that's who your father meant."

"Is it possible that my father was referring to Assistant DA James Barry?" I asked.

He went to say something, then stopped, his mouth open like a trout waiting to be hooked. "Yeah. I guess that's possible," he finally said, a question mark hovering over his words.

"Isn't it true that Assistant DA Barry was calling the shots on this case?"

Snyder appeared momentarily lost in thought. "Yeah," he mumbled.

"What happened at the meeting at the old Narcotics Unit that night?" I asked.

"What are you talking about? There was no meeting that night."

"You didn't get a call from Jimmy Barry or Vincent Chrystal to be at a meeting at the Narcotics Unit offices to discuss the retrial?"

"No," Snyder said, shaking his head. "There was no meeting."

"What about meeting at the Elks for a drink that night?" I asked.

"No. I know Tommy was found in the Elks' parking lot, but I assumed he went there because it was deserted—the Elks was closed for a few weeks for renovations. I'm not sure what time it was, but at some point, I got the call there was an officer down at the Elks. By the time I got there, the crime scene folks were all over the place. They told me that Tommy had shot himself. From there I headed to the hospital. Like I told you, Tommy was a friend. To this day, I don't know why he did what he did."

"Other than the original DNA on the semen, did you receive or see any other DNA results from the lab in the Barr case?"

"No. Like I told you, when I overheard Kelly bitching, I went and looked and couldn't find anything. I didn't even know about the results that surfaced after Riccoli was convicted. I'd never seen them before that. Reed was in charge of them."

"How come?" I asked. "If you were the lead, why weren't all lab results going to you?"

"Usually, they did. But after we got the results back on the semen, we indicted Riccoli. After that, Jimmy, I mean Assistant DA James Barry, told me he needed me working on other things for the trial and he said Reed would handle the lab results." His expression suggested he was starting to connect the dots.

"Are you aware that there was a third set of DNA results that were never disclosed?" I asked.

Snyder's head moved back, and his eyes narrowed into a squint. "Third set? No. There were no other DNA results. I checked the file."

A good liar can look you in the eye and tell you whatever they want and be so sincere you want to believe them. A bad liar trips all over themselves trying to stay ahead of you. Snyder was either a good liar or telling the truth. His credibility was also helped because I knew that when I had pulled the original file there were no results in there.

"What do you know about Reed trying to kill Lieutenant Kelly?" Lisa asked, shifting gears on him.

"You can't be serious. You think I had something to do with that?" Snyder asked incredulously.

"You want us to believe it was just a coincidence that Reed came after Lieutenant Kelly right after you confronted her about the security guard at the nursing home alerting you to her talking to her father about the Sherry Darling case?" Lisa fired back.

Snyder moved his gaze from Lisa to me and then back to Lisa. "Look, it's no secret that I thought we should have fired Kelly the day he started telling everyone he was a woman."

"You mean she," Lisa interrupted.

"What?" Snyder said.

"You just referred to Lieutenant Kelly as he. I presume you misspoke."

"Yeah. Whatever. Look, from my perspective we're a law enforcement agency, not a mental health clinic. So, I would've fired . . . *her*. On top of that, I didn't think she deserved the promotion and I was livid when they put her under my command. And of course, what's the first thing she does? Reopens a case involving another tranny. I needed this crap like a hole in the head. But when Lieutenant Kelly first paid Reed a visit and then was overheard questioning her father, I got a call from the chief saying that 'folks'—the chief's word, not mine—weren't happy Kelly was sniffing around this case and they wanted the investigation closed. I was just doing what I was told to do—shutting it down."

Lisa gave me a nod. My turn again.

"Tell me, Captain, at any point in time on the night Sherry Darling was murdered, did you go to a condo owned by Ron and Elizabeth Furst?" I asked.

Snyder shifted uncomfortably in his chair and his face reddened. I suspected that under different circumstances he'd have been halfway across the table trying to get his hands on me, because he was about to put himself in the soup and he knew it. "I want to speak privately with my union rep."

"Captain, you're free to speak to Lieutenant Conover, but regardless, you're obligated to cooperate and tell the truth," Lisa said.

"Let me see if I can help you along, Captain," I said. Then, even though I knew Reed had lied to us, I laid out those portions of what he said that I thought were accurate, knowing

Snyder wouldn't hesitate to pounce on me if I got something wrong.

"Around ten thirty P.M. that night, you got an urgent call from Reed to come to the condo owned by the Fursts. When you got there, Reed, Sergeant Kelly, the chief of Harrison PD, Ron Furst's chief of staff, and Furst's doctor were already there. The room was covered in blood. There was a dead body lying on the floor and Furst had some pretty serious cuts—so serious they needed to get him to a hospital because his doctor was afraid he was going to bleed out. Everyone agreed that the story would be that Furst had accidentally cut himself while using a power saw. Do I have it right so far, Captain?"

He rubbed his eyes, then ran his hands down the sides of his face. "Yeah," he said, his voice barely audible.

"Reed was the first there," I continued, "and Ron Furst had told him to get my father there. My father figured that they could fix it so that if anyone was called in to investigate, my father's squad would get the call. His squad was Reed, you, and Hammond. But Hammond was never called to the scene. Why was that?"

"Kelly said he didn't want Hammond called. I got the sense that something had happened between Kelly and Hammond, but I never knew what it was."

I speculated that it had something to do with my father's drunken ramblings to Hammond that my mother had died, but I'd never know for sure.

"Did you ask anyone what had happened?"

"Yeah, of course. There was a dead body lying on the floor and the county executive looked like he was about to bleed out."

"What did they tell you?"

"Everyone just kind of looked back and forth at each other. Finally, Kelly motioned toward the body and said, 'She broke in with a knife, cut up the county exec, and then slit her throat.'"

"Based on the scene in front of you, and the way people were acting, did you believe what Sergeant Kelly told you?"

"I didn't."

"Did you follow up to see what really happened?"

"No. I didn't want to know."

I raised an eyebrow, but I knew it got worse, so I moved on. "What happened next?"

Snyder glanced nervously around the table, shook his head, and sighed. "After they left to take Furst to the hospital, me, Reed, and Kelly just kind of stared at each other until Kelly finally said, 'I guess the son of a bitch expects us to clean up his mess.' We all put on nitrile gloves and gathered up sheets, towels, bedding—anything that had blood on it—and stuffed them into black garbage bags that the chief of staff had gotten for us before he left. The victim was lying on an area rug. Up until then, based on the long blond hair and clothing, we assumed the victim was a woman. We agreed we'd strip the remaining clothes off the body in case there was any DNA on the clothes, put the body in a couple of trash bags, dispose of it, and then take the clothes, rug, and other bloody stuff to dump somewhere else. When Kelly flipped the body over, we saw that the victim was a man dressed as a woman."

I wanted to scream "She was a transgender woman!" but I swallowed the words. I didn't want to risk stopping him now.

Snyder's gaze settled on me, a look of disdain solidifying

on his face. "When Kelly saw it was a guy, he totally lost it. He started calling him a fucking faggot. Screaming that he got what he deserved, just really railing on the guy. Then he walked over where the knife was lying on the floor, picked it up, walked back to the corpse and . . ." He hesitated. "He . . . he cut off the victim's scrotum and penis," he said, his eyes never leaving mine.

There it was—the one thing I had hoped Reed had lied about, and Snyder just confirmed it was true. The mutilation had been done in a fit of rage by my very homophobic and transphobic father. All this time, everyone assumed Sherry had been murdered because she was trans. I still didn't know who killed her—Elizabeth, Ron, Sam, Reed, or Padraig—but I was no longer convinced that her being trans was the reason.

Snyder went on to explain that they threw the bloody stuff into the trunk of Reed's car, then they put the body in the trunk of my father's car. First, they found a dumpster outside the Grand Motel, a fleabag place in the south end of town, and got rid of the evidence in Reed's trunk. The original plan was to throw the body in the Dagda River, but because of a drought the river was too low, so they took it to a dumpster in the alleyway next to the Collister Motel and dumped it there, hoping that when the garbage truck picked up the trash, the body would wind up in the landfill. They figured even if the body was found, it would just be another dead fag whose murder went unsolved. What they hadn't counted on was that when the body was discovered, it turned out to be someone who had just been on *The Michael Dobbs Show*, and all hell broke loose.

"Captain, based on what you saw the night of the murder,

you knew that Joseph Riccoli had not murdered Sherry Darling, correct?" I asked.

"Based on what I observed, that was my assumption."

"But you allowed Riccoli to be tried not once, but twice,
when you knew beyond any doubt he was innocent, correct?"

"I . . . I didn't know who killed . . . the victim."

"Captain, you have an obligation to be truthful. You knew
it wasn't Riccoli, didn't you?"

He nodded.

"For the record, Captain, your answer was 'yes'?"

He glared at me and managed to squeeze out an angry
"Yes."

"And whoever killed her was still free, correct?"

"Yes."

"And after Riccoli was convicted, he was sentenced to be
executed? And you still said nothing. Why?"

He looked up, his eyes burning with something—anger,
resentment, but certainly not remorse. "Because I was told
that if I knew what was good for me and wanted to continue
my career in the office, I'd keep my mouth shut."

"Who told you that?" I asked, even though I was fairly
certain I knew the answer.

"Your father, Francis Kelly, who at the time was my sergeant," he said, his words coated in venom.

I was about to fire back, confronting him with his sworn
duty as a law enforcement officer, when Lisa jumped in.
"That's all for now, Captain Snyder. You're free to go. I'll get
back to you after I discuss the situation with District Attorney
Graham."

After Snyder and Conover left, Lisa took out her cell phone.

"I just got a text from Detective Mills, who is at Ron Furst's house. Detectives from the Brisbane DA's office discovered a Colt .38 Detective Special snub-nose revolver, serial number 1589R, in Furst's gun cabinet. They've seized it pursuant to the warrant and are on their way back to have ballistics run on it." She turned to me. "Mills is still at the house and wants to know what she should do."

Before I could respond my phone vibrated. I looked down to see a message from Coffler.

"Tell Stacy to meet us outside Elizabeth Furst's room," I said.

When Lisa gave me a quizzical look, I read Coffler's text out loud.

"Elizabeth willing to continue statement. When can you get here?"

CHAPTER 40

I LOOKED AT MY Fitbit—10 A.M. The Sunday crowd at Denny's was growing, and I began to wonder if Jimmy Barry was going to show.

The last forty-eight hours had been a whirlwind. After leaving Graham's office, I met Stacy at the hospital to finish taking Elizabeth's sworn statement that filled in the details of what happened the night Sherry was murdered. And despite Reed's claim that she hadn't witnessed what happened, she had provided us with a detailed account of Sherry's murder. Hell hath no fury, as they say.

Then, before Brian flew back to LA on Saturday, we met for breakfast at his hotel at 6:30 A.M. He needed to know how our mom had died. This time, unlike when I heard it from Elizabeth in her hospital room, I wasn't wearing the protective armor of being a cop. This time, it was raw and emotional— the pictures in my head were far too vivid. I could see the scene unfold. Barr coming up from behind the car. Mom not even realizing he was there. The bullet being fired directly into her left temple. The spatter of blood and tissue inside her car. Her red hair matted with blood. Her smile, her laugh, her joy, gone—forever.

Brian and I had hugged each other and cried until there were no more tears. I was still struggling with the jumbled-up mix of emotions. She hadn't deserted us. She had loved us. But she was gone and there'd never be a chance for the reconciliation I always hoped would happen someday.

After I left Brian, Stacy, Lisa, and I met Ray Ashley at Memorial Hospital. Reed had looked worried when we walked into the room. He had every reason to be.

"Hello, Mr. Reed," I'd said as we gathered around his bed. "We've come to tell you that there's no deal. You lied to us, and not only are you going to be charged with attempting to murder me, but we're going to be charging you with the murder of Tom Hammond."

"No!" he had screamed. "I swear to you, I didn't murder Hammond." His eyes had darted frantically from me to Ashley and back.

"That's not what ballistics show, Barry. It was your gun that killed Tom," I pronounced.

"Barry, shut up," Ashley ordered. "What's going on?" he had demanded of Lisa.

Lisa had handed Ashley a copy of the inventory records. The first was a photocopy of the serial number entries for Hammond's and Reed's duty weapons. The second a copy of what the forensic people had uncovered—the serial numbers were Wited-Out and changed.

"As you will see, Mr. Ashley, the weapon used in the shooting of Detective Thomas Hammond was your client's.

We're prepared to file capital murder charges against your client. On top of that, we have evidence that he lied about who murdered Sherry Darling, and we now believe your client was part of a conspiracy to murder her."

The fact that his gun had been used to kill Hammond had the desired result. It took several hours of negotiations, but, based on Reed's new proffer, we ultimately struck a tentative new plea deal, subject to us confirming one key fact. The new deal was far less favorable to Mr. Reed. This one called for him to spend time as a guest of the state for being part of a conspiracy to kill Tom Hammond, as well as for attempting to murder me, the length of his stay to be determined based on the extent of his cooperation and his honesty. But this time, what we learned from his new proffer had been worth it. It gave us Tom Hammond's killer, provided us with another eye-witness to Sherry's murder, and gave me a stark reminder to never accept anything at face value, even a jail record.

After we'd finished with Reed, Stacy and I spent most of Saturday afternoon tracking down a retired DCDAO detective who had been in the Narcotics Unit twenty years ago. Late in the afternoon, we finally connected with Eric Morris, who confirmed what Reed had told us in his new proffer. Game on.

Now I waited impatiently in Denny's to see if Jimmy Barry would show. I had called his cell last night and left a message that I needed to talk with him and he had a choice—we could do it at the DCDAO or we could do it at Denny's. When he'd called back this morning, he had cursed me out, but when I told him he could talk to me or the Attorney Ethics Board, he chose me at Denny's. All things considered, probably not his best decision, but it really didn't matter what he decided to do, it was just a question of how many moves I had to make before I had him in checkmate.

I texted him that I had a booth in the back. And then, there he was. When he saw me, he sauntered over, looking none too happy.

"Good morning," I said as he slid into the booth.

"Fuck you, Kelly," he replied, coming out of the box swinging. But it was what I needed. It refocused me.

"Nice to see you too, Jimmy. I'd use your dead name, but I know how hard that can be for some people."

"Dead name? What the fuck are you talking about?"

"You know, the name you were given at birth. Trans folks call it our dead name."

He glared at me. "Like Liam Kelly?"

"Yeah, Seamus. You have the right idea."

I watched for a reaction, thinking I had drawn first blood, but his look remained inscrutable.

"What the fuck is this about?" he spit out. "You demand that I meet you on a Sunday, threaten me with going to the Attorney Ethics Board, and now use a name I haven't used in thirty-something years."

"Really, Jimmy? Do I really have to spell it out for you? I mean, you've always struck me as an intelligent guy." I paused, allowing myself a derisive grin. "Especially for someone who never graduated college, or law school, or passed the bar," I said, presenting him with the information that Becca had uncovered for me. "Although, that does explain why you never ran for DA. You had managed to avoid getting caught all these years, why run the risk that someone poking around in your background would discover the truth?"

"So instead, you're going to turn me in. Is that what this is about?"

"Actually, I don't give a shit about your legal career, Jimmy. I was surprised to find out that we live in a state that doesn't criminalize the unauthorized practice of law. So, the worst thing that happens to you is you get put out of business and fined. But like I said, I could care less. That's not what this is about."

"What do you want, Kelly? Money to keep your mouth shut?"

I snorted. "No, Jimmy. I don't want money. I want answers—just some honest answers."

I half expected him to pull a Jack Nicholson on me and tell me I couldn't handle the truth, but he didn't, so I continued. "Authorized or not, you've been at the legal game a long time, so I presume you've already put together that we're in a Denny's, not an interrogation room at the office, and I haven't read you your rights. Meaning, you're free to go any time you'd like. This is not a custodial interrogation and Miranda doesn't apply, but Jimmy, you are a suspect," I said, leaving out that I was wearing a wire and there were four detectives from Brisbane sitting in a van in the rear parking lot listening and ready to burst in if things went south.

We were interrupted by the waitress pouring more coffee for me and asking him if she could get him anything to drink, which he brusquely refused. I was going to suggest he could order whatever he wanted for lunch, kind of like a last meal, but I decided not to antagonize him any more than I already had.

"Let me start, Jimmy, by giving you some information.

Thirty minutes ago, your father was picked up for questioning in connection with the murder of my mother, Maureen Kelly. We believe that on the afternoon of December 6, 1982, it was your father who shot and killed her."

"You're out of your fucking mind. I don't have to sit here and take this crap!" he hissed, putting his hands on the table and starting to slide toward the end of the booth.

"Don't be an asshole, Jimmy. Sit and listen."

His scowl conveyed he didn't like my attitude, but he didn't leave.

"That was forty years ago. If you're stupid enough to charge him, he'll walk. Who you going to call as a witness, your demented father?" he said dismissively.

I ignored him. "We've also developed information concerning the murder of Sherry Darling, a.k.a. your sister. You remember the case. The one where you tried Joe Riccoli twice for capital murder, both times withholding DNA evidence that exonerated him. We have evidence that you knew the whole time who the real murderer was, but said nothing— something that if you had a law license could get you in trouble, but losing your license is obviously not a worry for you."

I stopped and leaned forward. "Jimmy, even without a law license, you're smart enough to know that anything we could charge you with in connection with Sherry's death is barred by the statute of limitations. So, I wouldn't have wasted your time if that was what this was about. No, this isn't about my mother or your sister, it's about Tom Hammond. You remember him. You called him a 'good cop.'"

His brown eyes were cold, giving me nothing.

"Here's what I need from you, Jimmy. I know who murdered Tom, but I need to know who ordered it. Did you do it on your own or was Ron Furst behind it?"

"He took his own life," he said. "You know that. I know that. This is bullshit, Kelly. You're just on this power trip, trying to prove yourself, even though you're clearly a fucked-up mental case."

"Here's the problem with the 'he killed himself' story, Jimmy. Hammond was shot with Barry Reed's gun. After Hammond was shot, the killer took his weapon and put Reed's gun in his hand. Then the records of the DCDAO were tampered with, so that the serial number for Reed's gun was changed to make it look like it was Hammond's gun, and vice versa. So, when the weapon was brought in from the scene of Hammond's shooting and checked, it showed that it was Hammond's gun, and the story went out that poor Tom had died by suicide. But we both know that's not what happened."

As I was talking, I saw two of the detectives from the backup unit take seats at a table about fifteen feet away. My seat had been well planned so that Barry had his back to the room and was unaware they had moved into place.

"What really happened that night," I continued, "was that you called Tom and told him to come to a meeting at the old building where the Narcotics Unit had its undercover office. Reed was also at the meeting. You discussed retrying the case, and at that point Tom asked about DNA evidence that had been buried, DNA that he had learned about from my father. You gave him a song and dance about my father being a drunk and he didn't know what he was talking about. Problem was, Tom was a good cop. He told you he had called the state forensics lab and they were sending him a copy of the results—all the results. That was a problem, because unlike my father and Reed, Tommy wasn't going to play ball and keep the results buried. So, when the meeting was over, you suggested the three of you head over to the Elks for a beer. Tommy left to go to the Elks, and you had Reed give you his gun. When you got to the Elks, Tom was waiting in his car because the Elks was closed. You got in his car, and shot him. You wiped your prints off Reed's gun, put it in Tom's hand, took his gun, and left. How'd I do, Jimmy? Sound right to you?"

Barry let out a grunt. "Even if what you say about Hammond being shot with Reed's gun was true, and I'm sure it's not, your theory is that I somehow got Reed's gun and shot Hammond with it? Come on, Kelly, give me a break. It's total bullshit. Sounds to me like Reed is the guy you should be questioning, not me."

"You know, Jimmy, that was my initial reaction too. Reed's gun—Reed did it. Makes sense—until it doesn't." I allowed myself a hint of a grin. "I'm not sure if you remember a detective in the Narcotics Unit who retired about ten years ago as a sergeant, but back in 2004, he was a detective—Eric Morris. Most people called him Mo. Good guy, good detective. If he'd been white, he probably would have retired as a captain or maybe even chief. Remember him?"

"Sure, I know Mo."

"Good. Then you know Mo is a straight shooter. I spoke with him yesterday. And he remembers the night Hammond was shot. He had been working OT and was at the Narcotics building when you, Reed, and Hammond met. He's sure it was that night, because he remembered it was the night everyone got a call, 'officer down.' and everyone headed to the Elks or the hospital," I said.

Barry was a good poker player because, if he was worried, there still was no tell. "Yeah, so what. I had a meeting with Reed and Hammond. Big fucking deal. That doesn't translate into I killed him."

"No, you're right, it doesn't. But Mo was also certain that you and Hammond left around the same time. And after you left, Mo said Reed invited him for a beer—an invite that stuck in Mo's mind, because Reed was a bit of a . . . how do I say this nicely? A fucking racist. So, Mo wound up going with Reed to The Goalpost to have a beer, and they were sitting there when the 'officer down' call came in and they all took off for the Elks."

I stopped and leaned forward. "Here's the thing, Jimmy. Reed knew what was going to go down. And he knew that his gun was going to be used to shoot Hammond, so he wanted an alibi in case things went sideways. He and Mo were together the whole time. That's how we know you did it, Jimmy. You shot Detective Tom Hammond to prevent him from finding out that there were multiple sources of DNA found on Sherry Darling—DNA results you had directed Barry Reed to bury on orders from Ron Furst. Furst was worried because, even though the sources of the DNA that were found were unknown at the time, he knew that if a real investigation was ever done, it might uncover that the DNA belonged to him and his wife, Elizabeth. And you knew from your conversations with Furst that he murdered Sherry. I think I know why Furst did it, and my hunch is that you felt you had to go along to protect yourself and your family from Furst, but feel free to fill in the blanks for me."

Barry's eyes met mine, and for the first time I saw fear. This was always the most dangerous time with any suspect. The time when they knew they were caught, the time when they felt trapped, the time when they were desperate. Reaching down, I slowly wrapped my hand around my gun, which I had placed next to me in the booth so I wouldn't have to draw it out of my holster. I let my gaze fall on his hands, both still on the table.

"You're full of shit, Kelly. I don't remember Mo being there."

"He was there, Jimmy. You have to hand it to Reed, he was smart enough to make sure he had an alibi. Kind of telling that you don't."

He shifted in his seat, seeming to weigh his options.

"So, remember when I said you were free to leave? Well, I take it back. You're under arrest for the murder of Detective Thomas Hammond of the Donn County District Attorney's Office. You have the right to remain silent—"

He suddenly slid out of the bench, pushed his jacket back, and reached for a gun in his belt. "Don't," I yelled, raising my arms, my gun now pointed at his face.

There was a cacophony of screams when people saw my gun. But before all hell could break loose, one of the detectives in the backup unit grabbed Barry from behind and slammed him face first into the table. In seconds he was disarmed, cuffed, and pushed back so he was once again sitting in the booth opposite me, now sporting a fat lip and a bloody nose.

I put my weapon back in my holster and finished reading him his rights.

"I want a lawyer," he hissed.

"A real lawyer, or one like you?" I said, unable to resist one last dig.

I nodded and the two backup detectives pulled James Barry out of the booth and led him out of the restaurant. Five minutes later, Lisa and Stacy slid into the booth across from me.

"You okay?" Lisa asked.

"Never better," I said. "Where do we stand?"

"I just spoke with the folks with Dawson County DA," Lisa said. "Declan Barr took the Fifth and demanded a lawyer. For now, since all they have is Elizabeth's statement, they didn't feel they had enough to charge him, and he's been released."

I knew on a professional level that it was the right move to hold off charging him, but it was still a kick in the gut. He was the person who murdered my mom. He was supposed to be locked up. *Shit.*

"They still haven't gotten the ballistics back on the gun seized from Ron Furst's house," Lisa added.

"And if there's a match?" I asked.

Lisa looked pained. "It was forty years ago. Unless they can tie Ron Furst directly to the murder, the statute of limitations has run on everything else—blackmail, extortion, being an accessory after the fact—all time barred."

"What about Otto Furst?" Stacy asked. "According to Elizabeth, he ordered it."

"It's the same problem that they have with Barr. All they have is Elizabeth's statement. It's probably not enough. Plus, he's ninety-six years old. Nobody wants to prosecute someone who's ninety-six."

I wanted to scream *We know who did it! We know!* And

yet, as my mind screamed at me, I also played back all the meetings I had sat in on when we had to tell a victim's family that we just didn't have enough admissible evidence to charge the person we suspected of killing their loved one. And now I knew how they felt. Frustrated. Impotent. Vengeful.

Somewhere off in the distance I heard Lisa's voice as she continued. "I think we have a solid case against Jimmy Barry for ordering the hit on you and for the murder of Detective Hammond. My guess is that given Barry's long connection to the DCDAO, the AG's office is going to want to handle the murder prosecution."

"Will you handle it?" I asked, coming out of my fog.

She gave me an appreciative smile. "No, Lauren. Assuming they seek the death penalty, they'll have a special trial team, which specifically handles death penalty cases. I will, however, recommend that you be part of the team on the Hammond case."

"Thanks," I said with a nod of appreciation. "Where do we stand with Sherry?"

Lisa sighed. "I have a meeting Monday with Graham and folks from the AG's office. Obviously, everyone wants to make sure we have a solid case before we go after Furst. But between Elizabeth and Reed, I think we're good."

"Can we talk before the meeting?"

"Sure. Is there any reason we can't do it now?" she asked.

"Yeah," I said. "I don't have the information yet." I turned to Stacy. "Were you able to make contact?"

"Yeah. Here's his cell," she said, handing me a piece of paper. "He doesn't trust us, but he's willing to meet tonight. You want me to be there?"

I thought for a moment. "No. It might work better if I'm alone."

Lisa looked confused. "What are you two talking about?"

"I want to talk to Padraig Barr," I said.

"Why?"

"Because I think he may be able to tie up some loose ends."

"But I thought he was in custody when Sherry was killed," Lisa said.

"According to his rap sheet, he was. According to Reed, he wasn't. And remember, at the time, he also had a brother who was part of the DA's office." I shrugged. "Time to find out the truth."

"Be careful. I don't like the fact that you're meeting him alone," Lisa said.

"No worries. I'm going to meet him in a very public place. A place I know has really good bouncers," I replied, knowing that neither of them had any idea as to where I was referring to.

I headed out. I had three more stops to make before meeting with Padraig—the first two were courtesy calls, the last one was to fill in the last piece of the puzzle.

CHAPTER 41

"YOU SAID YOU HAVE news about Tommy?" Joan asked, rubbing her hands together nervously as we sat at her kitchen table.

"I do, and honestly, Joan, I don't know if it will make things better or worse."

"Just tell me, please. Nothing you tell me is going to bring Tommy back. I just need to know what happened."

"We've just arrested former Assistant DA James 'Jimmy' Barry for Tom's murder."

She gasped and clasped her hands in front of her face. She slowly lowered them until they were folded in front of her lips. "What can you tell me?" she finally asked.

I explained what we had on Barry and how we believed the events unfolded the night Tom was murdered. When I was done, she looked at me, wiped the tears from her eyes and thanked me for believing her.

"I found out a few other things," I said.

She looked puzzled. "Such as?"

"I know my mother was raped by Ron Furst and I also know he's my brother Brian's father. I am fairly certain that my mother was killed by Declan Barr when she showed up at Furst Realty, and that her murder was ordered by Otto Furst. Whether anyone will ever be prosecuted for her murder is doubtful. But who knows."

There was one other thing that Eliza Furst had said that hadn't made sense to me at the time. Otto Furst had told my father that if my mother talked it not only could ruin Ron, but him as well. What did my mother have on Otto? And then, as I tried to fall asleep that night, it had come to me— Joan Hammond had been raped by someone in the office and had warned my mother. My guess was that someone had been Otto.

"I also pieced together one last thing," I said.

"What?" she asked.

"No," I said. "You told me once before the subject of who assaulted you wasn't open for discussion, and I respect that. Maybe someday soon, after that person has passed, we can discuss it, but not now."

Joan hung her head. "You're a good detective."

"Thanks. But there's one question I still have that hopefully you can answer. How did my father find out Brian wasn't his son?"

Joan sighed. "About a week before all this happened, Brian had been sick and needed blood work done. When your father picked up the results, he saw Brian's blood type. I guess he knew his blood type and your mother's, and being a detective, he knew that Brian's blood type couldn't result from a combination of the two. Of course, his immediate reaction was that your mother had cheated on him, so when he confronted her, she was forced to tell him what happened. That's when he went crazy and headed to Ron's to kill him."

I closed my eyes and nodded. A blood test had changed all our lives. How totally serendipitous.

I stood to leave. "Thanks, for your help," I said. "When things calm down, I'd love to have lunch and hear more about my mom."

"Of course," she said, reaching out and hugging me. "Thank you for all you've done. I think our sons believed me when I told them that their dad would never have taken his own life, but now . . . now they'll know for sure."

We embraced and I told her about the funeral plans for my mom, before we said our goodbyes.

MY FATHER WASN'T IN his room so I headed down to the day room at the end of his hallway. He was sitting in an arm-chair, facing a picture window that looked out on the fields behind the facility. There were two other people in the room, a woman in a wheelchair in the corner of the room who appeared to be sleeping, and a man parked in front of a television watching a Spanish-language soccer game.

I pulled out a chair and took a seat at a table about twenty feet behind where my father sat. I watched him, trying to wrap myself in what it must have been like for him, knowing his wife had been murdered, and who had done it, yet convinced if he came forward, he'd risk not only his life, but my life and Brian's as well—Brian, who wasn't even his child. How different all our lives might have been if he had never gone after Ron Furst that day. Would my mother have accepted me as a trans woman? Would she have accepted Brian, her gay son? Would I have come out sooner? I'd never know. Life was like that. The road not taken often looked better in the rearview mirror. But who knew for sure—who knew?

What I had learned about my father over the last few weeks had given me a different lens to view him through, a perspective that gave me a better understanding of why he had always been so angry and bitter. But even that didn't provide him with absolution. Brian and I had survived because we had each other. We survived despite my father, not because of him.

My phone vibrated and I looked to see a text from Becca.

We're in the room. Where are you?

The day room. Give me five minutes and I'll bring him back, I replied.

I walked over to where he was sitting and sat down in the armchair next to him.

"Mr. Kelly," I said.

He looked up, a faraway look in his eyes. Then "Kelly" seemed to register. "Yeah. Kelly. That's my name."

"Mr. Kelly. I'm with the Donn County District Attorney's Office and I'm here because we solved the murder of your wife, Maureen Kelly. She was murdered by Declan Barr. We know he used your gun and we know the murder was orchestrated by Otto Furst."

It was one of the few times I could recall when he didn't look at me and ask me who I was. His eyes seemed to clear, then grew moist. "Thank you," he said.

"You're welcome," I replied.

"Are my boys safe?" he asked, his voice quivering.

"Yes sir. They're safe."

His head dropped to his chest and a sigh escaped his lips. "Good," he whispered.

I let about fifteen seconds pass, then I stood. "Mr. Kelly," I said.

He looked up. "Who are you?" he asked.

"I'm here to take you back to your room," I said, putting my hand under his arm and gently lifting. He slowly stood and I guided him back to his room where Nora and Becca were waiting.

He smiled when he saw Nora.

"Hi, Grandpop," she said, going to him and giving him a hug.

"Hi," he managed with a mixture of confusion and surprise.

"We bought you some new music," she offered, leading him over to his chair. When he was settled in, she went to the Bose docking station, put in the iPod, and looked surprised to see the immediate recognition in my father's eyes as Glen Campbell started singing "Gentle on My Mind." He closed his eyes and seemed to be transported to some other time and place, his lips moving as he silently sang along with the music.

Nora walked over and put her arms around me. "I'm sorry about Nanny, Mads. I know I didn't know her, but I feel like I did."

"Thank you, hon. You would have loved her and she would have adored you," I said, hugging her back. "And I'm sorry about all the unwanted publicity."

She leaned her head against my chest. "It hasn't been too bad. Most of the kids have been asking me about Uncle Brian, not you."

"It's nice to have a famous uncle," I replied. "Remind me to tell you later who'll be coming to the funeral with him next week." She looked up at me quizzically. "Not now. I'll tell you when we leave."

Later, as I headed to my next stop, I allowed myself a smile over my daughter's desire to squeal with delight before realizing that being excited about who was coming to her grandmother's funeral was totally inappropriate. There was no question, however, that Brian had been on the money—the thought of meeting Charlene Fox in person had sent Nora over the moon.

It was a little after four when I walked into Eppie's. After handing the bartender my card, I told him I was here to see the owner, Robert Eppie. When he asked if I had an appointment, I told him no, but I'd be happy to call the Sheldon PD to help make one. Two minutes later, Robert came to the door that led to the back and waved me in.

"Why are you back here threatening me?" Robert demanded once we were in his office.

"No threats. I just need some answers."

His eyes narrowed. "I'm listening," he said, in a tone that bore the scars of being abused by people like me with power.

"How's Billie doing?" I asked, catching him off guard.

"The same," he said.

"How long had Padraig Barr been running part of his prostitution operation out of The Hawk?"

He stared at me, trying to size up what I knew. "Started sometime in 1999."

"What happened?"

"A guy came in one day and said he was here on behalf of

someone else, and from now on, I was to pay ten percent of my profits to this someone else. I told him to get the fuck out. The next day, Billie got jumped and got the shit beat out of him. The same guy came back the next day, and said now I had to pay fifteen percent of my profits, or the next time Billie would have his throat slit. So, I started paying."

"And the someone you were paying was Padraig Barr, correct?"

He nodded.

"And what happened?"

"Word on the street was Barr had been pimping cis girls for years. One night he came in and saw the show and he decided he could reach guys who were into something a little different by pimping out some of the girls who were in the drag show. They always needed extra money, especially those who wanted to have surgery."

"Was Sherry one of the girls he pimped?"

"No. Not right away."

"At some point did Padraig set Sherry up with Ron Furst?"

"Yeah."

"Why?"

Robert laughed. "Because Padraig was pissed at Furst. See after Barr stole part of my business, Furst decided he wanted a piece too. So, one day I got a visit from a couple of detectives from the Harrison Vice Squad who told me I needed to pay two grand a week to stay open. When I told Barr, he told me not to worry about it because his dad and Furst were tight and he'd straighten things out. But a week later, Barr came to me furious and told me to pay the money. Apparently, Furst had outgrown his need for the Barrs and told Padraig to go fuck himself. That's when Barr enlisted Sherry. I mean if you saw pictures of Sherry, you know she was a beautiful woman. No one ever clocked her as trans. And Barr's plan was to set Furst up with Sherry and then blackmail him."

"And the night Sherry died?" I asked.

"I don't know what happened. Before that night, Barr seemed confident I wasn't going to have to pay anymore. After Sherry was killed, I had to pay Furst four grand a week. I managed to hang on for a while, mostly because Barr disappeared, but Furst kept upping what he wanted until it got to the point I couldn't survive. That's why we closed."

"Did Billie know all about this?"

"Nah. Billie knew that Sherry was Barr's sister, and that he was getting her work, but he didn't know the rest. Only people who knew the whole story were Barr and me."

I nodded, satisfied that even though Billie had misled me about knowing who had set Sherry up with her sugar daddy, she hadn't known who Sherry was seeing. And shame on me for not asking Robert. Although if I had asked two weeks ago, before I had gotten some of the backstory from Reed, I'm not sure Robert would have been as forthcoming.

"Thanks, Robert," I said with a weak smile. "Please give Billie my best."

I WALKED INTO TESH'S around 7:30. I had called ahead and Gee was nice enough to save me a table in the back. When I got there, Gee was acting as hostess.

"Kelly!" she said, when I walked up to the sign that said PLEASE WAIT HERE TO BE SEATED. "I heard the news about your mom. I'm so sorry. How you doing?"

"I'm doing," I said.

She gave me a gentle smile. "I'm here if you need anything."

"Thanks. Maybe when things settle down a bit."

She nodded. "Your guest is already here." Her expression shifted. "This is business, isn't it?"

I nodded.

"The guy you're meeting, I've seen him in here a couple of times. Should I know who he is?"

"Sherry's brother, Padraig," I said.

She leaned back as if I had pushed her gently. "Kelly, it's a Sunday night—family night," she said. "There's not going to be trouble, is there?"

"Hopefully there'll be no problems, but just in case, you have a bouncer on tonight?" I asked.

She nodded. "Same guy as the night Sam came after you. Please, Kelly. I don't need any problems tonight."

"I'll be a good girl. Promise."

She sighed, shook her head, and then led me back to the table where Barr was already having a beer.

"Mr. Barr," I said, extending my hand. "Lieutenant Lauren Kelly."

He looked at my hand, but didn't take it. "I'm not a happy man, Lieutenant," he said.

I took a seat. "And why is that, Mr. Barr?"

"My father has been questioned in connection with a murder forty years ago, and then my brother Jimmy was arrested for a murder twenty years ago. What are you gonna try and pin on me?"

"Nothing," I said. "But you should know a few other things. The murder your father is under investigation for is the murder of my mother."

His mouth opened, then closed. "Your mother. Fuck. Okay."

"And your brother was arrested for the murder of a detective who was investigating the murder of your sister, Sherry. All I want from you is information."

"I didn't have a sister Sherry. I had a brother Owen."

"Stop," I said. "I know that other than your grandmother, you were the one member of the family who spoke with Sherry."

"Whatever," he said. "So, I spoke with her. Big fucking deal. That don't answer the question, what do you want from me?"

"Your help."

"My help? Why the fuck should I help you?"

"I can think of a few reasons. Like maybe you want to get off your chest what's been eating at you for twenty-plus years—that you're the reason your sister was murdered."

"What's that supposed to mean?" he said, the muscles in his neck tightening.

"It means, you pimped your sister out to Furst, so you could blackmail him and force him to stop taking kickbacks from bars that were already paying you for protection. Unfortunately for you and your sister, Furst had grown so powerful he was no longer dependent on you or your father to do his dirty work. So, when Furst saw Sherry on *The Michael Dobbs Show*, he figured out what you were up to, had you locked up, and then eliminated your sister." I folded my hands and placed them on the table. I had changed only one fact, but if Barr wanted to play ball, I'd know if he was being honest. "How am I doing?"

He snorted. "You're close, but you don't have it right."

"What'd I miss?"

His eyes bored into mine, as if taking my measure. "You missed the fact that I was there when that piece of shit slit Sherry's throat."

He must have correctly read my expression that showed I had already figured that out, because he continued before I said anything. "Jimmy knew I was going there that night and why. So, he had helped my mom bail me out that afternoon. But Jimmy also knew the people who ran the jail, so they made it look like I was still locked up. That way, when I killed Furst as I planned, I'd have an alibi. That night I drove Sherry to Furst's condo and waited outside. The plan was, when she came out, she'd let me in and I'd deal with Mr. Furst once and for all."

"What went wrong?"

"Fucking A, man—everything went wrong," he said, his voice a disgusted snarl. "First, Sam Furst and some other dude showed up, and I saw them waiting across the street. I'm wondering what the fuck are they doing here. Then the fucking wife showed up and goes bursting inside. Sam, the guy who's with him, and I see the wife go in, so we made a dash for the door. Sam didn't know what to make of me being there, but I told him we have to get in there or something bad was gonna happen. The three of us ran upstairs and the wife was swinging a knife at Sherry and Furst. I really think she was trying to kill Ron, which would've been fine with me, but Furst was using Sherry like a human shield. Sam and the other dude ran over and grabbed the wife, pulling her away. I screamed for Sherry, but before I could get to her, Ron picked up the knife, grabbed Sherry by the hair, and . . ."

He stopped, unable to continue. My preconceived notions must have been on full display, because I was taken aback by his show of emotion. Not something I generally encountered from tough guys.

"You saw it happen?" I asked.

He bit down on his lip. "Yeah." He looked up at me. "I know you think I'm a piece of shit and life means nothing to me. Well, you're wrong. Sherry was staring at me as he did it, her eyes pleading with me to save her." He looked down at the table. "I failed her and I see her face and the fear in her eyes in my sleep," he said softly. "You were right, Lieutenant. She's dead because of me." He looked up, and his eyes found mine. "I fucked up. I underestimated Ron Furst."

"What happened next?"

He lowered his eyes and covered his mouth with his fist. "I ran to Sherry, hoping I could stop the bleeding," he said, his words coming slowly. "I grabbed her blouse off the bed and tried to wrap it around her neck, trying to save her, but her eyes rolled back and she was gone. When I looked up, Ron was pointing a gun at me. He told me to get the fuck out, he'd deal with me later." Barr looked at me, this guy who had been to jail for attempted murder, and he had tears in his eyes. "I left, but—"

"But?"

"I still managed to fuck up Jimmy's life too."

"How's that?"

"Because Furst told Jimmy that if anybody found out what really happened, Furst would expose Jimmy as a fraud and then have my mother, father, sister, and Jimmy killed, saving me for last. So, Jimmy did whatever he had to do to make sure the truth stayed buried."

"Did you and Sherry have an argument over the phone in the days before she was murdered?" I asked, remembering something Riccoli had told me.

"Yeah, we did. I was pissed about her doing that stupid talk show. I know she did it for the money, but it was stupid. I called her and told her we were done—this was the last week, because I figured Furst would lose his mind if he saw the show, worried that she might expose him. She was upset and gave me a hard time because she needed money for her fucking surgery, but I told her this was it. Then when I got busted, I figured Furst was behind it. That's when I decided, fuck the blackmail, I was just gonna kill the motherfucker." He rested his head on his hand. "Another one of my fuckups. Smelling that he was on to me, I should never have let her go that night. I should have just given her the money for her fucking surgery. But I was so hell bent on making Furst pay for fucking me over, I . . ." He stopped. "Yeah, I fucked up big time," he said in a whispered voice, lowering his head and closing his eyes.

When he finally looked up, I said, "There's still one part I don't understand."

"What's that?"

"Furst was rich and powerful; he had a reputation for harassing women, even in some cases, sexually assaulting them," I said, thinking of my mom. "Why would he pay money—in Sherry's case, a lot of money—for something it seemed like he could get for free?"

Barr made a face. "Are you really that fucking clueless, Lieutenant? Furst knew Sherry was trans. He got his rocks off because she had a little something extra. Not my cup of tea, but some guys are into that."

Shit! I never saw that coming. That's why Sherry was making good money and why she wasn't worried about him finding out she was trans. *He knew.*

"I know you can't help Sherry, but there may be a way you can help Jimmy," I said.

"How the fuck can I help him?"

"If you're willing to testify truthfully as to what Furst did, maybe your brother gets offered a deal with a chance for parole, as opposed to facing the death penalty."

"Great fucking deal," he said sarcastically.

"A chance at getting out is better than getting the needle. And maybe, you finally get some peace."

"I'm not a big fucking believer in the afterlife, Lieutenant."

"Neither am I, Mr. Barr. So maybe it will give you some peace that you helped avenge her death by taking down the guy who killed her."

A hint of a grin grew on his lips. "I'm glad you didn't give me some bullshit about getting justice. There is no fucking justice in this world. But avenge my sister. I like that. I can do fucking revenge." He reached his hand across the table. I took it and shook it.

CHAPTER 42

IT WAS LATE TUESDAY morning when Stacy and I walked into the interrogation room. An hour earlier County Executive Ron Furst had been arrested on a warrant charging him with first-degree murder. This being Donn County, the warrant used Sherry's birth name in identifying the victim, but as much as that irked me, Furst's arrest was what was important.

I laid a file folder down on the table as Stacy and I took our seats. Opposite us were Furst and his distinguished lawyer, Sinclair Brinley, who, being the bombastic asshole that he was, spoke first.

"This is outrageous. We will be filing claims against the county, the DA's office and the two of you personally for malicious prosecution, false arrest, false imprisonment, and defamation."

"You may want to add the Attorney General's Office," I said.

"And why would I add them?" Brinley demanded.

"Because if you look at the arrest warrant and the initial

complaint, Mr. Furst is being charged by the Attorney General's Office, not the Donn County DA's Office. He was just brought here because he'll be processed here, then taken upstairs for his initial appearance on the complaint and for bail to be set. Given Mr. Furst's role as the county executive, after that, I assume the case will be moved to a different county."

"This is—"

"Outrageous," I said, cutting him off. I shifted my gaze so I was looking directly at Furst. "You should know that a little while ago other detectives from Brisbane County spoke with your son, Samuel."

"You have no right," Furst shouted, as Brinley quickly put his hand on Furst's arm to silence him.

"Actually, Mr. Furst, we have every right given that he's a witness as to what happened the night Sherry Darling was murdered."

"He wasn't even there," Furst fired back.

"Ron. Let me handle this," Brinley said, trying to keep Furst under control. "Who the hell is this Sherry Darling person? The complaint says Owen Barr."

"Same person," I replied. "And actually, Mr. Furst," I said, returning to his claim Sam wasn't there, "having watched Sam's interview, I know he admitted he was there, although he claims he didn't see who actually killed Sherry, just that it wasn't his mother, because he and Barry Reed were holding her. Mr. Reed has also confirmed he was holding your wife back, the only difference being Mr. Reed did see who killed Ms. Darling. Mr. Reed also confirmed that he and Sam were there that night because the plan was that they were going to grab Sherry when she left your condo and kill her—all on your orders."

"There's no way my son would have talked to any of you."

I smiled. "Actually, you'd be surprised how many people waive their rights and talk to us, especially to avoid being charged with conspiracy to commit murder," I said, trying my best to sound flippant.

Furst's eyes narrowed, his anger building. "Where is my son now?" he demanded.

"Truthfully, I don't know, sir. After the interview, he was free to leave. Would you like to respond to some of the things Sam and Mr. Reed told us?" I asked in my most innocent voice.

Furst glared at me. But before he could say anything, Brinley spoke.

"My client had no intention of talking to you. He is invoking his Fifth Amendment privilege."

"That is his absolute right, Mr. Brinley, and we will of course respect Mr. Furst's right to remain silent."

"So, I assume we're free to go," Brinley said.

I looked at him. Sinclair wasn't a criminal defense lawyer and I wondered why he didn't have the good sense to have one of the lawyers in his firm who practiced criminal law come with him. Sinclair was a rainmaker. He was the guy who had the connections. You called him if your company was having trouble getting whatever it needed to get done—Sinclair always knew someone who could fix it. But here, now, he was out of his league, and it showed.

"As I said, Mr. Brinley, when Mr. Furst leaves this room, he will be handcuffed and taken upstairs to the courtroom for his arraignment and to have bail set."

"Are you out of your mind? You intend to drag the county

executive out of here in handcuffs like some common criminal?"

I shifted my gaze to Furst, whose face was red, his rage
barely contained. I made sure I was looking directly at him
when I responded to Brinley. "Mr. Furst will be treated in the
same manner as all people charged with a crime—no better,
no worse. Everyone is equal under the law," I said, even though
I knew it was bullshit. Too often I had seen that there was one
set of rules for the rich and powerful, another set for the poor
bastards who had no money. "First Assistant Attorney General Max Gibney of the Criminal Division will be handling
your arraignment." I shifted in my chair, my eyes landing on
Brinley. "As well as the press conference after that," I added.

Furst leaned forward, his hands grasping the edge of the
table. "I will fucking kil—"

"Ron!" Brinley screamed. "Stop!"

I sat back, once again turning to Furst. "I believe you've
tried that already," I said, holding Furst's gaze as if we were
kids playing the staring game, neither of us blinking. When he
finally looked away, I said, "You should also know that search
warrants have been issued and all of Mr. Furst's cell phones,
computers, and mobile devices are being seized." I slid copies
of the warrants across the table to Brinley.

"What the hell is going on? According to the complaint,
this guy died over twenty years ago. None of those devices
could be relevant to those allegations. They didn't even exist,"
Brinley fumed.

"The person involved was a transgender woman, and she
didn't just die, Mr. Brinley, she was murdered," Stacy replied.
"Her throat slit so violently that she bled out in less than half

a minute. But you're right, it did happen over twenty years ago. But there's probably cause to believe that your client was attempting to prevent this investigation from going forward, including using various means to try and obstruct the investigation, including conspiring to murder Lieutenant Kelly," she said with a nod to me. "If we're wrong, then I assume your client has nothing to worry about. If we're not . . ." Stacy paused. "Any other questions, Mr. Brinley?"

"No," he said through clenched teeth.

Stacy and I stood and two other detectives entered the room and escorted Furst out to take him up three floors to the courtroom where he'd be arraigned. We found Lisa and Max Gibney waiting in the room where they had watched our interview of Furst. We had met Gibney for the first time yesterday, when we were called to a meeting he was having with Lisa and DA Graham about whether to charge Furst with the murder of Sherry Darling. We had told him that we had three eyewitnesses, Elizabeth Furst, Barry Reed, and Padraig Barr, as well as a fair amount of circumstantial evidence—including Furst's DNA on the victim; Reed's testimony that he was told by then Assistant DA Barry to bury the DNA evidence so that the person who it belonged to wouldn't be implicated; Reed's and Snyder's testimony about disposing of evidence after the murder; and finally, Reed's attempted murder of me, which Reed was told by Barry had been ordered by Furst.

Despite my concerns that the AG's office might drag its feet given Furst's clout, after a brief conversation with Lisa and Graham, Gibney signed the complaint and went before a judge to have the arrest warrant issued.

THE COURTROOM WAS PACKED for the arraignment. Reporters, supporters of Furst, and to my pleasant surprise, a handful of LGBTQ+ activists that I recognized from a few Pride events I had attended the last couple of years.

Gibney asked for a million-dollar cash bail because the crime was murder. Brinley argued that given who his client was, he wasn't a flight risk, and so his client should be released on his own recognizance. Judge Fiore split the baby, so to speak. He allowed Furst to post a personal recognizance bond in the amount of a million dollars, meaning that Furst signed an agreement saying that if he didn't appear, he'd owe Donn County a million bucks. Fiore also cautioned Furst about public comments on the case, indicating that he wasn't imposing a gag order, but would reconsider if needed.

After he banged his gavel and left the bench, the gaggle of reporters scurried forward, one group heading toward Gibney and Lisa, the others toward Brinley and Furst. Gibney told everyone that he would hold a press briefing outside the DA's office in about fifteen minutes, then he, Lisa, and Stacy headed out. Me being a bit of a voyeur, I hung back, listening to the reporters firing questions at Furst—and he didn't disappoint. He began by claiming he didn't even know the person he was accused of murdering, and that the charges were a political witch hunt. Then, catching me watching, he added that these charges were trumped up by a mentally ill member of the DA's office who should have been fired for trying to pass himself off as a woman. So much for the judge's words of caution. Before Furst could say more, Brinley grabbed him by the arm and quickly led him out of the courtroom.

I thought I'd feel differently. But there was no sense of elation, no joy. I had done what I set out to do: I found Sherry's murderer. But I could already envision that as part of his defense. Furst would put Sherry on trial—cis or trans, always blame the victim. She'd be portrayed as some trans sex worker who got what she deserved. And in the current environment around trans people, maybe he'd be successful.

My thoughts were interrupted when a few of the reporters recognized me and hurried over to where I was standing. "Lieutenant Kelly, do you have any comment on what County Executive Furst just said?"

"None," I said, as I made my way out, now with a renewed purpose. If this case ever went to trial, I'd be one of the main witnesses for the prosecution and just maybe I could make sure that who Sherry really was—a vibrant, funny, loving woman—wouldn't be lost forever.

AFTER THE PRESS CONFERENCE, I had driven out to Franklin. It was around three thirty when I walked into O'Donnell's. Joe Riccoli was at his usual spot in the back. I bought him a beer and told him that Ron Furst had been arrested for Sherry's murder, then proceeded to give him the rest of the sordid story and how it had all come to pass. When I finished, he chewed on his lip as we sat there in silence.

"You going to be okay, Joe?" I finally asked.

"I guess," he said, pushing his half-full beer into the middle of the table. "Maybe I won't need to numb myself anymore," he said, putting his fist up to his mouth. "I always blamed myself. Since we had argued that day, I thought that maybe she was upset with me and had done something stupid that got her killed." He paused and sighed, his eyes firmly fixed on me. "I suspect that knowing what happened won't take the pain away, but it may make it bearable. Maybe I can live now."

We walked out of O'Donnell's together, the sun low in the sky, and I handed Joe a piece of paper.

"What's this?" he asked.

"The location of Sherry's grave," I said.

He looked at the paper then back at me. "Thank you, Lieutenant," he said, extending his hand. "From the bottom of my heart, thank you for everything."

We shook hands and I watched him get into his truck and drive away. I knew what Joe meant. Knowing what had happened to my mom hadn't taken the pain away, but I guess sometimes all we can do is ease the pain and go on as best we can.

I MADE IT BACK to the office before 5 P.M. and was finishing up some paperwork, when I looked up to see Captain Snyder standing in my doorway.

"Captain," I said.

He made a noise that was a cross between choking and a snort. "Not anymore," he replied. "I put in my retirement papers this morning. I knew that I was going to be officially placed on administrative leave tomorrow, and the IA was going to start. So, I decided to get out while I could. I don't need to deal with all that shit."

He looked at me expectantly, waiting for me to say something. I had nothing to say. He, my father, Reed—they had all fucked up. I knew there were extenuating circumstances, but they were sworn law enforcement officers who had ignored the basic requirement of the job—enforce the law. God knows how different things might have been had they simply done their jobs.

"Got it," I finally said.

"Just so you know, I had no idea about Tommy. He was a friend. I know you think I did a lot of shitty things, and I can't say you're wrong, but I swear to you, I thought he took himself out. I never for a moment—Ah, fuck," he mumbled, his face twisting in pain.

"I believe you," I said softly—and on this one, I did.

He was quiet for a few seconds, his head slowly bobbing. "I have to give you credit for having . . . guts. I don't like you, Kelly, but I've come to respect you. See you around," he said, turning and heading down the hallway.

My cell phone vibrated and I saw that it was Becca.

"Hey, I saw you called earlier. Sorry, I was at my publisher in a meeting with my editor and someone came in with the news that Furst had been arrested, and we all wound up huddling around the television. How are you?" she asked.

"As my Irish ancestors would say, I'm grand. I was just calling to warn you that your father is really pissed at me."

"My father has been pissed at you since the moment he met you," she replied.

I managed a laugh. "Yeah, you're right, but I think we're now on a level where he just might spontaneously combust if he hears my name—especially if it comes from you or Nora. Just wanted to warn you."

"Thanks for letting me know," she said, and I could hear the smile. "I won't call and ask him how his day's been."

"Good idea."

"And Lauren, I know it's only the first step and who knows what will happen . . . but good for you. I hope you nail Furst."

"Thanks. I really appreciate all the help you gave me. Not sure I would've solved it without you," I said. "And Bec . . ." The words wouldn't come. *I'll always love you; I'll miss you; I want you to be happy; good luck*—all were stuck somewhere. Instead, all I managed to croak out was "Thanks, again."

"You're welcome."

"Maybe you can turn this into your next novel."

"Who knows?" she said. "Stranger things have happened."

CHAPTER 43

AS MY BROTHER PREDICTED, the church was packed, mostly with celebrities and people in the biz. But as we escorted my mother's casket down the center aisle, I saw a few people from the office, including DA Graham, Stacy and Lisa, and sitting in the back were Joan Hammond and Gee. My mother had been a devout Catholic during her short life, and so my brother's people had prevailed on the Cathedral of St. Mary Magdalene in downtown Harrison to be the venue for her funeral mass.

As Brian promised, Charlene Fox had flown in for the funeral. Her gentle embrace of Nora at the funeral home before the mass had been both genuine and comforting. Like Brian, despite her fame, she had retained a private side that was very real and vulnerable, and even though Nora was completely starstruck, Charlene had put her at ease.

When we took our seats, the pew in which we sat had me on the aisle, Brian next to me, Charlene, Nora, Becca, and Aunt Maeve, who had flown up from Florida for the funeral.

Missing was my father. Brian and I had talked to his doctors about bringing him to the funeral, but they had recommended against it. I had so many feelings about my father—anger, bitterness, forgiveness, sadness—all of them vying to take center stage. But I knew each would always be part of a chorus, none able to drown out the others.

Brian, being Brian, gave a moving eulogy about the women neither of us had ever gotten to know. There wasn't a dry eye in the church when he finished. I will confess that my emotions ran the gamut—from relief that we knew what happened to the overwhelming sense of loss for never having known the woman who so clearly loved us.

After the funeral, there was a full police escort to Holy Name Cemetery. I had requested it—not because of who I was, but because my mom was the wife of a member of the DCDAO at the time she was murdered. The graveside service was brief and everyone was invited to a repast at the Marriott where Brian and his entourage were staying.

We let everyone leave until the only ones standing at the gravesite were Brian, me, Aunt Maeve, Nora, Becca, and Charlene. Brian and I linked arms, and I'm not sure why it happened then, but I started sobbing. All I could see were the pictures of my mom with me blowing out the birthday candles, and lying on the floor holding my baby brother in her arms with a smile that would have lit up any room. Brian pulled me in close and I buried my face in his chest. Nora came up beside me and wrapped her arm around my waist and joined our embrace.

I'm not sure how long it was before we let go of each other, but when we did, I went over to Aunt Maeve and gave her a hug, and thanked her for all she had done after Mom disappeared. I could see a tinge of guilt in her eyes, and I shook my head. "You did all you could. No regrets." She threw her arms around my neck and pulled me close. Finally, I went over and gave Becca a hug and thanked her for all she had done to bring my mom home. When she whispered in my ear "Remember, she always loved you," I almost lost it all over again.

Brian turned to the others. "Can you give Lauren and me a moment alone with our mom?"

The others nodded and headed back to the limos.

"Your eulogy was beautiful," I said.

"Thanks," he said. "But I feel so weird. We just buried a woman who was murdered more than forty years ago. A woman who I have no recollection of. A woman who's my mother. I guess for you it's different. I mean, you told me that you thought Mom left because of you. Does it help knowing that she didn't?"

"No, not really. I guess whatever damage that did just became baked into me at some point. For me, I always held out the hope that someday I'd see her again. Maybe make things right between us. I know how stupid that sounds, but I clung to that like a life preserver in an open sea. And now it's gone, and I'm just bobbing all alone in the ocean."

"You're never alone," he said, putting his arm around my waist. "We still have each other."

"Thanks," I replied, leaning in.

"I worry about you," he said.

"Don't worry. Work will keep me busy."

"Well, from what I hear, you've managed to piss off

some pretty powerful people. Aren't you worried they'll come after you?"

"Too late to worry about it now," I said with a shrug. "For a while, I was concerned that they might mess with Nora or Becca, but with Becca's father so heavily involved with defending Furst, I'm comfortable they're safe. And it wouldn't make a whole lot of sense to come after me now. I'm an investigative witness. If something happened to me, someone else would take my place. Then he'd have to deal with an FBI Special Agent. Not sure even Furst would want to go there."

Brian gave me a quizzical look. "FBI?"

"Long story," I said, allowing myself a whisp of a grin. "Bottom line is that I should be fine."

"No chance of getting Declan Barr for killing Mom, or Otto Furst for ordering it?"

"Probably not. Case is too old. The star witness is dying of cancer, and while I can see all the dots as plain as day, they don't think they can convince a jury beyond a reasonable doubt. That said, I know who did it."

Brian gave me a strange look. "You're not thinking of taking matters into your own hands, are you?"

"Never," I said, allowing my eyes to leave my intent unclear. "But if they so much as jaywalk, I'll be there."

"I hear Becca's getting remarried," he said, changing the subject.

"She is." I shrugged. "Other than in my fantasies, it was never going to work. The bottom line is that I've only ever wanted her to be happy and, from what I hear, Roger Martin's a nice guy. I'm happy for Becca. And it'll be good for Nora too—something a little more run-of-the-mill than I can offer."

His eyes showed his sadness. "Speaking of family—I guess you can tell me now. Ron Furst is my biological father, right?"

"Yeah," I said. "When did you figure it out?"

"I guess I knew when you got the results so quickly that it was someone you were already investigating, and then when you arrested him, I figured he was the guy. Plus, his picture was all over the news and it's kind of weird, because I realized I look like him."

"So how you feel about it?" I asked.

"I guess it's kind of like the damage done to you believing it was your fault Mom left. Whatever damage Frank did, it's now baked in." He gave a short chuckle. "You know what's ironic, as awful a father as Frank was, I'll always think of him as my father. The other piece of shit who raped Mom—he's nothing to me. I hope with all my heart that you nail that bastard and he never sees the light of day."

"I'll do my best," I said. "You going to be okay?"

"Yeah. I'll be fine. The show is still going strong. I have a couple of movies lined up when I get a break from the series. Things are good."

He looked at me and smiled. "You know, if you ever wanted to, I have some friends that would probably love to turn your story into a movie. Interested?"

"No, thanks. I have a few more years to go. Then I can start looking at the next chapter. Besides, I would never do that to Becca and Nora—especially Nora."

"What are you going to do with Dad's house?"

"Clean it up, sell it, and put the money aside for Nora. By the way, I never told you that the attorney for Joe Riccoli told me that Dad . . . well, Frank, paid him fifty thousand cash to represent Riccoli on the retrial."

"He did?"

"Yep. He used half the money Otto Furst gave him to pay for the lawyer."

"Wow! I would never have guessed he was capable of something like that."

I nodded, electing not to tell Brian some of the other things he had been capable of.

"I'll be flying back right after the repast. The studio chartered a jet." He pulled me close and hugged me. "You're the only family I have, please come visit."

"I will."

"Bring Nora with you. I'll have Charlene take her shopping."

"Just what I need. A spoiled little rich girl."

I SLEPT LATE ON Sunday and had just finished grinding the beans to make coffee when my cell phone rang. It was Gee.

"Hi," I said.

"Hey, what are you doing?"

"Just about to make some coffee."

"Look," she said. "I know from personal experience that sometimes the toughest time when someone dies is after folks have gone home. You feel like some company?"

"Sure. When do you want to get together?"

"How about as soon as you open the front door."

"What?"

"Just open the door, Kelly."

I went to the front door. Gee was standing there holding two grocery bags.

"You going to invite me in?" she asked.

"Yeah, sure. Come on in," I said, stepping aside. "What's in the bags?"

"Brunch," she replied, as she walked by me and headed for the kitchen. "Don't worry. I'm not moving in; and it's not a date. I just love to cook. You make the coffee. I have the rest covered."

I followed her into the kitchen, where she placed the bags on the counter and turned and looked me up and down.

"Nice PJs," she said, admiring my flannel pajamas. Then she walked over to where I was standing, wrapped her hand behind my head, and kissed me deeply. "God, I've been waiting to do that," she said, when we separated. She held up a hand. "I know. I know—we have to wait," she said, rolling her eyes. "I'm still a potential witness. So, for now I'm just here to offer support and make breakfast. The kiss was just a show of support." She gave me a crooked smile and looked at me like no woman had ever looked at me. "But when the case is over . . ."

I made my way to the counter, a little weak in the knees, put some more coffee beans in the grinder and looked back over my shoulder at Gee, feeling urges I hadn't felt in a long time. "Um, I hate to be the one to break it to you, but it could be a while before the case is over."

"How long?" she asked.

"A year—maybe longer." I shrugged. "Not sure I'm worth the wait."

"I can be a patient woman when I have to be, Kelly," she said, smiling.

"Thanks," I replied, knowing that patience had been in short supply in my life both as the receiver and as the giver.

"Let's break some eggs and make an omelet," she said.

"How about peppers, onions, and mushrooms?" I suggested.

She fixed me with an icy stare. "My patience isn't unlimited, Kelly."

"Got it," I said. And for the first time in a long time, I allowed myself to relax and not worry about the future—or the past.

EPILOGUE

THE COLD WINDS WHIPPED across the open expanse of the cemetery. I tried to stay warm, huddled between Gee on one side and Joe Riccoli on the other, with Padraig Barr next to Joe, all of us looking at the newly installed gravestone.

SHERRY DARLING
NOVEMBER 20, 1977—APRIL 12, 2001

"She wouldn't want any prayers," Padraig said, "but I feel like we should say something."

There was silence as we all looked at each other.

"I'll go first," Gee said. "Damn, woman. You were the fiercest woman I've ever known. You gave me the strength to be me every single day I knew you. I hope wherever you are, you and Tony are hanging out together. And, Sher, who would have guessed that Kelly was one of us?"

Padraig looked at me and I nodded for him to go. "I wish I had done better by you. Not just in the last moment of your life, but when you were younger. I should have stood up for you with Dad. The fact that he's an asshole is no excuse. You were my sister—even though we all had trouble figuring that part out. You were always a girl and I don't know why we just couldn't accept that. I know this headstone doesn't make up for not being there for you, but it's my way of saying I'm sorry, and I love you."

I stared at the headstone, wishing there were words that could capture all the emotions I felt. "I should have taken your hand that day in detention. I wish that I had gotten to know you better, but even from afar, I always admired your courage and willingness to be yourself no matter what anyone else thought. Wherever the winds have taken you, Sherry, I want you to know that you continue to inspire and motivate me. I'm a better person because I knew you."

Joe cleared his throat. "I'm a plumber. I'm no good with words," he said, then sighed. "I loved you, babe, with all my heart. There wasn't a more beautiful woman on the planet than you, and every day when I saw you, I pinched myself because you were in love with me. I'm sorry we fought that day. I wish . . . I wish . . ." Joe put his head down and wiped away a tear. "I wish you were still here. Thank you for being a part of my life and loving me. I miss you every single day. I love you."

After a few minutes, we all exchanged hugs and headed to our cars.

"What do you think happens to us when we die?" Gee asked as we walked down the stone path leading to the parking lot.

"Fade to black," I said.

"That's it? No heaven or hell? That's pretty bleak, Kelly. Why even try to be good if there's no afterlife?"

"Because if this is all we have, why not try to leave it a little better than when we got here?"

She looked at me. "Is that what you're trying to do, Kelly— leave it a little better?"

"Yeah, Gee," I said, reaching out, taking her hand and giving it a squeeze. "And maybe making it a little better while I'm here too."

ACKNOWLEDGMENTS

THERE ARE ALWAYS SO many people who go into making one of my books possible. To start, there is my amazing agent, Carrie Pestritto at Laura Dail Literary Agency, who has more faith in me than I have in myself. This is our sixth book together. Fortunately, for both of our careers, the first one was never published. Thank you for believing in me.

A very special thank you to my extremely patient editor at Soho Press, Alexa Wejko, who worked with me for months to make this a much better book than the one that went out on submission two years ago. Additional shoutouts to Managing Editor, Rachel Kowal, and freelance copy editor, Trista Smith. I'm sure both of them wondered numerous times, *How can she be this old and not know where a comma goes?* And to the entire team at Soho, what a joy to work with all of you. Thank you for giving my book a home.

I owe a major debt to Andrea Robinson, an independent editor, who has taken the messy first drafts of all my books and helped shape them into something that was not only readable, but marketable. Thank you, Andrea, for your advice and for being part of my publishing journey.

To my family—kids, grandkids, siblings, in-laws, nieces, nephews, and cousins—there is no acknowledgment that will ever capture what all of you mean to me. I am here because of you. To my mom, whom I miss every day—you were there for the bumpy part of my journey. Thanks for always loving me. To my dad, who missed all the drama in my life, but was always there for me when I needed him—thanks, Dad. Most of all to Jan, who has been the most important person in my life since I was seventeen—with all my heart, thank you.

To those who have read drafts along the way—John Hayes, Lori Becker, Gerry Carbine, Lisa O'Connor, David Liss, Lori Linskey, Mike Stafford, and Janet Bayer—thank you—and an added apology to anyone I accidentally left out. For me, there is nothing scarier than sharing a work in progress. I truly appreciate that after you read whichever draft I sent you, none of you suggested that I return to the practice of law full-time—even if you may have thought it.

To the many friends I have made in the writing community over the last five years—no offense to lawyers, but you folks are a lot more fun. And to all in the Queer Crime Writers group, what a wonderful and supportive group of authors—thank you.

To my legal family at Dilworth Paxson, LLP—thank you for allowing me the freedom to continue pursuing my writing career while practicing law with all of you.

To you, the readers—none of this means anything without you. Whether you bought, borrowed or found this book in the trash, thank you for taking some of your precious time and reading it.

Finally, and most importantly, to all my siblings in the trans and nonbinary communities—please don't give up hope. We will get through these horrible times. I am proud to be a trans person. I am proud of all of you. I am proud to stand with you. I love you.